# Deadly Pleasures

Mary Firmin

# Deadly Pleasures

iUniverse, Inc.
Bloomington

# Deadly Pleasures

*Copyright © 2011 by Mary Firmin*

*All rights reserved. No part of this book may be used or reproduced by any means, graphic, electronic, or mechanical, including photocopying, recording, taping or by any information storage retrieval system without the written permission of the publisher except in the case of brief quotations embodied in critical articles and reviews.*

*This is a work of fiction. All of the characters, names, incidents, organizations, and dialogue in this novel are either the products of the author's imagination or are used fictitiously.*

*iUniverse books may be ordered through booksellers or by contacting:*

*iUniverse*
*1663 Liberty Drive*
*Bloomington, IN 47403*
*www.iuniverse.com*
*1-800-Authors (1-800-288-4677)*

*Because of the dynamic nature of the Internet, any web addresses or links contained in this book may have changed since publication and may no longer be valid. The views expressed in this work are solely those of the author and do not necessarily reflect the views of the publisher, and the publisher hereby disclaims any responsibility for them.*

*Any people depicted in stock imagery provided by Thinkstock are models, and such images are being used for illustrative purposes only.*

*Certain stock imagery © Thinkstock.*

*ISBN: 978-1-4620-4237-1 (sc)*
*ISBN: 978-1-4620-4239-5 (e)*
*ISBN: 978-1-4620-4238-8 (dj)*

*Library of Congress Control Number: 2011913384*

*Printed in the United States of America*

*iUniverse rev. date: 10/5/2011*

In loving memory of my wonderful husband William J. Firmin who recently passed away.

# Prologue

Sherrie Weston scrambled onto the big brass bed and rolled over onto her back. Naked but for a red satin garter belt trimmed with lace and equally red mesh stockings, she struck a lewd pose for the fat, sweaty trick ogling her from the foot of the bed.

*This guy loves garter belts,* thought Sherrie.

A sudden sweep of euphoria mellowed her out from the top of her platinum head to the tips of her painted toenails, and she thanked the universe she'd snorted multiple lines of coke before George Fisher arrived, or she'd never be able to carry out her plan. On top of the other drugs in her system, it was enough to fly her to the fucking moon.

She set down the ground rules. "No games today, George, I had a rough night." *And tonight is going to be worse.* Sherrie tried not to think about the session she had planned for later that evening. To distract herself, she fixed George his favorite scotch-no-ice from the bottle on her dresser.

George took the proffered glass and smiled around the cigarette pinched between his small, nicotine-stained teeth. He moved into the narrow space beside her bed, tugging at his tie. His piggy face oozed perspiration; his eyes glittered, and his fingers, thick as sausages, plucked the cigarette from his pale, wet lips. "That's okay, babe, I just got time for a quickie."

Trying to conceal her disgust, she watched him lean toward the nightstand and stub out the butt in a green ashtray next to a porcelain-framed photograph. Slowly, George lifted the scotch to his lips and studied the picture of Sherrie and her best friend, Allison Graham. Sherrie closed her eyes; dear, sweet Allison had been brutally murdered less than six months ago, her naked body tossed on the beach like so much garbage. It hurt to think about it. Suddenly, as if he found the image of the two friends' offensive, George reached forward and knocked the picture to the floor. Glass and porcelain shattered into a thousand pieces.

Even through the haze of drugs, Sherrie hated him. Hated him more than anyone she'd ever known, except for—she stopped herself. Tonight would come soon enough. As for George Fisher, she'd always known he was a freak. It just made it so much easier to stick it to him for a change. "Come to bed, babe!" she cooed.

In a flash, George was out of his shirt and pants and was peeling down his extra-large boxers. The bed dropped six inches when he belly flopped aboard, and with not even a "brace yourself, momma," he was on top of her, pumping away.

Pressed deep into the mattress, Sherrie thought about her dead friend, Allison, and remembered her words: "Always lay it on them first, before they get off." So she gave him a couple of "do it to me, baby's," and hit him with the big one. "Georgie?"

"Yeah, baby," he growled. "Do it to me."

"Georgie-e-e, I want twenty-five thousand dollars."

"Give it to me, baby." His body slammed into her.

"No, baby, you give it to me—twenty-five grand. Bring it the next time you come." She smiled at her own pun.

"I'm cu—"

"Remember the pink garter belt, George?" She smiled at the picture of him that came to mind. "And the lacy pink bra?" She knew he knew what she meant.

"Ugh. Oh, God. Aghhhh." His skin turned the color of beets. Sweat dripped from his face onto her breast. His mouth contorted, sucking air.

"Do it, Georgie. Oooh, Georgie-e-e." Sherrie bucked her hips up and down, faster, faster, trying to get it over with. But he wouldn't or couldn't climax. He raised himself up and continued to grunt—awful piglike grunts, like he was in pain. Not the usual guttural moans. All of a sudden his body stiffened and went into spasm. One final groan, one heaving shudder, and he collapsed on top of her. *That's more like it.* "Okay, George, get off."

He was heavy. Sherrie pushed. He wouldn't budge. She pushed again. Nothing moved. She was pinned down. Deadweight. It was hard to breathe. "Dammit, George, move."

Deadweight? That's when she knew. And that's when she screamed, and screamed, and screamed.

# Chapter 1

*Bayside Yacht Club, Marina del Rey. August 16th*

MEGAN RILEY STRUGGLED to sit up on the white canvas mat, lying on the top deck of the mega yacht, where she was sunbathing. She stared at her friend in astonishment. "Have you lost your mind?"

"Just a thought." Rachel Feinman turned onto her stomach to cook the other side of her perfectly tanned body. Her back was naked but for a silver thong that disappeared between her round, golden buttocks.

*Rachel has really lost it this time,* thought Megan. *Her cheating husband's antics have finally driven her around the bend.* "Are you suggesting that the three of us …?" She gestured grandly to include Alexandra Grant, whose husband owned the ninety-five–foot yacht where they presently languished. "… Alex, you, and I hire a good-looking guy to get it on with?" Megan could see the muscles in Alex's smooth belly quivering from contained laughter.

Propping herself on one elbow, Rachel swished back her lush black hair to reveal ample, sun-browned breasts. "Yes, that's exactly what I mean."

"Where did y'all get such a crazy idea?" Alex blurted in her quaint Southern drawl. "I mean, that sounds like somethin' the men would do."

Rachel shrugged. "You're absolutely right. I heard David telling

Gino Rosario about four guys at the studio who share a girlfriend. They pay for her apartment and give her a monthly salary just to be on call whenever they want a little action."

Megan couldn't believe what she was hearing. Did men actually do these things? Or was it a product of David Feinman's overactive screenwriter's imagination? Distracted by the sharp ring of a cell phone, she fished in her crocheted bag.

But Rachel already had hers in hand. "Hello?" *Pause.* "Oh, hi, Helen." Distastefully she mouthed the words, "Helen Jennings."

Helen was the club gossip. Rachel could count on large doses of calumny and character assassination if she stayed on the phone with her. Helen Jennings was also known as the "Top Bitch of Bayside." Though others tried, she retained the title hands down.

"You're kidding!" Rachel said, arching her permanently lined eyebrows. "No, I believe you, Helen. Go on."

Obviously, even the jaded Rachel was captured by this conversation. Megan figured it had to be really choice stuff or she wouldn't give Helen the time of day.

Minutes later, she clicked off the phone and took a deep breath. "George Fisher died in bed with a hooker."

Both Megan and Alex shot up from their mats.

"He did what?" Stunned, Megan couldn't finish the sentence. She was speechless. Was this some kind of joke?

Tiny Alex covered her flat chest with ten delicate fingers and blurted, "You can't be serious."

"It's true. George died of a heart attack. But that's not all …" Rachel paused, slowly reeling them in. "The poor girl was trapped beneath him. She screamed for fifteen minutes before the next-door neighbor came to the rescue. The woman had to call the fire department to come and 'un-hooker' old George." She raised her palms. "Helen's words, exactly. 'Un-hooker him.' I can't stand it." That's when Rachel fell back on the mattress, her body convulsing with laughter.

For a long moment, Megan exchanged a dismayed look with Alex and then shifted her gaze back to Rachel, who was rolling around the mat.

"I think the whole thing is appalling," Alex drawled, adjusting her red bikini bottom over protruding hip bones.

But Megan felt a sudden rush of sadness and, unexpectedly, fear. For George? Hardly. While she felt bad about his death, she'd barely known the man, and what she knew of him she didn't like. He was, how old? Forty-one, maybe forty-two, about ten or so years older than herself.

She could not think of a single thing to say.

But of course Rachel could. "Well, I think it's hilarious. Ol' grabby George died in the saddle." Still chuckling obscenely, she added, "I'll bet he'd be the first one to say it's a hell of a way to go."

"You ought to be ashamed of yourself," said a shocked voice coming from the direction of the stairwell.

Megan turned to greet the new arrival. "What took you so long?" She'd driven her friend Kathleen Rosario to the yacht club but left her in the ladies' locker room visiting with Senator Rattner's wife. Megan had walked down to the *Ecstasea's* dock by herself. But that was almost an hour ago.

Ignoring Megan's question, the lanky redhead marched across the teak deck, tossed her backpack beside the last vacant mat, and towered over Rachel. "What about George's poor wife?" she demanded, her lips compressed, like a disapproving nun's. "How do you think she feels?"

"Jesus, Kathleen, will you lighten up?" Rachel rolled her eyes. "She'll probably mourn all the way to the bank. And when she finds out how much money old lover boy had stashed away, she'll head straight for Neiman Marcus!"

Alex chuckled. "Neiman Marcus? That's funny."

Despite herself, Megan smiled.

She glanced over at George's fishing boat, moored directly opposite the transom of the *Ecstasea*. The sign on the back of the hull read *Happy Hooker*. How appropriate. How sad. And how terrible for George to die the way he did, exposing all his nasty secrets. Shuddering, she remembered the circumstances of her own father's death, the shame she'd felt—and the heartrending grief.

*Forget it, Megan. That was a long time ago.*

Flopping back on the mat, Megan tried to get comfortable.

Silently she renewed her daily vow to lose ten pounds—by the weekend. Maybe then she could wear something other than this lousy black bathing suit—like maybe a sexy bikini.

*Dream on, girl.*

But the new arrival, Kathleen, seemed unwilling to let go. "One day it could be your turn, you know. Your comfortable little lives won't always be so perfect."

Her childlike voice didn't wield enough power to be threatening. In fact, scarcely anyone took Kathleen seriously, including her soon-to-be ex-husband, Gino Rosario. But Megan did, and she was especially glad she had, that night a few months ago, when Kathleen threatened suicide. The doctors claimed that Megan's fast reactions had saved her friend's life.

Silently, Kathleen unbuttoned her lace cover-up, revealing a pale, shapely body in an emerald tank. The rich color of the suit complemented her glorious auburn curls, but the usual glow on her lovely face was sadly diminished. Suffering, for months now, through a heart-wrenching divorce from her TV-anchorman husband, Kathleen was so vulnerable she was apt to cry for no reason at all. Still sniffling, she folded her long, slender body onto the down-filled pad.

From a prone position, Alex voiced her agreement with Kathleen. "She's right. The whole family's gonna suffer because of George's disgustin' behavior and the circus surrounding his death."

Megan sighed. No one was laughing anymore.

"According to Helen, the police are going to release the body tomorrow," Rachel said. "But they still want to question all of George's friends." She tried to attach some softness to her next words. "Apparently the house where he passed on was close to the beach where the other prostitute's dead body was found. Five or six months ago, remember?"

Megan was jolted. "You mean the Bondage Murder?"

"That's the one."

"Not far from your house, Megan, if I remember rightly," said Alex.

Megan nodded. "Three blocks away." She recalled the precise moment Kathleen's husband had announced the discovery of the girl's body on the late news. Just thinking about it renewed her terror.

"But why are the authorities so interested in George's death if it was supposed to be of natural causes? Do the police think George had something to do with the Bondage Murder?"

"That's preposterous," Rachel dismissed. "Old George was basically a wimp."

"I guess they'll be speakin' to my Charlie," Alex murmured. "He and George were fishin' buddies."

Suddenly, Kathleen sat up. "Wait a minute! I saw George Fisher with some woman in the Venice Liquor Store about a week ago. I saw him. I know I did. He was talking to her, their heads real close, at the back of the store. She had white, spiky hair, big breasts. And she was young, younger than either one of his daughters."

"Built like the proverbial brick shithouse, I'll bet," Rachel snickered.

Megan gave her another scathing look. "Rachel."

"Well," she said, "that's the type he liked."

"Yes, I could see where he might have a heart attack if she was the one." Kathleen gave a sage nod. "She looked kind of scary to me."

"Everybody looks scary to you," snapped Rachel.

The conversation ceased against the deep roar of a 747 taking off from LAX. Megan raised her eyes to watch it disappear into a cloud bank. She mulled over her own screwed-up life and the recent breakup with her fiancé, Brian Mason. She felt a familiar twinge of self-pity.

First, her three-year marriage to Stephen had ended in divorce. Now, her engagement to Brian was over. Maybe she was incapable of having a successful relationship. Maybe two or three years were all she could manage.

It was a painful time to remember.

New in Los Angeles—with no family, no friends—Megan had been heartbreakingly lonely, so she'd latched onto Stephen like a drowning woman. She knew now she'd married him for all the wrong reasons. When he moved on, she was alone again. But she'd worked very hard to get her real estate license, and then she had spent the next five years making a name for herself in the business. Along with success, her drinking had accelerated, and she'd been easy pickings for the likes of Brian Mason. Now that relationship was over too.

And here she was, thirty years old and still looking for Mr. Right.

But this time Megan wouldn't have to drink. This time she had the love and support of her three best pals, not to mention all her new friends at the AA meetings.

She glanced at Alex, who was opening a bottle of Dom Pérignon with an experienced hand. Having recently passed the golden age of forty, though she'd never admit it, the petite blonde was totally obsessed with her weight and survived solely on lettuce and champagne. Alex Grant held the mistaken belief that her waif look pushed back the years, when, in fact, she was so painfully thin she looked anorexic. Megan pondered what she would do if anything happened to her husband, Charlie. After all, he was quite a bit older than Alex.

The Grants' custom-built Christensen was the largest, most expensive cruiser in Marina del Rey. Moored in front of Bayside Yacht Club, the *Ecstasea* had its own heated spa on the forward deck and four staterooms. The sophisticated art-deco salon, complete with player-piano bar and spiral staircase, had recently been featured in *Motor Yacht* magazine.

Charlie's family also held controlling stock in Grant Aviation, as well as dozens of real estate investments, not the least of which were 220 condominiums in the Marina he was trying to sell off as timeshares. Add that to the penthouse where they resided, and Megan was sure the Grants had more money than they could count.

Megan concluded that if anything happened to Charlie, Alex would simply buy a new husband—maybe two or three. Or at least that's the way it used to be before the crash of the economy these last couple of years. Megan wasn't sure how much damage, if any, had been done to the Grant family fortune.

Alex filled the fluted wine glasses with a flair that suggested the abundant Bayside lifestyle was her due, while Megan was not even sure how much longer she could pay the monthly fees. She'd joined the yacht club in order to meet and procure wealthy real estate clients, but lately her sales were almost nonexistent.

Unfortunately, Megan had no one to depend upon but herself and was now painfully aware she'd soon have to dip into her small emergency fund.

"Champagne, Megan?"

Megan stared at the bottle for the longest time. She could almost feel the icy bubbles tickle the back of her throat. She shook her head. "No, thanks, Alex."

"Oh, I'm so sorry, honey. I keep forgettin'." Alex blushed. "How long has it been now?"

"Ninety-seven days clean and sober." *And it isn't always easy.*

"Why, I think that's commendable, darlin'." Alex emptied a bottle of Perrier into one of the fluted glasses and handed it to Megan.

Sipping it, she turned her attention to Rachel, who had quickly drained her glass and held it out for a refill.

Stunning Rachel Feinman, with her perfect yuppie family, seemed to have it all. She was rich, thin, and gorgeous, married to a handsome screenwriter husband, and the mother of two adorable little girls.

But Megan knew differently. Trouble was brewing in that paradise too!

She could tell from the way Rachel was acting that David was up to his old tricks—being emotionally unavailable, staying out all night, and God knows what else. Megan flashed on the last miserable months of her own marriage and shuddered.

"While we're on the subject," Rachel's matter-of-fact voice brought her back to the present, "I booked the club dining room for Thursday, December 2."

Megan looked at her quizzically.

"You know, for the Mothers in Recovery luncheon?" Rachel prompted.

"Of course." The luncheon was for Megan's new cause.

Mothers in Recovery assisted female addicts and alcoholics who were pregnant. The program also maintained a facility to handle their special-needs children, but it was extremely costly, so Megan had volunteered to chair a fund-raiser. It was her way of giving back for her sobriety.

"By the way, I spoke to Charlie," Alex said. "We'll be sending a large donation."

"Thanks, Alex."

"When can I help with the babies?" Kathleen pleaded.

"Anytime you like. I spoke to—" but Megan was interrupted by the sound of a deep masculine voice calling from the dock below.

"Hello? Is there anyone aboard? Ahoy there!"

"Now, who can that be?" Donning the strip of red material that was her top, Alex rose from the mattress and leaned over the side. "May I help you?"

Megan couldn't hear the reply.

"Mr. Grant is out of town," Alex said. *Pause.* "All right, come on up. Through the salon and up the spiral staircase; we're on the top deck."

"Who is that?" Rachel asked.

"He says he's a police detective. He wanted to see Charlie, but now he's going to speak to us."

"What do you think he wants?" Megan asked.

"He probably wants to know more about George Fisher." Alex patted her sleek, blonde hair. "George is—I mean was—our neighbor on the dock."

Megan lapsed into silence. Again she asked herself the question: Why were the police investigating an accidental death?

## CHAPTER 2

SUDDENLY, HE WAS there on the deck, the most fabulous-looking man Megan had ever seen, probably in his late thirties. He wore Ray-Bans, a brown leather aviator jacket, and beige chinos, and he didn't look the least bit like a policeman.

That's when Rachel scrambled for a towel to cover her bare chest. Despite her best efforts, one ruby nipple escaped concealment.

*So much for Rachel's modesty,* thought Megan.

"Good afternoon," he said. "I'm Detective Matt Donovan, Los Angeles Police Department." He displayed his badge to Alex and then handed her a business card, which she tucked inside her red bikini top without even looking at it. "Mr. Grant is out of town?"

"Yes, he's visiting our factory in San Diego." Alex checked her watch. "But he's due back any time." She then introduced her three companions.

Megan watched the detective scribble their names in a crumpled black book. In fact, she couldn't take her eyes off him. To put it mildly, Matt Donovan was your classic tall, dark, and handsome. But when he removed his sunglasses, he epitomized Megan's vision of an IRA rebel, with his shock of curly, dark hair peppered with gray, and pride dancing in those moody, blue eyes. "Black Irish" is what her father would have called him.

"Would you mind answering a few questions about Mr. Fisher?" He smiled at Megan and moved closer.

"Of course not," she murmured, shocked to feel herself blushing.

"You all know about Mr. Fisher's death?" he asked.

Alex answered, "Yes, Rachel told us all about it. It's terrible, terrible."

"Then you're aware of the circumstances?"

"Isn't it just awful? Dying in bed with a ... well, you know. Poor, dear Junie," Rachel purred, feigning sympathy for George's wife.

Kathleen gave her a disbelieving look.

"It doesn't surprise me," blurted Megan. "George fancied himself as a ladies' man. Besides, he was carrying a lot of weight. He drank way too much and smoked like a fiend." She had to force herself to stop chattering. *What the hell is wrong with you?*

"Did you know him well, miss?" His laser eyes turned on her again.

Squirming like a nervous child, Megan replied, "Not really, no more than anyone else at the club. He was around the bar a lot."

"Have you ever seen either of these women with Mr. Fisher?" He moved even closer and handed her a photograph.

The clean smell of his lemony aftershave was so distracting she was forced to pull back. To cover her discomfort, Megan examined the picture a little longer than necessary. There was nothing unusual about it—two young women, probably in their late teens, wearing blue jeans and skimpy tops, smiling for the camera.

Shaking her head, she passed it on.

Silently, Rachel and Alex also shook their heads.

But Kathleen pointed to one of the girls. "That's the one I saw with George in the liquor store last week."

"Are you sure?" he asked.

"Positive." Kathleen glanced back at the photo. "That's her, all right. I recognize the bleached blonde, spiky hair and all that heavy makeup. You know, cheap-like."

"Definitely Sherrie Weston," he said, almost to himself.

Rachel prodded him for details. "Is she the one George was with when he died?"

"Yes."

"Then who's the other girl?" Megan asked.

"Allison Graham."

"Wasn't that the B—" Megan hesitated.

But Rachel didn't. "Not the Bondage Murder?"

The detective nodded.

Megan pressed her lips together. She knew it. He thought there was a connection to George Fisher's death.

Suddenly, she heard the loud whirring of a helicopter circling above them. A funnel of air whipped towels, mats, and magazines around the deck.

Rachel's towel blew into the water, exposing her completely. Megan smiled inwardly as Rachel grabbed a straw hat and tried to conceal her bosom.

From the corner of her eye, Megan watched the detective's reaction. He didn't even glance in Rachel's direction.

Shading her eyes with her hand, Alex looked skyward. "Here's Charlie now. He'll be on board any minute. Would you care to wait?"

"Yes, please, if you don't mind."

"You can wait in the salon, if you like."

"Thank you." His blue eyes lit up when he smiled. "I'll do that."

Megan followed the detective's broad back until he disappeared down the stairs to the deck below. Only then did she shift her gaze to the circular pad near the clubhouse, where the shiny, black helicopter had landed. The name Grant Aviation was painted on its side in large silver letters. Seconds later, two men jumped out. Their clothes and hair were blowing in the turbulence of the still-whirling blades. One of them waved, and the chopper rose.

Megan watched it fly away until the sun, reflecting on the two-storied glass wall of Bayside Yacht Club, impeded her vision. The noise faded until the only sound left was the soft flap of canvas on a sailboat coming about in the channel.

Then, silence.

Lying back on the mat, Megan experienced a strange mixture of sadness and anger as she pondered the girl in the photograph. Allison. Allison Graham. Strangely, she felt more empathy for the murdered girl than she did for George.

She prayed the police would find the killer. Even though it wouldn't bring her back, it would honor the young woman's life if her assailant was brought to justice.

"George Fisher was a prime example of male double standards," Rachel complained, out of the blue. "Men really do have the advantage over women ... no matter how feminist we think we are."

Alex nodded absently. "I suppose."

Relieved to take her mind off the gruesome murder, Megan sat up again. "You're absolutely right. Since men control the money, they can set up some bimbo any time they want, and who's to know? Who knew about George Fisher's little love nest on Venice Beach?" She made a vain attempt at the lotus position. Failing miserably, she inhaled a deep yoga breath.

"You have control over your money, Megan," Kathleen said, peering over her large dark glasses. "You make a fortune selling real estate."

With a sweep of her long fingers, Megan waved away the remark. "Not anymore, I don't. I used to be top gun in our office, but lately no one is selling anything." *And I've used up most of my savings,* Megan thought, *feeding all my bad habits.* For a long moment she stared at the water. A fat brown duck paddled into view. He plunged his head underwater, looking for lunch, but came up empty-beaked. She shifted her gaze to Rachel. "Gross inequities still exist between men and women—and in matters of sex there will always be a double standard."

"Not necessarily, my dear, things are changing," Rachel demurred. "I'm reading this book called *Erotic Wives,* and, despite the dangers of multiple partners, many of today's women are indulging in guilt-free, extramarital sex. They're having hot and heavy affairs when their schedules allow—during lunch hour, on business trips, on the way home from work."

Hooting with delight, Megan clapped her hands. "It's about time. More women are wearing the pants nowadays. Why shouldn't they take them off as much as the damn men do?"

Rachel took a lingering sip of champagne. "One working mother compared her illicit sexual experience to a month's stay at a health spa."

"Really?" Megan asked. "Maybe we should get that guy's phone number." *Or,* she said to herself, *the good-looking detective's.*

"We could open a bordello for women." Rachel drew a line in the air to depict a headline: "R & R for the Overworked Woman of the Twenty-First Century."

Everyone laughed, almost hysterically. *Good.* It was time to lighten up. Relief came with laughter. Megan had learned that from her AA meetings. The news of George Fisher's untimely death combined with viewing the pictures of the murdered girl had been traumatic for them all.

Megan moved her legs aside as Rachel, still chuckling, stepped over her to the bubbling spa. A cascade of jet hair rippled down her back, like a black satin sheet, reaching all the way to her thonged buttocks. Rachel's entire body was tanned to what Megan enviously called "goddess gold." How she hated her own pale skin. It never tanned. Large pink blotches just appeared all over and—

"I think maybe I'll find a lover," Rachel said, sinking deeper into the tub. "It might be fun to have a cute little boytoy waiting in the wings."

"Boytoy," Alex mused. "Great sex whenever you want it with no obligations."

"I'm not so sure you're that sophisticated," Megan observed. "Or that any of us are." *Besides,* she thought, *that would make us all cougars, and we already have enough of those hanging around the club.*

Rachel crooked her mouth into a little smile, her red lips floating above the waterline, like a crimson blossom. "Well, if we were gutsy like Cher or Madonna, we'd do it."

"The only one of us who could afford it is Alex." Megan gave her a friendly nudge. "Just one less trip to Rodeo Drive, right?"

Alex smiled.

"Gino found a way to do it, and we're not that rich." Kathleen's green eyes brimmed with tears. "Maybe if we could've had a child …"

*Silence.*

The conversation died, as it always did when Kathleen brought up the divorce and the tragedy of her infertility.

Megan scrambled to her feet. It was time to go. "Let's get moving, Kathleen. I have an appointment to show Charlie's time-shares at five o'clock."

Rachel's eyes gleamed. "That's it—a time-share boytoy. Get it?"

The words tumbled from her lips as the fantasy took form. "We'll find us a good-looking guy, set him up in an apartment, and take turns just like the guys do."

Megan stared at her as if she was a madwoman, but it didn't seem to diminish Rachel's enthusiasm one bit.

"You are really gross," Kathleen observed.

"You're spoofin' us again, ain't you, Rachel?" asked Alex.

Rachel grinned. "No, I'm not. I think it's a fabulous idea!"

"It's original," Megan said. "I'll give you that."

But Rachel would not be stopped. "I mean we certainly don't want to fool around with people we don't know, not with AIDS and other STDs floating about—not to mention date rapists and Bondage Murderers. At least this way we can investigate his background and know who we're dealing with."

Astonished, Megan checked each of their reactions.

Deep in thought, Kathleen stared pensively at the dark blue water. Alex gazed upward at the puffy clouds scudding across the sky. Rachel, her eyes bright with anticipation, wiggled her toes in the spa.

*My God, they're actually considering it.*

Ascending from the bubbly water, like Venus rising, Rachel reached for a towel. "Well? What do you think?"

*Silence,* again.

Finally, Megan broke the ice. "What I want to know is who'd be in charge of scheduling?"

Alex was quick to answer. "Not you, Megan."

"Definitely not Megan," Rachel agreed. "We'd never get a turn."

The mood lightened. Even Kathleen smiled.

Megan grinned. Rachel was joking again. Wasn't she?

Dropping the towel, Rachel wrapped herself in a skimpy sarong and slipped into her gold sandals. "It's late, I have to go. I want to be there when the kids get home from school."

Rising awkwardly to her feet, Alex muttered out loud, "I suppose I should spend some time with my husband." She didn't sound thrilled with the prospect.

"Tell Charlie I'll let him know how the showing went."

Alex nodded. "And I'll have him mail our donation to Mothers in Recovery."

"Thanks; it's a good cause, and they really need the money." Gathering her belongings, Megan headed for the stairwell.

Halfway down the spiral staircase, she suddenly giggled. "Time-share boytoy? I love it."

"You would, Megan," Kathleen teased as she followed behind.

"I still think we ought to do it," Rachel said, already at the bottom.

Megan laughed again ... and thought about the detective.

*There* was a man she wouldn't share with anyone.

But surely the girls weren't serious about hiring a boytoy, were they?

# Chapter 3

Matt Donovan stood on the dock at Bayside Yacht Club and looked back at the two yachts. George Fisher's blue-and-white fishing trawler *Happy Hooker* had probably set him back a couple hundred grand, and Charles Grant's mega yacht *Ecstasea* was worth at least two million.

His conversation with Mr. Grant, of Grant Aviation, had been over in ten minutes, and Matt had learned nothing. Zilch. But he hadn't expected much, knowing from experience that when scandal reared its ugly head, the rich closed ranks and protected their own. Even the guilty were not given up so easily.

But that valet of Grant's, Sy Neang—he sure was strange. Charles Grant and Sy Neang—now there was an interesting duo. According to Mr. Grant, Sy Neang was Cambodian and had been with him since the early nineties while on a U.N. Peacekeeping Mission in Cambodia. While the valet had remained in the background during his entire conversation with his boss, Matt had felt a weird undercurrent flowing between the two of them. But he just couldn't put his finger on it.

He shrugged it off—for now.

Matt stared at the water and considered the four women aboard the *Ecstasea*. They were classy, all of 'em. But if he were to choose one for himself, it would be that cute honey-blonde with the lively hazel eyes and well-curved body, Megan Riley. Not as sexy-looking as the redhead, and not even close to the beauty of the dark-haired one, but there was a quickness and vitality about Megan he found hard to resist. His own life had been empty of that kind of energy for a long, long time.

*C'mon, Matthew, calm down, boy. She's way out of your league.*

Besides, what kind of ditsy female hung out on a yacht all day long? He shook his head and turned toward the parking lot, automatically surveying his surroundings.

The Bayside Clubhouse was a two-storied, octagonal building constructed mostly of glass. Expensive motor yachts and high-tech racing craft were tied up alongside eight private docks. He imagined it cost a bundle to belong to this joint.

Placing his hand in his jacket pocket, Matt fingered the crumpled business card he'd found in George Fisher's personal effects. He pulled it out and stared at the shocking-pink rectangle for a full minute.

PARTY FAVORITES
*We fill all your party needs.*
Sherrie Weston    (310) 555-9988

He turned it over. Scrawled on the back in blood-red ink was the name Allison Graham and the number 310-555-2754. Did George know Allison? He definitely knew Sherrie. And the card connected Allison and Sherrie, along with the photograph.

A call came through on his cell as he opened the car door. Matt unfolded the telephone. "Donovan here."

The dispatcher relayed the message, "One-eighty-seven at 42 Beachview Ave."

The address was a familiar one. "I'm on my way," said Matt.

When Matt arrived at Sherrie Weston's house, a uniformed officer was encircling the picket-fenced yard with yellow tape. The white clapboard bungalow, although charming, was badly in need of paint, the lawn sparse and brown.

"Here we go again, Gonzales," Matt said, referring to the death of George Fisher, which had occurred only yesterday in this same house. "Is Bentley here yet?" he asked, referring to his partner, Angelle Bentley.

"I ain't seen her, and I was first on the scene."

Two technicians, brushing the front door for prints, mumbled a greeting as Matt climbed the porch steps and entered the house.

Sherrie's living room was dark, all the drapes drawn, the blinds on the front door pulled down. The whole house was ransacked, drawers dumped onto the floor, pillows slit open, stuffing strewn everywhere. The cheap wooden tables were turned over as if the intruder had been looking for something taped on the underside.

The medical examiner emerged from the hallway, leading to the rear of the house, and approached Matt. Stooped and frail, Dr. Tom Wilson's hair stretched across his bald head in thin, gray ribbons that matched his etched, gray face. From his expression, poor old Tom looked like one of his dead patients, and Matt felt a deep concern for his longtime friend.

"Down the hall." Doc Wilson jerked his head in the direction of the bedroom. Clutching a yellow paper in his gnarled hand, he read from it, his neck pushed forward from his hunched shoulders like a shortsighted turtle's. "According to her driver's license, the victim's name was Cheryl Louise Weston."

"Aka Sherrie Weston."

Doc nodded and continued, "She was an addict. I'd guess probably heroin, from the tracks on her arm. Cocaine too—there's residue on the kitchen table. Time of death, as far as I can tell right now, was late last night or early this morning." Doc Wilson peered over his glasses at Matt. "Looks like the cause of death was asphyxia by ligature strangulation, but there were also multiple stab wounds and lots of spatter."

"Like Allison?"

"Not quite. The ligature's still there. A wire coat hanger wrapped around her neck. One thing I haven't figured out yet. There's some kind of black soot in the wound. It must have come from the hanger, but how? Crime lab boys will find prints if we're lucky."

"Any handcuffs?" Matt asked.

"Not this time. She's tied to the bed with rope. I told them not to touch her until you got here."

"It's a repeat, isn't it, Tom?"

"I'm not finished. There's postmortem amputation of the right breast, invasion of body cavities with a foreign object, and severe trauma to internal organs."

"Any sex paraphernalia around?"

"Nope, he must have taken it with him."

"Weapons?"

Tom shook his head. "The cuts were deep. It's probably a knife with a long, thin blade. We can't find that either."

"No physical evidence?"

"Nothing visible, but maybe I'll find something when I get her downtown."

"The MO's a match with Allison," said Matt.

The coroner nodded. "Some of it is."

"Jesus, that's what I was afraid of. The bastard's already got a taste for it. I'd bet there've been others and nobody's connected them." Matt turned away in disgust.

"The good news is we have something to work with. We've got an actual crime scene here, and he didn't clean her up this time." He pulled his turtle neck back in place. "Don't worry, Matt; eventually they all leave something."

"Yeah, right."

"This guy had a good time. We've got a sexual psychopath on our hands here."

"And there's no guarantee he'll stick to hookers," snapped Matt. "Who found the body?"

"That crazy old lady, the one who lives next door. She was in hysterics when I got here. I told her you'd want to speak to her, but she went home to lie down."

"Oh, brother, not her again. All I need is a loony witness." He placed his hand on the little man's arm. "How's the wife?"

Tom winced, his first sign of emotion since the beginning of the conversation. "The cancer's eatin' her up, Matt."

He wanted to put his arm around Tom's hunched shoulders, even though he knew it wouldn't help. "I'm sorry, man."

"Yeah." He wiped his steamy glasses and put them back on. "You're probably the only one I know who understands what it's like to watch your wife fade away in front of your eyes. It's a bitch, Matt." He moved down the hallway toward the small bathroom near the kitchen.

*Yeah, it's a real bitch.* He knew all about it.

Matt's wife, Constance, had died from ovarian cancer three years before. After her death, the only thing that kept him going was the knowledge that he had to care for their sixteen-year-old daughter, Julie. Walking down the hallway, he forced the memories down but found them immediately replaced by his worries about Julie's safety in the insanity of New York City. With effort, he cleared his mind and concentrated on the work at hand.

Pulling on plastic gloves and the required booties to cover his shoes, he stood on the threshold of Sherrie's bedroom and surveyed the mayhem.

The window was covered with black paper. The place was trashed.

A police photographer clicked pictures of the female body, as well as the numerous ropy striations of blood splashed on the wall behind the bed.

"I'm outta here, Matt." Pushing past him, the photographer left the room.

Matt's eyes were immediately drawn to the grisly sight on the king-sized brass bed. Sherrie was spread-eagled, face up. Naked. An angry circle of jagged flesh replaced her right breast, an array of stab wounds on her torso, and even her bare legs told of the attacker's frenzied state of mind. Matt closed his eyes for a moment and then propelled himself into the suffocating room.

The stench of violent death was heavy in the air and the hot, metallic odor of blood so overpowering he could almost taste it. Blood was everywhere, soaked into the mattress, dried on the gleaming headboard, and spattered in grotesque designs on the wall. For at least thirty seconds, Matt felt the anguish full on and had to turn away to get a grip on himself.

He approached the corpse and examined the bindings. Sherrie's arms and legs were tied to the bed with a series of complicated knots. When he saw the extent of the rope burns on her bruised and bloodied wrists, he knew she had not given up without a fight.

Stuffed between her teeth was a black leather ball gag. Pale eyes, open and glazed, stared back at him. Stark, raving terror was grafted in horrifying detail on her once-pretty face.

*Jesus, what the fucking bastard had done to her!*

Matt closed her eyelids and gently covered her nakedness with a soiled sheet. His feet crunched the broken glass on the floor near the bed. He reached down to gather up the shards of glass, mixed with shattered porcelain, and placed them in an evidence bag.

Matt recalled his conversation with Doc Wilson, who had attended the scene after George Fisher's death-by-sex, and noticed the broken frame and the photo of Sherrie Weston taken with Allison Graham. Since Doc Wilson had performed the autopsy on Allison six months earlier, he knew that Matt was working on the Bondage Murder investigation and had called him, immediately, to suggest he might want to interview Sherrie.

Even though George had apparently died from natural causes, Matt had spoken briefly to Sherrie about his death and the murder of her friend Allison. She had given him the photo only if he promised to bring it back. She had been too shaken up to speak to him at the time, and Matt had realized she was still pretty high from whatever drugs she had taken. He had decided not to take her in since he believed she had also been a victim. But now both girls were dead.

Allison and Sherrie had been friends; that much he knew. He withdrew the photo from his pocket and stared at it, willing it to talk to him. *How well did George Fisher know AllisonGraham?* After his death, Matt had found her telephone number in his pocket, written on the back of Sherrie Weston's pink business card.

*And I'd make book some of his buddies at Bayside knew 'em too.*

Tom Wilson called from the bathroom. "Matt?"

"Yeah, Tom." He slipped the photo back into his inside pocket.

"Come in here."

Tom was standing in the tub with a pair of tweezers in his hand. His neck was in a forward position as he examined the contents. "I found these hairs caught in the drain."

"Do they have follicles?"

"Uh-huh."

"And there's how many?"

Looking up, Tom smiled. "There are at least half a dozen pubic hairs. They could be the killer's or any one of her tricks. But it looks to me like the killer took a shower when he was finished. This is one tidy fucker. No prints, no semen, nothing. But he forgot the trap in the bathtub drain. And I'll bet you ten to one when I spray the bathroom with Luminal, it'll light up like a fucking Christmas tree."

"Matt!" The voice came from the kitchen.

"I'm in here, Fred."

"We got perfect prints on the kitchen cupboards, also on the dirty dishes and coffee cups in the sink. They belong to the victim and at least one other person."

"Great. Maybe we're finally getting somewhere. Oh, and be sure to bag her hands. We need to check her fingernails."

Back in the bedroom Matt took another look at Sherrie.

What the hell was the killer looking for to turn the house into such chaos? Money? Jewels? Stocks and bonds? Yeah, right. Nobody in his right mind would expect to find anything of value in a small-time hooker's pad. Drugs? Maybe. And why were all the windows covered with black paper? To keep the nosy neighbors out?

Then he had an idea. He explored the walls from the baseboard all the way to the ceiling. Halfway around the room he focused on a heart-shaped wreath made of dried flowers and pink ribbons. Hidden in the center was a small round hole. His gaze moved over the room. He searched the nearby closet. Nothing. He pushed the clothes to the left.

*What do we have here? Aha, a secret door.*

Crude, but it was a door all the same. Matt pried the cheap plywood away from the wall. In a small cubbyhole he discovered an expensive video camera angled perfectly toward the bed.

Matt wedged his way into the small space to retrieve the disk. It was gone. He scrounged around on the floor, but the area was empty of all but the camera. At least now he had an idea why the house had been torn apart.

Someone must have been looking for the DVD that came from that camera. But who? The murderer? And did he find it?

Brushing himself off, Matt hollered. "Hey, you guys. Take a look at this."

Within minutes, five techies were crowded inside the closet, trying to get a better look.

"Look, man, *Totally Hidden Video*," yelled Fred, the fingerprint man.

"Naw, it's *Candid Camera*," cracked the photographer. "But I'd lay odds whoever starred in these movies was doing more than smiling."

The others laughed.

Matt didn't. "Better get in there, Fred. See what you can find in the way of prints."

"You got it."

That's when Detective Angelle Bentley entered the room, and everyone turned to look. Her exotic presence was out of place in the grim surroundings. "Sorry I'm late."

"Yeah, I was beginning to wonder," Matt quipped.

He had decided at their very first meeting, only two weeks ago, that this slender Haitian beauty, with skin the color of milk chocolate, should be on some sandy beach, not wading through ghastly crime scenes wearing her sensible shoes and that god-awful navy-blue suit.

The guys backed away from the closet and stood in a semicircle, waiting to see how she reacted to the murder scene and the blood-splattered walls.

For a second, Angelle's tawny face registered shock, but only for a second. Then she walked to the bed, drew back the sheet, and calmly examined Sherrie's body. "Who found her?" Her tone was crisp, businesslike, with only the faintest touch of a Caribbean accent.

"The same crazy neighbor we spoke to yesterday." Matt could see the guys were disappointed Angelle had handled the crime scene so well. So they trudged single file back to their own work. As soon as the last one disappeared, Angelle covered her mouth with her hand and left the room.

When she returned, Matt made no reference to her behavior. How could he? He'd felt the same damn way.

"It's the same MO as Allison Graham. He's a serial, Angelle. I can feel it."

Her expression rigid, she nodded. "I'll take a look through the rest of the house."

He followed her into the living room and watched as Angelle dropped to her knees and began scouring through the debris. She held up a bondage magazine.

Matt knelt down beside her. His gaze was glued to the cover of *SLAVES* magazine, displaying a long-legged, masked woman dressed for bondage in black leather. "Holy shit," he said. "I'd hate to run into that broad in a dark alley." The dominatrix wielded a dangerous-looking whip with shiny metal casings on the tips of the lashes. Bright red nail polish, like drops of blood, was splattered on the magazine cover.

"Look, there's a name written down." Angelle peered closely. "It's … Michael Harrington. I can barely read the phone number."

"Check it out, would you? I gotta go see the old lady next door."

Outside, Matt gulped the fresh sea air. He'd never get used to this crap if he worked it for a hundred years.

# Chapter 4

Matt climbed the three steps to the neighbor's porch and rang the bell.

The door opened a tiny crack. "Yes?"

He flashed his badge. "Mrs. Zuckerman? Detective Matt Donovan, Homicide. Remember me? I spoke to you yesterday."

"Come in, young man. Come in." The door opened wider.

Matt entered, closing it behind him. "Thank you."

The old woman moved slowly, maneuvering her considerable bulk by leaning heavily on an old broom handle. "I'm not a bit surprised, you know?" She scrunched her wrinkled lips into a know-it-all smirk. "When that girl moved in six months ago, I knew she was trouble, though I must say I didn't expect this. I told Jack Simmons. He lives next door on t'other side. 'Yup,' I says to Jack, 'this girl's gonna be trouble.' And I was right. Men were runnin' in and out of that cathouse all hours o' the day 'n night. Know what I mean?"

"Yes, I do, ma'am." Matt gazed around the dingy living room in amazement. Years and years of dirt grimed the windows, and what looked like a twenty-year supply of newspapers and magazines was stacked in every corner. The whole place smelled rank, as if something had died under the floorboards.

Gingerly, he sat on the edge of the faded green couch and took out his crumpled notebook. "What time did you discover the body, Mrs. Zuckerman?"

She took a deep breath. "I was waiting for Oprah to come on, mindin' my own business, when a knock comes to my door, somewheres before three o'clock. It was the UPS man." Her voice sank to a whisper. "He says to me, 'Will you take this package and give it to the folks next door? I've tried to deliver it twice and nobody's ever home.' Well, I knew she was in there. She hadn't left the house since the fat guy died, yesterday."

"How do you know she didn't leave the house? You couldn't possibly have been watching every minute."

"Well, I know she didn't drive her car nowhere, that's for sure. When she started up that old Mustang in the alley, everybody in the neighborhood knew it. Jack Simmons says she don't have no muffler."

"Okay, but she could have walked somewhere?"

"I woulda seen her." She sounded confident. "Yup, I stay on top of the comings and goings 'round here."

He'd bet his entire paycheck on the truth of that statement. "Did you see anyone go to the house, yesterday, after the police and the coroner left?"

Tilting forward, she squinted. "Nope, and the only way I'd miss 'em is if they sneaked in 'n outta the back door in the middle of the night. I don't sleep much, you know." She leaned back again. "Just that upstart young man."

"What young man?"

"Who?" For a moment, she appeared lost.

He tried not to lose his patience. "The young man who visited Sherrie yesterday. What did he look like?"

"Tall, good-lookin'. Cocky, if you ask me."

"Was he dark-haired? Blond?"

"Dirty blond." Her eyes brightened. "He looked like that guy on the cover of *People* magazine. Rick Holt. He looked like Rick Holt."

"Rick Holt? Gimme a clue, Mrs. Zuckerman. Is he an actor, a ballplayer, a politician?"

"An actor. Yup, he's an actor. Supposed to be the sexiest man in America or somethin'. I think they're wrong, though. JR's the sexiest guy in America." Struggling to her feet, she hobbled to the corner and rummaged through a pile of old magazines.

Finally, she handed one to Matt.

Matt scanned the *People* magazine. It was so old and filthy he couldn't decipher the date. The headline read: "Nick Nolte. The Sexiest Man Alive."

"You mean Nick Nolte?" Dammit, a defense attorney would rip this poor lady to shreds in minutes. The magazine must have been twenty years old.

"Yeah, he looked like him, only a whole lot better-lookin'. Tall guy, lotsa muscles, he was ridin' one of them big bikes, like the Hells Angels. It made a hell of a lotta noise, too."

He wrote down NOLTE TYPE and glanced up. "Can you tell me what he was wearing?"

"Blue jeans, tight leather jacket, cowboy boots." She raised her eyes to the ceiling. "His name was … lemme think. Michael. Yup, that's it. Sherrie called him Michael. I heard her."

"Did he mention his last name?"

The old lady hemmed and hawed. "He said it, but I can't remember."

But she'd remembered every other goddamn detail. "Do you know what time it was?" Impatient now, he snapped the question.

She rolled her eyes. "Lemme see. I was outside in the front yard, waterin' the lawn. About six thirty, seven, maybe later. I remember thinkin', that George feller ain't even cold, 'n here she is off again with some other guy."

Matt cut her short and showed her the snapshot of Sherrie and Allison. "Do you recognize the other girl in this photograph with Miss Weston?"

Plopping back down on her chair, she shook her head. A couple of bobby pins spilled onto her lap. Silently, Matt watched her gather them up with bent, arthritic fingers and felt a sudden wave of sympathy for her. He tried to soften his tone. "Did you hear anything unusual last night? Noises? Cries for help? Sounds of a car or motorcycle?"

"Nothin' like that."

"How did you get into Sherrie's house?"

"When she didn't answer I went 'round back. The door was open." Twirling a single lock of unwashed hair around her gnarled finger, the old woman paused. "I called her name a few times, and then I went in. Found her in the bedroom. Crucified on the bed, she was, her tittie gone." She scowled and let go of the greasy ringlet.

Matt caught a glimpse of bewilderment in her squinty, colorless eyes, but it passed quickly. "Where's the package from UPS, Mrs. Zuckerman?"

"Right here." The old woman reached down beside the armchair. Setting a small square box on the table, she leaned closer and whispered, "One of them packages wrapped in plain brown paper. It's prob'ly porno."

He examined it. A slit in the package four or five inches long revealed a couple of DVDs in clear plastic containers. "I suppose you've already checked these?"

"No, sir." She placed her hand on her heart. "I swear that's the way they was when the guy gave 'em to me." She paused. "Do you think it is?"

"Is what?"

"Porno?" She gave him a coy smile.

Matt stood up. "I think that's it for now, Mrs. Zuckerman." After writing a receipt for the DVDs, he fished for a business card. "If you remember anything else at all, please call me at this number."

She followed him to the front door.

Matt turned. "One more thing, Mrs. Zuckerman, please don't speak to the media until we notify next of kin." He knew it wouldn't do any good, but he had to say it.

Outside, Matt tried to ignore Marcia Waters and her cameraman, but the pushy reporter followed him to the house of the neighbor, Jack Simmons, asking one question after another.

Finally, he stopped in his tracks and turned. "No comment, Miss Waters." He pushed the microphone away from his face.

Grumbling to herself, Marcia Waters stood her ground defiantly. Then she followed Donovan up the steps to the neighbor's verandah still trying to question him.

Ignoring her, Matt knocked at the door of Jack Simmons's house.

A bald, heavyset boxer type answered. He wore dirty blue jeans and a gray sweatshirt with the words PITBULL GYM painted across the front.

Matt identified himself, displayed his badge, and asked Mr. Simmons if he had heard or seen anything unusual last night.

"I didn't see nuttin' or hear nuttin'." Simmons's nose was flattened on his face and made him sound nasal and punch-drunk. One eye was half-closed, and his mouth twitched nervously. He did not look pleased to see the badge.

"Did you see anyone entering or leaving the house at any time yesterday?"

"I didn't see nuttin' or hear nuttin'." Again, his mouth twitched, and his good eye blinked.

"Did you hear a car in the alley?"

"I didn't see nuttin' or hear nuttin'."

"What about Sherrie's car?" he snapped. "Did it come and go at all last night?"

"I didn't hear …"

Matt knew he was lying. "I know, I know. You didn't hear nuttin' or see nuttin'."

In the hope of scaring him, he asked, "Where were you last night, Mr. Simmons?"

Scowling, the old man curled his lips in classic Stallone fashion. "Over at the strip joint with a buddy o' mine."

"And his name, please."

"Benny Donato."

"And his telephone number?"

Simmons frowned. "I dunno. He's in the book, I guess, lives in Mar Vista."

"What's the name of the club?"

"I can't remember. Hot Girls Go Wild? Sumpin' like that."

He knew the place. A tacky joint in Culver City called Hot Girls in the Wild.

"Thank you, sir."

The door slammed shut in his face.

Matt shook his head in disbelief. What the hell ever happened to the days when people cooperated with the police?

Suddenly, he realized that Marcia Waters was talking to Mrs. Zuckerman.

*Shit.* He hurried over to break it up.

# Chapter 5

D<small>EAR GOD, PLEASE GIVE ME ONE MORE COMMISSION AND I PROMISE I WON'T PISS IT AWAY.</small>

Megan usually chuckled each time she read the sign pasted on her dashboard, but not tonight. Tonight, her heart pounded in her chest, and her grip on the steering wheel tightened as she drove into the underground garage of her Venice apartment.

This was not like her. Why was she so paranoid?

Had George Fisher's death unnerved her? Or was it seeing the photo of the murdered girl? After all, Allison Graham's killer had never been caught, and almost six months had passed since her body was found on the beach, only three blocks from this very spot. Of course she was scared. Who wouldn't be?

She pulled into a parking space near the elevator. Keys clenched tightly in her fist, she alighted from her vintage black Mercedes and, balancing several manila folders, her briefcase, and her shoulder bag, crossed the cement floor of the dark, musty garage. Eyes wary, Megan scanned each shadowy corner and crevice.

Ever since the night of Allison's murder, she'd been apprehensive—especially at night and always in the deserted garage. In fact, she couldn't walk through any desolate place without thinking of the girl on the beach, and today's reminder had served only to exacerbate that fear. Pushing the frightening thoughts from her mind, she focused her attention on the hiss and roar of the surf. The sound of the ocean usually calmed her, but tonight was the exception. She heard a noise. *Slam.* Was it a car door?

"Who's there?" Her voice echoed in the silence. She stood quite still. Then she saw a shadow.

Someone was there, near the laundry room.

"Hello?"

No response.

*Okay, run like hell, Megan.*

And she did.

Reaching the entrance to the building, she fumbled with her keys. *Damn.* The contents of the files fell to the floor. She groaned. *Get the key in the hole, girl.*

At last, she turned the key and opened the door.

"Megan," said a man's voice. He was close. She almost fainted.

"Megan?"

Terrified, she turned and squinted at the tall sandy-haired figure. It was her ex-boyfriend, Brian Mason.

"Dammit, Brian," she hissed. "You scared me half to death. What the hell are you doing sneaking around here at this time of night?"

"Christ, Megan," Brian mumbled as he picked up a fallen file and shoved it into her hand. "I've never seen you so jumpy."

"Of course I'm jumpy. We're living in a damn war zone. Don't you ever watch the news? What do you want, anyway?"

"I need a couple more business suits for work."

"Why didn't you call me first?" Trying to control her temper, Megan knelt to pick up the rest of the scattered files.

Brian crouched beside her to help, his gray eyes meeting hers. "You know I can't keep all my stuff on the boat. I'm looking for an apartment." He breathed ninety-proof fumes in her face.

Megan turned away. "You can't stay, you know!"

"Who the hell wants to?"

"Well, just as long as you know." She stood up.

Brian held the door open.

She tried to avoid body contact as she pushed past him into the hall, and she kept her distance while he pressed the elevator button. Megan could not shake the apprehension she felt in his presence. Was she afraid Brian might do something to cause her to drink? Or was it more than that?

The elevator light was out.

Her knees trembled when the door slid closed, and the darkness of a tomb enfolded them. But Brian did nothing, said nothing, and within seconds they were on the second floor.

He opened the door with his own key. Once inside the townhouse, Megan dropped her burdens on the bleached oak floor in the hall. "I'll take my keys now, Brian."

Without a word, he dropped the keys into her outstretched hand and headed upstairs to gather his belongings.

Megan put them in her purse, walked to the CD player, and slammed on the switch.

The sweet voice of Carrie Underwood emanated from the speakers as she entered the kitchen.

After banging around for a minute or two, she returned to the living room with a turkey sandwich and a cup of instant coffee. She was still furious with Brian for appearing on her doorstep without calling. Kicking off her shoes, she curled up on the deep cushions of the white sofa to eat her sandwich. The living room was dark and lonely, and she could hear Brian rummaging in the second-floor closet.

A familiar feeling of abandonment swept over her, but this time she didn't wallow in it. She stopped it in its tracks. *Get real, girl. Brian didn't leave you; you kicked him out almost three months ago.* Still, the feelings were same.

The food sank like a rock in her stomach. She couldn't finish the sandwich.

Leaning her head back on the cushion, she recalled the night of their breakup. Brian had come home late, much later than usual, from his job as a stockbroker at James Farnsworth Investments. He was drunk and barely able to walk.

She had been shattered. He was supposed to be clean and sober. Hadn't they joined AA together?

Megan had known, immediately, that she could not continue to live with Brian. Not if she wanted to stay sober. She promptly asked him to leave. But Brian wouldn't go.

For once in her life, Megan had stood her ground and insisted he leave the apartment that very night. Finally, after a terrible row, he'd grabbed a few of his things and left for Bayside Yacht Club to stay on his boat. And he was still living there.

Brian's clatter on the stairs brought her back to the present. As he appeared in the living room, she turned. His arms were filled with suits, jackets, and shirts.

"Can I use the phone?" he asked.

She nodded and turned off the music.

Brian tossed the hangers over the armchair, sauntered to the dining room, and opened the shuttered doors concealing the wet bar. "I'll just have a little toddy for the body while I'm here—since it is my booze."

"Then why don't you take it all with you?"

"Don't worry, my dear, I'll get it next time."

Megan struggled to keep her mouth shut. She didn't want an argument. She just wanted him to leave. Fast.

He poured himself a large glass of Johnnie Walker and drank half of it down. "Mind if I get some ice?"

She shrugged.

Brian returned to the living room, stirring the drink with his middle finger. "I just need to make a quick call. Do you mind?" Placing the glass on the coffee table, he reached into his inside pocket and pulled out a mangy-looking address book held together with a rubber band.

Megan decided it must have gone through the laundry; there was no other explanation for its sorry condition. When he removed the elastic, several pages fluttered to the ground. Brian crawled around in an effort to retrieve them, but Megan turned away, declining to help.

While he made his phone call, she took a long hard look.

Brian had the kind of boyish charm she found hard to resist, even now. His rumpled hair was rust-colored, like a brick, and, as always, she felt a compulsive desire to pat it into neatness. She sighed, thinking of the times when Brian had made her believe she was the most beautiful woman in the world—usually, as it turned out, when he wanted something.

Suddenly glancing up, Brian caught her looking at him. He

smiled, his gray eyes sparkling. But Brian's eyes sparkled all the time, laughing at some secret joke he never shared—at least not with her.

Megan smiled back, in honor of the good times.

When they were first introduced, she'd been divorced for three years. At that time, she spent a lot of time at work and was already drinking heavily. So when she met Brian, she was pleased to find a man who drank the way she did. Besides, Brian had made her laugh, made her feel like a woman. And yes, she had to admit—he was fabulous in bed. So Megan clung to him, just as she'd clung to Stephen.

At first, Brian took her to romantic places: Malibu, for picnics and sunsets; sailing trips to Catalina; exciting trips to Mexico and Las Vegas. But, as both of their addictions progressed, their lives had changed, and not for the better.

The relationship became a roller-coaster ride filled with manic ups and depressing downs. To counter her hangovers, Brian taught her the sorcery of drugs. He had a pill for everything, and Megan was a willing guinea pig. Finally, he thrilled her with the magic of cocaine, which allowed her to drink longer and still function normally.

Or so she thought. In time, Megan learned there was a heavy price to pay for all those feel-good drugs. And she'd paid it. Now, a week after receiving her ninety-day chip, she would not trade one moment of sobriety for Brian Mason or anyone else.

Brian was winding down his telephone conversation. "Okay, great. Yes, David, I'll see you tomorrow. Say hi to Rachel. Bye."

So, he'd been talking to her friend Rachel's philandering husband—another real winner in Megan's estimation.

She watched him gather his clothes.

"Thanks for the use of the phone." He walked to the door and turned. "Megan?"

"Yes."

"How would you like to go for dinner this weekend?" Brian stared at the floor, shuffling his feet like a little boy.

For a moment she felt a familiar tug on her heartstrings. "Please don't make this any harder, Brian. You know why I can't. I'm sorry."

His eyes narrowed and his mouth twisted downward, but the look passed quickly. "Let me know if you change your mind."

She didn't hear the door shut.

In the solitude of the empty living room, Megan almost had second thoughts. Brian had always claimed to love her, desperately. And he did, sometimes to the point of obsession. But he'd never really been around when she needed him—like the night of Allison Graham's murder. She remembered Gino Rosario, Kathleen's ex-husband, who had announced on the late TV news the discovery of Allison's body, just a few blocks from Megan's condo. Brian hadn't showed up all night. But he often didn't come home when he stayed out late with the boys. That night, Brian had slept on his sailboat, *Dreamer*.

*Get a grip, girl. Surely, you're not one of those dependent women who need a man around all the time, even when it's the wrong man.* Why couldn't she just accept it? Her relationship with Brian was a fiasco. It didn't work then, and it would never work now. Especially when he was drinking, and she was sober.

Suddenly, without conscious thought, Megan picked up Brian's drink and brought it to her mouth.

Holding the glass to her lips, she inhaled the sweet, woody smell of the scotch. It made her warm all over. She wanted it. "What the hell are you doing?" she cried and dropped the glass. It bounced off the coffee table and fell to the floor, scattering ice cubes everywhere. Megan stared at the pool of liquid as it formed an ever-widening circle on the beige carpet. Terrified, she stepped back.

The urge to drink was powerful, insidious—appearing when she was most vulnerable. Then she had a horrible thought. Had Brian left the half-full glass on purpose? Surely he wouldn't do that? But in her heart she knew he would.

Trembling, she knelt on the floor to clean up the mess.

Spying a slip of paper under the table, she picked it up. It was a page from Brian's phone book. She set it on the glass tabletop and finished her cleaning.

Afterward, she marched to the wet bar and emptied out every single bottle of liquor on the shelf. Even the Grand Marnier, which was her favorite.

"Dammit, I will not drink no matter what," she mumbled out loud.

The conflict churning in her gut was unbearable, but Megan had a solution for that and it wasn't booze or drugs. She went to the kitchen, opened the refrigerator door, and removed all her goodies, placing them on the counter. Compulsively, Megan prepared her famous Chocolate Quick Fix. She poured thick, dark syrup all over two scoops of Häagen-Dazs chocolate chocolate chip ice cream and added a scoopful of walnuts, some real whipped cream, and four maraschino cherries.

*Damn!* The chocolate overflowed. She licked the syrup off her fingers and the sides of the bowl and carried it to the living room.

*Hell,* she thought between mouthfuls, *maybe I should find a lover.*

She didn't want anything serious, just an uncomplicated, happy-go-lucky affair with a hot sexy man. Her mind flashed on the detective. No way. Megan knew, intuitively, a relationship with Matt Donovan would be anything but uncomplicated.

What she needed was the boytoy she and her pals had talked about on the yacht. She licked the back of her spoon, set it down on the table, and picked up the page from Brian's address book. She could see it was the D's. Darren Davenport, David, Danielle. Hmm, who was Danielle? Denny Daniels was a drug connection. Then, underlined in red, Destiny La Cunt? *Wha-a-a-t?* She read it again. That's what it said. And there were four little stars beside the name. Brian was such a pig!

Megan ripped the page into tiny pieces and placed them in a small crystal box on the coffee table. She picked up her spoon and devoured every last bite of the Chocolate Quick Fix. At least she wasn't drinking.

But who the hell was Destiny La ... whatever?

And what was her connection to Brian Mason?

# Chapter 6

Before leaving the crime scene, Matt spent another couple of hours on Beachview Avenue questioning the rest of Sherrie Weston's neighbors. The quiet street leading to the beach was eerily empty. And as usual, when any of the neighbors were questioned, no one heard, and no one saw, anything.

Tom Wilson, the medical examiner, had agreed to work late and complete Sherrie's autopsy, so Matt had joined him downtown for the entire procedure. But he was back in Venice by nine fifteen and decided to stop by Gold's Gym on his way home to work out some of the tension.

Although he was tired, he surprised himself with a fairly decent workout. Even at that late hour, Gold's was like a meat market—beautiful bodies everywhere. More goddamn action than the *Dating Game*.

He could have hooked up with someone, but instead he ate alone, as usual.

While driving home, Megan Riley popped into his mind again. She'd been doing that all day. *Shit*. What the hell was wrong with him? It was not like him to be so attracted to someone since the death of his wife.

Because he lived on one of the Venice walk streets, which were only wide enough for a small sidewalk, he parked the car in the alley, vowing, as he had for the past six years, to paint the house before summer was over. The shit-colored brown was even getting on his nerves now. Maybe he'd paint it white. He knew he should sell it. The place had too many memories. But he just didn't have the heart.

Entering through the kitchen door, he went straight to his bedroom, turned on the overhead light, and then pushed the button of the answering machine on a side table next to the unmade bed.

"Hi, Daddy, I'm just calling to see how you're doing. Everything here is perfect. I've got a callback tomorrow for a cosmetic ad. This could be the big one. I'll let you know what happens. Good night, Daddy, I love you."

Matt smiled. Nothing warmed his heart more than the sound of his daughter's voice. God, he missed her. Julie was the sweetest, most beautiful—he stopped the thought. No sense making himself any lonelier than he already was.

He checked his watch. It was way too late to call New York.

He hit the button again.

"Hello, Matt, this is Angelle."

He loved his partner's voice and was charmed by her accent. Actually, he liked Angelle Bentley altogether. She was quiet, unassuming, and she definitely knew what she was doing when it came to detective work. Those years she'd spent in Miami as a DEA officer had taught her a lot.

"I found a Michael Harrington in the telephone book. He lives at the Marina. We can pay him a visit in the morning. I also went through the evidence taken from Sherrie's Mustang. Found some interesting stuff—traces of heroin, a box full of pills, a bunch of pretty sexy underwear, and some nasty leather goods. I did not find her trick book in the house, or anything else of interest. Did you watch the DVDs the neighbor gave you? If it's not too late, call me back. Bye."

DVDs? *Damn.* How could he have forgotten the disks in the UPS package, the ones the neighbor had given him? Was it only this afternoon? He'd been so damn busy, it seemed like a week ago. Anyway, he figured they were probably just porn, like the old lady had said.

They were in the trunk of his car. He pulled on some gloves just in case.

On his way back into the house, Matt tore open the plain brown wrapper. As expected, there were two DVDs. He read the small label attached to each plastic cover.

*Fantasy Films? Whoa, real Academy Award stuff.*

He turned on the TV and popped one of the disks into the drive.

Murky black-and-white film, crappy music, no credits.

The old lady was right—it was porn. But Matt hadn't expected to recognize the bedroom of Sherrie's house on Beachview. Black paper on the windows, just like today, except there was no body on the bed, and the place looked a hell of a lot more tidy.

Sherrie came on-screen wearing a black see-through nightgown. With a sexy move, she slid the straps off her shoulders. It fell to the floor in a dark puddle. Naked, she lay down on the bed. *Shit.* Watching her on-screen, alive and well, was like a dream.

*No, more like a friggin' nightmare.*

The last time he'd seen Sherrie Weston she was a pale husk on the mortuary table. Just hours ago, he'd watched Tom Wilson slice her body open in a Y-cut and saw him weigh and measure her organs and place them in plastic bags to be stored in the freezer.

Sickened, Matt tried to concentrate on the screen.

There was more. Much more. Some guy? Who was this guy? *Holy shit.* It looked like George Fisher ... wearing ladies' friggin' underwear. George was grinning foolishly. He was tiptoeing onto the screen in strappy high heels, wearing a pink lacy bra over his white hairless chest and an oversized garter belt slung below his huge belly. The black mesh stockings were a special added touch, thought Matt. What a sight!

Was somebody filming this piece of shit or was it a do-it-yourselfer?

He stopped the tape. There was no disk in the camera when Matt discovered it. But maybe Sherrie had filmed others with her hidden camera. Maybe even the killer.

He started it again. The action went on for another fifteen minutes. More and more of the same boring shit, but he ran it through to the end on the chance there was something other than George Fisher on the DVD. Nothing.

He ran the second DVD. It was an exact duplicate.

Maybe whoever owned the disks had sent her these copies.

Maybe she planned on giving one to George for a present. Not likely. She probably wanted an extra one so she could stash it someplace and collect from George, indefinitely.

Fantasy Films. *Hmm.* He reexamined the small labels on each of the disks.

There was an address in San Francisco. And he would get there as soon as he could. Matt knew from experience. It would all come together and he'd find the sick son of a bitch if it was the last thing he did.

He glanced at his watch, again. Now it was too late to call Angelle.

Matt headed for the shower.

"San Francisco, open your pearly gates," he sang, lathering his body with Irish Spring.

Drying himself, he switched on the TV. Maybe he could catch himself on the eleven o'clock news.

† † †

Megan jolted awake. She was in a cold sweat, shaking.

For a minute or two she felt disoriented. Then she heard the sounds of the ocean. Her ocean.

A dream. It was only a dream.

She turned on the light. She was in her own room, thank God.

Megan recalled going to bed, remembered tossing and turning for over an hour.

Then the dream.

The detective was telling her about the Bondage Murder, showing her a photo. But it wasn't Allison who was dead. From above, she could actually see herself lying on a table in the morgue, her body mangled and broken. Then Megan was inside her head, looking out, feeling the cold steel on her back, and seeing the bright sterile lights overhead.

Her ex-husband, Stephen, was there, laughing.

But there was another man. He wore a dark green parka with a fur-trimmed hood concealing his face. Megan recognized the jacket. She knew who it was. He tossed back his head to drink, and the hood slipped. It was a terrible sight. But the eyes? The sad, gray eyes of her dead father were very much alive as he handed her the bottle ... and she drank from it.

Fire burned all the way to her gut.

But she drank it. She drank it all.

*Oh, my God.* She'd broken her sobriety.

No, no. It was only a dream. A "drunk" dream. Her body shook and wouldn't stop. She said the Serenity Prayer, the Lord's Prayer, and a full string of Hail Marys. Nothing worked. She tried to talk herself sane.

It hadn't been the best of days. First, she saw the photo of the murdered girl, and then Brian scared her half to death and left his damn whiskey to tempt her. Of course the giant ice cream sundae she'd consumed before going to bed hadn't helped either.

Who wouldn't have nightmares?

Megan hadn't dreamed of her daddy for a long time. Right after his death, the dreams of her father came every night.

Her mind flashed back to her painful childhood in Buffalo, New York, and her daddy. She would never, ever, forget that day. It was etched in her mind forever.

On January 28, her twelfth birthday, she'd been on her way to school with her best friend, Dolores. She was excited about her special day. Giggling and daydreaming of streamers, balloons, and presents, the two girls had plodded through a fresh fall of snow and stopped at the old family Ford parked at the curb.

Someone sat in the driver's seat, someone who wore a dark green parka.

Was it Daddy? Drunk again? Passed out? He surely must be freezing. Her heart raced just thinking about it.

She'd pulled open the car door and tried to wake him up, felt the coldness of his hand, his cheek. Emotions, bleak and raw as that icy day in January, assailed her. Pain swooped down and seeped into that hidden place deep inside, the secret place in her belly where unresolved feelings are converted into fear, anxiety, and rage.

Her chest tightened. Even now, the memories affected her, deeply.

The autopsy said he died of a heart attack. But Megan knew,

even as a child, it was the bottle of cheap wine between his legs and the many others before it that had killed her daddy. She'd never celebrated a birthday since.

Four years later, almost to the day, her mom had a stroke. Confined to her bed, it took her mother another four years to die—forty-nine months and seventeen days, to be exact. Megan had been her sole caretaker, and when it was all over her teenage years were gone.

Not long after the funeral, alone and with little money, Megan had headed west.

And ten years later here she was. Part of that time she'd spent educating herself, several years on a failed marriage, and then another dreadful relationship with Brian.

*Stop thinking about the past, girl.* She blinked away her tears and grabbed the remote. *Mindless TV, that's what I need.*

Gino Rosario materialized on-screen. As always, she wondered what her friend Kathleen saw in him. He looked like your typical gigolo, with his greasy black hair, suave manner, and slick Armani suits. As far as Megan was concerned, Gino was a walking, talking case of infidelity, and she didn't think his new girlfriend would have any luck with him, either.

"Another gruesome Bondage Murder in Venice last night," Gino was saying. "Our reporter, Marcia Waters, was on the scene this afternoon as police were investigating. Marci, won't you tell us what's happening?"

Instantly alert, Megan sat up and pulled the comforter to her chin.

The camera focused on a shabby clapboard bungalow with a white picket fence. Several curious neighbors congregated at the gate; some waved at the camera while others stared blankly.

A slender blonde woman stepped into the picture. "Yes, Gino, Marcia Waters here. Once again we're here at Venice Beach, this time at 42 Beachview Avenue, the home of an unidentified woman. According to police, she was murdered sometime Tuesday night or early this morning. It is unclear if this death is connected to the other Venice homicide the press is calling the Bondage Murder. If you recall, Gino, the body of Allison Graham was found on the beach, not far from here, in March of this year."

The house looked familiar to Megan. Beachview Avenue? She didn't know anyone with that address. Maybe she'd been in the area, checking out property.

Suddenly, her ex-boyfriend, Brian, came to mind. Could she have gone there with him? But why? Megan racked her brain and couldn't come up with an answer. Nor could she shake the haunting feeling of déjà vu.

The reporter tried to question the policeman who stood guard at the white picket fence. "Officer, can you tell us about the murder victim? Has she been identified yet?"

"I'm sorry, miss. No comment."

"Who discovered the body?"

But the cop was adamant. "No comment, ma'am."

The camera swung over to a neighbor's house, where Detective Matt Donovan was talking, animatedly, to an elderly man on the rickety porch.

The reporter ascended the steps of the veranda and shoved the microphone toward him. "Detective Donovan, is there anything more you can tell us?"

Megan turned up the sound.

"No comment." He pushed the microphone away.

Immediately, the reporter made her way to another house where an old woman stood on the porch, watching all the action.

Marcia began plying her with the questions. "How well did you know the victim Mrs. …?"

"Zuckerman. Z-u-c-k-e-r-m-a-n."

"Ahem, yes, Mrs. Zuckerman, did you know her well?"

"Better than she thought I did." The old lady rocked back on her heels.

"Do you know what time the body was discovered?"

"I should. I was the one as found 'er."

The reporter's face lit up. "Oh, really?"

"You shoulda seen her, tied up on the bed she was, one … missing." The word was beeped out.

"Oh, no." Marcia Waters looked visibly shaken.

Mrs. Zuckerman continued. "Yup, it don't surprise me, though.

The goings-on in that house for the last coupla years, I could write a book, I could."

The reporter's face brightened again. "I'm sure our audience is eager to hear your story."

Matt Donovan reappeared on the screen and took Mrs. Zuckerman's arm. He turned and aimed his killer smile at Marcia and then directly into the camera.

Megan felt an involuntary thrill and leaned back into the pillow.

As he led the old lady back into the house, the detective turned. "I'll have a press conference, Ms. Waters. Very soon, I promise."

Marcia Waters assumed a sincere expression as she made her closing statement. "Well, that's it for now, Gino. The police apparently want to keep the lid on this, the second Bondage Murder on the Westside. Remember, you heard it first on Channel Three. This is Marcia Waters in Venice, saying good night, and back to you in the studio, Gino."

Gino came back on-screen, showing an obsequious smile. "That is quite a story, Marcia. Keep up the good work and get back to us if there's anything new to report."

Megan clicked off the set.

She jumped out of bed and walked to the window. A thick blanket of fog crept over the sand, obliterating her view of the ocean. On the boardwalk, yellow halogen lights surrounded by an aura of moisture cast little light, adding to the eeriness of the landscape. Listening to the soft swoosh of surf stroking the beach, she wondered if the waves were the last sounds Allison Graham had heard before she died. Or was she murdered somewhere else and then dumped on the beach?

Megan crossed her arms over her breasts, and a cloud of sadness settled on her heart. Who could have killed those two young women so brutally?

# CHAPTER 7

MATT AND HIS partner, Angelle Bentley, sat on the dock for at least thirty minutes, waiting for Michael Harrington to show up.

He didn't mind the wait; in fact, Matt reveled in the early-morning peacefulness of the Marina—so cool and quiet, the water calm with faint threads of mist lingering on its surface. It was a rare moment for him to feel so relaxed.

Looking around at the assortment of power yachts and sailboats, Matt tried to estimate the cost of Michael Harrington's thirty-foot schooner moored on the end slip. The sailboat was old but appeared in mint condition. Someone had spent plenty of hours keeping the white paint pristine, and even more time varnishing the gleaming teak rails. But it probably wasn't worth much, maybe twenty grand. A pittance compared to the high-powered cigar boat in the next slip.

In the silence, Matt considered Angelle. Perched on a gray steel dock box, her legs dangling, she stared into space.

He'd called her Angel from the second day they'd worked together. It suited her. Angel Bentley. From what she'd told him, she'd arrived in Los Angeles only three months ago, along with her eight-year-old son and her mother. After three years with the Drug Enforcement Agency in Miami, most of it undercover, she wasn't used to working with a partner. And it showed. But Matt knew, instinctively, that Angelle Bentley was a good cop, and her reputation as an expert in Caribbean cults had preceded her to Los Angeles. He knew she had witnessed many vicious and bloody crime scenes in her pursuit of drug lords and the ritual murderers who killed in the name of Santeria and Voudon, yet she still maintained a level of empathy. He admired her for that.

When Captain Rick had first introduced them a couple of weeks ago, the strength in Angelle's handshake had impressed him. Her face was unusual, structured like one of those African masks you see in the museum with high cheekbones and arched brows. She had the most unusual eyes. Matt had once seen a lion in the zoo with those same amber eyes. The haunted expression in them did not belong on a woman so young, and they told him that Angelle Bentley had suffered more than her share of pain. But right now, squeezed into her navy wool suit, she looked hot and restless.

Luckily, Matt had left his jacket in the car and wore only a light cotton shirt and chinos. He raised his face to catch the rays.

Presently, a tall athletic young man walked down the dock. He wore pale-blue Levi's, seemingly painted on his long muscular legs, and a denim shirt of the same color. Under the brim of his jaunty captain's hat were two very blue eyes.

"Michael Harrington?" Matt displayed his badge. "I'm Detective Donovan, LAPD, and this is Detective Bentley. We'd like to ask you a few questions."

Michael looked surprised. "Questions about what?"

"Do you know a young woman named Sherrie Weston?"

"Yes, is she in some kind of trouble?"

Matt glanced toward Michael's sailboat, rocking gently in the wake of a passing yacht. "May we board? This may take a little time."

"Of course." Michael climbed over the gunwales and offered his hand to Angelle.

A cracked white leather banquette formed a semicircle behind the steering wheel of the boat, and a couple of aluminum chairs were set out for guests.

Michael ducked under the heavy boom wrapped with canvas and sat down on the leather seat. He gestured toward the chairs. "Can I get you a cold drink?"

"Not for me, thanks." Angelle dropped into one of the chairs.

Matt sat down and pulled himself closer to Harrington. "No, thanks."

Leaning back, Michael stretched his powerful legs. "Okay, shoot."

"How well did you know Miss Weston?" Matt asked.

Harrington quickly drew back his legs. "Something's happened to her?" There was a distinct tone of concern in his voice.

Matt assessed his body language. Fear? Guilt? "Miss Weston was murdered in her home early Wednesday morning."

"Murdered?" Visibly shaken, he groaned. "But I just saw her Tuesday evening." For a brief moment, Michael closed his eyes. When he opened them and spoke, his voice was almost belligerent. "You do know that some guy had a heart attack right there in her house?"

Matt nodded but volunteered no further information.

Obviously disturbed by Sherrie's death, the young man ranted on. "And when I saw her she really looked bad, like she was on something. She told me she hadn't eaten in days."

Leaning forward, Angelle said one word. "Heroin?"

Michael's jaw tightened. "Yes, and God knows what else."

"How well did you know Miss Weston?" she asked.

"Barely. I worked with her at Party Favorites."

"Were you dating her?"

"What you mean is, was I a trick?" Vehemently, Michael shook his head. "Look, all I did was drop by the house to see if she was okay. Rosa—that's my manager at Party Favorites—she asked me to check up on her." He glanced at Matt and then back at Angelle, finally realizing he might be a suspect. "I worked with her. That's all."

Matt had tried to contact Party Favorites after finding the card in George Fisher's pocket but so far had not made a connection. He reminded himself to follow up again.

"Do you know of anyone else she might be seeing?"

"The truth is, dammit, I hardly knew the girl."

"When did you two meet?" Angelle asked.

"Three or four months ago. No more than that. I met her at work."

She lowered her voice. "S&M, Mr. Harrington? Ever try a little recreational bondage?"

"S&M? Are you kidding?" Michael stared directly into Angelle's eyes, a small smile playing on his lips. "Not me, ma'am, I like my sex straight with lots of moonlight and no complications."

Angelle did not avert her gaze. "What time did you leave Sherrie's house?"

"Must have been seven, seven thirty. I felt sorry for her. She looked terrible. I fixed her something to eat, talked for a few minutes, and then I left."

Lifting her eyebrows, Angelle shot Matt a swift look. "You cooked for her?"

"Uh-huh, I made her a boiled egg and toast. Like I said, she hadn't eaten in days." Michael paused. "Sherrie was quite taken with the coat hanger trick."

Matt jumped on that one. "And what is the coat hanger trick?"

"It's something my dad taught me when I was a kid. You place a slice of bread on top of a folded coat hanger …" He hesitated, looking from one detective to the other. "You don't believe me?"

"Show us how it's done," Angelle coaxed.

Michael disappeared below.

Waiting, Matt directed his attention to the water, where two sleek kayaks were skimming along, propelled by two muscular young men. Over on the next dock, a cute little blonde in Daisy Mae cutoffs hosed down the deck of a small catamaran. Matt took a deep breath, inhaling the tart, briny smell of the sea. He saw a fish leap out of the water and then another. Obviously, an underwater predator was chasing its prey.

Michael came back to the deck, carrying a wire coat hanger.

He folded the hanger in half, allowing a space a couple of inches deep. This, Michael explained, kept the bread raised up from the flame of the gas burner so it wouldn't catch fire.

So that's why there was soot on the hanger. Matt leaned forward to examine the wire contraption. He took the folded wire from Michael and straightened it out. "This is very imaginative, Mr. Harrington. Did you then lengthen the same coat hanger and strangle Sherrie Weston with it?"

Michael had a bewildered look on his face, and his left eye twitched nervously. "What the hell are you talking about? Of course I didn't."

"But Sherrie Weston was strangled"—Matt manipulated the hanger into a noose and held it up—"with the very same coat hanger you say you used to make toast."

"Why the hell would I want to kill her?" Harrington raised his voice, a manic glaze on his startling blue eyes.

Matt shrugged. "Maybe you were in love with her and didn't want her to turn any more tricks."

"Look, this is really crazy." Michael glanced at Angelle, almost for support. "The whole time I was at the house Sherrie was trying to get rid of me. Maybe someone else was there with her."

"Did that make you angry, Michael?" Matt asked, using his Christian name for the first time.

"No, goddamn it, it didn't. I keep telling you I hardly knew the girl." The alarm on Michael's face was evident.

But Matt persisted. "Did you go back to Sherrie's house later that night?"

"No, I did not, sir."

"So where were you on Tuesday night?"

"I took the boat down the coast to Paradise Cove."

Matt scratched his head and remained skeptical. "Alone?"

"Yes, alone."

"Do you do that often?"

"Yes, I do." Michael must have realized how lame his alibi sounded, because he stood up, ending the interview. "And now, I don't think I'm going to say anything more without consulting a lawyer. I know that much about the law."

That was Matt's cue to quit. He didn't want the slightest doubt cast on the integrity of his interrogation of Michael Harrington.

Heaving a deep sigh, Matt rose from his seat. "As far as I can figure out, you were the last person to see Miss Weston alive, other than the murderer. Take it from me, Mr. Harrington, you'd better contact your attorney at once, because I will be back, with an arrest warrant. My advice is that you come down to the station, voluntarily, and make a statement." He didn't have a speck of physical evidence to link this kid to the murder; he just wanted to scare him. Maybe then he would come in on his own.

From the terrified look on young Michael's face, it looked like it was going to work.

# Chapter 8

Megan drove up to the parking valet at Bayside Yacht Club, quickly exited her black Mercedes, and tossed her keys to the uniformed attendant. As usual, she was late for her luncheon date with the girls and hoped she wasn't the last one there.

Hurrying through the brass-and-glass turnstile door, she entered the sumptuous lobby of the club. The marble tile sparkled, reflecting the heavy furniture and antique brass lighting fixtures.

*A lot of spit and polish goes into this place,* Megan thought. That's when she slipped and almost lost her balance on a slick patch of tile between two hand-woven Kashmiri rugs. Promptly, she righted herself.

Greenery was in abundance in the two-storied entryway, and tall potted palms arranged like soldiers guarded the paneled walls. Every mahogany table—and there were many—held a porcelain pot or Chinese footbath filled with English ivy, exotic orchids, and other fascinating arrangements. In fact, the money this club spent on flower arrangements was mind-boggling. Megan wished they would donate some of that cash to Mothers in Recovery. But she had been pleased when the club had offered the entire dining room, free of charge, for the charity luncheon in December.

Megan checked her watch and quickened her step as she rounded the corner to the dining room. She smacked into a very hard body. She lost her breath and her purse.

"Why don't you look where—" Muttering to herself, she dropped down to the floor to pick up her purse. As she rose from this position, she lifted her gaze all the way up the entire six feet of muscle towering over her.

It was him, the handsome detective.

"Are you all right, miss?" Matt Donovan's voice was filled with concern.

The old gray-haired maître d', with whom the detective had been conversing, hovered over her. "Miss Riley, can I get you something? Would you like to sit down? Can I get you some water? An aspirin?"

Impatiently, Megan brushed him away. "I'm fine, Pierre, thank you."

"I'm very sorry. I just didn't see you coming." Matt was still apologizing as the maître d' half-carried, half-pushed her across the ballroom floor to a window table overlooking the harbor.

"Really, I'm fine. Thank you, Pierre." Megan scanned the empty dining room. After all that, she was the first one there.

"You sure you're okay?" Matt leaned over and searched her face with his hypnotic eyes.

"I'm perfectly fine." She didn't mean to sound irritated, but that's the way it came out.

"Good," said the detective curtly. "Then I'll be on my way."

She watched as Matt, followed by Pierre, stalked across the floor and practically ran over Rachel Feinman. She felt bad that she hadn't been more gracious. *Oh, well.*

Seeing Rachel as she approached, Megan was shocked. Her usually impeccable friend was in total disarray. Tiny wisps of dark hair escaped haphazardly from her upsweep, and her navy cotton shirt and white pants looked like they had been slept in. "My God, girl, you look ghastly," she said, unable to stop herself.

"Thanks a lot. That's just what I needed to hear." Rachel took the seat held out for her by the waiter. "I've been up all night. What I need is a drink." She ordered a Bloody Mary. "Megan?"

"I'll have a Diet Coke." When the waiter was gone, Megan reached over and patted her friend's hand. "Tell me what happened."

"David's cheating on me," she blurted.

"Are you sure?" For Rachel's benefit, Megan registered surprise, but the news only confirmed what everybody had always suspected.

"I saw him with my own eyes." Rachel burst into tears. "Oh, God, it was so humiliating. I hung around outside the porthole of our boat, like a creepy, peeping Tom watching them make out. But I had to be sure. Can you understand that?"

Megan loved her casual reference to the boat. David's fifty-five-foot yacht *Father's Office* was anything but a mere boat, and it had always been a major problem in Rachel's marriage. David spent most of his time on *Father's Office*, claiming it was the only place he could find the peace and quiet to create. Why he needed so much peace to write the blood-and-guts screenplays for which he was so famous, Megan couldn't imagine. She'd always figured it was a different kind of piece that kept David out all night. Apparently, she was right. She tuned back in to Rachel.

"I wish I'd had the courage to drag the bitch out of his bed," Rachel spat. Then she uttered the final indignity. "She was so young, Megan. Why did she have to be so goddamn young?"

Leaning closer, Megan asked, "Did David see you?"

"I don't think so. He was still whispering sweet nothings in her ear when I left."

"What did you do?"

"I slunk into the night, like the gutless wonder that I am." Tears flowed freely through Rachel's mascara and down her cheeks in thin black rivulets. She hurried to wipe them away as the waiter approached with their drinks.

As the server set their glasses on cocktail napkins, Alex Grant, dressed from head to toe in white linen, joined them. She pointed to the Bloody Mary. "I'll take one of those, please."

"Yes, ma'am," and the waiter was gone.

Trying to bring Alex up to speed, Megan blurted, "Rachel caught David in bed with another woman last night."

Without so much as a flicker of an eye, Alex drawled in her know-it-all voice, "Now you listen to me, Rachel, honey. You're gonna do exactly like the rest of us women. You're gonna make the most important decision in your whole life." She paused, waiting for her reaction.

There was no response at all from Rachel.

Megan tried to read her expression. Her eyes were dark bottomless pools, betraying absolutely nothing. The long night of stress had carved deep lines into Rachel's forehead, and her generous mouth was pulled into a tight, peevish line.

Alex continued the tirade, her Southern drawl barely softening the bitterness she so obviously felt. "Now, honey, you can wait for David to come home—and you might even confront him. But he's gonna deny it to the death. He'll accuse you of spying on him. The fight will rage on, and on … no one ever wins. And you'll probably end up divorcin' him."

"Oh, my God," Rachel groaned. "What about my kids?"

Megan knew she didn't have the answers. That was for sure.

But Alex had plenty. "There is another alternative. You can ignore the whole episode. Forget you ever saw it. When David comes home you'll smile sweetly and say to him, 'How was your day, darlin'?' No accusations. No recriminations. No fights. And your marriage goes on like before."

Rachel looked appalled. "I don't know if I can do that."

Alex was quick to answer. "I did it with my first husband, and I did it with Charlie. And we all know Junie Fisher was doin' it for years with ol' George."

"What do you think, Megan?" Rachel asked.

"It looks like Alex has it all figured out." What else could she say? Get angry, leave your husband, and deprive your kids of a father. No, Rachel had to come to that decision all by herself.

Rachel looked even more miserable.

So Megan changed the subject. "Not to diminish your problem, Rachel, but Kathleen had a pretty rough night too. I tell you, if I'd had that bastard Gino Rosario in my hands this morning, I would have strangled him. When I went to meet the broker this morning, I found Kathleen huddled in the corner of the living room in exactly the same condition Gino left her last night. The poor dear had been crying for hours. At first I thought he'd hit her, but he hadn't—at least not with his hands. But the verbal abuse must have been horrendous. It took me forever to get her cleaned up and into her car before the broker arrived to show the house. I had to stay for a while to speak to the clients, and when I finally got here I found her in the ladies' room, still trying to pull herself together."

"What do you expect from a bastard like Gino?" Alex spat.

Still self-absorbed, Rachel didn't appear to snap out of it until she actually saw Kathleen crossing the room. "Oh, dear, she looks terrible."

"Yes, she does," agreed Megan. *Even though she's been primping in the powder room for heaven knows how long.*

But at least Rachel now had someone else to worry about other than herself.

*Why is life such a bitch? And full of so much pain.* Megan was glad her two-year relationship with Brian Mason was over. Glad he'd shown his true colors last night by leaving his drink on the table to tempt her. And especially glad she'd run into the detective again—and with such a bang.

As she approached, Kathleen's face looked swollen, her eyes bloodshot and puffy. Luckily, Megan had managed to get her fairly well put together in jeans and a white shirt before she had left the house. And the additional blush she had recently piled on helped considerably.

Rachel slid her arm around Kathleen. "You poor baby."

Lifting a tear-stained face, Kathleen moaned. "Gino said he's going to marry Jennifer. She's seven months pregnant. And he wants the money from our home to buy a house for Jennifer and the baby—my baby. That should be my baby." Her entire body shook as she spoke.

"You'll find someone else. I know you will, Kathleen." Megan tried to offer even a small ray of hope. *And maybe even have a child of your own.* She didn't say this out loud, but who knew what was down the road? They were performing all kinds of miracles in fertility these days. There might even be one out there for Kathleen.

An eerie silence descended on the table, and Megan could see that each of her friends was wrapped up in her own thoughts, her own dilemmas. Maybe she was the lucky one. Even if she didn't have a lot of money like the other girls, Megan was doing okay. And, with the help of AA, her life was beginning to sort itself out. Maybe having a husband really wasn't the answer to all of life's problems. In fact, it looked to Megan like having a husband was the cause of a lot of them.

Lunch was a solemn occasion with little small talk, and Megan was sipping the last of her cappuccino and enjoying its aroma, when the widow Fisher breezed into the dining room.

Squeezed into an abominable black suit, not unlike a sausage, and wearing flat Ferragamo shoes, George Fisher's wife, Junie, scurried across the polished floor. "I'm so glad to see you all. You are coming to the memorial for dear, dear George?" She handed Megan a slip of paper and then adjusted the black fedora resting on her dark frizzy hair. The hat was her only salute to modern fashion. "Here's the address and a map. We're having a wonderful reception afterwards—here at the club. I do hope your husbands can make it, too. You can come alone, dear," she said, patting Kathleen's arm. "I'm sure Gino will come by himself of bring his girlfriend."

Kathleen burst into tears again.

"Oh, my word," Junie cried. "Did I say the wrong thing?"

"We'll take care of her." Megan reached for Kathleen's hand as Junie left in a flurry.

"Well, so much for love," Alex said, the bitterness seeping back into her voice. "It's just another party according to Junie Fisher."

"What *about* love, Alex?" Rachel said in her cynical voice. "What do you think love is?"

Alex smiled. "Well, for me, and y'all know this is just my opinion." She stared at the expectant faces. "Love is a grand passion … passion without reason … crazy and irrational, with no end but itself." She paused. "Until it runs out of steam. Then, what do you have left?"

Megan sipped her coffee. *A lot of damn suffering*, she thought to herself.

But Alex wasn't finished. "I'll tell you what's left. Just your silly dreams of what coulda been or shoulda been—if only." She lowered her lashes. "You see, my first husband, Richard, was my knight in shining armor. I would've laid myself down in front of a speeding train had he asked me to."

"What happened? What happened to Richard?" Kathleen pleaded.

"It's not a happy ending." Alex fumbled for a tissue in her white Chanel bag.

"Go on," Megan urged.

Wiping the single tear from her eye, Alex continued. "Love flies out the window when poverty limps in the door, especially when it's accompanied by drunkenness, infidelity, and the odd Saturday night beating."

In her wildest dreams, Megan would never have imagined Alex as a woman who would put up with that sort of abuse.

"I was seventeen when I married him. He was the man of my dreams: tall, athletic, studyin' to be a navy pilot." She stopped and didn't speak for the longest time, as if she were reliving that period of her life. She attempted to say something further, but nothing came out. Swallowing hard, her next words spewed from her mouth. "When Richard was killed in that automobile accident, I was glad."

Shocked, Megan pulled back.

The waiter hovered around the table. "Can I get you another drink, ladies?"

"Why the hell not?" Alex's voice rang with false gaiety. "Give us another round."

Leaning forward, Rachel touched Alex's hand. "But if you believe that love is this raving passion, what do you think about plain old sexual desire?"

Megan could hear the anxiety at the root of Rachel's question and tried to think of something to say—anything that might heal the wounds her friend was carrying—but she couldn't. She couldn't think of a single thing. Rachel was going to have to live with the humiliation of David's infidelity for a long, long time. Maybe she'd never get over it.

A feeling of futility swept over Megan. *Doesn't anyone have a relationship that works? Is there no hope at all?*

Still contemplating the answer to Rachel's question, Alex swished the ice around in her empty glass. "Sexual desire is just a basic instinct, a bodily function, like eating or drinking. Something built in to guarantee the survival of the species."

A long silence followed.

In her usual attempt to lighten things up, Megan added, "And, since God is very smart, *She* made it fun and called it lust with a capital L."

The laughter that broke the pensive mood was not without a touch of hysteria.

"What about Charlie, Alex? Are you in love with him?" Kathleen asked, twisting her napkin into a long, thin roll.

"Charlie's one of the best things that ever happened to me. If he hadn't found me in little ol' Pensacola, Florida, I'd still be workin' in a dead-end job or married to some underpaid sailor."

"Yeah, but how is he in bed?" Rachel demanded.

Alex's face colored slightly, but she answered. "Oh, we've had a few memorable moments. On a moonlit night when the champagne is flowing, you close your eyes, your fantasies take over, and sometimes there's satisfaction. But for the most part, the sex act with Charlie has always been … basically an act of gratitude!" With that, Alex shrugged her fragile shoulders and smiled, wistfully.

Megan stared at her friend. *Well, I guess that says it all.*

But, she wondered, how many more secrets were her three friends still keeping?

# Chapter 9

When Angelle returned to the station after finally meeting with Rosa at Party Favorites, she hailed Matt while he was still in the lot, parking his car. Walking together into their office, she told him that Rosa Martinez had been visiting her family in Mexico for the last few days, and that was why they could not reach her.

Apparently, Rosa had assumed control of the operation in April of this year. Since there was no profit margin, the previous owner, Ray Jennings, had simply signed over the business. The present mission of the company appeared to be providing strippers, both male and female, to perform at parties and showers and to deliver birthday and congratulatory telegrams.

"Did Sherrie Weston ever work there?" asked Matt.

"Yes, as a stripper, but only for a short time."

"What about Michael Harrington?"

"He's been there for about three months. And yes, Rosa did send him to Sherrie's house. She hadn't been able to contact her for a few days, and she had a job for her, delivering a birthday telegram. Apparently, Rosa is short on help."

"Well, at least Michael's story checks out. But this does not totally exonerate him. We don't have motive yet, but we sure have opportunity."

"I'm checking on the previous owner of Party Favorites, and I'll let you know when I get the info."

"Good work, Angelle. Write up the report and put it in the murder book."

Back in his office, Matt was cornered by his ex-partner, Joe Schumann. "Hey, Donovan, got a minute?"

"Yeah, what's up?" Matt sat down at his desk, and the overweight cop flopped onto a steel folding chair opposite him.

Joe's face was round and flat, except for a bulbous nose displaying a red vein for every year the aging detective had devoted to booze. Steel-colored hair fringed his balding head, like a monk's tonsure, and quick eyes, alert and hard as tiny brown pebbles, probed Matt's brain. But Matt stared him down.

The defiance fading, Joe lowered his eyes. "What I wanna say is this. Can I get in on the new case wit' you and Angelle?"

"You mean the Bondage Murders?"

"Yeah, I only got six months before I retire, and I'd like to go out on something really worthwhile here."

It was hard to imagine Joe Schumann looking sheepish, but sheepish he was. "Sure, pal. Why don't you run it by Captain Rick? I was going to ask him for a couple more men anyway. But first, I want you to check out this movie with me and Angelle."

Elated, Joe stood up and yelled across the crowded office for one and all to hear. "Hey, Angelle, come on, we got a porno to watch."

A loud clamor arose from the rest of the guys. They wanted to see it, too.

*That was a dumb move, Joe.* "Believe me, you're not missing much." Matt tried to console them as he headed for the conference room.

The remainder of the afternoon was spent with Joe and Angelle, running and rerunning the film of George Fisher and Sherrie Weston.

By the time Matt had seen it three more times, his mind wandered. He thought about Megan Riley. Strange. She'd been anything but friendly when he'd slammed into her at Bayside this morning. And it sure as hell wasn't his fault; she was the one who ran into him. He couldn't get Megan out of his mind and kept trying to figure some way to meet up with her again—away from the investigation.

The police shrink he'd talked to after his wife's death would have a field day with that one. Since his wife's passing, Matt had not been attracted to anyone, not even the beautiful Angelle. Not that he'd get mixed up with his partner.

Matt zoned back in on the tape. Over and over it played till he knew every single blemish on Sherrie Weston's body and was sick to death of looking at George Fisher in his transvestite outfit—the pink garter belt and bra revealing more of George's pale flesh than Matt cared to see. "Number one question," he said. "Did George know she was taking these films?"

Angelle shook her head. "I doubt it."

"I can't get over his fucking stockings," Joe said for the third time.

"Did this video have anything to do with George Fisher's heart attack?" Matt asked.

"Maybe, maybe not." Angelle tapped her pen on the table. "Since the two disks weren't delivered by UPS until after Sherrie's murder, chances are George didn't know about them yet."

"On the other hand," Joe argued, "maybe George knew about the disk and she was getting him an extra one. You know, so he could watch it at home and jack off. Pardon me, Angelle, masturbate."

"Good point," she agreed. "Some couples like to star in their own porno movies. In fact, I saw a story about it on cable TV a couple of weeks ago."

"Everybody wants to be a star," Joe lamented.

"That may be true in George's case," Matt said, thinking aloud. "But what if Sherrie had a film of Allison's murder and decided to blackmail the killer? He sure as hell wouldn't like having a film floatin' around of him playing with his whip and handcuffs and whatever other crap he fools around with. Maybe he murdered Sherrie to get his hands on that film."

"And had a good time while he was at it," said Joe.

Angelle looked thoughtful. "I find that hard to believe. Allison was her best friend. Surely, Sherrie would have turned him in if she knew who killed her."

"Maybe, maybe not. The money would be awfully tempting to someone like Sherrie." Matt changed the subject. "Tom Wilson called this morning. He found blood other than Sherrie's in the grooves of the claw feet of the tub—Allison's blood type. He sent it to Cellmark for DNA." He sighed. "I say it's the same perp. He tortured and killed Allison in the house on Beachview Avenue, cleaned up the mess, and then carried the body to the beach."

After a moment's silence, Angelle said, "Tell me more about Allison Graham."

Before Allison's murder case was set aside, due to the lack of any feasible leads, Joe had been partnered with Matt. He slid a thick file across the table. "Here's the murder book."

Matt opened it up and lapsed into the impersonal drone of policespeak. "Allison Graham was a nineteen-year-old hooker from Mobile, Alabama." He handed Angelle a shot of Allison's body lying on the beach.

Glancing at it, she inhaled a deep breath.

Fishing in another file, Matt retrieved a similar crime scene photo of Sherrie Weston and gave it to her.

"The mutilation is identical. They must be connected."

"Right." He continued to read. "Allison Graham. Caucasian, five feet, 110 pounds, blonde, fair complexion, heavy into coke, heroin, and amphetamines."

"They're all on something," Joe muttered.

Matt shrugged and then continued. "Cause of death was asphyxia by ligature strangulation, ligature unknown, except in Sherrie's case. They both had multiple stab wounds and the same mutilation of the right breast."

There was a loud knock, and a uniformed cop stuck his head in the door. "There's someone here to see you, Matt."

"Who is it?"

"He says his name is Michael Harrington."

*Well, well, well, the mountain comes to Mohammed.* He'd wondered if Michael would come in of his own accord. Although it still didn't make him any less of a suspect, it certainly made it a lot easier on Matt. "Put him in number three. We'll be right there." Casting a quick nod toward Angelle, he kicked back his chair.

Outside the door of interrogation room #3, Matt grabbed Joe's arm and looked him straight in the eye. "Not a word, you hear?" He knew from past experience how caustic Joe could be.

Joe nodded.

Matt opened the door. "Mr. Harrington, thank you for coming in." He took a seat opposite the worried-looking young man.

Angelle sat down next to Matt while Joe, his lips pressed tightly together, leaned against the wall behind the suspect.

The room, like a blank check, gave away nothing: gray walls, brown floor, a long scarred table bathed in the light of two ceiling fixtures, one brighter than the other.

It reeked of stale coffee, tobacco, and sweat.

From the grim look on Michael Harrington's face, you'd think he'd already received the death sentence.

After he was read his rights, Michael signed the required releases, and Matt began his questioning. "Let's see, now where did we leave off?" He scratched his head for a minute. He already knew Michael's story had checked out.

"Right. I wanted to ask you about Miss Weston's mental and emotional condition at the time of your visit. Would you say she was nervous or angry?"

Michael answered promptly. "'Disturbed' would be the word. She kept looking at the bedroom door. I told you before. I think there was someone else in the house."

"Or she could have been expecting someone? Possibly a trick?" He checked Michael's face for any sign of deceit. There was none. Matt waited for a reaction, but the kid's face remained blank. "Was she frightened?"

"No, just jumpy. Like I said, I thought she was coming down from the drugs."

Angelle leaned forward. "Besides heroin and coke, what else was she using?"

"Who knows?" Michael shrugged. "You'd have to be blind not to notice the track marks on her arm. But it could have been anything."

"How was she dressed?" She lowered her voice. "Or was she?"

Surprised at Angelle's question, Michael took the bait. "Goddamn it, of course she was dressed. She was wearing some kind of red see-through nightgown."

Matt took over. "Did she always dress like that when you came to visit?"

"Look, I keep telling you, it was the first and only time I ever went to that house." Michael was beginning to act really pissed off. "This is what I get for trying to do somebody a good turn. I told you before, my boss, Rosa, wanted me to check her out. See if she was dead or ali—" He caught himself and stopped.

That's when Joe put in his two cents. "And what about Allison Graham? Are you the one who sold her the drugs?"

Spinning to face him, Michael sputtered, "Dammit, what are you talking about? I didn't sell drugs to Allison Graham, or Sherrie Weston, or anybody else for that matter."

Joe stepped out of the shadows. "How did you get the body to the beach?"

Matt sighed, but he let Joe run with it.

"You cleaned Allison's dead body up in the bathtub at Sherrie's house, didn't you? And then you carried her to the beach. My guess is you were going to drop her into the fuckin' ocean, but somebody came along and saw you."

Michael shook his head the whole time Joe was accusing him.

"Well then, let's get back to Sherrie. You went to her house for a little S&M. Stop me if I'm wrong, buddy." Joe didn't take time to breathe. "You tied her to the goddamn bed. Then you pulled out your fuckin' whip and your knife. You beat her till the skin on her bare ass was shredded and then stabbed her all over her body. An' after you got your rocks off doing that, you sliced off her goddamn breast and took it home with you, you sick son of a bitch." Now Joe was really in Michael's face.

"Okay, that's enough." Matt's words were a command.

Michael Harrington looked at the aging detective as if he'd just dropped from outer space, too stunned to say a word. He sat up straight, opened his mouth, closed it.

Joe melted back into the darkness.

Suddenly, Michael leaped to his feet.

Matt shot up and held his arm to deter him. "Mr. Harrington,

I'm afraid I have to ask for your fingerprints, also a sample of your DNA."

Before he could finish, Michael shrugged him off, rounded the table in a flash, and headed for the door. "No way. My lawyer warned me not to come alone, but I thought if I showed good faith you guys would—"

Matt stopped him. "In that case, Mr. Harrington, I'm arresting you for the murder of Sherrie Weston."

It was the only way to get his DNA.

# Chapter 10

It was almost five o'clock, and Megan was seated on the sofa in Charlie's plush, white office located atop Grant Enterprise's timeshare building. Spotless windows on six sides of the octagonal room afforded spectacular views of Los Angeles, Marina del Rey, and the sparkling Pacific Ocean.

Megan inhaled the pine-scent freshness of the room and looked around. The entire space was immaculate—the desk, the coffee tables—not even a paper clip was out of place. Just like Charlie's boat, the *Ecstasea,* everything was in total order.

While he was on the telephone, Megan inspected him at leisure. Everything about Charlie was average, from his slight frame and medium height, to his forgettable face. His features taken singly were quite good. It was only when you jumbled them all together that his face was kind of odd. She couldn't explain why. Dull thinning hair, the same color as Charlie's chocolate brown eyes, was obviously dyed and wound around his head to make the most of every strand. He caught her looking at him and stared back, his gaze so hard and penetrating, Megan had to turn away.

When he resumed his telephone conversation, she sneaked another peek. He wore an expensive blue suit and a designer silk tie, clipped with a diamond bar. Charlie Grant had all the accoutrements, but they didn't seem to help his look. He was definitely not handsome, and there was nothing very redeeming about his personality, either. Megan could see why his wife, Alex, was so disillusioned. If good old Charlie didn't have all that money, Megan was sure that pretty Alex would be gone in a flash.

She pondered her own financial condition. Until now, Megan had always made enough money selling real estate, but the truth was, she longed for relief of the financial burden she'd carried for so long—even when she was married to Stephen.

Sometimes she envied Alex and Rachel. It wasn't just the money. More than anything Megan yearned for a family. She wanted a real family, a Walton kind of family, with brothers and sisters and cousins and aunts and uncles, having picnics and spending Christmas together. Recently, she felt her own biological clock ticking.

Suppose she never had children?

Maybe that was why she'd been drawn so easily into supporting Mothers in Recovery. She loved to be around the new babies, helping with their care and feeding, and it would behoove Kathleen Rosario to become equally involved.

"Well, Megan," Charlie began, replacing the receiver, "I guess we didn't have much luck with the group from Korea." He came from behind the desk across the expanse of white Berber carpet and sat opposite her in a plush, creamy armchair.

"Not true, Charlie. They're open to buying two, maybe three units, but only if they can buy them outright. No time-share."

"Well, maybe they can do that." He smiled. "We've decided to put all the units on the auction block."

Megan's mouth dropped open.

Before she could say anything the telephone rang, and Charlie picked up an extension on the table beside him. "Grant here."

Her mind was racing. What did this mean? Was the bank calling the loan? Did Grant Enterprises need to bail out as quickly as possible? *Trust Charlie to make it sound like his idea.* How much trouble were the Grants really in? *Oh, dear, does Alex know about any of this?* Megan doubted it.

Charlie hung up the receiver and stood up. "I promise, Megan, you'll be the first to know what's going on so you can get your clients in line for the auction." He reached into his inside pocket and produced a piece of paper. "But just to make you feel better, I'd like to give you this."

Charlie beamed as Megan accepted the check for ten thousand dollars made out to Mothers in Recovery. She gasped. "I don't know what to say."

"No need to say anything. It's a worthy cause, and I'm happy to help." He moved from behind the desk. "So is Alex."

Picking up her briefcase, Charlie walked her to the door.

She heard herself speaking. "I'll call you when I hear from the clients." She paused. "And thanks again, Charlie. You have no idea how much—"

"Yes, yes, dear. Good-bye." He hustled her forward and opened the office door. "Stay in touch," he added absently, closing the door behind her.

Standing in the hallway outside his office, Megan tried to analyze their meeting and recover from her shock at Charlie's gift. In fact, all the way to the center to deliver the check, she reviewed every detail of the conversation.

She considered Charlie's condo project and promptly decided he was in trouble. Of the 220 luxury town houses Grant Enterprises had built three years ago, there were still a 196 left. That was a huge overhead to cover every month and definitely not a money-making proposition.

So why the big check for Mothers in Recovery?

A horn suddenly honked behind her, bringing her attention back to the heavy traffic on Pacific Avenue. Turning right into the less chic area of Venice, where the recovery home was located, Megan swung another right and drove alongside the railway tracks running through the shabby semi-industrial neighborhood.

The structures on one side of the street were an eclectic mix of newly renovated houses, filthy shacks, and an occasional apartment building. On the opposite side, several commercial enterprises advertised their products and services with cheap signs.

Megan parked in front of a five-unit building.

As she walked toward the rear apartment, she heard the insistent wail of a baby. Megan smiled.

The ten thousand dollar check burned a hole in her pocket.

Everyone was gone for the day, and Matt was alone in the office, his feet propped on the desk. Like a squirrel worrying a nut, he chewed on the end of a pencil with his two front teeth and gazed at the web of earthquake cracks in the ceiling.

Michael Harrington's attorney had showed up, and the kid was out in three hours. But by that time, Matt had obtained the fingerprints and DNA swabs he needed.

Harrington admitted they would find his prints in Sherrie Weston's kitchen but insisted he hadn't gone anywhere near the bedroom. From the evidence, so far, he appeared to be telling the truth. And since DNA testing would take a while, Michael had been released from custody with orders not to leave town.

Late in the day, Matt received a call from the coroner, Tom Wilson.

Fibers had been found in Sherrie's wounds from the rope used to tie her to the bed. He could find nothing special about the rope. It was a popular brand of nautical line used on a million yachts in California. The Luminol he had sprayed in the bathroom revealed plenty of blood evidence—some old, some new. Whoever had cleaned up was efficient. Tom expected to find DNA in the blood evidence from both Sherrie and Allison.

He believed that Alison was murdered in the same house as Sherrie and then dumped on the beach.

According to Angelle, Michael's story about sailing to Malibu checked out. His neighbor on the dock had seen him pull out of the slip in the evening but didn't know what time he came back.

The information Angelle had obtained from UPS and the property management company was invaluable. A Mr. Troy Hanover owned the Beachview house where Sherrie's murder had occurred. And surprise, surprise, he lived at the San Francisco address from which the DVDs of George Fisher and Sherrie Weston had been sent.

Matt called Troy Hanover's number, and an answering machine informed him that Troy was out of town for the weekend. He wondered if he was visiting Los Angeles and just how long he'd been here. Long enough to murder Sherrie Weston?

He racked his brain. There was no sign of breaking and entering, so Sherrie must have let the murderer into the house herself.

But who? Was it a dope dealer, a friggin' movie director from Fantasy Films, or a trick? Maybe the trick was into bondage. He tied her up and went berserk. Too late … she's dead. Maybe it was all about money. Sherrie tells the killer she's got a video of his sex games, tries to blackmail him. He goes crazy. She's dead.

He played another scenario. Sherrie gets a dope delivery. She's short on cash. The dealer takes it out in trade, but the guy's a fruitcake. They get wasted and go too far with the fun and games. According to lab tests, the amount of heroin in her system was monumental. She was flying high when she died.

The telephone rang. It was his superior, Captain Rick Kasabian, summoning him to his office.

Wearily, Matt pulled himself to his feet and headed for the glass-enclosed office.

As he entered, Matt remarked, "I didn't know you were still here, Rick."

The deep voice of the beefy captain rumbled like a California earthquake. "Yeah, I got a lotta work here, Matt, a lotta work. Take a seat."

As always, Matt half-expected the desk to shake when the captain spoke. Rick's jowly face housed bovine eyes, which were benign at the moment, and great dewlaps of flesh hung on his thick neck. To the uninitiated, the captain looked soft and out of shape, but Matt would rather tackle a grizzly bear than take on Captain Rick Kasabian.

"We just got word in from up north." He handed Matt a fax. "They picked up your stuff on the computer. There was a murder in San Francisco a while back. It could be related to ours."

In Matt's mind, a red light flashed the name Troy Hanover. "No kidding? Let's see that." He read from the flimsy fax paper. "Jane Doe, found in a vacant lot in the Haight. Whipped, strangled, and one breast removed. A heroin addict, presumed a prostitute. They found her on June 2 of this year, time of death, May 27." Matt shot him a look of rage. "Dammit, this was more than two months ago. Why the hell didn't I get the information till now? Why didn't they put this case in VICAP? Somebody screwed up." The Violent Criminal Apprehension Program had been originated in 1985 and provided a database of crimes and criminals that could be accessed by law enforcement all over the country. But if the case hadn't been entered, how could he know about it? He had been checking VICAP daily since March, when Allison was murdered, and found nothing.

Rick shrugged. "We do the best we can. Be grateful they picked it up now."

"It's the same guy, Rick. I think we've got a serial sexual sadist."

"Don't even mention those words. I shudder to think what the fucking press will do with it."

"Tell me. Marcia Waters from Channel Three News already called three times today, and she doesn't even know about this one.

"You know the sad thing about all this, Rick? If these girls weren't hookers, we wouldn't be dropping their cases so quickly. The press and every politician up for election would be all over us, making statements and shoving their faces in front of the cameras." But the facts were obvious; hookers had little publicity value.

The captain didn't even respond. He simply lowered his eyes to the pile of paperwork. "Interview over."

When Matt walked back to his desk, the telephone was ringing. "Matt Donovan here."

"Hi, Daddy."

His face broke into a smile. "Is everything okay?" That was always his first question—ever since Julie had signed a modeling contract with one of the largest agencies in the country eight months ago and moved to New York. Matt had this unreasonable fear that one day he would get a telephone call like the one he'd made to the parents of Allison Graham and others. He knew it was foolish, but he just couldn't help it. Too often he'd heard the families of victims say they never thought it could happen to them.

"Couldn't be better, Daddy, how about you?" Julie sounded happy.

Picking up the photograph on his desk, Matt smiled. In the picture his daughter had both arms wrapped around him, her head on his chest. Julie's lovely mouth was captured in a shy grin, and her straight blonde hair shimmered over her bare shoulders. She was so beautiful. Every time he looked at her, he was reminded of his wife, Constance. They were so much alike.

"I'm fine, sweetheart, just fine."

"Daddy, are you sitting down?"

He dropped into his chair, praying it wasn't a disaster. "I am now. What's up?"

"I got the job. Daddy, I got the job." Julie's voice was jubilant.

"Job?"

"Don't you remember? The cosmetic ad." She bubbled with excitement. "I got the TV commercial, the print work, the personal appearances. Daddy, I'm the new Avalon girl. Can you believe it?"

He loved to hear her laugh. "Honey, I'm so proud of you. The Avalon girl? Hot damn." Matt had no idea what that meant.

"I am going to make so much money. And who knows where it will lead. I could end up a movie star. Oh, Daddy, I can't believe this is happening."

"Well, I can. You are a beautiful young woman, Julie. I only wish your mother could see you. She'd be so proud."

"I know, Dad," she said, softly. "But she can see us both from up there. And she's taking care of us, you know?"

"Yes, I think so, too." He tried for a fatherly tone. "I hope you're saving your money, sweetheart. Sooner or later this modeling thing will be over and you'll want to go to college."

"Daddy."

"Okay. Okay. I won't mention it again."

"I'm going to say good night now. The Avalon girl has to get her beauty sleep, you know?"

He smiled. "If you get any more beautiful, the world couldn't handle it."

"You think that because you're my daddy."

"The Avalon people made you their girl, didn't they?"

Julie laughed. "But I'm still your girl, Daddy. Good night. I love you."

"I love you, too, baby." He hung up the receiver. God, he missed her.

Matt was being paged by the duty officer.

"Yeah," he called. "I'm at my desk."

The officer had a small washed-out-blonde lady about forty-five years old in tow. "Matt, this here is Mrs. Weston, Sherrie's mother. She just got in from Tallahassee."

The woman had apparently come directly from the airport. Gripping a plastic suitcase as if it contained her last earthly possessions, she stared up at him with lackluster eyes.

Hurriedly, Matt shoved the pictures of the mutilated girls into a folder and sat her down. *Jesus.*

† † †

When Megan came home from the AA meeting in Brentwood, the first thing she did was call Kathleen. "Hi, honey. Were you sleeping?"

"No, not yet, I took half a sleeping tablet a while ago, and I'm waiting for it to work."

*At least she's coherent,* Megan thought, recalling Kathleen's suicide attempt. "You're sure you only took half?"

"Don't worry, Megan. I'm all right."

Unable to contain her excitement, Megan blurted, "I called to tell you that Alex and Charlie donated ten thousand dollars to Mothers in Recovery. I gave it to the housemother today. She's going to put it in the building fund so we can buy the house next door and create a nursery. Then when the women go back to work, they'll have a secure place for their children."

"That's wonderful news."

"I know. Listen, I asked Roxie if you could help with the babies. She said you could go by any time you want."

"I'd really like that, Megan." There was a long pause. "Can I call you tomorrow? I'm beginning to fall asleep."

But she wanted her friend's promise to devote some of her free time to the babies, knowing that the true beneficiary of such an action would not be the children, but Kathleen. "If you like, I'll go with you."

"Yes, I would like to do that, but right now I'm really tired."

"I'll call you tomorrow."

Megan hung up and dialed again.

"Hello?" Rachel wasn't sleepy. She sounded angry.

"It's Megan. How are you doing?"

"David's gone." Her voice was tight.

*Oh, no, not again.* "Did you have a fight?"

"Sort of." Rachel began to sound weepy. "I—I—I guess I just lost it."

"You didn't tell him what you saw on the boat?"

"No, I did exactly what Alex suggested. But it wasn't easy." Rachel began to cry in earnest. "He's such a bastard."

"Do you want me to come over? I'll leave right now."

"No, it's too late." Rachel sniffled. "I'm okay."

"You will call if you need me?"

"I will. I promise. Good night, Megan, and thanks."

She hung up, knowing exactly how Rachel felt. Betrayed. Lonely. Unforgiving. She'd felt it with her failed marriage and her breakup with Brian.

Suddenly, Megan was alarmed. Unlike with Kathleen, she didn't worry about Rachel committing suicide. She was more concerned about what Rachel would do to her husband if she caught him screwing around again. She had visions of David, lying in a pool of blood. Hell, she was going to Rachel's house, right now.

Twenty minutes later, Megan pulled up in front of the Feinman's house in Brentwood just as Rachel's red Jaguar screamed out of the driveway.

Megan honked. Rachel ignored her.

*Where would she be going at this time of night? What if she's looking for David? Oh my God.* Megan followed her.

Rachel raced down San Vicente Boulevard, turned right on Seventh Street into Santa Monica Canyon, and headed for Pacific Coast Highway. Megan was trying to keep up with the Jag when a thought occurred to her. How would Rachel react if she knew Megan was spying? Maybe she ought to go home and mind her own business.

No, Rachel was acting too weird. She would keep her distance and find out what she was up to. This could be another crisis—and Rachel might need help.

She followed her down Pacific Coast Highway and almost to Malibu before Rachel slowed down, obviously checking the street numbers. Halting suddenly, she parked on the shoulder.

Megan made a U-turn to the ocean side of the highway, where all the houses were in darkness. She crouched in the front seat and watched Rachel lock her car and then walk to a small guard hut at the foot of the cliffs. Where the hell was she going? And what if she caught David in the act again?

Megan squinted at the shack.

She wrote down the number 51532.

A cable car rumbled down a narrow track on the side of the mountain and halted in front of the guard hut. A young man climbed out, and Rachel spoke to him. She tried climbing aboard the car, but he stopped her. They argued. Then, apparently not getting her way, Rachel stomped back to her car.

Megan hunkered down again as the Jaguar made a screeching U-turn and headed back toward Brentwood.

"Now, what the hell was that all about?" she said aloud.

All the way home, Megan wondered if she would ever be able to confront Rachel about this midnight outing. But at least she had the address, and Megan was going to check it out tomorrow—right after George Fisher's funeral.

# Chapter 11

Megan leaned back into the soft glove-leather seats and reveled in the luxury of the Grants' white Rolls-Royce. Charlie drove while Alex pouted.

Watching them from her seat in the back, Megan could see that Alex was not pleased to be attending George Fisher's funeral. The only reason she came, as she'd told Megan and Charlie repeatedly, was out of respect for the family.

Tired of hearing Alex's complaints, Megan was glad to get out of the car no matter how lavish the upholstery.

The towering pinnacles of the church cast a gloomy shadow, despite the fact that the sun shone brightly on profuse bursts of purple bougainvillea climbing the stone walls.

Charlie clutched his wife's elbow as he guided her down the gravel path.

"Damn," Alex complained and lifted her tiny foot, showing the signature red sole. "The heels on my Louboutins are going to be ruined."

"C'mon," Charlie grumbled, dragging her along.

Megan suppressed a smile. Alex was perfectly dressed for a funeral: not too much—a burgundy silk David Hayes suit with a fluff of white lace at the collar—while Megan, uncomfortable in a tight black pantsuit, felt like a peasant.

"Alex, Charlie," a man's voice called out.

Megan turned and saw David Feinman trying to catch up with them. He looked like quite the stud in his black silk jacket and light gray pants. It was quite an occasion to see the tall, slender screenwriter wearing anything other than designer jeans.

Rachel, her hair done up in a chignon, trotted behind, buttoning the jacket of her charcoal-gray suit. "Hi," she said. "Has Kathleen arrived yet?"

"We just got here ourselves," Megan answered vaguely, trying to hear what David and Charlie were saying as they shook hands and slapped each other on the back.

But Rachel wanted her attention. She linked her arm in Megan's and whispered, "The son of a bitch came home at seven o'clock this morning."

"Did you confront him about what you saw on the boat?"

"No, I didn't say a word, but I wish I had. We had a big fight."

"Oh, Rachel, I'm so sorry."

"I'm not. Two can play at that game." Her voice bristled with malevolence. "I want to do it. I want to hire a lover. It's my turn now, Megan, I want to have some fun."

The men caught up with them at that crucial moment, and all Megan could do was stare at Rachel in dismay before David whisked her into the church.

Inside to greet them were several somber-faced ushers wearing dark three-piece suits. Megan found herself being guided into a pew next to the feuding Feinmans.

She checked out David. To use Rachel's own words, he had the eyes of a poet and brown Byronesque curls crowning his long, lanky frame. In another time he could have been a dashing pirate sent to woo his heroine. But today, David was just another cheating husband.

Finally settled in her seat, Megan looked around the charming chapel and gazed up at the beautiful cathedral ceiling with its exquisite, hand-painted beams.

The pews were almost full. The entire Bayside Club membership appeared to be present, and pleasantly sober for a change.

Junie, the black-lace-covered widow, was seated on the side of the altar to the right of a gray leatherlike coffin smothered with white orchids. Her two daughters clung to each other while their husbands oversaw the children. *No wonder she's got her face covered—after what the bastard did to her.* Megan hoped her own animosity wasn't too apparent.

The commodore of the club, Dr. Richard Henderson, and his wife, Gloria, were seated across the aisle. Beside them sat Senator Harley Rattner, his spindle-necked wife, and their weird daughter, Bonnie-Sue. Out of respect for the funeral, at least she'd removed most of her earrings and took out the studs from her nose and eyebrows. A sleek gray dress replaced her usual black Goth costume.

The senator turned and nodded solemnly.

Megan reciprocated, as did the others.

At that moment an usher led Kathleen to Megan's row.

Her manner dour, Kathleen inched her way along the pew, maneuvering past Alex and Charlie Grant until she reached Megan.

Then Brian Mason showed up wearing the obligatory funereal attitude. He didn't look thrilled to be there. Megan didn't even acknowledge his presence.

She'd hoped to arrive at the church earlier in order to have a word with Rachel about her midnight trip, but Megan couldn't get away from the office in time. "Can you believe all these people?" she whispered to Kathleen.

"Shhhh," murmured the nasty club gossip, Helen Jennings. She was sitting in the row behind them, wearing a ridiculous black lace hat.

Who the hell was she to talk? Helen rarely kept her own mouth shut—like the other day when she could hardly wait to call Rachel and spell out the sordid details of George's death.

Rachel interrupted her thoughts. "Is she here?"

"Yes, of course." Megan pointed her chin toward the altar. "She's up there next to the coffin."

"No, not his wife, Junie. I mean George's Lolita. The one he was with when he died." Rachel craned her neck in all directions.

"You don't think she'd have the nerve, do you?" Alex countered in a shocked voice.

"It's hard to say." Rachel raised her eyebrows. "For all I know he could have put the bitch in his will. George really was a bastard."

Megan caught David and Charlie exchanging horrified glances.

The organ began to play a chorus of "Amazing Grace" in slow, muted tones.

A long string bean of a man dressed in black ministerial robes and a white clerical collar advanced toward the podium. The gray-haired reverend had to practically fold his body in half to speak into the microphone. When he leaned forward, his horn-rimmed glasses slipped to the edge of his nose. Nervously, he adjusted them and cleared his throat. "Good morning."

"Good morning," the crowd answered.

Megan noticed that Rachel said nothing. She just pressed her lips together in a tight, angry line.

"We are gathered here today to celebrate the essence of a wonderful man taken from his family in the prime of his life."

"Pshaw," Rachel spat.

Megan fumbled for a handkerchief.

David gave them each a threatening glance.

"The loss to the community is indeed a tragedy. George Fisher was a man of many good works. He did not like to advertise the wonderful things he did, for he was a private man."

"You got that right," Rachel said from the side of her mouth.

Megan tried not to smile, especially when she saw Alex's shoulders shaking with laughter. It was hard to maintain an appropriate demeanor.

Charlie nudged his wife. "Cut it out, Alex." He shot Rachel a dirty look.

Everybody was on edge, Megan thought, including herself.

She glanced at Rachel, still wishing she could ask her about last night's mystery ride to Malibu. Maybe an opportunity would present itself later. Although, she didn't look forward to admitting she had followed Rachel.

The minister droned on. "His beloved wife of twenty-three years and his two treasured daughters will surely miss him most of all, for he was the center of their existence."

Suddenly, Junie burst into great sobs, and her young daughters rallied to comfort her.

"How long do you think it will take for the widow to get merry?" Rachel asked, a wicked gleam in her eye. "After the will's read?"

"Oh, Rachel, stop. I can't stand it." Giggling, Alex covered her mouth with her hand.

Charlie frowned at Rachel again. But she snubbed him.

After a long half hour of eulogizing, the pastor directed them to pass by the coffin on the way out. The family would receive everyone at the back of the church. There would be a graveside ceremony at Inglewood Cemetery, a reception at Bayside Yacht Club right after the interment, and everyone was invited. The reverend stopped to take a breath. "The family thanks you for your attendance."

"I just came to see if he died with a smile on his face," Rachel mumbled.

Megan knew that all the anger and resentment that Rachel was carrying around was going to destroy her if she didn't put a stop to it.

Then she glanced at Alex, who stumbled out of the pew behind her husband, Charlie, still attempting to conceal her laughter.

Megan cast her eyes down so she wouldn't fall over the kneeler, but in a headlong effort to keep up with the others she walked into a man who had stepped into the aisle at the very same time. He grabbed her elbows to keep her from falling. Equalized by the strength of his arms, she lifted her chin and looked straight into the sapphire eyes of Matt Donovan. The faint scent of lemons lingered about him as he held her a little longer than necessary.

"I'm sorry, miss. I guess I wasn't looking."

"Excuse me!" Helen Jennings's voice in the background sounded irate. "We need to pass by here." She pushed her way around them, holding onto her hat.

Praying her embarrassment wasn't too obvious, Megan retrieved herself from his arms. "This is getting to be a habit, isn't it, Detective?"

He laughed, and his eyes crinkled.

"You got me." Matt scratched his head, ruffling his dark curls. "I guess I'd better stop following you around."

*I wish.* "Well, we do keep running into each other. Literally."

"You're Megan Riley, right?"

"And you are Detective Donovan." She liked the sound of his name. Don-o-van.

"You remembered."

"It's not every day I get questioned about a murder."

He smiled that darling smile again. "And is that Miss or Mrs.?"

Megan promptly responded. "It's Ms."

"Yes. Well, I hope you're not hurt, Ms. Riley." He moved on down the aisle and then turned around and came back. "Ms. Riley, I wonder …?"

At that moment Brian came up behind her and placed a proprietary hand on her arm. "Who's that, Megan?"

The detective immediately turned and walked away.

"It's none of your damn business," Megan said, knocking his hand away.

She hurried outside. Too late. Matt Donovan was gone.

By the time Megan arrived at the yacht club, after the graveyard ceremony, it was one o'clock. Slipping her high heels off under the table, she wiggled her toes.

Funerals made her nervous, and watching the family's trauma only reinforced her own desire to be cremated, her ashes scattered at sea.

*Okay, that's it, Megan. No more thoughts of death.*

Feeling very much alive after her encounter with the detective, she smiled.

Convinced that Brian had purposely interfered, Megan glanced around the room, looking for her ex-boyfriend. And there he was. Where else but the bar, chatting with David and Charlie? They were probably reminiscing about George Fisher and their boring fishing trips.

The grieving family sat en masse in demure propriety at the head table, receiving condolences from members of the club and other friends. Even some of the waiters and waitresses stood in line to pay their respects.

Senator Harley Rattner hovered behind the widow's chair with a condescending attitude while his wife remained quietly in the background, clutching her daughter's arm. Bonnie-Sue still stuck out like a sore thumb with her punk hairdo. From the look on her face, Megan expected her to bolt at any moment.

Helen Jennings selected a table nearby. Megan wondered about her three companions. They hadn't been with her in church. From Helen's reputation as a celebrity hunter, she figured they had to be VIPs. Fascinated, Megan watched the club gossip prance around the table, wearing her giant hat and seating her guests in some kind of demented order.

Finally, Helen turned toward Megan and cooed, "How are you, dear? You haven't forgotten the wedding shower for Ginny Barnes at my house next week? There's going to be some hot surprises." She positively beamed fellowship and good will, the exact opposite of her nasty behavior in the church.

"Yes, I'll be there." Megan gave her a sugary smile. *Ugh.*

Alex and Rachel returned from the restroom.

"Did you see Helen Jennings with her coven of bitches?" Rachel asked.

"You're incorrigible." Megan laughed. "But funny."

"Well, she is a bitch. And everyone knows she's a black-belt starfucker."

Smiling, Megan placed her hand on Rachel's arm. "By the way, I have some good news. Well, it's good news for Mothers in Recovery."

"You knew that the club offered to give us the room for nothing, didn't you?" Rachel asked, her eyes lighting up.

"Yes, but this is even better." She paused. "Alex and Charlie gave us a check for ten thousand dollars."

Rachel swung her attention to Alex. "That is truly fabulous. I'll see what I can wring out of my husband. That way there'll be less for his bimbos!"

"Here comes Kathleen." Alex waved.

But Kathleen was waylaid by Helen Jennings, who began making introductions.

The minute she broke free of Helen's hold, Kathleen rushed to the table, dropped into the chair beside Megan, and declared, "I'm so happy to sit down."

Casually, Rachel asked, "Did you check out Helen's boots?"

"What boots?" Kathleen's face was blank.

"Her social-climbing boots." Rachel's palm hit the table with a bang.

Everyone muffled their laughter, including Megan.

Then, Rachel whispered, "Did you tell Alex yet?"

"Tell me what?" Alex asked.

"No, and I'm not going to," Megan countered. "You must be crazy."

"She didn't tell me nothin', honey," Alex complained.

Rachel took a deep breath. "We're in. At least I am."

"You're in what?" Alex looked perplexed.

"The boytoy thing."

"You're kidding?" Then, after a small hesitation, she admitted, "But I must say I thought about it a few times myself."

"I've thought of nothing else," Rachel quipped. "What about you, Megan?"

"It crossed my mind."

Rachel raised one eyebrow. "How about you, Kathleen?"

"Oh, my." Kathleen shook her head. "I couldn't do anything like that."

"Oh, come on." Rachel put on her best persuasive manner. "You all know that men use women as sex objects. Why can't we do the same for once?" She brightened. "Let's live a little. All we ever do is sit around and complain about what cheaters these men are and never have the guts to do anything about it. Here's our chance to get even."

"Well, I don't know, Rachel." Kathleen turned to Megan and whispered, "What do you think?"

Megan shrugged. "We could never agree on the same guy, so it'll never happen. Go for it, Kathleen."

"I'll take that as a yes from you, Megan." Rachel grinned.

But Megan was curious. "Why would you want to do a time-share thing? You're an attractive woman with plenty of money. You could find your own lover. So could Alex."

"Now, if I was to participate …" Alex dragged out her answer, apparently thinking as she spoke. "It would just be for the fun of it.

Besides, I think Megan's right. There's no way y'all will ever agree on the same guy. We can't even agree on a place to have lunch."

"Don't be surprised if we do," Rachel cautioned. "I'm really quite serious. The way I look at it, if we're all in this together, it will obfuscate who's doing what to whom. Then, if somebody gets caught, she can blame it on the others. Megan's single, and so is Kathleen. Alex and I can say he belongs to one of you. Besides, I want a lover, now. And I'd hate to have to go out and kiss all those stupid frogs again."

Megan stared at her. "You've got it all figured out, haven't you?"

"I've had quite a few nights alone, lately," Rachel reminded her. "It gives me plenty of time to think."

*That's true for both of us,* Megan thought. "Oh, what the hell, it might be fun."

Kathleen appeared confused by the whole conversation.

"And what about you, Kathleen?" Rachel asked. "We're in; how about you?"

"I—I—I really don't know."

"Oh, do it, Kathleen," Rachel urged. "For once in your life take a risk."

Checking her out, Megan could see Kathleen visibly waiver. She didn't want to offend her friends, so Megan knew she'd eventually agree. She always did.

With a look of trepidation on her face, Kathleen glanced from one to the other. "I don't have to have sex with him, do I? I mean, I could just go out on a date with him or watch TV or something, right?"

Rachel laughed aloud, drawing stares from the other guests. "Honey," she said in her best Mae West voice, "you can do anything your little heart desires. You call the shots when you're paying the bills. That's why guys do it."

"Okay, we're all in. What do we do next?" Alex appeared anxious to get on to the more technical aspects.

Megan grinned. "Is Alex ready or what?"

Rachel whispered, "Now we need to find the right guy."

"Just make sure he's got a fine body!" Alex said.

"Ye-e-a-h." Rachel leered. "And at least half a brain."

"And he must be ... sensitive," Kathleen breathed.

Megan stared. She could hardly believe it. Kathleen was not only in, she was involved.

"And I truly do like 'em blond," Alex drawled.

Megan was aghast. "What the hell do you expect for your money? Brad Pitt? Lighten up, ladies. We're talking about a roll in the hay here."

"Oh, Megan," Kathleen moaned. "Why must you always be so honest?"

Rachel's eyes flashed. "I have just the right guy. But he isn't blond. Sorry, Alex."

"See? What I want doesn't count," complained Alex.

Megan interrupted. "Shhh, the guys are coming."

"Just meet me at my gym." Rachel lowered her voice. "Power Workout, Brentwood. Five o'clock today. Agreed?"

Before anyone could respond, Charlie, Brian, and David rejoined them.

"Hey, this is a funeral," Charlie said. "You're not supposed to be having such a good time."

Brian placed a bottle of Perrier and a glass in front of her. "Cool it, Megan."

She gave him a dirty look.

That's when she saw him again, the detective.

He passed by the table and smiled at her.

Her stomach contracted.

*What the hell are you thinking?* asked the little voice in her head. He was probably married with five kids. The little voice never said anything nice to Megan. But he had inquired if she was Miss or Mrs. So why did she tell him Ms.? She should have said Miss. *Stupid, Megan, stupid.*

David Feinman nodded in Matt's direction. "There's the detective who wanted to question me about George Fisher."

"Oh, really," said Rachel, "you never told me."

"I don't tell you everything," quipped David. "My secretary told him I wasn't there."

Rachel flashed Megan a knowing look.

"He spoke to me too," Charlie said. "How about you, Brian?"

"Why would he talk to me?"

"He questioned everyone who knew George Fisher. He obviously thinks there's a connection between George's death and the Bondage Murder."

"Holy mother, here comes Gino." Kathleen stood up, prepared for flight.

Megan watched him saunter across the room. "You can guarantee that Gino Rosario would make a grand entrance."

"Hi, folks." Gino flashed his blinding white teeth. "I just came to tell Junie the good news. It comes across my desk first, you know."

"Get to the point, Gino." Megan clutched Kathleen's knotted fists and sat her down again.

Ignoring them both, the obnoxious Gino exulted, "The cops finally got around to identifying the victim in the latest murder." He paused. "It was Sherrie Weston."

No response.

"You know," Gino said, impatiently, "the girl George was screwing when he had his heart attack."

Brian nudged Charlie and grinned. "Well, I guess old George won't be a suspect."

Megan didn't react. What did this mean?

Gino put on his sleaziest smile. "Poetic justice, huh?"

"You're sick." Megan turned away, and once again her eyes met those of the detective. And then the tapes in her head began to play.

Why was Detective Matt Donovan attending the funeral? Did he suspect someone in George's family of murdering the girl? Or did he think it was one of his friends? Or even a club member?

No. That was impossible.

She looked around the room. Or was it?

# Chapter 12

After George's funeral, Megan went directly to her office and headed straight for the computer. Scrolling the property tax files, she checked out 51532 Pacific Coast Highway, the site of Rachel's midnight visit.

A Destiny La Conte owned the property.

When she finished computing the figures, Megan estimated the house and land value at more than four million dollars. Obviously, Ms. La Conte was loaded.

But was she one of David's girlfriends?

Megan turned her chair to the expanse of office window that faced out on the busy Marina. It was a hot, windy day. The colored flags and yacht club pennants attached to hundreds of boats flapped about in the breeze. The sky was an incredible cerulean blue that rarely appeared in Southern California skies anymore. For a moment Megan responded to its beauty.

But only for a moment. Then she sat upright.

She remembered the entry in Brian's address book that read Destiny La C.... She couldn't even say it to herself. Could *her* real name be Destiny La Conte?

The similarity in names was too much of a coincidence.

How many Destinys could there be on the Westside?

She couldn't wait to get home and piece together the page from the address book. Obviously, Brian Mason knew this person called Destiny.

And if he did, he could have introduced her to David.

Had Rachel expected to find her husband there? Or was there another reason?

And why was there a guard posted at the cable car of Destiny's house?

Megan quickly packed her briefcase and left the office.

All the way home she wondered how she'd gotten railroaded into the boytoy thing. Unlike her rich friends, Megan didn't have the money for that kind of nonsense. Nor did she have the guts to tell them she didn't. And even if she did, she'd much rather write a check for Mothers in Recovery.

Despite her convictions, Megan felt compelled to go along with their crazy scheme—for now. She was certain each of them had definite ideas on the kind of man they wanted and would never compromise. The whole thing would blow over. Besides, whoever they chose had to agree to their little plan. And that was even more unlikely.

She reached her apartment.

She had only thirty-five minutes left to change, piece together the page of Brian's phone book, and get to Power Workout.

Less than an hour later, after leaving her belongings in a lavender locker in a purple dressing room, Megan worked her way to the coed floor of Rachel's gym and checked out the crowd. Power Workout was one of those Brentwood designer gyms where the elite came to meet. Where soft rock blared from hidden speakers and emaciated women wearing perfectly matched outfits flirted with out-of-work actors with hard, sculpted bodies.

Convinced Kathleen wouldn't even show up, Megan was surprised to see her already there, sporting a stiff upper lip and listening to Rachel, whose face was flushed with excitement. Excited by revenge or lust? Megan couldn't tell.

Alex was busy checking herself out in the mirror and sucking in her nonexistent stomach.

Greetings were exchanged. But not much else was said. They all knew why they were there, and they were obviously unwilling to talk about it.

The walls of Power Workout were painted in soothing pastels of pink, lavender, and pale gray. The carpet was a blend of all three colors, and the workout machines were a startling purple. Megan checked out the equipment and decided to try the treadmill. It looked the least dangerous.

She stepped on the belt like she knew what she was doing and pressed a couple of buttons. It started. Marching stoically on the machine, Megan realized if this boytoy thing continued for long, she might even get in shape.

Within ten minutes, she'd worked up a sweat.

Boytoy? They must be totally insane, all four of them.

Watching Kathleen as Rachel instructed her on the correct way to use the weights, Megan marveled at her shy friend's change of attitude.

Even Rachel seemed less tense, and she hadn't mentioned David once.

Rachel really looked stunning. Her sleek, dark hair was woven into a classic French braid, and her ebony eyes sparkled with an air of expectancy, giving her the youthful bearing of a teenager. A slinky red leotard transformed her sultry beauty into movie-star glamour and outlined every curve in her body.

David Feinman must have been a complete and utter fool. How he could even think of cheating on this exquisite woman was beyond Megan. And then she had a terrible thought. If Rachel Feinman couldn't keep a man interested, what hope was there for her?

She picked up her pace to keep up with the treadmill and turned to Alex.

Anorexic Alex, in her pale blue tights, sat on a bench unenthusiastically curling a two-pound dumbbell. At the rate she was moving, Megan figured it would take her thirty-five years to lose three pounds. But Alex didn't have to worry about losing weight, not the way she starved herself.

And of course, Kathleen looked absolutely smashing in a forest-green leotard, her hourglass figure fairly oozing sexuality. But her stiff upper lip was gone, replaced by the pained look of a virgin about to be sacrificed.

Would she ever get over Gino? If only Kathleen could become involved with something other than herself. Or find another man.

Megan glanced in the mirror, detesting the black bicycle pants and black oversized T-shirt she wore to cover her hips.

*Got to lose the weight. Got to lose the weight.* This was her new mantra.

The treadmill's speed increased again. "What the …?"

"Uh-oh, here he comes," Rachel squealed and pumped the weights faster.

"Where is he, Rachel?" The treadmill picked up speed; Megan breathed harder.

"I can't stand this. I'm so embarrassed." Kathleen jumped on a nearby Lifecycle and began to pump the pedals, pretending she didn't know them.

"I still—*gasp*—can't see him," Megan puffed.

Alex pointed. "Over there by the door."

Rachel exploded. "Don't be so damn obvious, Alex. And don't point!"

Megan got her first look. "Oh my God. Check out that body. He's incredible. Should I talk to him?"

"No, you can't talk to him. He's Rachel's choice. You'll get your chance to pick someone," Alex said in her bossy voice.

Megan glared at her, ready to challenge the rules they'd already agreed upon, but was distracted by the runaway treadmill. She could hardly keep up. How the hell did you stop this thing?

"He's coming this way," Rachel said, trying to look cool.

Striving desperately to keep up with the machine, Megan watched the muscle-bound trainer strut across the workroom floor and head straight for Rachel.

When he got there, he looked her up and down, stripping her with his eyes. "How ya doin', babe?"

"Hi." Rachel smiled her cockeyed smile.

His mouth curved into a smirk. "Hey, babe, weren't you here the other day?"

*Yuck.* His whole macho attitude was a complete turnoff. In fact, the only good thing about this guy were his baby blues.

"I don't think he's our man," Alex sang.

"You got that right," Megan muttered, praying the treadmill would stop before she dropped.

"Well, er—er—" Rachel seemed lost for words.

*Alex, can't you see she's in trouble?* Megan's mind was running a mile a minute. So were her feet. *How do you shut this crazy thing off?* She fumbled with the controls, gave up, and yelled, "Do something, Alex, or get me off this sucker."

But Alex just stood there, staring stupidly at the jerk.

A quick glance toward the purple Lifecycle told Megan that Kathleen had reacted as expected. Her eyes were tightly shut, and she was pedaling maniacally.

By this time the machine from hell was rolling at such a fast clip Megan could only stay on by taking short, quick steps. Dear God, the whole damn thing was not to be believed—like a Laurel and Hardy movie.

Alex finally came to her senses and elbowed the guy out of the way. "We really must be going," she said in her Rodeo Drive voice. Then, taking poor, deflated Rachel by the arm, she steered her toward the locker room.

Megan was flying now and perspiring heavily.

Without missing so much as a beat, the weight lifter turned to Kathleen on the bicycle. "Hi, babe."

In her hurry to get away, Kathleen caught her foot on the pedal and almost fell off the bike.

The killer treadmill slowed down. *Thank you, God.*

Now considering it a sworn enemy, Megan jumped off quickly in case it started again of its own volition. Knees shaking, arms flailing, she struggled to keep her balance. She reached out for support. One of her hands caught the handrail, breaking a nail way down past the quick.

That was the final straw.

Wiping away the sweat on her face with a towel, Megan sucked on her damaged finger and followed the green streak that was Kathleen to the locker room. The only way her legs would move was in teeny-weeny steps, as if she were still on the treadmill. Before leaving, she turned around to see what *he* was doing. The jerk was so self-absorbed he hadn't even noticed their exit.

Rounding the corner into the purple dressing room, she found Alex and Rachel holding their sides, screaming with laughter.

"He was so dumb," Rachel cried. "Boy, I can sure pick 'em."

"But he had a great body!" Alex moaned.

"What's wrong with you, girl?" Megan mumbled around her hurt finger, which was still in her mouth. "He was really a creep."

When Alex didn't respond, Megan studied her broken nail and pumped her knees up and down so her legs wouldn't cramp.

"Okay, girls, onward and upward. Who's next?" Rachel wiped the tears of laughter from her eyes.

"I got one," Alex yelled. "I do. It's my turn."

"Let's get out of here first," Rachel said. "You can tell us later, over a drink."

"You'll have to go without me," Megan said. "I'm off to a meeting."

Kathleen protested. "When can you stop going to those dumb AA meetings?"

"They tell me I have to keep going until I want to go."

On her way back to the locker room, Megan ran her fingers through her hair.

She wished she'd found a way to discuss the Malibu jaunt with Rachel, especially since Megan had discovered that the address Rachel visited belonged to the same Destiny in Brian's address book. She desperately wanted to know who this woman was and what she had to do with Brian Mason and David Feinman.

Megan was determined to find out.

# CHAPTER 13

It was Friday night, and Matt checked the clock on his bedside table. Ten o'clock.

Working in front of the mirror, he greased back his hair in a ducktail, gigolo style.

*Sheee-it*. He almost had enough to tie in one of those skinny little ponytails. It was just as well he didn't; he wouldn't want to drive the girls and boys wild altogether.

He posed. Looking good.

He wore black jeans, a black T-shirt, and black Reeboks. To complete his ensemble, he pulled on a tight leather jacket.

Giving his hair one last slick, Matt left the house.

Traffic was slow on Pacific Avenue, but the leather clubs he and Joe Schumann planned to cruise didn't get started till at least midnight. Matt hated this kind of sleazy duty, but they had to start somewhere. Seeing an opening, he hit the gas pedal.

When he arrived at the Whipping Inn, a crummy bar on Culver Boulevard, the joint was filled with male hustlers, pimps, biker types, and a few worn-out female hookers.

Joe was waiting at the bar.

Matt chuckled. They were dressed almost identically.

He climbed on the vacant stool next to Joe and ordered. "Bushmill on the rocks."

The bearlike bartender grunted and retrieved a bottle of Irish whiskey from the back bar. Stretched over his fat beer belly was a white T-shirt emblazoned with the words: LAPD ... THEY'LL TREAT YOU LIKE A KING.

"Jesus, will they ever give up on that King shit?" Matt asked.

Joe shrugged. "You got me."

Smiling, Matt commented, "I like your outfit."

"It's my S&M getup. Yours too I see." Joe took a swig of his Coors beer.

Matt's drink arrived, and he took a small sip.

Joe spoke up again. "I saw Marcia Waters on the news tonight."

"So?"

He looked at Matt through the mirror. "She went on forever about a serial killer connection to the murders."

Matt groaned. "After hearing about the case in San Francisco, Rick let the cat outta the bag. I guess she just ran with it."

"I think it's a nutcase. That would explain the missing boobs."

"I just don't want to put ideas into anyone's head, Joe. All the freaks in town could start cutting up broads just to be part of the action."

"True." Joe finally turned to face him. "Who knows the way these friggin' weirdos think?"

Matt sipped his drink and said nothing, just stared into the smoky mirror behind the bar and watched the action. The place looked like the alien bar scene in *Star Wars*, and the patrons were almost as way out.

"Well?" Joe asked. "Are you ready for a night on the town?"

"Ready as I'll ever be."

"I'm warning you, pal. You're gonna get your fill of debauchery tonight. Of course, I seen it all in Hollyweird, and if it ain't happened there, it ain't happened."

"I can believe it." Matt tossed back the rest of his drink. "Let's go." He backed off the stool and headed for the door.

The Whipping Inn was mild compared to the S&M bar Joe took him to next. Deep in a sleazy industrial district, the underground sex club was reached by passing through several blocks of boarded-up stores near Venice Beach.

Matt parked at the end of a graffiti-covered alley littered with motorcycles, within walking distance of a run-down warehouse. A row of Mercedes, Beemers, even a Rolls-Royce convertible, were parked alongside a loading dock near the dimly lit entrance. The cars were guarded by a tough-looking hombre wearing a ten-gallon hat and a fringed suede jacket.

"Where's his goddamn horse at?" Joe asked out of the side of his mouth.

Matt stood in the shadows while Joe spoke to the bouncer, who turned out to be a young Asian man.

Turning to Matt, Joe tipped his head. "This asshole thinks he's a fuckin' ninja."

But the guy heard him and walked toward Joe, one hand in his pocket. The ninja was backed by a tough-looking female punk rocker wearing a shocking pink leather dress with spaghetti straps. Her hair matched the color of the dress and was buzzed to about one inch in length. A small diamond stud pierced her left nostril, and a row of golden rings curved around her ears. She carried a vicious-looking riding crop and looked ready and able to use it.

"What is this?" Joe smirked. "Fucking Halloween come early?"

"Hey, man. You got no beef with us." The Asian had a Bronx accent.

Matt tried to pacify him. "Look, buddy, we're not looking to cause any trouble. We'd just like to take a look around, find out if you've seen any weirdos lately."

"Are you kidding or what? You two are the weirdest dudes been around here in a long time." The Asian snorted when he laughed.

"Very funny, asshole." Joe flashed his badge. "Just let us in or you're gonna find out how fuckin' hysterical we can be."

The bouncer nodded, and the punk rocker stood aside.

Matt followed Joe down the long eerie passageway.

One entire wall was painted black. On the other, the words Club Damnation were scrawled in vivid red script. Orange flames lapped at the Gothic lettering in a graphic portrait of hellfire. Skull and crossbones, swastikas, and pornographic images were illustrated in Day-Glo colors all over the wall.

Matt could hear death-metal rock blaring from giant speakers in the cavern ahead. For a minute Matt thought his ears would burst. This was definitely not his kind of music.

The chamber at the end of the tunnel was a scene from a horror movie. A giant birdcage stood on a shelf behind the wooden bar, which ran the full length of the left side of the room. Inside the bamboo cage, a naked man crouched on his knees, hands tied behind his back, his mouth stretched into a permanent yawn by a black rubber ball, not unlike the one they had found in Sherrie's mouth. A studded dog collar, leash attached, was tied securely around his scrawny neck. Sitting at the bar, a tall cadaverous woman, wearing a tight black dress and thigh-high boots, held the leash.

Each time she yanked on the strap, the man's head slammed into the bars of the cage, and everyone applauded.

But there was more.

Various-sized tables were arranged in a semicircle around a small stage. Nailed to the back wall was a wooden X about seven feet high.

Joe whispered, "It's a St. Andrews cross."

"What the hell is that?"

"Just watch. I saw a lot of this crap when I worked vice in Hollywood."

Suddenly, a deep voice streamed over a scratchy loudspeaker, interrupting the acid rock. "And now, Club Damnation is proud to present The Brides of Discipline."

Two hefty beauties entered the stage followed by a naked man. Identical platinum wigs veiled the women's pale shoulders.

The audience screamed their appreciation. Several motorcycle types threw their Nazi caps in the air, and one woman, shrieking with delight, lifted her fleshy breasts right out of the leather bustier that encased them.

"Holy shee-it," Matt exclaimed.

The Brides secured the male to the St. Andrew's cross by fastening chains in complicated patterns around his anemic-looking body. One of them covered his shaved head with a black leather hood that totally encased his face.

Muffled cries escaped from behind the mask.

Ignoring the scene onstage, Joe straddled an empty stool. "Let's talk to the barkeep."

Matt stood behind him but still couldn't take his eyes off the bizarre spectacle on the platform. With difficulty he turned his attention to the bar.

The middle-aged bartender's head was shaved. He wore a black wifebeater and jeans. His entire head and body were covered with tattoos. He also had holes in his ears the size of quarters, containing round black studs. Multiple piercings in his nose, lips, and eyebrows were apparently not enough; he had two horns, made of either bone or metal, implanted under the skin on his forehead.

"Gimme a coupla Becks." Joe's tone was tough.

The barman returned with two bottles of beer, no glasses. "Twelve bucks."

"Twelve bucks?" crabbed Joe. "Are you outta your fuckin' mind?"

"Cover charge." The bartender nodded toward the stage. "We've gotta pay for the entertainment here."

Joe removed a twenty dollar bill from his wallet and set it on the bar. He placed another one right beside it.

The bartender reached for the second bill.

Joe slapped his hand. "Later, asshole."

"Waddya want?"

"I'd like to know if you've seen any nutcases lately. Somebody who likes to get violent, and I don't mean this showbiz crap." Joe jerked his head toward the stage. "I mean violent for real, especially with women."

"Mister, look around. The place is loaded with shitheads and weirdos. Violence is the only game they know." He jerked his head. "Take your pick."

"This guy likes hookers—small, blonde hookers."

A flash of recognition swept across the bartender's face. It was gone in a second.

Joe reached over and grabbed him by the neck. "Now, asshole, I need to know, right now. This motherfucker is a killer, and I need to know anything you even think you know."

The bartender pushed him away. "Get your fucking hands off me."

Joe almost climbed over the bar. One of the beers hit the cement floor.

Matt jumped in, holding them apart. "Cut it out, Joe."

Joe struggled for a minute. Then he stepped back.

"Look, we're just trying to do our job here." Matt played good cop and tried to calm the bartender. "Some son of a bitch is out there cutting up hookers. We need all the help we can get."

"Okay, okay. Some dude came in a couple of weeks ago. Asked me if there was a bondage parlor I could recommend. He said he was partial to blondes."

"What did he look like?"

"Shit, I dunno. You know how many assholes I see in this joint every night?" At the word "asshole," he stared at Joe.

Joe was ready to go at him again. Matt stepped between them. "Please."

"He had a hat on. Like a fedora. It was pulled down over his eyes. I couldn't see his face. And kind of like a trench coat. That's all I know." The bartender grabbed the wet twenty dollar bill off the bar and stuffed it in his pocket.

"Where did you tell him to go?" Matt asked.

"The only place I know is the House of Destiny."

"Where the hell's that?"

"It's on the Pacific Coast Highway, near Malibu."

"What's the address?"

"I don't know the street number."

Joe pushed Matt out of the way, but the bartender backed away before he could grab him. He leaned against the back bar, palms in the air. "No shit, man. I've never been there. Honest."

Joe picked up the remaining beer and poured it over the bar. Grasping the neck of the bottle, clublike, he slapped the palm of his hand with it.

The bartender watched him, eyes wary. "But I think he had."

"What do you mean?" Matt asked. He was instantly alert.

"He acted like he knew where it was."

Joe's jaw tightened. "Let's get outta this sewer."

"One more thing," Matt said. "Did you ever hear of an operation called Fantasy Films?"

The barman shook his head.

"What about Party Favorites?"

The aging Goth shook his head again and wiped his sweaty hands on his shirt.

Following Joe toward the exit, Matt took one last look at the show. One of the Brides was attaching nipple clips to the prisoner on the cross.

What a lovely way to spend an evening.

During the next few hours, Joe took him to the Meat Market, Devil's Playground, and the Sex Bazaar—with no results. Matt was discovering how the heterosexual bondage clubs in this town kept themselves below the radar. He couldn't help wondering who they were paying off.

After calling it quits around four in the morning, he still didn't know the address of The House of Destiny.

"I'll talk to vice tomorrow. They'll know where it is," said Joe on their way out of the Sex Bazaar.

Matt dropped him off at the Whipping Inn to pick up his car. "Thanks a lot for the cultural tour, Joe." He grinned. "That's one you won't find in the Chamber of Commerce brochure."

"You got that right." Joe leaned in the window. "I hope we get the fucker before he gets horny again."

"So do I. See you tomorrow."

On his way home, Matt prayed there would be no more victims tonight.

# Chapter 14

As she cleaved through the crowd on Venice Boardwalk, Megan was wearing the formfitting sweater and tights that made up her Rollerblading outfit, a matching yellow-and-white helmet, and thick, protective pads covering her knees and elbows.

On this hot muggy day in August the place was a madhouse, surreal, like an outrageous carnival—and her favorite place to spend a Saturday morning. She glided by a small group of spectators gathered at Muscle Beach, where four overdeveloped young men, and one Amazonian woman, strutted their stuff and lifted mammoth weights. As she moved through the crowd, Megan's ears were invaded by a cacophony of sound: acid rock, Spanish guitars, steel bands, even an Indian sitar.

Her body moved to the Latin beat.

Suddenly, she was thrust into a pocket of people and a tunnel of smells—sweat, perfume, cigarette smoke, grease, and marijuana converging with myriad odors from the sidewalk stalls where every food imaginable was offered, from teriyaki tacos, to Indian curry, to Polish Louisiana sausages.

Squeezing her arms to her sides, Megan maneuvered her way through the hordes and continued to skate on the periphery.

Beyond the food stands was an open market where vendors sold T-shirts, socks, dresses, purses—the list was endless.

Interspersed with the shops and stalls was a generous sprinkling of tattoo parlors, advertising the booming trade of body piercing. On a sidewalk sign, in large bold letters, one such outfit declared itself the foremost expert in Los Angeles, specializing in "tits and clits."

Distracted by the outrageous sign, Megan collided with another female skater.

Laughing, they brushed themselves off.

She mingled with a crowd gathered to watch a young man riding on a unicycle while juggling three knives and a live chain saw. The knives flashed angrily in the sunlight.

*And I thought selling real estate was tough, especially in this down market.*

Smiling, Megan skated from one attraction to another, pausing to watch various acts: two karate experts kicking and grunting on a large tatami mat; a man with Rasta curls inching his way under a limbo stick; three carbon copies of Madonna, wearing latex and feather boas rock'n and roll'n on the sidewalk.

Megan continued on, heading toward Santa Monica. And then she saw the street sign. Beachview Avenue.

Wasn't that where the murder took place?

She had to see. She had to.

Matt Donovan walked slowly along the boardwalk, trying once more to assimilate the facts of the case. There had to be a connection between the two Venice murders and the one he'd just heard about in San Francisco. He planned to fly up there Monday and hoped to contact Troy Hanover, the owner of the house on Beachview.

For now, Hanover was the only link to both places.

Unfolding the piece of paper Joe had given him this morning, Matt read:

> House of Destiny
> 51532 Pacific Coast Highway
> Password: Justine

Justine? What the hell did that mean? But his mind refused to work. He knew from experience he had to blank out his mind, and then he could come back to the problem later with fresh eyes.

So he shut everything out and thought only about Julie.

He visualized his beautiful daughter, and love flooded his being. The world was all right again. Sadly, Matt realized this was the only way he could feel love anymore.

How his heart ached for the family life that had ceased the minute his wife, Constance, had died. Poor Julie had been forced to take over the household—tough for a sixteen-year-old whose father was so absorbed in his own grief he was paralyzed. No wonder she'd decided not to go on to college. She'd have had to continue living with him. No, that's not true. Julie wanted to be a model; that's why she went to New York.

He smiled. She was so excited about her cosmetic ad. As far as Matt was concerned, she should get every job she applied for, but maybe he was prejudiced.

He concentrated on the crowd and studied each individual face.

Was he here today, the Bondage Murderer, the cold-blooded killer of two, possibly three young women? As if life hadn't handed them enough crap and desperation, enough to drive them into the streets to sell their bodies. This son of a bitch had to come along and rob them of their futures.

*Morbid thinking, Matt, morbid thinking.*

Turning at Beachview Avenue, he headed for Sherrie Weston's house. He wanted to check it out one more time.

Megan stood in front of the small cottage on Beachview Avenue, where the second Bondage Murder had occurred. She contemplated the yellow tape wrapped around the white picket fence.

*Darn it.* Why did the place look so familiar? Had she really been here before? Somehow, she knew she had. But why? And when? She looked around. The street was quiet, deserted, except for a few kids playing football. Megan opened the gate and then lifted the crime scene tape to gain entry.

Once inside the front yard, it was déjà vu all over again.

Sidestepping on her Rollerblades, she stopped at the foot of the three steps leading to a long covered porch. The glass-paneled entry door was flanked by wood-framed windows.

A flashback. Herself, on this veranda—or one like it.

She was waiting, and it was dark. She was scared. Again, she had a sense of Brian. Why Brian?

Megan reached back into her subconscious and tried to extract the information, but it lingered there on the edge of memory. She conjured up the names in Brian's address book and wondered if this place belonged to a drug dealer. She'd rarely accompanied him to buy drugs. But how could she be so sure?

She'd done a lot of things when she was drinking and using that she couldn't remember.

As for Brian's address book, yesterday, after comparing the two Destinys, Megan had dialed the phone number. An answering machine had picked up and said, "The House of Destiny. Please leave a message." It was a woman's voice, trying very hard to be sexy and inviting.

Convinced the place was a brothel, Megan would be forever grateful to the young gatekeeper who had refused entry to Rachel. Or there might be another dead body ... David Feinman's.

She continued to walk around the exterior of the house. With skates on, it wasn't easy. All the blinds were closed so she couldn't see inside. The small backyard was empty except for a pile of newspapers and a cracked plastic garbage can so dirty she couldn't even discern the color.

Turning, she headed for the front of the house.

And then she saw him. Matt Donovan. He had one long leg over the picket fence. For a moment Megan was paralyzed. Then she snapped to. Slowly she began to walk backward. What would he think if he saw her here?

He'd ask her a trillion questions. And she wouldn't have any answers.

*Move it, girl.*

Reversing herself, she hurried as fast as was possible on rollerblades and headed toward the back gate.

It was locked. In desperation, she rattled the chain.

What the hell was she going to do?

Matt entered the house with a key and wandered through the cluttered rooms.

Sometimes, at deserted crime scenes, thoughts came to him—impressions, intuitions.

He stood silently in the bedroom, taking in the bloodstained bed and walls.

He could almost hear Sherrie's screams when she realized she was going to die—felt her pain and terror. And panic. How she must have panicked when the long, thin knife plunged into her body. Was she still conscious when he strangled her? Thank God she'd been dead when the bastard sliced off her—

What was that? He listened.

Someone was outside.

He rushed to the front porch and got the surprise of his life.

"Detective Donovan." Megan Riley looked flushed. "I thought it might be you."

"What are you doing here, Ms. Riley?" He knew his tone was brusque. But he damn well wanted to know.

"Oh, I was just passing by and I thought I saw you come in here." She looked uncomfortable. "I just live a few blocks from here and I was skating an' all …"

Familiar with that particular fault of human nature that requires they stop to watch a gory car accident or walk by the scene of a crime, Matt was slightly disappointed. But he couldn't help wondering if maybe there was more to this than met the eye. Did Megan Riley know the victim? Or even the murderer?

Without thinking, Matt turned, locked the front door, and, surprising even himself, said, "Ms. Riley, how would you like to have a cup of coffee with me?"

Megan promptly agreed.

They were seated at a bistro table in a small café on the busy boardwalk. Matt sipped his coffee and watched Megan skim the foam off her cappuccino. She was dressed in full Rollerblading regalia, so skating was obviously a pastime she enjoyed.

He wondered if she had a steady boyfriend.

Lifting her eyes, she smiled, and his stomach flip-flopped.

Totally without guile, her eyes were clear and pale. Not quite green, not quite brown. Freckles trailed like fairy dust across her nose, over her cheekbones, and her smile was fresh as a spring day. What the hell was wrong with him? He'd just caught this woman at a crime scene. "Was there any other reason you were at Sherrie Weston's house?" he asked.

Megan shook her head. Then, as if she couldn't bring herself to continue the lie, she said, "I saw the house on TV, and it looked vaguely familiar. When I saw the street sign, I decided to check it out."

"And was it?"

"What?" she asked.

"Familiar? Had you seen the house before?"

Megan shrugged. "I must have passed by it when I was working. I sell real estate here on the Westside, and I patrol these streets all the time looking for property."

"You mean canvassing? Like knocking on doors?"

She smiled. "No. I'm usually just checking out property that's on the market or comparing prices. That sort of thing."

And he bought it. He bought it because he wanted to.

Matt was pretty sure that this woman had nothing to do with the Bondage Murders. In fact, Michael Harrington was the only suspect they had, and there was very little evidence to make an arrest, let alone get a conviction.

So why was he even questioning Megan Riley? Because he knew it was the perfect opportunity to get to know her better.

Matt had decided to enjoy the day and Megan's presence.

On the other side of the table, Megan watched the detective as he stared at the waves cresting on the beach. His blue eyes were almost the same color as the Pacific Ocean and much more serene. A brisk wind had suddenly come up and was beating the waves into foamy whitecaps. She patted her hair down and tried to anchor the flimsy napkins on the table with silverware.

She did feel a little guilty. At first, she had thought about trying to deceive him. But what she had told Matt was mostly true. Megan only hoped he believed her.

"Are you from LA?" he suddenly asked.

She smiled. "No, I came here from Buffalo, New York. And you?"

He grinned. "I'm a local boy. Born 'n raised in California. I went to Venice High when there was no graffiti on the walls and no drug-sniffing dogs patrolling the halls. I still live in Venice, in my parents' old house."

Dying to find out if he was married, Megan asked, "Does your family live there with you?"

"No, my parents are dead."

"Oh." *But do you have a wife?*

"What about you? Where's your family?"

Megan tried to sound nonchalant. She didn't want her emotions showing through. "They're both gone. My father died when I was twelve, and my mother passed away a few years later."

Before she knew it, she was telling him about her mother's slow death, how she'd taken care of her all those long, lonely months that had turned into years.

What was she doing? She never talked about this to anyone. It was way too painful. And the last thing she wanted to be regarded as was a martyr, or a victim, especially by Matt Donovan.

"Do you have any brothers and sisters?"

She shook her head.

"So you came to California alone?"

Megan could feel the empathy radiating from his eyes. "It was rough at first. I didn't know anybody, but I managed." She cocked her head to one side and fiddled with a napkin. "I got a job as a waitress for a couple of years, went to City College at night."

"Is that when you got your real estate license?"

"No, I made the mistake of getting married first."

He was quiet for a moment. "Are you still married?"

She shook her head. "It lasted three years."

"I'm sorry." Matt put his hand on hers. She felt his heat.

She automatically pulled away. "Don't be sorry. He was kind of a jerk. After the divorce, I studied for my real estate license and eventually started working at it five years ago. I work on the Westside, mostly Venice, Santa Monica, and the Marina."

That's when Megan realized she wanted to reach out and touch him. Instead, to cover her uncertainty at this turn of events, she checked her watch. "I'm afraid I have to go." For a change, thank heaven, she was not rushing in where angels feared to tread. She'd been hurt once too often. "I have a showing, and I need to go home and change."

She was grateful for the perennial reason of having a showing. It had given her many easy escapes from all kinds of unwanted situations.

Megan held out her hand to him. She felt the shock when he touched her.

She tried to look directly into his eyes but failed.

"I'm sure I'll be seeing you again, Megan." He held on to her for a moment.

Gently, she slid her fingers from his hand.

"Yes, I'm sure you will."

And Megan skated off down the boardwalk … without looking back.

## Chapter 15

Dressed in what he considered to be his black S&M outfit, Matt sat in the darkened car and waited for Angelle. He rehashed the day in his mind.

The timing of his arrival at the house on Beachview had been completely unforeseen. But he found it to be more than fortunate.

The time he'd spent with Megan at the beach had been a joy. Not since his wife passed away had Matt felt so much at ease with a woman.

But, from an investigative standpoint, the tour of Sherrie's house was a complete waste of time, and tonight's trip to the House of Destiny would probably be the same.

*Shit.* All he could do now was keep following the leads.

At ten minutes past ten, his partner hurried out of the house and jumped in the front seat beside him. The team had agreed that having a woman present would cause less suspicion, and Matt wanted to be undercover until they discovered what was going on up there.

Matt was stunned. Angelle's exotic face was expertly made up, her hair curled and styled. She wore a shiny black trench coat and looked like she'd stepped from the cover of a magazine.

"Wait till you see what I've got on," she giggled. "Actually, it's what I haven't got on."

Clearing his throat, he mumbled, "I guess we have to look like we fit in." Making no other comment, he headed for the beach. "Joe said this place is near Malibu, 51532 Pacific Coast Highway. The house is on top of the hill so we have to ride up on a cable car. I just give the bouncer the magic password and we're on our way to the stars."

When they arrived at the Malibu address, Matt parked the car on the highway and then steered his partner toward a small wooden structure at the side of the road.

There was no one in line at the guard hut. Following Joe's instructions, Matt slipped the guard a twenty. "Justine," he whispered, feeling like an idiot.

The gatekeeper pocketed the bill, and Matt and Angelle boarded. It was that simple.

They were the sole occupants of the cable car as it creaked and rumbled its way up the hill to a garishly lit adobe mansion on the edge of the cliff.

The small car swayed from side to side. *"Mon dieu,"* Angelle said. "Do you think she'll make it?"

"I hope so." Matt felt a little queasy himself.

But even with edgy nerves, he couldn't ignore the spectacular view of the coastline that unfolded as the funicular neared the crest. Santa Monica Bay, which curved from Point Dume to Palos Verdes, was necklaced by a million twinkling lights. Overhead, hooked onto a magnificent vista of stars hung a silvery quarter-moon.

The hilltop mansion was ablaze with light, and loud music emanated from the open windows, ravaging the silence of the secluded mountaintop.

Angelle rang the bell. "A place like this must cost millions."

To Matt's surprise, the door was opened by a peculiar, bandy-legged man wearing tight white leggings and an intricate, red leather mask to match his flattened brassiere and miniskirt. The little man's skin was blotched with age, his lips painted crimson.

"Welcome, welcome. Come in, join the party." He gestured to the left with an effeminate wave of his hand. "The cloakroom's that way. Do you have a mask?"

Matt shook his head.

"Pick one out. They're in there."

Angelle dropped her coat on the bed while Matt rummaged in a large brass chest and selected two masks.

He turned, and his mouth dropped open. His partner wore

skintight, black leather pants that clung to her curved buttocks and shapely legs. Barely covering her ample breasts was a short beaded T-shirt.

"Like it?" She twirled for him to see.

"I guess so." Matt cleared his throat and handed her a black sequined mask. He couldn't turn his eyes away. Angelle's hair hovered about her shoulders, like a cloud of mist, and the glitzy mask added even more appeal to her sexy outfit. "Shit, Angel. Don't leave my side, no matter what." He adjusted his own mask that was decorated with silver studs and tried to lighten things up. "I feel like the Lone friggin' Ranger."

Angelle laughed, breaking the spell.

Megan had attended an AA meeting in Malibu and spent another hour having coffee with her sponsor, so it was after eleven o'clock when she arrived at the cable car leading to Destiny La Conte's house.

She slowed the car to get a better view of the people waiting at the foot of the hill.

Megan decided she was going to get in there. She pulled onto the shoulder and waited for the traffic to subside before making a U-turn. Luckily, it was late and few cars traveled the highway. She turned and parked just beyond the guard shack.

She glanced at her watch. It read 11:08.

What if the place was a brothel? *Well*, she thought, *it must be a pretty busy one.*

First, Rachel made her visit. She was obviously trying to find David. And then there was Brian. He had the phone number in his little black book. And hadn't he given her four damn stars? Who else was she likely to find at Destiny La Conte's house?

The same beachboy bouncer was checking people out, both men and women. Some were allowed entry, and a few were rejected. Megan wondered what she had to do. Slip him a fifty-dollar bill? Well, she was willing. She had to know what was up there.

Just when she'd begun to lose her nerve and was about to leave, a white limousine pulled alongside the guard shack. Two couples practically fell out of the backseat and lurched toward the gatekeeper.

This was it, now or never. Dare she?

Megan jumped out of her car and joined the group.

She checked out the women and their much older boyfriends. Never in her entire life had she seen so much gold lamé, leopard print, and rhinestones. Feeling grossly underdressed in her gray slacks and white cable-knit sweater, she chatted with the drunken foursome, pretending she belonged.

She heard one of the men say the password, Justine. And after an animated exchange of banter and cash, the guard allowed the couples on the cable car. Megan slipped on with them. Lurching up the mountainside in the cramped, swaying car, it took all of her efforts to keep the bald-headed guy's hands off her breasts.

† † †

Matt led Angelle across the adobe-tiled hallway into a white Sante Fe-style living room littered with naked and near-naked bodies. All were masked. One older lady wore only finger paint and was still in the process of dressing with the aid of an artistic male in a black G-string. He smirked at Matt as he daubed the woman's buttocks with royal-blue paint.

"Jesus, save us," Angelle whispered under her breath.

In the dining room, food and drinks were plentiful. A dozen or so people, all masked, sat on the floor and ate with their hands, laughing and shoving food in one another's faces.

*It's a bacchanal,* thought Matt.

Holding his partner by the elbow, Matt continued to inspect the house. At the rear of the dining room, men and women passed back and forth through the open glass-paneled doors. He steered Angelle toward the opening.

Out of nowhere a spidery middle-aged woman dressed in a gold-sequined dress and a white feathery mask grabbed Matt by the arm and dragged him into the corner. He tried to shake her loose, as he would a deadly tarantula, but she hung on.

The mask slipped, revealing a pasty face. Translucent skin stretched across her cheekbones, obviously from too many face-lifts, and kohl-lined eyes sloped upward, like those of an Egyptian queen. One more desperate effort and Matt finally broke away.

The woman leaned against the wall, laughing, her mouth a purple slash against yellowing teeth.

Matt shoved his partner through the patio door. "What the hell was that?"

Angelle didn't answer.

The yard was poorly lit, but a large round structure loomed in the darkness and seemed to be attracting the crowd.

He preceded Angelle into the darkened amphitheater.

Arranged in-the-round, the small auditorium was filled with wooden bleachers, forming two semicircles. Centered in a patch of sand was what looked like an obstetric table. Couples, threesomes, and even foursomes draped over the benches in various coital and precoital positions.

"It's a fucking orgy," Matt exclaimed.

"No kidding."

Matt found an empty row, and they sat down. Angelle, glued to his side, stared dead ahead. Before long, a spotlight beamed on the circular patch of sand.

The little man, now dressed in tails and twirling a top hat, stepped into the limelight. He was followed by two males wearing black leather; they yanked on a long silver chain. The chain was attached to a harness like contraption worn by a naked girl who stumbled on stage. Tall and slender, her long dark hair arranged to conceal her breasts, she limped into the spotlight. Her lovely face showed no sign of emotion.

"She's drugged," said Matt.

Angelle nodded and turned away.

"Justine," the diminutive ringmaster proclaimed, with a flourish of his hat.

The two men strapped the girl down on the table, and the little man disappeared, reappearing almost immediately with a long wicked lash. He cracked the whip at the young woman, and she cried out. The crowd roared.

Angelle jumped from her seat and headed for the door.

Matt caught up with her outside.

Megan and her newfound friends rang the bell, and a woman wearing only body paint opened the front door. She directed Megan and her snickering companions into the darkened room off the hallway and instructed them to don masks.

Seeing this as an opportunity to dump the two couples, Megan slipped into the adjoining bathroom and closed the door.

When the giggling subsided, Megan assumed they were gone and ventured outside. She dipped into the large brass trunk and pulled out a feathery mask. Not her style. Digging deeper, she came up with a Minnie Mouse face. Perfect.

The hallway, elaborately floored with hand-painted Mexican tile, disappeared into the confines of the house. Megan turned right and entered the living room, which appeared to be where the action was. She was right.

Two couples, intricately entwined, were having at it on the living room rug. Megan thought she would choke on the spot. The other guests ignored the action on the floor and sipped their wine. They nonchalantly reached for the hors d'oeuvres, carved in lewd shapes that were carried around on trays by topless waitresses. In fact, the essence of sex dominated every aspect of the goings-on in this party house.

And that's what it was—a party house.

At that moment a hand moved up her leg … fingers with nails … long nails. Megan jumped away and looked down. A naked woman leered up her skirt, beckoning her to join her on the floor. With a loud screech, Megan fled.

She passed a gold baroque mirror over the fireplace and caught a glimpse of herself in the ludicrous Minnie Mouse mask. Dumb. But she was grateful for the anonymity it afforded. Megan escaped into the dining room.

No salvation there. A dozen naked people, behaving like beasts, smeared food all over themselves and each other. The whole scene made her sick to her stomach.

French doors led to an outside garden, and Megan made a dash for it. On the stone patio, she paused to catch her breath.

Standing under the light, she removed the mask and wiped her forehead with the sleeve of her white sweater. That's when she saw him.

Was it Detective Matt Donovan? She would know him anywhere, by the cut of his body, the tilt of his head, and all that curly dark hair.

Mask or no mask—that was Matt.

He had his arm around a young woman, an incredibly gorgeous woman.

*Please don't let him see me.* Megan spun around and rushed back into the dining room, searching for a place to hide. She dived under the table and tugged on the tablecloth to better hide herself. As she curled up on the floor, she realized she was still holding the mask in her hand.

She should have known. Any guy that good-looking had to have a girlfriend.

But what the hell were they doing here?

That was obvious—Matt and his friend were into kinky sex!

But what if he'd recognized her? She had taken off her mask for a moment. What would he think, seeing her here in this—this disgusting orgy house?

Suppose he was out there right now, getting it on with that crowd in the living room. He might be there all night. She could be here all night. Maybe she'd have to stay under the table for hours. That's when she started second guessing herself.

She should never have come here. Her behavior had now bypassed impetuous, proceeded to reckless, and was bordering on damn crazy. As always when she was desperate, Megan whispered the alcoholic's prayer: "Please, God, get me out of this one, and I promise I'll never, ever do it again."

Matt caught up with Angelle outside the amphitheater. She was apparently very upset at the treatment of the young woman. Her fingers fluttered at her brow in a gesture totally out of sync with her appearance. Not knowing what else to do, Matt put his arms around her to comfort her.

He looked over Angelle's shoulder, and, for a moment, he thought he saw Megan Riley standing under the light.

Nah, that was impossible. Not here, in a place like this.

Angelle righted herself. She looked embarrassed at her own behavior. "I couldn't watch anymore, I'm sorry."

Matt moved on. "Let's find the owner of this joint, see if our guy's been here. Then we can get the hell out."

With Angelle hard at his heels, Matt reentered the house.

Approaching one of the masked diners, he inquired after the owner. He was directed to a woman draped across a white armchair, fondling the breasts of a plump young woman. It was the same scrawny broad in the sequined dress who had grabbed him on the way to the garden.

Matt stood in front of her. "Ma'am, I'd like a word with you."

"No need to be so formal, darling." The woman smiled, still fingering the girl's nipples.

He took off his mask and flashed his badge. "Detective Matt Donovan, LAPD."

"Run along, dear," she instructed her protégé and then turned to Matt. "How did you get in here?"

"We used the magic password," Angelle snapped.

Matt took charge. "Are you the owner of this house?"

"Why yes, darling, I am."

"What is your full name?"

"My name is Destiny La Conte." Eyebrows arched, she indicated the badge in his hand. "Is that thing real? Or is that how you get your kicks?" She offered her wrists. "Would you like to handcuff me, Officer? Hmmm?"

"I'd like to ask you some questions, ma'am."

She dropped her hands. "Oh, damn."

He gave her the description of the suspect the bartender at Club Damnation had provided, but Destiny denied ever seeing him.

Assessing him with veiled eyes, she pursed her purple lips and made a declaration. "Matt. I can call you Matt, can't I? This is a very distinguished crowd we have here. Guests must be highly recommended before gaining admission. In fact, if anyone gets too kinky or causes unnecessary pain—especially when it hasn't been specifically requested, you understand?—well, we ask them to leave right away."

"Yes, I can see it's a classy place," Angelle snipped.

Matt jumped in again. "Am I correct in assuming this is a private residence, Ms. La Conte?"

"Yes, darling, it is." Destiny cast her gaze around at the carnal scene in the living room. "Care to join us in some fun?"

Matt pulled out pictures of the two murder victims. "Have either of these women ever been here?"

She looked agitated but recovered quickly. Taking her time, Destiny pointed to Allison. "Yes, this one."

"Was she with anyone in particular?"

"Yes, she always came with the same man. But that was months ago."

"What was his name?"

She crossed her legs. "I don't know."

"Can you remember anything about him?"

Destiny shook her head. "All my guests wear masks."

"Was he tall or short? Blond or dark?" Angelle demanded.

"He was sort of medium."

Angelle rolled her eyes.

Matt asked, "Are you familiar with the Bayside Yacht Club?"

He could see a flicker of recognition in her eyes.

"Mrs. La Conte, may I remind you—" He paused.

"Yes. And you may consult my lawyer if you have any further questions, darling." The woman gave Matt a coquettish yellow smile.

"How about Fantasy Films?" Angelle asked. "Did you ever hear of them?"

Destiny looked down her nose. "I've never heard of it."

"Party Favorites?"

She shook her head.

Angelle persisted. "Do you know a Michael Harrington?"

"Should I?" Destiny turned to Matt, smiling her purple smile. "Is he as good-looking as you?"

Giving Matt a phony grin, Angelle said, "Oh, he's much better-looking."

"Then I don't know him. I'd remember." She stood up, her eyes wandering around the room. "Will that be all?"

"For now." Knowing he wouldn't get any more information, Matt handed her a card. "I'd like to stay in touch in case Allison's companion shows up here again."

Her interest perked. "Is this an invitation, darling?"

Ignoring the question, Matt hurried after the infuriated Angelle.

After a few more minutes, Megan furtively lifted the cloth and peered into the dining room. Matt was nowhere in sight. She moved to the other end of the table, facing the living room. From there, she could see an unmasked Matt and his girlfriend, even more gorgeous without the mask, speaking to a weird-looking woman.

Suddenly, the girlfriend became angry and stomped away. Matt ran after her as the older woman laughed boisterously.

What was that all about? Megan would kill to know.

As Matt clung to the railing, and Angelle clung to Matt, the cable car trundled down the hill. His mind was on Megan Riley and the brief moment he thought he'd seen her on the patio. He knew that was impossible. She'd never come to a place like this.

Or would she? How could he be so sure? He barely knew the woman.

Still, as he immersed himself in the beauty of the night, thoughts of Megan lingered. The sky was crystal clear, a million stars flaunting their glory. The lights on Palos Verdes' Peninsula vied with their brilliance—and lost. To the north, the long finger of light, which was Malibu Pier, pointed to the horizon, where a silvery slice of moon sank lazily into the sea.

"I think Destiny knows more than she's willing to admit," Angelle said.

Matt agreed. "Yeah, I think so too."

# Chapter 16

Megan awoke on Sunday morning with a sense of impending doom, fearing she hadn't heard the last of the House of Destiny. After her flight from the orgy house on the mountaintop, she'd been plagued by the same three questions.

First, had Matt Donovan recognized her? Second, why the hell was Rachel trying to get into a kinky sex club? And third, was Brian Mason going up that hill to visit four-star Destiny La Conte while he was still living with her?

Whatever possessed her to go up there in the first place?

She must have been totally nuts. Any number of things could have happened. Suppose Brian had been there, or David? What the hell would she have done?

*Darn it.* She had to learn not to be so compulsive. Surely, that kind of behavior had gotten her into enough trouble for any ten lifetimes.

She was fixing herself a cappuccino when a broker from her office called and told her she'd written an offer on the Rosario home. Megan prayed it would be a sale.

Within an hour, Megan found herself seated at a table in the Bayside Yacht Club with Kathleen Rosario. Sunday brunch was in full swing, and the place was packed.

Megan was extremely grateful that Gino wasn't there but

wondered where she might find him later. Maybe he was on his boat with his girlfriend.

Kathleen suggested they eat first, obviously trying to put off making a decision on the house. On her way to the buffet table, Megan waved to Alex and Charlie Grant, who were seated with Senator and Mrs. Rattner and the commodore of the club, Dr. Henderson, and his wife.

She passed the Feinman table, where Rachel and David sat in stony silence, watching their two lively children interact. The family picture they presented did not jibe with the activity at the House of Destiny or with Rachel's lust for a weight lifter.

Brian was at the bar. He waved.

Megan ignored him.

After loading up her plate at the buffet, Megan returned to the table. Kathleen nibbled on a thin slice of papaya. *No wonder she's so slim.* Having chosen an omelet, ham, potatoes, and a blueberry scone with maple walnut butter, Megan began to feast.

"I really must start my diet on Monday," she heard herself whine, not convincingly, knowing in her heart that once again she'd spent the whole weekend in another "farewell to food" and still wouldn't start the damn diet on Monday.

Kathleen watched every single bite that went into her mouth. Trying desperately to ignore her mournful eyes, Megan swallowed the last mouthful of blueberry scone.

"Those people want to buy the house, don't they?" Kathleen asked.

*Please don't cause a scene.* "Yes, they do, dear."

"I suppose it had to happen sometime." Her voice was small and plaintive. "Where will I go?"

Megan watched the tears form in her friend's eyes. They escaped and rolled down her perfect cheekbones. "Don't you fret. Everything is going to be fine. To be honest, I think you'll be much better off out of that house and away from all the memories. You can start a whole new life." She reached across the table and patted her hand. "You won't have to worry about money. When the dust settles, there'll be at least two million dollars for you. If you invest it wisely, you'll have more than enough to live on."

"Megan, it's more than losing the house, even more than losing Gino. All my dreams of love and family are shattered." Kathleen's hands formed rigid fists, and her baby voice escalated. "Marriage vows don't mean anything anymore. All that 'till death do us part' garbage is obsolete. Everything I was ever taught is untrue. It's all lies, all of it, lies."

People at the next table stared, and Megan shuddered at her rage. She knew Kathleen viewed the world through veils of romantic illusion, but the cruel reality of the last few months had finally been brought to bear. Now, she would have to face the truth and deal with it. And that wasn't going to be easy.

"Look, honey, my family are Irish Catholic, like yours, and I don't think it's a sin to get a divorce. Maybe God isn't a Catholic or a Jew or any special religion. Maybe He doesn't have any hard-and-fast rules. I mean, maybe He or She just wants you to be a good person and be happy."

It didn't seem to be the right time to mention the time-share lover, but maybe it wasn't such a bad idea. Kathleen had laughed as much as anyone over her escapade at the gym. At least it had taken her mind off Gino and his new family for a while.

Jumping to her feet, Kathleen sounded breathless. "I have to go. I can't sit here a moment longer."

Megan grabbed her hand. "You're not going to do anything stupid, are you?"

Kathleen stared at her, a wild look in her eyes. "I'm just so confused right now. Please take the papers to my attorney, Megan. I'll do whatever he says."

Worried to death, Megan wouldn't let go of her friend's hand. "Promise me you'll call if you start having crazy thoughts."

"I will, I promise," Kathleen said, pulling away. "I just want to get the whole thing over with and get on with my life."

And then she was gone.

At exactly that moment, Megan saw Detective Donovan amble into the busy dining room. Immediately, her heart sank. The exotic-looking young woman was right behind him. Then, a pleasant thought occurred to her. Maybe this woman was a cop.

Megan tried not to stare as the detective spoke to the maître d' and was directed toward the commodore of the Club, Dr. Henderson.

As Matt and his lady friend walked toward the table, Megan saw Charlie rise from his chair and head for the restroom.

He signaled to David Feinman.

David got up and followed Charlie. Then, Brian slid off his bar stool and meandered across the room to join them.

Very interesting, but her first concern was Matt. She was pretty sure that he had recognized her last night at the House of Destiny, and she didn't want to have to answer any questions. So she headed for the ladies' room.

Rounding the corner to the hallway, she realized that Brian, David, and Charlie were in the corridor with their heads together. The conversation ceased the moment they saw her. "Hi," she called.

"Hi," answered all three in unison.

Was this a private conference?

Megan entered the ladies' lounge and, not knowing why she did it, quietly reopened the door to the corridor and caught part of the discussion.

"We've got to get our stories straight." David sounded frustrated. "Charlie? You didn't say anything about Gino's divorce party, did you?"

"Definitely not, that would really open a can of worms."

"The detective hasn't talked to me yet," Brian said.

David spoke so softly she had to strain to hear him. "Me neither … yet. Has he spoken to Gino?"

"I doubt it," Brian chuckled. "If he had, Gino would be screaming about his precious career by now."

"David, I think you're making too much of this whole thing." Charlie seemed annoyed. "Pretty soon the whole damn mess will blow over and be completely forgotten."

"I wish I could be sure of that. Not that I have anything to hi—" David's voice faded away.

Megan heard the men's room door open and close, and then all was quiet. She couldn't believe it. They had a divorce party for Gino Rosario. Were they planning to give the bastard a baby shower too?

And what had happened at the party to make David so upset? These guys were definitely hiding something. But what?

When she rejoined Alex in the dining room, Matt and his girlfriend were gone.

Should she call the detective and tell him what she'd overheard? Or was she just looking for an excuse to see him again?

## CHAPTER 17

Early Monday morning, Matt took a flight to San Francisco, but due to a foul-up at LAX, he'd sat on the runway for almost two hours and arrived later than planned. By the time he reached Homicide Division of the San Francisco Police Department, it was midmorning, and the joint was a madhouse.

He followed the uniform to the second-floor office.

"Hey, Jaybird," the officer called. "There's somebody here to see you."

A tall, thin man approached, holding out a slender hand with extremely long fingers. "You're late."

Matt took the warm, moist hand. "I'm pleased to meet you, too." If he hadn't been so pissed at the guy's attitude, he would have smiled. Jaybird looked like a French fry. Long and thin in blended shades of yellow, from his straw-colored hair and sallow skin, right down to his chicken-fat slacks. Even his head was long and narrow with small ears sticking to the sides, like a couple of dried apricots.

"Likewise, I'm sure." Jaybird grinned, displaying predictably yellow teeth. His voice sounded garbled, like marbles rolling around a track. Grumbling all the way, he led Matt down a hallway into a small room containing a desk littered with files. "All the paperwork's in there. We never did get an ID. Our plates are full up here, and we gotta set priorities. Not much time for this Jane Doe shit."

*Well, screw you and the horse you rode in on.* "I do have one more question," Matt said. "Ever hear of an outfit called Fantasy Films?"

"I'll see if I can find somebody to check the porno file." Jay slammed the door when he left.

Matt sighed. He'd hoped for more help. *Not only did this guy not enter the case into VICAP, but now he's giving me nothing but crap.*

He read the coroner's report who had estimated that her death occurred on May 27. Pinpointing a set time was even harder.

Matt removed a photograph of the dead girl from the file.

She was naked, lying on a stainless steel table.

The week-old corpse was not pretty. The medical examiners declared both the scene and the body had been badly contaminated by rainy weather, the foraging of animals, and time.

According to Jay Santini's notes, not much effort had been made to identify the remains. When they had established that the crime was committed elsewhere, and the body dropped in the Haight, chances of discovering her identity were greatly diminished.

No one had claimed her, so the Jane Doe was buried in a pauper's grave on city property. Unexpectedly, Matt experienced a surge of anger over the young woman's death and her life.

He thought about Julie, his Julie. *Don't even go there.*

Matt continued to fumble through the reports. Santini's questioning of the kid who'd found the body appeared thorough, as were countless interviews of everyone in the neighborhood.

Things would be a whole lot easier if they had a goddamn crime scene. He checked it all again—nothing that he could see.

Matt left the police station without speaking to Detective Santini again and found a small Italian restaurant nearby.

All through lunch, he considered his findings and could come up with nothing, other than the MO, to connect Jane Doe to the LA murders. But Matt knew in his gut it was the same guy. He couldn't understand it. The Jane Doe had to have been murdered somewhere. Recalling the carnage in Sherrie's house, he figured there had to be plenty of blood. Why hadn't someone reported it?

*Dammit, somebody knew something.*

Pulling out his notebook, Matt wrote down the similarities. The murders were identical in so many ways. All three women were small blondes. He assumed the Jane Doe was a hooker, like the others, and an addict. They all had a breast removed and were taken from the scene. Did they know each other? Did they know their killer?

He glanced at his watch. *Time to go.* Matt called for the check.

† † †

His next stop was the home of Troy Hanover, the owner of the house Sherrie Weston had rented at 42 Beachview Avenue in Venice, which was also the address for Fantasy Films, and who had also sent her the DVDs.

Without too much difficulty, he found the elegant Victorian town house on one of the hilly streets overlooking the bay.

He rang the bell. It played a chorus of "Feelings."

Opening the door, Troy Hanover looked like an eight-by-ten glossy with his black hair, awkward smile, and strong, chiseled features. Graying sideburns gave him an air of maturity, and Matt figured him somewhere between forty and fifty.

"You must be Detective Donovan?" The minute he spoke in his faux British accent, the intense air of masculinity surrounding him disappeared.

"Yes, I am." Matt displayed his badge.

"Troy Hanover. Do come in." Once inside, Hanover carefully closed and locked the heavy mahogany door. "I was sorry to hear about the unfortunate death of my tenant, Ms. Weston."

Even though it was the middle of the day, the elaborate crystal chandelier in the two-story hallway was on, its twinkling lights reflected in the shiny peg 'n groove planks of the floor. A graceful mahogany staircase ascended to an upstairs landing.

"Come into the drawing room, please." Hanover seated himself in a gold brocade wing chair and gestured to another one like it. "How may I help you?"

Matt sat down, placing his file on the delicately carved coffee table. "Mr. Hanover, do you own the house at 42 Beachview Avenue in Venice, California?"

"Yes, I do, although I've never seen it."

"Never seen it?"

"Yes, it was left to me by a friend who recently passed away." He bowed his head in sorrow. "He left me everything he owned."

"And what was your friend's name, sir?"

"Raymond Jennings. He used to live in Santa Monica, but he moved up here early this year, in April. Six weeks later he was dead."

"How did he die?"

"Hit-and-run. It was shocking. They never did find out who did it." He swallowed hard. "I really miss him."

"Forgive me for asking, but how close were you to Mr. Jennings?"

Hanover was unabashed. "Ray was my partner. He was a warm, generous lover." He cast his eyes around at the roomful of antiques. "I inherited everything when he died. This house alone is worth almost two million dollars. He paid cash for it out of his divorce settlement. We were going to live here forever."

His grief looked genuine enough to Matt. "We traced a package sent from this address and delivered by UPS to the house in Venice. They identified the sender as Fantasy Films."

"That was Ray's company. He owned it when he lived in LA and continued to work it up here. Actually, he did much better with it in San Francisco. Gays and lesbians go for that sort of thing. I guess we're more open about our sexuality."

"What kind of company was it?"

"Just a small operation. Ray filmed people in the act of making love. Nothing illegal," he hurried to add. "You know, some couples wanted a record of their lovemaking on film, so they could enjoy it later. People who don't want to put a lot of money out for their own equipment. Ray provided a camera and the house in Venice as a set. The rest was up to them. He made a little money in Los Angeles. Not much."

"And the film you sent to Sherrie, where did it come from?"

"Oh, that. You mean the one with the transvestite and the blonde? I presume the blonde was Sherrie Weston."

"You don't know her?" Matt asked, surprised.

"No, I never actually met her. But she wrote to Fantasy Films and asked for a certain DVD and one extra copy. I don't think she even knew that Ray was dead, so I didn't say anything. I just sent back the two copies she requested. After all, she said she was one of the participants and that she'd paid Ray for the taping in the first place."

"As far as you know, did Mr. Jennings film anyone without their permission?"

Hanover acted shocked. "I hardly think so, Officer. That would be illegal."

"So you don't think Mr. Jennings could have been blackmailing anyone?"

"Absolutely, positively not." He shook his head, vigorously. "He'd never do anything like that. I'm sure of it."

"When did Mr. Jennings's accident occur?"

"I'll never forget that day. It was May 27."

*No shit?* That was the same day the medical examiner had fixed the time of death for the Jane Doe. He squinted at Hanover. *If the coroner was right, is it possible the same person had also killed Ray Jennings? Too far-fetched? Not really. Maybe Ray knew the killer.* Then he had a sudden thought. "Was Mr. Jennings a member of the Bayside Yacht Club in Marina del Rey?"

"Yes, he was. How did you know?"

*Bingo.* "Just a lucky guess."

"I think his ex-wife, Helen, still belongs to it."

"Was Mrs. Jennings bitter about the divorce?"

"You mean, do I think she killed him?"

Matt nodded.

Troy's pause spoke volumes. "Who knows? The woman is a twenty-four–carat bitch."

"Did she know that her husband was homosexual?"

"Not until he told her, right before he left. I guess it came as quite a shock. We'd been seeing each other for a couple of years, and she hadn't suspected anything. I don't think anyone knew he was gay."

"I wonder if it was enough of a shock to put her over the edge."

"Possibly. Although she seemed to handle it fairly well after the initial impact. The marriage was on the rocks for years. If you ask me, Helen's number-one priority was getting ownership of the family home in Santa Monica and as much money as she could get her hands on." Troy Hanover leaned forward. "I tell you she was not thrilled when she had to refinance the house earlier this year to pay Ray his half of the equity. Have you ever met her?"

"No, I haven't had the pleasure."

"No pleasure there, sweetie. The woman is cold as a witch's tit." Troy's own bitchiness came to the fore. "You should have heard her when the will was read and Ray left all of his assets and his insurance to me. Well, you can imagine."

Matt steered the conversation back to Fantasy Films. "Did Mr. Jennings keep copies of any of his other films?"

"Yes, he did, but I threw most of them out when I closed the office after his death. Now I just keep a mail drop. Sherrie was lucky. It was only by chance her disk was available."

*I don't think I'd call her lucky.* "Have you ever seen any of these women before?" Matt showed him the pictures of Sherrie and Allison, as well as the morgue photo of the Jane Doe.

After a quick glance, he turned away. "Just Sherrie. From the video, you know."

Matt placed the photos back in the file. "Mr. Hanover, I have to ask you this to clear the record. Where were you the night of Mr. Jennings's death?"

Hanover appeared unshaken. "I was in Santa Maria, visiting my brother and his family. They'll vouch for me."

"Ever hear of Party Favorites?"

He nodded. "That was Ray's business too. He had it before he came to San Francisco, turned it over to someone who worked for him. I can't remember her name."

Matt was out of questions. "Thanks again. You've been a great help."

Troy Hanover followed him into the hallway.

Matt turned and asked, "Do you remember where you were on Tuesday, the night of August 16?"

"You mean last week?"

"Yes, the night of Sherrie Weston's murder."

Hanover thought for a moment and then looked relieved. "I was at a party at Craig's house." He gave Matt the phone number.

Matt scribbled it down. "Oh, and there's one more thing, Mr.

Hanover. Does the name Michael Harrington mean anything to you?"

"No. Should it?"

"You never heard Mr. Jennings mention the name?"

"No. Was he one of Ray's lovers?"

"I don't think so. But I can't be certain."

Opening the front door, Hanover explained, "Ray had a whole other life before he and I met. I didn't ask too many questions."

"Yes. Well, let me know if you find any films or if you think of anything else." He handed him a business card. "Thanks."

For several minutes, Matt stood outside the house on the steep sidewalk and gazed across the bay to the island of Alcatraz and the ruins of the old penitentiary. It was beautiful but ominous.

His mind produced nothing but questions. What if Hanover was the real bitch in Ray Jennings's life? Suppose Mrs. Jennings was simply the poor jilted wife?

But the yacht club connection was now clear. And Ray Jennings had once owned Fantasy Films, Party Favors, and the house on Beachview Avenue.

Matt could hardly wait to meet the wife.

Also, he was itching to find out if Michael Harrington knew Ray Jennings—and how well.

† † †

Megan sat in the beauty salon, wondering where the weekend had gone. She checked out her friends and herself in the salon's floor-to-ceiling mirrors.

What a sight they were, dressed in ugly black smocks with matching turbans, waiting for their "Special Hour of Beauty," compliments of Alex Grant. A study in black-and-white tile, the Elegant Lady Salon was not a place Megan could afford on her own.

But the special—which included a manicure, a pedicure, and a facial—was far from the real reason she sat so patiently with her feet in a container of sudsy water. No, they were all here to check out Alex's selection for boytoy, a young hairdresser at the salon.

Smiling, Megan recalled the fiasco with Rachel's weight lifter. Still, undaunted by failure, here they were again.

"If he's not here by the time they've finished with my nails, I'm leaving," Rachel complained. "I don't intend to sit here all day."

"I have to be at my attorney's office and sign the real estate papers at ten o'clock," Kathleen put in. "And I know you want me to do that, don't you, Megan?"

"I wouldn't worry about that," Rachel barked. "Lawyers always make you wait. Now I'm the one who's kept waiting."

Rachel, who had given up her career as a successful corporate attorney for marriage and family, was obviously regretting her choice.

Megan studied Kathleen. No sign of tears. Wonderful.

Their little diversion was taking Kathleen's mind off the sale of her house and helping her through the trauma. Laughter really was the best medicine. As a matter of fact, Rachel didn't seem quite as angry, either, not since they'd started their adventures into boytoy land. She'd told Megan, only this morning, that she no longer wanted to kill David. Just maim him a little—"like, Bobbitize him."

"He-e-e-re's Ronnie-e-e-e!" Alex's imitation of the late Ed McMahon left a whole lot to be desired.

Ronnie was all duded up in a white western-cut shirt, buttoned at the neck, tucked into tight blue jeans, tucked into black cowboy boots. Megan couldn't believe her eyes. Except for his cowboy outfit, Ronnie looked like he'd just stepped down from the ceiling of the Sistine Chapel. He looked, for all the world, like one of Michelangelo's angels. His skin had the milky veneer of the white marble of the Pietà, and a shock of golden curls haloed his round baby face, like an aureole.

"Hello-o-o-o, Ronnie," Alex cooed.

Megan had never heard Alex coo before. It was quite an experience. She turned to look and was equally surprised by the coy expression on Alex's usually implacable face.

"Hi, Alex, are you here again?"

When Ronnie spoke, his mouth spread into a cutesy smile, revealing deep dimples in both cheeks. Dimples that Megan had an incredible impulse to pinch.

Alex introduced him, and Ronnie offered his limp fingers to

Megan, nodded briefly at Rachel and Kathleen, and then moved on to the back of the shop.

Megan was disappointed he had no wings, just a great rear end. Like his other cheeks, very pinchable.

"Well, what do you think?" Alex asked excitedly.

"To tell you the truth," Rachel said, "I've never had the urge to screw a Botticellian angel."

Megan laughed. "He's darling, but he does look like a baby. What do you think, Kathleen?"

"Well, he is kind of young."

"I want to know what the hell you girls are looking for," Alex snapped. "The perfect man? 'Cause I'm sorry Brad Pitt is still unavailable, and so is Matthew McConaughey."

"Wow, there's a hunk!" Rachel smiled.

"Does anyone else have a suggestion?" Megan asked, ignoring them both.

"No," Rachel said. "I don't."

But Alex challenged Megan. "How about you, Megan? Why don't you find somebody?"

Before she could respond, Rachel jumped in. "Now, girls, let's not get into an argument."

"I—I—I think I know someone," Kathleen said hesitantly.

"You?" they asked as one voice.

Megan listened to Kathleen's story about a male model she'd recently seen at a clothing store on Venice beach and agreed along with the others to check him out on the way to Ginny's wedding shower.

"I still like Ronnie," Alex whined.

Megan laughed. She was beginning to have a really good time.

# Chapter 18

Matt ate breakfast with Joe in a local coffee shop on Culver Boulevard. When he was finished, he leaned back in the red plastic booth and surveyed the clientele. A bunch of cops sat at a long Formica counter and made jokes about their latest arrests, a sad-looking homeless woman struggled with the lid of a plastic container, and a couple of young mothers maneuvered baby strollers down the slender aisles.

Joe had just finished slurping up the remains of his pancakes and eggs when Angelle walked in.

After the waitress refilled their coffee cups, Matt repeated what he'd learned about the death of Jane Doe and told them of his conversation with Troy Hanover regarding the hit-and-run of Ray Jennings's and his connection to Bayside.

According to Angelle, there was nothing incriminating, and no porn, found on any of the videotapes or DVDs they had confiscated from Michael Harrington's sailboat. But she still had stacks of film to screen. His background had been checked out, and nothing extraordinary was found. Except for a couple of parking tickets, he was clean. His enrollment in UCLA film school had been corroborated. His family were deceased, and he was obviously a loner.

The DNA tests on the hair found in the bathtub wouldn't be back for several days, so there wasn't much else she could do on Michael Harrington.

Joe cracked fresh peanuts with his teeth and spit the shells into an ashtray. "I did a whole day of hard canvassing in the neighborhood, showed everybody the photo of Allison and Sherrie. I got the same old crap—nobody knows nothin'." He picked a back tooth with his pinky. "What about that weirdo who lives next door to Mrs. Z.? Jack Simmons?"

Matt tapped his pencil on the table. "His story checks out. He was at a strip joint with a friend. He came home around one thirty."

"I still think the killer is a homo," Joe said.

"What difference does that make?" Angelle snapped.

"Whoever murdered these broads was a woman-hater, so maybe Harrington was makin' it with Ray Jennings before he kicked off. Gays go in for this S&M sex. They got their own leather clubs and all kinds of other weird fetish crap. I remember when I was in Hollyweird—"

Matt cut him off. "There'll be no gay-bashing here, my friend."

"You're quite right, Matt." Angelle glared at Joe. "This killer doesn't have to be homosexual, and it doesn't have to be Michael Harrington."

"Harrington's prints were all over the goddamn kitchen," Joe argued.

Defending Michael yet again, she countered, "If it was Harrington, why weren't his prints in the bedroom? What do you think he did? Strangle Sherrie with a hanger he'd already used to make toast, take off his gloves, and then go into the kitchen and spread his fingerprints all over the dishes?"

It didn't make much sense to Matt, either. But maybe the guy got nervous and forgot about the prints in the kitchen. "Angelle, call your friend at the property management, and get a history of everyone who lived in the Beachview house for the past five years. But right now, you and I are gonna pay Mrs. Helen Jennings a visit."

As they left the restaurant, Joe followed Angelle, wiggling his hips.

Matt shook his head. Joe was a walking goddamn lawsuit.

A couple of hours later, Matt parked his car in front of Helen Jennings's beautiful two-story house in the high-priced district north of Montana Avenue. He gestured toward the For Sale sign planted in the front yard. "It looks like she's planning to move."

"Wow," Angelle said. "How could two people find each other in such a huge house?"

Matt lifted the lion's head knocker and clanged it a couple of times. "Maybe that's the point."

A uniformed butler answered, "Yes?"

Impressed, Matt asked politely, "Is Mrs. Jennings at home?"

"Who should I say is calling?" He spoke with a thin, nasal voice much too small for a man so large.

Matt showed his badge and tried not to laugh. "I'm Detective Matt Donovan, and this is Detective Bentley, LA Police Department. We need to ask Mrs. Jennings a few questions."

"One moment please." He halfway closed the door.

Matt rolled his eyes at Angelle. She smiled.

"Oh, this is a terrible time for this to happen." In the background was a woman's voice, thick with a fake English accent, not unlike Troy Hanover's. The door flung open. "Come in, come in. I don't have much time. There are seventy-four women practically at my door, and I'm not even close to being ready."

The place was a beehive of activity. Trays of dishes and glasses seemed to float in midair as tuxedo-clad young men carried them past. Two hefty women barked orders at the waiters, and a huge clatter of dishes came from what was obviously the kitchen. A pert, redheaded woman in a black-and-white maid's uniform was rearranging a vast array of flowers in the hallway.

Mrs. Jennings led them into a paneled den and sat down behind an imposing walnut desk, instructing them to take the chairs facing it. "Now, what can I do for you?" she asked, her stubby fingers fidgeting with a pink spongy roller perched like an awkward bird on top of her head.

He figured Helen was somewhere in her fifties. "Mrs. Jennings, we'd like to speak to you about your husband."

"He's dead."

"Yes, I know. I spoke to Troy Hanover in San Francisco. You do know Mr. Hanover?"

Mrs. Jennings's face turned practically orange, and she took a moment to pull herself together. "Mr. Hanover and my ex-husband were very good friends. But you didn't come here to tell me that, did you?"

"How familiar are you with your husband's business, Fantasy Films?" Matt asked.

"My husband had retired early from the film industry, and Fantasy Films was his hobby." Mrs. Jennings spoke slowly, as though talking to a child. "Among other things, Raymond was a voyeur. He thought he'd discovered a wonderful way to get paid for doing something he loved to do and would have done for free. I'm afraid he didn't make a lot of money from the enterprise."

"How about Party Favorites?" Matt asked.

"Another of his failed ideas."

"Did you and your husband own a house at 42 Beachview Avenue in Venice?"

"Yes, we did. Raymond took it as part of the divorce settlement." Her voice was cold and unforgiving.

"And are you a member of the Bayside Yacht Club?"

"Yes, I am. What does that have to do with it?"

Matt took another tack. "Are you aware that a fellow member of your yacht club, George Fisher, recently died of a heart attack?"

"Yes." Nervously, Helen played with a glass paperweight on her desk.

"Did you know he died in the house on Beachview Avenue?"

She glanced up quickly. "I didn't ask his wife where he died. One doesn't ask that question when one knows he died in the arms of a whore."

Angelle spoke for the first time. "Did you know Mr. Fisher's lady friend was a victim of the Bondage Murderer?"

"Is that a fact?" Helen unrolled the pink roller and brushed back the little curl. "And what does that have to do with me?"

Angelle replied. "We strongly suspect that the first victim, Allison Graham, was murdered in the same house, the house at 42 Beachview Avenue—the one you and your husband once owned."

"I wouldn't know anything about that." Her lips tightened.

"Did you know your husband had camera equipment installed in a secret closet and was videotaping certain events?" Matt asked.

"You mean my ex-husband, sir." Helen's voice dripped with venom. "I told you Raymond was a voyeur, and that's all I know. It shows you how little he confided in me after twenty-six years of marriage." She stood up in anticipation of dismissing them. "I really do have to get back to preparing my party. I presume you know my ex-husband's lover now owns the house on Beachview." Her greedy smile was revealing. "But I own this one."

Matt didn't trust the woman, and her condescending manner bugged the shit out of him. "Did your husband leave any videotapes or DVDs here when he moved away?"

"No, he did not. And even if he did, I threw out everything that belonged to him months ago. Now, you'll have to excuse me."

Rising to his feet, Matt asked, "Where were you at the time of your husband's death?"

She smiled. "I was on a cruise to Catalina with my friends, Senator and Mrs. Rattner. You can check with Dr. Henderson. He's the commodore of Bayside Yacht Club. Now, if you have any more questions, speak to my lawyer." Retrieving a card from a marble box on top of her desk, she handed it to Matt. "Good day." With that, Helen Jennings slammed the door, leaving them in the hallway.

The butler showed them out.

Climbing into the car, Matt let out slow whistle. "No wonder old Ray found himself a boyfriend."

"I'll check with Mr. and Mrs. Henderson about the cruise," Angelle said as she slid into the passenger's seat.

Gunning the old blue Chevy he'd taken from the police motor pool, Matt swerved around the parking attendant who was setting up signs. "And you'd better get back to Harrington's boss at Party Favorites. We've got to find out about the previous owner, Ray Jennings, and his relationship, if any, with Michael Harrington." He added as an afterthought, "Show Rosa the picture of the San Francisco body too."

Matt knew in his gut that all these killings were linked, including the Jane Doe in San Francisco, and they were all connected in some way to Bayside Yacht Club.

All he had to do now was find out which one of the ritzy club members was killing women.

# Chapter 19

Megan, accompanied by Kathleen, was again seated in the backseat of Alex's Rolls-Royce. This time Alex, not Charlie, steered through Santa Monica traffic. And in the passenger seat, Rachel was the one complaining. "That was a wasted trip."

Defending herself, Kathleen whined, "How did I know he was married?"

"Couldn't you see the damn wedding ring on his finger?" Rachel asked. "Jesus, it was an inch thick."

"The first time I saw him I was walking on the beach, and he was strutting on a runway outside that clothing store." Kathleen pouted. "I didn't plan to look him up again."

"Stop bickering," Alex snapped. "Just forget it. He was too greasy-looking for me anyway."

Megan didn't even get into it. She didn't have the energy. And she was hot. The silk suit she had chosen to wear was uncomfortable and sticky after their trek on Venice Beach to see Kathleen's stupid model. She checked her watch: ten after two. They were late for the wedding shower at Helen's house.

Megan had been extremely busy the last couple of days, calling clients late into the night about Charlie's upcoming real estate auction. The entire morning had been spent checking property on the caravan list, looking for a condominium for Kathleen. And any spare second left over was used to tie down the loose ends of the Rosario deal. She was grateful she had a commission coming in.

Thankfully, the rest of the day was hers.

Megan had already decided to put Matt, and the House of Destiny escapade, out of her mind. In fact, she'd made up her mind to forget everything, even the conversation she'd overheard at the club among Brian, David, and Charlie. At present, she had way too much on her plate. And it was none of her business.

Obviously, Matt hadn't recognized her at the sex club or he would have questioned her by now. But Megan still wondered if he was there as part of the investigation or for his own perverted pleasure.

*Forget it. That's also none of your business.*

Alex pulled the car into the designated parking space in front of Helen Jennings's house. A uniformed attendant leaped to attention and then ran around the car, opening all four doors.

Megan was the last to get out. "Will you look at that? Helen's got her house on the market and she didn't even tell me, let alone give me a shot at the listing."

"Maybe she knows you don't like her," Kathleen said.

She didn't have an answer for that.

"I wonder why she's selling," Alex asked. "Do you think she needs the money?"

"I can't imagine." Megan only knew that Helen Jennings was divorced. Nobody seemed to know why. Her ex-husband, Ray, was a nice-enough guy, a good friend of Brian. A film producer or something, she'd heard he moved up north after the divorce.

A uniformed butler opened the door.

"Helen's going all out for this one," Alex whispered.

"Doesn't look to me like she's short of money," Rachel said, loud enough for everyone to hear.

Nose in the air, the butler pointed to a long table in the hallway laden with shower gifts. Megan deposited her offering, as did the others, and the butler led them into a humongous living room.

The place was absolutely smashing. High, beamed ceilings gave it the feel of a stark white cavern. Down-filled sofas and chairs, strategically placed around a beveled glass coffee table, centered the room, and bleached floors framed expensive Indian rugs scattered everywhere. An exquisite Chagall, in deepest shades of blue and green, hung over a marble fireplace. The painting and the rugs were the only color in the room.

Helen Jennings certainly knew how to live.

Their hostess entered the living room through French doors. Flashing a bright smile, she tried to tame her frizzy brown hair by patting it down with her fat little hand. Somewhere in her fifties, Helen was what Megan would describe as a solid woman, with short legs and a square body. At the moment, her long arms hung loosely at her sides, giving her a somewhat simian look. She had the thick, heavy features of a peasant, and her head was planted squarely on her shoulders. Funny, Megan had never noticed before: Helen had no neck.

"We've been waiting for you," Helen cried, air-kissing all eight cheeks.

"Oh, dear, are we late?" Rachel asked with mock sincerity.

Helen frowned. "Not that late, dear."

The determination etched in Helen's face suggested a terrible strength of will, a will made evident many times at the Women's Auxiliary meetings at the club. And those crafty eyes of hers, gloomy and cunning by turns—you never knew quite where you stood with Helen. A fact that made Megan feel very uncomfortable.

Ginny, the guest of honor, scampered into the room. "Megan, Rachel, all of you, I'm so glad you could come."

She was a tiny woman, a bit like a chipmunk. But Megan genuinely liked Ginny and warmly congratulated her on her upcoming marriage.

As she followed everyone outside, Helen put a hand on Megan's arm to detain her. "I've been thinking, Megan. Would you be interested in listing my house?"

*Are you kidding?* Megan wanted to jump for joy. The money from the sale of Helen's house would put her on easy street for a whole year. "Why, I would love to, but don't you already have a broker?"

"I'm not satisfied with the service, and the contract expired two days ago. I decided not to relist with them. I thought maybe ..."

Without hesitation, Megan jumped in, "Why don't I come by in the morning?"

Helen nodded and, hooking her arm in Megan's, led her outside to the party.

✝ ✝ ✝

Outside, on the terrace, Megan's pals waited with questions in their eyes. And as soon as Helen bustled off, Rachel spoke. "What did she want, Megan?"

"I'll tell you later." Grinning from ear to ear, Megan headed for the one empty table at the back of the covered lanai.

On the way, she scoped the property.

Helen's meticulous garden was breathtaking, boasting dozens of prize rose bushes, bursting with blooms. Bordered by beds of multicolored flowers, a perfect green lawn encircled an Olympic-sized swimming pool, shimmering in the sun. The far end of the patio thickly veiled with long strands of bougainvillea created a dramatic hot pink wall. This house was going to sell—fast.

Already feeling more secure about her financial future, Megan chatted her way through the labyrinth of tables and chairs. "Hi, Susan. I'm delighted to see you, Laura."

Rhoda Farnsworth waved be-ringed, clawlike fingers, diamonds and emeralds flashing refracted sunlight. "Hey, Alex, are you and Charlie heading for Catalina this weekend?"

"We sure are. Let us know if y'all wanna come with," Alex answered, but whispered to Megan, "Not on your life."

Megan spied the senator's wife, seated at a front table. "Hello, Mrs. Rattner." Bonnie-Sue, again not wearing her usual Goth attire of leather jacket and black jeans, looked even more out of place in her little black dress. That and the single strand of pearls were obviously her mother's idea. Megan could see the senator's daughter was not a happy camper. "Hi, Bonnie-Sue."

"Hey, Megan." Her voice oozed with boredom.

Mrs. Rattner patted her daughter's hand.

Approaching the rear table, Rachel snickered, "Not the A-seats, my dears."

"Quit griping and sit down," Alex said.

Rachel did and, at the same time, beckoned to the waiter. "We'll take some wine, and a Perrier for my friend here."

Taking a seat, Megan looked around and admired Helen's good taste. An abundance of white Battenburg linen, delicate china, and Waterford glass was made all the more enchanting by the contrasts of light and shade on the secluded terrace. Lush arrangements of fat pink cabbage roses, mingled with baby's breath, decorated the tables. Yanni's tinkling piano music flowed from unseen speakers, soothing her soul. Silently, Megan inhaled the scent of a thousand blossoms.

Checking out the crowd, she figured at least seventy-five women were in attendance, of various sizes and shapes. They were dressed in a fashion show of expensive outfits.

Alex didn't waste a second. "C'mon, girl, tell us what Helen wanted."

"She wants me to list the house."

"Are you kidding?" Rachel blurted.

Megan shrugged. "I'm surprised too."

"And you thought she didn't like you." Shaking her head, and her napkin, Kathleen smiled.

Within minutes, the waiter brought their plates. Shrimp salad, cold poached salmon, caviar, and steamed asparagus were creatively arranged on Limoges plates.

During lunch, the noise escalated a few decibels with each round of drinks—and there were many. Megan couldn't help noticing how heavily the wine flowed. This was one of those times she would kill for a drink but satisfied herself with an extra helping of lemon soufflé drowned in raspberry sauce.

Coffee was being served when Yanni's music was suddenly replaced by a pounding version of "The Stripper."

Megan looked up, startled.

Standing where everyone could see her, Helen proclaimed, "And now I'd like to present the real dessert. We have a present for you, Ginny! I now give you ... Michael Harrington."

The blond Adonis appeared from nowhere. He wore a brown sports coat, beige shirt, striped tie, and tan slacks. Megan glanced at the waiter pouring coffee into Rachel's cup, and she continued to watch as the coffee overflowed all over the Battenberg lace tablecloth. But neither of them seemed to care. Their eyes were glued on the hunk who had just stepped off a billboard into the party.

Loudly, Megan cleared her throat.

"Oops." The waiter set down the silver coffee server and sopped up the mess with Rachel's napkin, his eyes still on the dancer.

Rachel sang along with the stripper music. "Da dada dada dada dada."

But Megan could only stare. This was not the sort of thing one expected from Helen Jennings—or Ginny Barnes, for that matter.

And then, the dancer began to gyrate in time to the music.

Rakishly, he pulled on his tie, slid it off, and threw it to Rhoda Farnsworth at the front table. She blushed and braided it through her tiny, dazzling fingers.

Slowly, he undid the buttons of his shirt and bared his broad shoulders. With a sexy stripper move, he pulled the shirt back and forth across his naked back.

Alex stood up so she could see better.

"Take it off! Take it off!" Bonnie-Sue Rattner yelled, her face coming alive. She stood up to cheer him on, while her mother tried to pull her back on the chair.

Megan watched the audience. Everyone looked flustered and excited. *My God*, she thought, *you'd think they'd never seen a man's body before*. Was it the wine? No, because she felt it too. It was this guy's animal magnetism.

The stripper dropped his shirt.

"Oh, shit, he's fabulous," Rachel groaned.

She was right. Michael Harrington was spectacular.

Full hard pectorals stretched his skin tight across his chest, making his nipples stiff and alert. His body formed a perfect V from his wide shoulders down to a narrow waist. The silkiness of his smooth skin was dulled by a thin veneer of golden hair. Taut abdominal muscles rippled in strong ridges and disappeared into his slacks. Megan stared at the thick, tan fingers undoing his shiny silver buckle.

Alex dropped back into her chair and drawled, "Honey, will you check out those sexy hands?"

The stripper tugged on the belt, once, twice, pumped his slender hips, and then, slowly, ever so slowly, undid the zipper of his pants.

The women went wild. "Take it off. Take it all off."

His slacks fell to the floor, and he stepped out of them, wearing only skin-colored Calvin Kleins. Sunlight filtered through the latticed roof of the terrace, bathing his honey-colored skin in a golden glow, and Megan thought she would faint. His whole body appeared incandescent, as if lit by a fire from within. She expected Pegasus to arrive at any moment and fly him to the sun. But all too quickly the magic image passed, and he moved on to the next table.

Taking a deep breath, Megan tried to pull herself together.

By the time he arrived at the back of the patio, the dancer wore only a thong bikini consisting of a string of black leather. Megan stared at his body in awe. He was so masculine that some distant cavewoman instinct told her to grab him and run. Did cavewomen do that?

She scrutinized him a little more objectively, or so she thought. His chin was strong and square, his nose finely sculpted, and intelligence beamed from frank, sky-blue eyes. He was exceptionally handsome in a manly, virile way and, even in his bikini, projected a commanding and confident presence. The nearer he came, the surer Megan was that she'd melt from the intensity of his being.

He looked straight at her. She could feel his heat.

He knew. She knew he knew and was still unable to turn away. A hint of decadence glimmered in his sexy eyes, and his lower lip pouted. Provocatively, the dancer wet his lips. Megan licked hers too. She couldn't help it, even though she knew it was all part of his act.

Finally, he turned around. Dancing to the front of the room, he concentrated on Ginny, the bride, who was squealing ecstatically, her little chipmunk mouth working overtime.

Helen snapped pictures of him, one after another.

The other women had lost all control and were screaming their enthusiasm at each enticing bump and grind.

Semi-recovered from his steamy appeal, Megan was grateful to be back to her pragmatic self. She noted, with chagrin, the waiter wasn't. He still stared longingly at the stripper.

Checking out Michael's rear view, Megan couldn't resist a comment. "His buttocks are as tight as my twenty-four–hour girdle."

"He's a perfect ten," Rachel said.

"I think I just fell in love," Alex moaned, sighing like a teenager. "And I adore his blond hair."

"What a hunk," the waiter murmured.

Kathleen just stared, her lips slightly apart.

After much applause, the dancer waved and left the garden followed by Bonnie-Sue Rattner.

"By God, I think we've found him." Rachel raised her palm and high-fived Alex.

"Amen," the waiter agreed.

"Now all we have to do is proposition him." Scribbling a note on her cocktail napkin, Rachel handed it to the waiter. "Take this to that young man, darling."

"Amen," he repeated.

# Chapter 20

Matt followed Angelle past Sherrie's house on Beachview Avenue and wondered who the hell ripped the crime-scene tape off the fence. Undoing his tie, he opened the top three buttons of his shirt. "It must be ninety degrees today."

"Thank God we're at the beach," Angelle replied. "At least there's a breeze."

"Yeah." He laughed. "Sure hate to be in Hollyweird."

Mrs. Zuckerman flopped on the steps of her rickety porch in old-lady position, the skirt of her faded sundress draped loosely between widespread knees. Her doughy face was wet with perspiration, and trickles of sweat rolled down the wrinkled crevice between her white fleshy breasts. She was chatting with her neighbor, Jack Simmons, who still wore his Pitbull T-shirt and jeans.

The fat on the old woman's dimpled arms jiggled as she cooled herself with a bamboo fan. "Things been pretty quiet 'round here with that whorehouse closed up." No greetings or salutations for Mrs. Z., just straight to the point. Placing her hand under her left breast, she heaved it over the waistband riding high on her stomach. "Pretty soon we gonna be a decent neighborhood again. When I first moved in here, thirty-five years ago …"

"I'm sure it was wonderful, Mrs. Zuckerman," Matt said. "But right now, I want you to look closely and see if you can remember seeing this young woman around here." He showed her the picture of the San Francisco Jane Doe.

Mrs. Z. didn't bat an eye or register any shock at the decayed body in the picture. "She looks deader 'n Sherrie."

Matt nodded.

"Yup, she lived over there for a while." She flicked her eyes toward Sherrie's house. "Cindy, that's her name. Cindy sumpin' or other."

"Are you sure?" Angelle prompted.

"I ain't senile, you know?" The old woman snubbed her nose in contempt.

"Yes, I know that, but this is important." Angelle was insistent. "Do you remember when she lived there?"

"Waddya think, Jack?" Mrs. Zuckerman asked. "Five? Six months ago? Less?"

"I don't know nuttin'." Jack's voice was surly.

"You remember her. She had that little dog. The one that kept shittin' on your lawn."

"I tell ya, I don't know."

"Mr. Simmons, I need your cooperation here," Matt pleaded.

Mr. Simmons hung his head in stony silence.

*This guy is really pissing me off.* "Look, we're talking about three murders here, maybe more. I am going to find some way to take you in and book you, unless you tell me what you know about this girl."

"Okay," Jack Simmons exhaled. "The broad moved in early this year, February, maybe March. Anyway, she stayed a while 'n went up to Frisco. Said she could make more bread up there. Said this fag pal o' hers was gittin' her some high-rollin' clients."

"Thanks," said Matt. "Now that wasn't so hard, was it?" He was convinced Jack Simmons was not gay, as Joe had suggested.

Mr. Simmons sulked.

Matt threw Angelle a world-weary glance. "Mrs. Zuckerman, did Sherrie and Cindy know each other?"

The old woman shrugged. "I dunno."

"Did they ever live together?" Angelle asked.

"They could've. I didn't pay no attention."

*That's a laugh.* "Did you know Mr. Jennings well?"

"I did," Jack Simmons said. "Ray was a real nice guy."

"Mrs. Zuckerman?" Matt asked.

"Yup, said he was a sex therapist." Her lack of teeth showed when she smiled.

"What?" Matt was completely taken aback. "A sex therapist?" Was this Ray's way of covering up his sexual activities and films?

"That's what he said." She fluttered the fan.

"Did you know Ray Jennings was dead?"

"No-o-o?" Mrs. Zuckerman drawled, shaking her head. "There's an awful lotta dead folks 'round here. Wouldn't you say?"

Matt shook his head. Nothing fazed Mrs. Z.

† † †

Ginny's shower was over at five thirty. By two minutes after six, Alex had parked the car on Abbott Kinney Road near Hal's Restaurant, where they had arranged to meet Michael Harrington.

Megan was first to enter the brick building, while her friends straggled in behind her. Wearily, she sank onto a bench in the foyer and waited. She looked around. At this early hour the place was almost empty, but a rush of yuppies would soon invade the scene.

When the other girls arrived, they were still arguing the pros and cons of what they were about to do. Megan spoke to the hostess, who led them all the way past the bar to a booth on the far wall.

Once seated, Megan scanned the brick ceilings. The place had a rustic feel and was very booze friendly; she knew this from her past experience. She glanced at one of the center tables where two weight lifter types were eating a humongous meal.

Alex was already checking them out. "If this guy Michael, doesn't want to play we can always come here. We can even hit Gold's Gym and World's Gym and—" Before she could finish, Rachel let out a nervous squeal.

"Look, he's here! He's here!" She could hardly contain her excitement.

Megan turned to look.

"Don't stare!" Rachel fussed. "Jesus, don't stare at him."

But Megan did. Michael was casually dressed in faded well-pressed jeans and a peach, cotton sweater that emphasized his wide shoulders and contrasted, dramatically, with his tan face. Blond hair—long enough to make her want to run her fingers through it, and short enough to curl into his neck—was streaked by the sun. She squirmed in her seat and glanced sideways at her companions.

Alex gaped, unashamedly, as did Rachel, despite her own admonition. Kathleen fiddled with her wineglass and cast quick, surreptitious glances at him while he spoke to the hostess.

Megan's eyes stayed on the stripper as he followed the girl to the back of the restaurant, where they were seated. He moved with just the right amount of swagger.

Surely any guy this hot-looking had to be an arrogant jerk, thought Megan.

*Don't do this,* her gut screamed. But she didn't want to listen.

Rachel had already talked to him at Helen's house, and she was planning to research him even further. So what could go wrong? *An awful lot,* said the wretched little voice in Megan's head.

So far, they knew that Michael Harrington was doing grad work at UCLA film school and didn't have a wife or a girlfriend. He'd agreed to listen but had no idea what they were about to propose. He probably thought they wanted him to do a strip routine at some girlie party. At the very least, the whole thing should be interesting.

"Over here, Michael," Rachel called.

He clasped her hand and held it. "Hello again, Rachel."

Michael's smile lit up the whole corner of the room.

"This," Rachel gestured, flamboyantly, "is Alexandria Grant."

Like visiting royalty, Alex nodded her greeting.

Rachel motioned in her direction. "Megan Riley."

"I'm pleased to meet you." *Damn.* She barely got her tongue around the words.

Michael nodded and reached for her outstretched hand.

His touch was cool but electric. Megan pulled back, flustered. He tipped his head, inquisitively, and held her eyes. She was physically unable to turn away, totally unprepared for the magnetism of his gaze, which gripped her and wouldn't let go. His eyes left hers—and she was freed.

Rachel was still talking.

*Isn't she overdoing it a bit? And who put her in charge anyway?* Megan saw him reach for Kathleen's hand and saw her blush, ever so demurely. *Give me a break.*

The waiter arrived to take Michael's drink order.

"White wine cooler, please." His voice was soft, polite.

Silence. He waited. Everyone looked straight ahead.

Alex coughed but said nothing.

*Dammit.* Someone had to start, so Megan asked the question, "Did Rachel tell you why we wanted to speak to you?"

"No, she didn't, and I must confess I'm curious."

Those eyes again. Megan tried to return his gaze.

It was impossible. *Damn.* She knew she was blushing, just like stupid Kathleen. But how could she approach it delicately? "It's rather a difficult subject."

"Well, why don't you just spit it out?" he said nonchalantly.

Rachel jumped in, guns blazing. "It's like this. We're looking for a lo—lov—" She stopped, mid-sentence.

"Oh, Rachel," Kathleen cried.

Megan wanted to disappear into the ether.

Michael raised one eyebrow, questioningly.

"We're looking for a—a—an investment," Megan blurted and then cast her eyes quickly around the table, expecting someone to challenge her.

Alex gaped at her. Rachel seemed equally surprised.

"Just what exactly do you have in mind, ladies?" Michael glanced at each one of them in turn.

"Well, we're actually looking for someone with a successful future ahead of him, and we'd like to invest in that future," Megan forged ahead, as if she knew what she was talking about. But the whole time she spoke, she sank lower and lower into the booth, praying the seat would swallow her up.

"And?"

"And what?"

"And what would you expect in return?"

"Well, he could act as our companion. Sometimes," Megan added, lamely.

"All of you together? Or one at a time?" Michael raised his eyebrow again.

Megan knew she was going to die right there on the spot. "Well?" Her eyes pleaded for help from the others. "Probably one at a time."

"And what kind of companionship do you have in mind?"

"Oh? C—c—companionable companionship," she stuttered.

That's when Rachel took over, using her arrogant lawyer voice. "Mr. Harrington, I think you know exactly what we mean. And if you don't, we've made a terrible mistake."

Michael turned his whole body toward Rachel and concentrated on her fully.

Rachel didn't flinch. It was courtroom drama, *L.A. Law* style.

"Is that the kind of guy you think I am?" he asked in a shocked voice. "A gigolo?"

At that, Rachel's manner crumbled. "No, no, that's not at all what I meant." Her face turned crimson. She stood up, poised for flight. "This was a crazy idea."

Michael began to laugh. He had a warm, unpretentious laugh that came straight from his incredibly flat belly. He placed his hand gently on Rachel's arm and sat her down.

Megan was mortified.

"I'm intrigued, ladies. And I'm most interested in hearing the rest of your offer. Now, tell me what you have in mind."

Tentatively, Rachel sat down and lowered her eyes.

Kathleen grabbed a menu and covered her entire face.

Alex simply giggled.

Baffled, Megan stared at him. Michael appeared to be very much in control of the situation. His eyes found hers, and the power grabbed her again. Quickly, bowing her head, she hunted in her bag for a makeup sponge to dab her face. She simply could not look him in the eye. "You tell him, Rachel. You're the business manager."

Rachel found her tongue again—in a big way. "What we had in mind was this." Now on the familiar ground of negotiating a settlement, she outlined the arrangement they proposed using Megan's theme of buying into his future. She told him they would invest in his next film project, paying him on a monthly basis. In a matter-of-fact voice, Rachel discussed scheduling and the rights of each woman to a certain amount of attention, proposing convenient days and frequent free time for Michael to study, make his movies, and tend to his own life. No demands would be made that he was unwilling to fulfill. In fact, she was brilliant.

Meanwhile, Michael listened intently, head to one side in that peculiar questioning mode of his. He said nothing, just listened. But, when Rachel told him they were willing to pay three thousand dollars a month plus expenses on an apartment, he lifted his head, raised both eyebrows, and Megan knew they had him.

"Okay, let me tell you where I'm coming from," he said, calmly.

*Here it comes. He sounds like Donald Trump. He probably wants more money.* And Megan couldn't afford what Rachel had already proposed, at least until one of her real estate deals paid off.

"I'm in my final year of film school, and the only reason I took the stripper job was because it paid well, and I could pick and choose my hours. If I went into something like this, my class hours would be inviolate. Is that understood?"

Megan nodded, as did the others. Rachel elbowed her in the ribs. She was glad he had a brain.

He went on. "I formally agree to serve in the capacity of escort and companion. Anything beyond that will not be part of the deal. Understood?"

Nodding her head in unison with the other three, who were hanging on his every word, Megan was absolutely amazed to what extent they seemed willing to make fools of themselves. She had the distinct feeling that every single one of them, herself included, would march off the edge of Santa Monica Pier if he instructed them to do so—one Svengali and four little Trilbys.

Michael Harrington had something they wanted, and he apparently knew it, so he continued to drive a hard bargain. "One more thing. I live on a sailboat in Marina del Rey and have no desire to move into an apartment. Any monies that would be used for living accommodations should be added to the three thousand dollars. That would bring it to, say, four thousand a month. Agreed?"

Four nods again. The man was a barracuda.

"Oh, and there's one more thing. I'll take an AIDS test if you all will, just in case."

*Great.* Megan had wondered how they were going to get around to that issue, but he'd done it himself. He knew what they were up to. Since when did escorts and companions need an AIDS test?

Everyone nodded.

"Okay, I'll do it." Just like that.

Megan said nothing, just stared at the long, honey-colored fingers wrapped around his glass as he lifted it to those full, sensuous lips. This guy had the potent charisma of a rock star, the kind of steamy sexuality that pushed teenagers to the brink and weakened the knees of old ladies. And now, he fairly beamed with satisfaction.

*You're getting sucked in, girl.* But Megan didn't listen to the little voice. She wanted some fun. And why shouldn't she? Brian was gone. Besides, Michael Harrington was a big step up from Brian. Wasn't she about to get a big commission from the sale of Kathleen's house? And then there was the listing on Helen Jennings's property. That was like having money in the bank. Oh God, she wasn't behaving rationally. What about all her good intentions? Sending the money to Mothers in Recovery? Not being so impetuous? Looking before she leaped?

But Michael rubbed his tantalizing hands together, and Megan was a goner.

"Well, it looks like we have a deal," he said. "When do you want to start?"

"Tonight," Rachel cried, enthusiastically.

At that, Alex got all excited. "Charlie's out of town, so let's celebrate. I'll buy dinner."

Kathleen nodded vigorously.

"I'd love to have dinner." Raising his drink, Michael made a toast. "Here's to a long and successful relationship."

For some reason she could not explain, Megan did not raise her glass.

# Chapter 21

It was noon the next day when Matt pushed the bell on the six-foot-high security gate of an older apartment building on Ocean Front Walk in Venice.

Brian Mason's name and home address had been on the list Matt had received from the secretary of state's office in answer to his inquiries about Fantasy Films. Raymond Jennings was registered as president, Brian Mason as treasurer, and four men from the San Francisco area comprised the board of directors.

"Do you realize we're only a couple of blocks from the spot where Allison Graham was found, and five blocks from Sherrie's house?" Matt said to Angelle.

"Looks like we've got us another suspect," she said, leaning on the bell again.

A woman answered, sounding very irritated. "Who is it?"

"Detective Donovan, LAPD, ma'am."

After a long pause, the voice said, "Come on up. I'm on the second floor, second door to your right."

When they stepped out of the elevator, Megan Riley, looking curvy and fabulous in a smart, beige pantsuit, awaited them in the hall.

Matt couldn't have been more surprised.

Ms. Riley, this is my partner, Detective Angelle Bentley."

"Oh, your partner," Megan exclaimed with a smile.

Strange, she seemed delighted to meet Angelle.

Still smiling, Megan led them into a small living room. "Let me get you some coffee."

Angelle declined.

"None for me, either." Matt looked around. The room was not elaborately furnished but comfortable: a white settee, glass-and-wood coffee table, lots of plants, great stereo equipment, and wonder of wonders, no TV.

But what a view. Matt walked to the open windows. To his left, Catalina Island graced the horizon, and to his right, the sun-drenched Santa Monica Mountains kissed the sea.

"I'll just have to throw out the rest of this coffee if you don't have some," Megan insisted, turning toward what was obviously the kitchen.

Angelle shrugged and sat on the couch.

Matt deposited himself beside her.

Silently, he stared out of the sliding glass doors and admired the panorama of sky, ocean, and beach. The sea was calm except for a white roll of surf, slapping the sand. It soothed his jagged nerves. But why the hell was Megan so at home in Brian Mason's apartment?

Megan returned with three cups and a large carafe of coffee, which she placed on the table. "Is this about George?" she asked, slipping into a chair opposite him.

"Not this time." He shook his head. "We've come to see Brian Mason."

"He doesn't live here anymore. Brian moved some time ago."

She didn't look too unhappy about it, which pleased Matt.

He studied Megan's face, recalling their pleasant conversation at the beach, after he'd finally set aside his original suspicions. But now the doubts were back. Jesus, he'd hate like hell if Megan was involved in this bondage crap. But he was pretty sure he'd seen her at the House of Destiny. He couldn't deny it. While standing under the light, she'd removed her mask.

As Matt tuned back in, she was saying, "Brian moved onto his boat until he can find an apartment."

Then Angelle asked the all-important question. "What was your relationship to Mr. Mason?"

"We were engaged to be married, but we broke it off."

*Good.* "What's the name of Brian's boat?" Matt asked.

"*Dreamer.*"

"Where is it moored?"

"Slip seventy-three at the Bayside Yacht Club."

Somehow, he was not surprised. "Do you know anything about his connection to Fantasy Films?"

"Fantasy Films. I never heard of it. What is it?"

"A movie company run by a man named Raymond Jennings," Matt explained. "Mostly pornos."

"You're kidding?" Megan's eyes widened. "He and Brian were good friends, until Ray moved up north after his divorce from Helen. I don't think Brian's seen him since he left."

"Mr. Jennings is dead. He was killed by a hit-and-run driver in San Francisco."

Obviously shocked, Megan whispered, "I'm sure Brian doesn't know. He would have said something."

Matt produced the morgue picture of the San Francisco Jane Doe and showed it to her. "Ever see this girl before?"

Megan paled and shook her head.

He set down some rules. "I must ask you not to discuss this conversation with Brian Mason or even let him know we've been here. At least until we can talk to him."

"Of course, but I'm sure you're mistaken. Brian couldn't possibly have anything to do with any of this."

"Can you be absolutely sure of that, Ms. Riley?" Angelle asked.

"Well, I'm pretty sure." Megan bit her lower lip.

Matt knew he should ask her about the House of Destiny, but not now. Was that another compromise? And then, he just couldn't resist it. "May I have your telephone number in case we need to speak to you again?" It was a crappy way to get a lady's number but, shit, he was out of practice. Matt hadn't asked anyone out in years.

After the detective and his partner left, unable to allow even a moment to dissect the conversation, Megan rushed to change into her jeans and a cotton shirt. She'd been due at a birthday party for Rachel's daughter almost an hour ago.

Grabbing the huge gift and her purse, she ran out the door.

This was a day of surprises. First, her appointment with Helen Jennings had been remarkably pleasant. Although Megan put it down to the fact, like Brian Mason, Helen was always nice when she wanted something.

Suddenly, another thought hit her. Why had Helen Jennings never mentioned to anyone that her husband was killed in a hit-and-run accident?

☦ ☦ ☦

Thirty minutes later, Megan parked her old Mercedes in front of the Feinmans' Tudor-style mansion in Brentwood.

As soon as she stepped out of the car, she heard children's voices raised in laughter and chatter. Balancing the large package against her hip, she rang the bell.

Before long, Maria answered the door. "Buenos dias, Miss Megan. Everybody is in backyard."

The garden was a double splash of sunshine that took Megan's breath away. Hundreds of plastic sunflowers were planted everywhere, but the vases of golden blooms on the tables were the real thing. Enormous sunflower plates designated at least twenty place settings, along with giant plastic cups splashed with the same motif. Bright yellow napkins were tucked into sunflower holders.

Suddenly, a bundle of energy wrapped herself around Megan's legs and hung on. "Meggie. Meggie. Come see the pony." Lisa looked up at her with chocolate-brown eyes bright with excitement. The birthday girl, herself, was a blossom, in her sunflower dress with its tiny skirt of overlapping yellow petals.

Megan smiled. Lisa had called her Meggie when she'd first begun to talk, and the name had stuck. "Okay, okay. Let me put the present down. It's heavy."

The child's eyes widened when she saw the package wrapped in cherub paper and tied with gold ribbon. Five golden angels dangled from the ribbon, one for each year of Lisa's life. "Can I open it?" she cried. "Please, Meggie. Can I? Can I?"

Before she could answer, Rachel's mommy-knows-best voice warned them. "First we have to cut the birthday cake, Lisa."

Megan barely had time to deposit the package on the patio with the rest of the gifts before Lisa dragged her off to the pony. "C'mon, Meggie."

Disguised as a unicorn, the pony's silver horn, lavishly decorated with roses and baby's breath, was lopsided. The flower-bedecked pony stood among the plastic sunflowers, patiently waiting for his next customer.

"Meggie," Lisa cried. "You ride him."

"I can't, honey. I'm too big."

But Lisa insisted. Worried she might kill him, Megan climbed on the pony and rode around the garden, her feet dragging on the grass. Delighted, Lisa ran alongside, clapping her hands.

Laughing, Megan finally dismounted and joined Rachel and Kathleen at one of the umbrellaed tables on the patio.

On her way to the party, Megan had thought a great deal about whether or not she should tell her friends about Detective Donovan's visit and his questions about Brian Mason and Ray Jennings. She decided to say nothing.

"David, the loving father, hasn't shown up yet," Rachel announced, her voice caustic enough to burn right through the glass top of the table.

"Don't fret, dear." Kathleen reached over and touched her hand. "There's still time."

"Frankly," said Rachel, "David's time is running out."

"Well, at least you've got a boytoy you can play with," Megan joked. "You won't miss David at all."

"I called Don Bradford today."

"Who's that?" Kathleen asked, confused as usual.

"You know. The private detective I used to work with. He's going to check on Michael Harrington. See if he's got a criminal record, make sure he's not a rapist or anything."

"Meggie! Meggie!" Lisa yelled from across the garden. She was knee-deep in cherub wrapping paper. "What's in it?"

Despite Rachel's tepid objections, Megan watched her open the lid of the pink, satin chest and stare at the contents.

"Oh, Meggie," Lisa cried, her eyes luminous.

The first thing the child reached for was the purple boa. She threw it around her neck in a manner that would put Gloria Swanson to shame. Next, she grabbed the Lady Godiva wig and slapped it on her head, followed by pink spangled sunglasses, crystal chandelier earrings, and three strands of pearls.

Megan chuckled.

Attacking the trunk with renewed vigor, Lisa dragged everything out—silver and gold necklaces, a box of fake emeralds and diamonds, a big fluffy powder puff, nail polish in seven outlandish colors, chiffon scarves, glitzy heels, even a rhinestone tiara. If it was wearable, Lisa put it on. The rest she set carefully aside, except for a tube of pink lipstick, which she smeared on her mouth.

"It's like a treasure chest." Kathleen's voice was filled with wonder.

"It's a dress-up kit," Megan said as she crossed the lawn with Rachel and Kathleen. "I always wanted something like that when I was a kid." Megan looked at her watch. She was having so much fun, the time had flown by. She turned to Rachel. "I have to go. I'm seeing a client."

Rachel called to her daughter. "Lisa, Meggie's leaving."

The child flung herself at Megan and covered her with greasy, pink kisses. Wiping them off with tissue, Megan headed for the house.

Trailing behind her, Rachel whispered, "If David doesn't show up before the party's over, I'm going out on the town."

Megan wondered if that meant another trip to the House of Destiny. "Rachel, please don't do anything rash. And don't even think of calling Michael Harrington until we have him checked out. For all we know, he could be a rapist."

"A rapist? Get real, Megan. Next, you'll be saying he's a murderer."

# Chapter 22

It was after lunch when Matt spoke to the dock master at Bayside Yacht Club, and he directed them to Brian Mason's slip, a few yards from the main clubhouse.

Mason's dock accommodated only small sailboats about twenty to thirty feet in size. Almost half the slips were empty, and few people were about.

Matt spoke to the one person on the dock. "Mr. Brian Mason?"

Barefoot and wearing only a pair of bright red shorts, Brian was hosing down his twenty-eight-foot ketch, *Dreamer*.

"That's me." He glared at them with bloodshot eyes, his sand-colored hair rumpled like he'd just fallen out of bed.

*He's a sleaze,* Matt decided.

Angelle displayed her badge first. "We'd like to ask you a few questions, Mr. Mason."

For a moment, Brian looked startled. Recovering quickly, he continued to hose down the decks. "Fire away."

"How well did you know George Fisher?" she asked.

"We did a lot of fishing together."

"And Ray Jennings?" Angelle posed the questions.

"I knew him too," he said. "So what?"

"What do you know about Fantasy Films?"

Mason turned red. "What about it?"

Angelle kept prodding. "Are you on the board of directors?"

"That corporation was dissolved when Ray died."

So he knew Ray Jennings was dead. Had Brian told Megan

that Ray was dead? "Were you on the payroll of Fantasy Films?" he asked.

"Look, I got nothing out of that company. I did it as a favor for a friend." Brian sounded agitated. "Even Ray didn't make any money."

"How did he go about finding clients?"

"He placed ads in the magazines and on the Internet. Got a real strong response at first, but not many people actually did it. Ray was pissed. He'd thought he was going to make a fortune."

"Where are the company records?" Matt asked.

Brian shrugged. "Ray took care of all that."

Matt paused. "But where are all the films and videos?"

"Ray kept all those too."

"Ever visit Mr. Jennings's office in Culver City?" Matt wanted to know.

"No. Like I told you, the whole thing was flaky. Like everything Ray did."

Then Matt hit him with the big one. "How well did you know Allison Graham and Sherrie Weston?"

"I never met Allison. But I saw George with Sherrie Weston a few times." Brian was beginning to look more and more unhappy with each question.

"When was that?" He had to drag every goddamn word out of him.

"I can't remember exactly."

Matt showed him the morgue photo of the Jane Doe, aka Cindy.

"She's the one Sherrie brought—" Brian stopped suddenly.

Matt prodded him on. "Sherrie brought Cindy where?"

Brian didn't answer. He just kept folding and refolding his wet cloth.

Matt tried threats. "You could be a witness in a murder case."

No reaction from Brian. He still kept folding the cloth.

"Or a suspect," said Matt. "It's your choice."

Brian let out a deep breath. "George's fishing boat, the *Happy Hooker.*"

"Who else was on board?" Angelle asked.

Brian shrugged and returned to washing his windows, as if what he said had no importance. "It was just a party for one of the guys at the club."

"What kind of party?" she insisted. "A birthday party?"

"No. More like a divorce party."

"A divorce party?" Angelle glanced at Matt.

"Yeah, George brought the two broads to do a live sex show. Just guy stuff, you know?"

She shook her head in disgust. "I'm afraid I do, Mr. Mason."

"A divorce party for whom, Mr. Mason?" Matt asked.

Mason looked the other way.

"Do you want to go downtown?" Matt snapped.

"Gino Rosario," he mumbled, almost inaudibly.

"You mean the TV anchorman, Gino Rosario?" Matt couldn't believe what he was hearing.

"Yes." Mason moved to another porthole, but first he rinsed out the cloth in a bucket of water.

Matt tried to keep the distaste from his voice but failed, miserably. "And when did this divorce party take place, Mr. Mason?"

Brian looked thoughtful. "I guess it was sometime in April."

Ray Jennings and Cindy were both killed late in May—and three months after that Sherrie Weston was murdered. "Who else was at the party?"

"C'mon, man," he moaned. "Gimme a break."

Matt took a step forward. "We're going to find out, Mr. Mason. So you might as well make it easy on yourself."

Backing away, Brian said, "Gino Rosario and me, George Fisher, David Feinman, and Charlie Grant. Oh, and that man of Charlie's, Sy Neang. He was the bartender."

"Was there anyone else?"

Looking miserable, Brian nodded his head. "Just the two bimbos."

"Bimbos, meaning Sherrie Weston and Cindy?"

Brian nodded.

Matt finished writing the names in his book. "Mr. Mason," he asked, formally, "where were you Tuesday, August 16, the night of Miss Weston's death?"

"That's easy." Brian grinned. "I had dinner at the club, and then I came to the boat."

"Did anyone see you?" Angelle asked.

"See me?" He looked perplexed.

"What Detective Bentley means is can anyone vouch for your being here?" Matt was getting ready to lose it.

"Am I under arrest?"

"No, sir." Trying to keep his cool, Matt softened his voice. "But we'd appreciate your cooperation."

"You're asking me to establish an alibi. I believe I should consult a lawyer before answering any more questions." Mason smiled as if he'd outsmarted them.

*Right.* "I have one more question, Mr. Mason. Have you ever been to the House of Destiny?"

Silence.

"Mr. Mason?" Matt pushed him. "The House of Destiny?"

"Yeah." Brian hesitated. "A coupla times."

"Did you go there with Allison Graham?" Matt just threw it in.

Brian got real testy. "I told you, I didn't know the broad."

"Then who were you with?" Matt moved closer.

"Ray Jennings took us—me, David Feinman, and Charlie Grant."

"When was that?" Matt was right in his face now.

"Must have been months ago." Mason took a step backward. "Way before Christmas, last year."

"Does that mean that you and your friends go in for a little S&M?"

"Are you crazy? I can't speak for anyone else, but I sure as hell don't."

"That's it for now." Matt snapped the notebook shut. "Thanks."

Without another word, Brian turned on the hose again.

The next stop was David Feinman's boat *Father's Office*, but it was late afternoon before Matt and Angelle got there.

The furthest end of the club was obviously reserved for the

more illustrious yachts. Matt estimated David Feinman's exquisitely designed Grand Banks was probably somewhere between fifty and sixty feet long. His knowledge of naval architecture was certainly expanding with this case.

After several minutes of banging on the side of the hull, Matt feared they had missed Mr. Feinman once again. But just as he and Angelle turned to leave, a male voice invited them to come aboard.

A freestanding small staircase led from the dock to a long causeway, which surrounded the main cabin from stem to stern. The house appeared to be quite spacious, and Matt assumed the sleeping cabins were below decks. He noted the pristine condition in which the vessel was kept, teak rails meticulously varnished, wooden deck well oiled, and paintwork crisp. This yacht cost mucho bucks just to maintain.

He found David Feinman working at a computer station, situated in a detailed work space in the corner of the main salon. He introduced the leggy blonde sprawled on the couch as his secretary, Sonja. She wore only a black bikini.

Glancing up, the blonde nodded and went back to her magazine.

"As I told you on the phone, I don't have much time." Feinman spoke rapidly, as if by doing so he could be rid of them sooner.

The Hollywood screenwriter had intelligent eyes and a smooth facade Matt suspected would be difficult to crack, so he didn't pull any punches. "I'll get straight to the point. Where were you on the night of Tuesday, August 16?"

Feinman smiled. "I was here, working."

"Was anyone with you that night?" Angelle move closer to the computer.

He gave her a provocative smile. "Yes, Sonja was here."

The blonde looked up. "I was here."

"You mean you were here all night?" Angelle acted shocked.

"Yes." Smiling, Sonja went back to reading her magazine.

Matt showed him the pictures of the three victims, Allison, Sherrie, and Cindy. "Do you know any of these women?"

Feinman barely glanced at the photos. "No, and they are definitely not my type. Anyway, I'm married." But he still cast another appreciative glance at Angelle.

*Well,* thought Matt, *that's lie number one.* Matt shoved the photos into David's hand. "Look again, Mr. Feinman. Are you sure you didn't meet any of these women at a 'divorce party' for Gino Rosario some months back?"

"Let me see them again." Looking a bit unnerved at the mention of the divorce party, David Feinman gave them a closer look. "Now which ones were at the party?"

"Why don't you tell me?" Matt suggested.

"It's hard to say. I recognize the blonde, George's girlfriend, Sherrie, I think. But this other one, it's hard to say." He held up the morgue shot of Cindy.

Matt kept going, but he doubted they'd get much more out of him. "Were you on good terms with Raymond Jennings?"

That brought a show of temper. "Ray Jennings? Hell, no! That asshole caused me nothing but grief."

"How's that, Mr. Feinman?"

"I was one of the investors in Party Favorites. But the whole thing went belly-up simply because all Ray wanted to do was mess with the help, male and female."

"What about the profits? Didn't he sell the business?"

"What profits?" David scoffed. "There was nothing left."

"Are you aware that Mr. Jennings is dead?" Angelle asked.

"Hit-and-run, I heard." No emotion, just the facts.

"Who told you about his death?"

David took a moment. "I think it was Brian Mason."

Brian again. But it was apparent that David Feinman hadn't mourned Ray Jennings demise, either. Matt selected the photo of Sherrie and Allison and pointed to Sherrie. "Did you know this was the woman Mr. Fisher was with when he died?"

Feinman shrugged. "George always had something on the side."

"And you, Mr. Feinman?" Angelle asked, pointedly.

He didn't answer. But the blonde lifted her eyes from the magazine and smiled.

Matt fanned the photos. "Have you had any contact with any of these women since the party on Fisher's yacht?"

"No, I have not." Feinman shook his head.

Slipping the photos back in his pocket, Matt hit him with the big one. "Tell me about the House of Destiny."

Surprised, Mr. Feinman asked, "What the hell do you mean?"

"Like how often you go there. Did you ever take Allison Graham?"

"Who the hell is Allison Graham?" David scrunched his face.

"The other young woman who's standing right next to Sherrie in this photograph." Matt shook the picture in front of his face. He was weary of all the friggin' games.

Feinman's bravado appeared to weaken, but only for a moment. "I've been to the House of Destiny once, with a few of the guys. Just for a lark."

Rubbing his forehead, Matt asked, "Who were you with?"

He told him the usual suspects: Ray Jennings, Brian Mason, Charlie Grant. "When were you there?" For all their money, these guys were just cheating assholes.

"A c-c-couple of months before Ray left town," he stuttered.

"That's it? That's the only time?"

"Were you up there for the bondage sex?"

"No, sir, I was not. It was a night out with the guys, that's all." His voice had regained its strength. "Now, if there are any more questions, you can speak to my lawyer."

*This son of a bitch lies like he breathes.* But Matt knew that was as far as he could go at this time. "Thank you, sir."

Back in the car, Angelle asked, "What do you think?"

"I think he's an egotistical jerk." Matt floored the gas.

Matt and Angelle entered the hushed atmosphere of Charles and Alex Grant's luxurious penthouse on the very top of the tallest building in the Marina. He glanced quickly at his partner, who appeared to be fascinated by the paintings and statuary lining the walls of the circular foyer.

A maid showed them to the living room, where Charles Grant

III awaited them. The interior of the apartment was awesome too. Even the pretentious Mr. Grant looked small in the huge two-storied living room, with its grand fireplace and pink marble floors.

The view was spectacular.

Tall etched-glass doors opened out to a large deck, displaying magnificent vistas of the Marina and the ocean beyond. Outside, the sky, laden with pregnant gray clouds, threatened to burst at any moment.

Matt took a place beside Angelle on a pale-yellow silk couch opposite a matching chair in which Mr. Grant relaxed.

Arranging his feet on the flowery rug positioned under the table, Matt glanced up.

On the wall behind Mr. Grant hung a massive oil painting of a handsome blonde woman dressed in black. Though small in stature, she created a powerful presence as her hypnotic eyes glowered down on their host.

Getting straight to the point, Matt showed Mr. Grant all the photos of Sherrie and Alison, along with the morgue shot of Cindy, and went through the routine.

Charlie Grant was no different from the other club members and gave him the same bullshit answers.

"Refresh my memory, sir. The first time we spoke. Remember? We were on your yacht. Didn't you tell me you didn't know either of these women?" He held up the picture of Allison and Sherrie.

Mr. Grant coughed, uneasily. "Yes, I believe I did."

Again, holding up both photos, Matt prodded. "You were never on George Fisher's boat when any of these women were present."

"Not that I can remember."

Matt shook his head and turned to Angelle, giving her the privilege of telling him. "Brian Mason says otherwise."

He put the question to Mr. Grant. "Were you not present at a 'divorce party' for Gino Rosario early in April?"

Quick as a flash, Grant changed course. "Oh. Were they the ones—"

"Yes, Mr. Grant." Angelle's voice dripped sarcasm. "Two of these young ladies performed a live sex act for the pleasure of you and your friends."

"Well, er, come to think of it, I must have seen them. But my recollection of the whole evening is rather hazy. You know how one tends to drink too much at those kinds of bachelor parties?" Smiling, he tried to draw Matt into his macho camaraderie. When he got no response, Mr. Grant reached for the photos and pointed to Sherrie. "Maybe this one. But I certainly can't tell anything from this." He placed the morgue shot of Cindy face down on the table.

Matt pressed on. "Was your attendant there?"

"Yes. I offered his services for the party. Sy played bartender and prepared the food."

Matt wrote himself a note to check out Sy Neang. "Did you have any additional contact with the women other than at the party on Mr. Fisher's boat?"

"Why would I? I'm a happily married man."

*But you look too damn nervous,* Matt thought. "One more thing: where were you on the night of Tuesday, August 16?"

"San Diego. I go there almost every week for a couple of days." He smiled. "And I have an office in the Marina."

"Is there someone in San Diego who can corroborate that?"

"Yes, my cousin, Frank Gleason. He runs Grant Aviation."

"Where can we reach him?" Matt wrote down the number and asked him, casually, "Have you ever been to the House of Destiny?"

Startled, Grant was slow in answering. "Er, only once, with Ray Jennings."

Pencil poised. "When was that?"

"Months ago. We didn't stay long. I'm afraid that sort of thing's not my cup of tea."

"Was there anyone else besides Ray Jennings with you?"

Once again, the usual suspects—Brian Mason, David Feinman. Grant rose from his chair. "Will that be all?"

"No, sir, but we'll contact you if there's anything else."

# CHAPTER 23

Megan was working late. Everyone else had left hours ago, and the real estate office was silent and empty. But try as she might, she could not concentrate and found herself moving paperwork around her desk, accomplishing nothing.

She recalled her conversation with the two detectives this afternoon and her relief when she'd learned that the stunning young woman was Matt Donovan's partner. And he hadn't even asked her about the House of Destiny. She'd worried for nothing.

Through Matt's well-placed questions about Brian, Megan had come to realize how little she knew about her ex-fiancé, even after their three years together. She'd never met any of his family. Brian had told her they were estranged.

But he did say he was raised in poverty on the wrong side of the tracks, and his teenage years were fraught with problems and arrests. Brian had never been in serious trouble, just underage drinking, possession of marijuana, and stealing a couple of hubcaps. He'd told her all the kids in his neighborhood did the same thing. He didn't have a record or he would not have passed the stringent qualifications for becoming a stockbroker and financial analyst.

Maybe she should have been more honest with Matt and told him about her feelings of déjà vu regarding the house on Beachview. But it was all so vague. It wasn't as if she actually remembered being there with Brian.

*Come on, what the hell does any of it mean?* She didn't really believe Brian was a murderer. How could she possibly eat, sleep, and make love with someone for three years and not know if he was capable of murder? But she hadn't known about his affiliation with Ray Jennings. And what about the strange conversation she'd overheard among Brian, Charlie, and David about the divorce party for Gino Rosario? Surely she should have mentioned that to Matt Donovan.

Well, she didn't, so she might as well forget it.

After completing her commission report on the Rosario house, Megan made sure that Helen's house was adequately covered for the weekend and the open house. She planned to leave for Catalina early Saturday morning with Charlie and Alex, and she couldn't afford to miss a single showing.

It was getting harder and harder to put a deal together in this terrible economy, and even after five years of making an excellent living in the real estate business, Megan was now having difficulty making ends meet. The high-rolling years were long gone. But she'd still written a check for Michael Harrington this afternoon.

Her stomach turned over at the thought of handing Michael a thousand-dollar check. For what? Sex? Reaching into her purse, she pulled out the check, stared at it for a moment, and then ripped it up and dropped it in the trash.

She'd think of something to tell the girls.

Glancing at her watch, Megan picked up the telephone.

One more call, and then she had to meet with Alex and Charlie at Bayside.

*And I am* starving. *Screw the diet.*

She dialed. Kathleen picked up on the first ring. She probably thought it was Gino. "Hello, my dear, Megan here."

"Oh, hi, how are you?" Kathleen's voice was flat.

*Uh-oh, she doesn't sound good.* "I'm just fine, honey, and you?"

"I guess I'm a little down."

*No kidding.* The lift Kathleen had experienced from their boytoy escapades had already passed, and she'd plunged deeper into her depression. "Well, I've got exciting news. I've found a fabulous town house with an incredible ocean view, and it's just minutes from where you are now. Twenty-four–hour armed security, your own state-of-the-art alarm system. Would you like to see it tomorrow?"

Silence.

Megan tried again. "You'll feel more comfortable when you're out of that house and away from all the memories."

"I guess."

She could hear Kathleen's sobs. "Please don't cry, honey. We'll get through all of this somehow. It will get better, you know." Did she really believe that? "Look. Why don't you meet me at the club for dinner?"

Ignoring the question, Kathleen asked between sniffles, "If I meet you at the club, will you stay with me overnight, Megan?"

"Of course I will, honey. But why don't you stay at my house? I have to get up really early in the morning for an important showing. Should I come by and pick you up now?" She strained to hear the answer.

Kathleen seemed to calm down. "No, I can drive."

"Please, sweetheart, don't cry anymore," Megan begged.

"I'm going to get dressed now, Megan. Good-bye. I'll be there soon."

"Okay, dear." Replacing the handset, Megan prayed that her friend would soon find relief from her terrible obsession with Gino.

*Better check my machine.* Megan dialed her home number and keyed in the code. Tapping her fingers on the desk, she waited. "Hi, Megan, Rachel here. I just wanted to let you know that I'm going to visit our friend Michael. See you tomorrow."

Megan couldn't believe it. Rachel had gone to see Michael Harrington. How could she be so dumb? No investigation. No AIDS test. She must be out of her mind. Hurriedly, she called the Feinman home, but Maria answered. Rachel had gone out over an hour ago. Declining to leave a message, Megan hung up.

Shaking her head in disbelief, Megan cleaned off her desk, locked everything away, and grabbed her umbrella.

On her way to the car, the storm accelerated, and gale-like winds blasted across the lonely parking lot. As she struggled to open the door, Megan's umbrella was swept away by a fierce gust. She dropped her briefcase at the car and took off after it.

*Gotcha!* But the umbrella was broken. Soaked to the skin, Megan swore at the weather.

On her way back, she saw the outline of someone sitting in a car parked a couple of spaces behind hers. It gave her the creeps.

Grabbing her wet satchel, Megan shoved it in the backseat.

Hurriedly, she jumped into the old Mercedes and locked the doors. Positioning the rearview mirror, she watched the mysterious figure lean forward and look through the glass of the windshield. Quickly, she turned the key.

A grinding sound, then the engine sputtered but didn't catch. *Rrrrrr. Rrrrrr.*

*Dammit.* It wouldn't start.

The headlights snapped on in the shadowy car behind her. Slowly, it inched toward her.

Megan had seen enough movies to know this was not a healthy scenario.

Panicked, she tried again. *Rrrrr. Rrrrr.*

*Clang.* The car hit her bumper.

She rechecked the locks on the doors and windows.

*Bang.* He hit her again.

What the—? *Damn.* She was scared half to death.

Gritting her teeth, she turned the key again. The engine caught. *Thank you, God.*

Slamming her foot on the gas, she screeched out of the parking lot, brakes squealing. The tires slid across the slick surface of the blacktop and screeched even more as she spun onto the street.

The other car followed and then sped up to pass.

She recognized the driver at once. It was Brian!

Furious, Megan slammed her hand down on the horn and floored the gas. "You jerk," she screamed. "What do you think you're doing?" But she knew. Brian was drunk again.

Brian's car roared past the Bayside Yacht Club entrance.

She yearned to overtake him and slam her car into his bumper. Instead, Megan turned into the driveway of the club, inserted her card, and drove through the gate.

Filled with rage, her body wouldn't stop shaking. She resolved to call Matt Donovan in the morning and tell him about Brian's threatening behavior.

† † †

Scrunched down in the front seat of the police-issue Cadillac, Matt sipped his coffee. He'd been sitting in the parking lot of the Marina, where Michael Harrington's boat was moored for more than an hour. He'd made the best of it by drinking a gallon of coffee and enjoying the night. There were some benefits to stakeouts. If nothing else, it was peaceful and quiet, unless something went down.

His decision to keep Michael Harrington under surveillance had not set well with Joe or Angelle, so Matt had taken the first watch. This was the shit work they all hated, but it had to be done.

The sudden appearance of lights pulling into the lot didn't faze him. He'd seen several cars coming and going in the short time he'd been there. Mostly, he assumed, they were visitors and boat owners going about their business. This particular dock had a lot of live aboards, so there was more activity than usual.

He went back to watching the weather happen. A streak of lightning flashed in the West, and a layer of dark clouds traveled slowly across a pale quarter moon, adding a ghostly aura to the night sky. No stars tonight, just a drizzling mist slowly turning to rain.

Matt was just about to head for the john when another car pulled in. He sank down in the seat and watched closely as the red Jaguar XJS pulled up within twenty feet of him. *Man, that's $75,000 worth of automobile.*

The driver turned off the engine and sat there, gazing through the windshield for the longest time. In the darkness he couldn't distinguish a face. But when the interior light went on, he could see it was a woman, refreshing her lipstick and rearranging her long dark hair.

It looked like ... no. But it sure as hell was ... Rachel Feinman. Her kind of good looks was hard to miss. What the hell was she doing here?

*Shit.* He had this terrible urge to urinate, but he didn't dare move in case he blew his cover. Mrs. Feinman started the car again and ripped it into gear. Matt's first thought was *Thank God she's leaving.* His second was relief; he was going to get to the john. His third was *Oh, shit, she ain't going.* He cursed the three cups of coffee he had drunk from his flask.

The rain began to fall in earnest as Rachel got out of the car and opened the gate leading to Michael's slip. Matt knew he had to give up the idea of the john and follow her. He could just hear himself explaining to Captain Rick. Sorry, sir, Mrs. Feinman got snuffed because I had to take a leak.

He eased out of the car and waited until Rachel was halfway down the dock. Then he saw Michael Harrington meet her with an umbrella. Why the hell didn't he have one of his own? He heard them laughing as they ran down the dock.

Then, silence.

Catlike, Matt moved along the floating dock and hid behind a dock box. The rain came down harder, and he was drenched. He stopped one vessel short of the sailboat at the streamlined cigarette speedster, like the one on *Miami Vice*. Dripping wet, he climbed aboard and huddled under an old tarp, trying to hear what was happening on Michael's boat.

Rachel Feinman was here, visiting with his murder suspect? Who would have believed it? Matt smiled. Her asshole husband, David, wouldn't.

Was Michael Harrington her lover? Man, this guy really got around, from the hooker to the screenwriter's wife. Did he have some kind of agenda? Was Rachel Feinman about to become his next victim?

Then Matt had a terrible thought. Did Megan know him too?

The rain beat down harder and harder, and Matt couldn't hold out one minute longer; his kidneys were about to burst. He undid his zipper and let go over the side.

Relieved, but drenched from the rain, he crawled back under the tarp.

This was the downside of surveillance.

A half hour later, the storm accelerated, and the wind whistled through the marina, like a banshee. Lines and halyards clanked around him, and with each gut-wrenching swell the craft Matt was hiding on rocked and banged against the dock.

Suddenly, a loud moan, building to a scream, came from Michael's sailboat.

He moved closer until he stood right next to the porthole.

It was obviously Rachel Feinman.

How did he know she wasn't getting hurt? How did he know it was a cry of pleasure? It was the voice of experience. Unfortunately, not his own—at least not lately.

Matt moved away and crouched down under his tarp again.

Time ticked away. His legs cramped, so he changed position.

*Shit.* How much longer was she going to stay? Matt peeked out from under the canvas. The rain had stopped, and the lovers sat on the deck, drinking wine.

In truth, Matt was relieved to hear them out there talking and giggling. He was glad he was right. It might have been hard to convince Captain Rick he didn't know the difference between an orgasm and a murder.

Matt wasn't too unhappy. Except for his foray to the porthole, the tarp had kept most of the rain off him, and it sounded like they were going to break it up for the night. Still, he couldn't wait to get back to his warm dry car and another cup of hot coffee.

† † †

In the dining room of Bayside Yacht Club, Megan had just finished her diet dinner of broiled whitefish and steamed vegetables and was dreaming about the dessert she'd just ordered—just to calm her nerves, of course—after the ordeal with Brian.

Her view of the marina was exquisite, as was the ambience of the club. Megan really enjoyed the soft background music, the fine white linen tablecloths, the ever-so-subtle candlelight, and the divine smell of gourmet cooking.

She tried to close out the sound of Charlie Grant droning on about plans for his upcoming real estate auction. She hadn't mentioned her encounter with her ex-boyfriend, knowing Charlie would make her do something unreasonable, like call the police and have Brian arrested.

Megan was just about to call Kathleen on her cell when she saw her crossing the room. It had taken her long enough to get here.

Flopping on the seat beside Megan, Kathleen immediately began to cry.

*Oh, God, what's happened now?*

Alex looked concerned. "What is it, dear?"

Kathleen went into a long story about an intruder trying to break into her house. Terrified, she'd called the police. But when the cops arrived, they'd found Gino at her back door and arrested him. But Kathleen had informed the cops, in no uncertain terms, that Gino was her ex-husband and they'd better let him go.

Of course, her indignation was directed at the police.

*This girl will never learn.* "Where is he now?" Megan asked.

"I don't know. He wanted his golf clubs, so I gave him his golf bag, and he left when the police did."

It was all very strange. "Do you think there could be another reason Gino was at the house?" Megan asked.

Kathleen didn't answer.

"Of course not," Charlie blustered. "He's entitled to go to his own home for his golf clubs, isn't he?"

Alex gave him a withering look. "Not unannounced, he's not. Can't you see how frightened Kathleen is? Why, Gino is darn lucky she don't have a gun. He could be deader 'n a skunk right now. We're all scared to death with this killer runnin' loose."

"Come on, Alex," Charlie scorned. "You don't think Gino Rosario is the murderer?"

"Not really," Megan joked. "It wouldn't be good for his image."

Nobody laughed.

Alex issued orders. "Charlie, get yourself to the bar and buy this little gal a drink. What would you like to drink, honey?"

"I don't care, anything."

Charlie wandered off, replaced by a tuxedoed waiter arriving with Megan's chocolate chip cheesecake. Picking up her fork, Megan paused and then immediately set it down. She'd lost her appetite.

When Charlie was out of earshot, Kathleen pulled two Polaroid shots out of her pocket and threw them on the table.

Alex picked them up first. "My goodness, child! Where did you get these?"

"Gino was in such a hurry to leave, they fell out of his golf bag. I think that's why he broke into the house. He wanted those pictures."

"You poor, poor dear," Alex whispered, handing them to Megan.

In the soft candlelight, the faces of the two women in the photograph were almost indistinguishable, but Megan recognized Gino in the middle. In the first shot she noted a life buoy, left of the threesome, inscribed with the name of George Fisher's boat, *Happy Hooker*. The second photo was actually pornographic—Gino making it with some girl in a cabin. Her heart ached for Kathleen. "What are you going to do?"

"What can she do?" Alex demanded. "She's already divorcing him."

"Happiness is the best revenge," Megan said, pragmatically. "Get a new man. Call Michael Harrington. Make a date with him. Enjoy yourself. Rachel went tonight. She didn't even wait to check him out, let alone get an AIDS test."

"You're kidding," Alex said.

Kathleen just gaped, openmouthed.

"Well, someone had to go first." Megan picked up the fork and took a small bite of dessert. "And you know, Rachel was chomping at the bit." She almost told them of her decision to drop out of the boytoy deal, but didn't.

Kathleen fingered the photographs. "What am I going to do with these?"

"Get rid of them, right now." Alex lit a match and grabbed the pictures out of her hand. "Shall I?"

Kathleen nodded.

Megan swallowed her cheesecake. "Wait—"

But it was too late. Depositing the charred remains in the ashtray, Alex put her arm around Kathleen. "There, there, dear, it's all over now."

Charlie arrived with drinks. "Megan, you're not going to like this, but Brian's at the bar, and he is bombed." He set down the glasses.

Megan groaned. "I knew he had to be drunk. Stalking me, driving erratically, he wouldn't do that if he was sober. Would he?"

Alex didn't answer; she just put her other arm around Megan. "C'mon, honey. You can't let Brian get to you like this." She turned to Kathleen. "You're stayin' with Megan tonight, aren't you, dear? It will do you both good to have company. Charlie will follow you home and make sure you're okay. Won't you, dear?"

"Sure, honey. I'd be happy to."

Before leaving the club, Megan took a long look at Brian, lounging on the barstool, and realized how much more his behavior had deteriorated in the last few months. His drinking was getting progressively worse to the point that Brian was almost a stranger. Or maybe it was her. Maybe she was the one who had changed.

But now she was beginning to wonder if Brian could be involved with these murders.

# Chapter 24

It was nine o'clock on Thursday morning, and Joe had just relieved Matt of his post at Michael's sailboat.

Arriving home, the first thing Matt did was pick up the phone and dial.

Megan's machine answered. He hung up quickly, without leaving a message.

Doubts assailed him. Why would he take a chance on dating a witness?

He answered his own question. Because Megan was the only woman he had been attracted to in the years since his wife, Constance, had died. He was certain Megan was not a murderer. And as long as he kept their friendship under wraps, who the hell would know?

On the other hand, why would Megan go out with him, a cynical aging cop?

Matt dialed again. This time, he called his daughter in New York. "Hi, Julie."

"Hey, Daddy." She sounded pleased to hear from him.

Smiling at her enthusiasm, Matt was grateful their relationship was such a loving one. He'd heard so many horror stories about raising teenagers. "How are you, baby?"

"I'm pretty darn good." Julie's voice was charged with excitement. "We start shooting the cosmetic ad on Monday. Can you believe it, Daddy? They're blocking off a whole section of Central Park so they can take pictures of me."

His cop mind kicked in. "How much security will they have?"

"Oh, Daddy, you always think the worst. Nothing's going to happen to me."

"You're right, honey." He sighed. "I guess your old dad sees so much garbage every day, it spills over."

"How are you getting along with your new partner?" she asked.

"Good. She handles herself well, seems to know what she's doing."

"Is she pretty?" Julie asked, always trying to hook him up with someone.

"Yes, she's very pretty. But that doesn't matter. It's her work that counts."

"You're so liberated, Daddy. I'm proud of you."

"Is that a crack?"

"No, it isn't. Just a minute, Kent's at the door."

Matt was already jealous of her latest boyfriend, and he hadn't even met him yet. "You go ahead, honey. I'll call you in a couple of days."

"Okay, Daddy. I love you."

"I love you too baby." He hung up and then stared into his hand at Megan's business card for the longest time.

*Damn.* He'd lost his nerve. He was too chickenshit to make the call. *Do it.*

He grabbed the phone. This time he dialed her cell phone. While he waited for her to answer, he almost lost his nerve again.

"Hello?"

"Megan. Matt Donovan here. Remember me?"

"Of course I do. How are you, Detective Donovan?"

He cleared his throat. "Matt. Please, call me Matt."

"What can I do for you ... Matt?"

"Listen, would you like to have a bite to eat with me sometime?"

She remained silent. And then she said, "I'd like that very much."

Matt grinned. He wasn't prepared for a yes. "That's great. That's great."

Silence again. "When, Matt?"

"When? Uh, how about tonight?" He hurried to add. "That is,

if you're not busy. Sorry, I guess this is kind of late notice. Never mind—"

But she interrupted him. "Tonight would be wonderful."

"Great. Yeah, that's great. I'll see you at eight." He hung up fast before she changed her mind.

He slapped out a rhythm on the coffee table.

He had a date. *Hot damn!* Matt had a date with a real lady.

That's when Tom Wilson, the medical examiner, called.

They'd found another mutilated body.

Megan entered a small banquet room, located on the lower floor at Bayside. She hurried past the waiters, who were getting ready to serve lunch.

The entertainment committee was holding its final meeting before the big bash in Catalina this weekend. Alex, resplendent in a gray Escada suit, sat at the head table, presiding over the board members, including a dour Kathleen on her right and Rachel on her left.

Megan took the empty seat beside Rachel.

She noted that Helen Jennings had positioned herself at the end of the table with Junie Fisher, Gloria Henderson, and the senator's wife, Anne Rattner. A few latecomers trickled in and located seats at the remaining tables.

Alex was speaking. "We must now decide on table arrangements for the Commodore's Ball in October." Since Charlie was up for commodore next year the Grants were involved in every affair the club had planned, and of course Alex had enlisted her three closest friends.

Megan tried to focus, but the tedious discussion about table decorations lingered on for forty-five minutes. Should they be black and white? Or black and silver? Or just plain black? On and on and on, they argued as if any of it were important. Sometimes, Megan thought she would suffocate in the mounds of trivia that permeated her life.

Finally, the members voted. Black and silver won. June Fisher consented to be in charge of the decorations, and everyone agreed it would take her mind off George's death.

While she had the chance, Megan studied Rachel. Dressed to kill in a sapphire St. John pantsuit, Rachel sat calmly in the chair, her hands in her lap, looking more relaxed than she had in a long, long time.

Did she actually have sex with Michael?

Megan didn't dare ask her, but she was dying to know.

Alex closed the meeting. Then, turning to Megan, she said dryly, "I see you arrived just in time for lunch, Megan."

"I planned it that way. Last time I came early, I got stuck with all the decorations for the Halloween party. Did you ever try to make a floor plan of Dracula's mansion? It's impossible, and I hated sticking all those stupid black bats all over the place."

Kathleen giggled. "This weekend when we're in Catalina we're going to do the circus clowns. Won't that be fun?"

Rachel rolled her eyes. "Sometimes I think Kathleen's in a time warp."

Alex smiled. "We're all in a time warp."

Turning to Rachel, Megan couldn't resist it. "How was Michael?"

Startled by the question, Rachel crossed her legs and whispered, "I thought we agreed it was our own business what we did with you-know-who?"

Rachel had sex with him. Megan knew immediately.

"I think you're exactly right," Kathleen said with a knowing look. "I'm not going to tell anyone what I do."

"None of us much care what you do," Rachel snapped. "I bet you won't even call him."

"Maybe I will," Kathleen said, defensively.

Powdering her nose, Alex asked, "She's gonna call this afternoon, aren't you, honey?"

"No, she's not. She's going with me to look at condominiums, aren't you?" Megan wanted to be finished in time for a leisurely bath and to get ready for her date with Matt.

Kathleen nodded to both of them, Megan noticed.

But Alex insisted. "You have to call Michael right now."

"She'll never do it," Rachel snapped.

"Oh, yes I will." Kathleen stood up. "But first I must speak to Junie Fisher and see how she's doing."

While she waited for Kathleen, Megan had better things to think about, like her date with Matt.

†  †  †

On the way to the murder site, Matt drove slowly up the long road, winding to the top of Balmoral Avenue in the Hollywood Hills. He glanced at Angelle, who sat next to him, clutching the armrest. He could tell from her white knuckles how much she hated the curving mountain road.

"There it is." Matt pointed to a house on the left side of the street with five or six vehicles in front, two of them squad cars. He made a quick turn in the driveway and parked halfway down the block.

Returning on foot, Matt entered the mini-estate through baroque, wrought-iron gates, and Angelle followed a couple of steps behind him.

The old two-story Spanish mansion was charming, the gardens lush and well tended. A high ficus hedge surrounded the property, guaranteeing the privacy and seclusion rich people seemed to crave. The place was crawling with cops, searching the grounds for clues. A coroner's van parked in the driveway supported two morgue attendants sipping coffee and eating doughnuts.

A uniformed officer stopped Matt at the front door. "I need ID, sir."

Matt flashed his shield. "Who found the body?"

"The maid did, sir, this morning. She'd been dead a while."

"No shit." He could already smell it.

The minute he stepped inside the door, the combined odors of decay, defecation, and death almost knocked him over. He took out his handkerchief and covered his nose.

Angelle rummaged in her purse for a tissue and did likewise.

Matt walked down the uncarpeted hallway toward an open steel door. "Holy shit!" he said, standing in the portal.

Inhaling deeply, he entered.

The room was a grisly nightmare made all the more revolting by the cold harsh glare of police floodlights. The mirrors on the walls and ceiling were splattered with blood, giving Matt the feeling he'd stepped into the deepest pits of hell. Fumes from the body, decomposing fast in the August heat, were almost suffocating. His stomach lurched. Quickly, he checked out Angelle. She stood firm, holding the tissue to her mouth and nose.

In a flash, Matt absorbed the contents of the room. Black carpet and the abundance of mirrors gave the room an abyss-like depth. An iron maiden stood in one corner and the replica of a guillotine in another. On one wall, every imaginable tool of sadomasochism was displayed: paddles, whips, chains, blindfolds, gags, handcuffs, clamps, vibrators, and an assortment of dildos. Suspension equipment, even a swing, hung from a scaffold.

Lifting the sheet, Matt assessed the corpse. The young woman was naked, lying face up on the black carpet. Her body appeared more a mass of blood and tissue than the remains of a human being. The killer had hacked her to pieces. He couldn't tell if the right breast was gone, her body was so ravaged.

"A ritual killer would be more precise," Angelle said, quietly. "This is the work of a madman."

Matt looked around at the roomful of activity.

A female photographer snapped pictures of the crime scene, and half a dozen lab and fingerprint technicians labored with frenzied intensity. He could feel the depth of emotion in the room. He heard none of the usual jokes and wisecracks.

Tom Wilson, the medical examiner, was deep in conversation with an athletic-looking man dressed in jeans and a polo shirt.

Matt walked toward them. "Hi, Tom, thanks for the call."

"I recognized the MO, and I thought you'd want to know." Doc Wilson identified the victim. "She called herself Darkness, but her real name is Bonnie-Sue Rattner. Matt, this here is Dan Coleman from Hollywood Division. He's in charge."

*Rattner, I know that name.* Matt held out his hand. "I'm Matt Donovan, Venice-Pacific. We got two of 'em in Venice and another possible in San Francisco."

Dan shook his hand. "Exact same?"

"Yours is much worse. If it's the same perp, he's escalating. Okay if I look around?"

"Sure." Coleman resumed his conversation with Doc Wilson.

Matt joined Angelle, who was exploring the contents of the windowless dungeon. He shook his head in disbelief. Lately, his sex education had been expanding rapidly, but the implements of sadomasochism he saw here were an advanced course.

He glanced at Angelle to see if she was still coping. But before he had a chance to ask, the two morgue attendants pushed him aside and approached the body.

"You through here, Dan?" the attendant called out.

"Yeah, take her away," Detective Coleman answered.

"Doc?"

"I'm finished."

The sound of the zipper closing on the body bag scraped across Matt's already-raw nerves. Leaving Angelle still investigating the dungeon, he ventured down the hallway.

Suddenly, a commotion at the front door erupted as two heavyset bodyguard types shoved their way past the officer on guard.

"Hey, you can't go in there," the young cop yelled.

"So shoot me," snapped one of the newcomers.

Matt moved back against the wall as they rushed toward the torture room. What the hell was that about? Coleman seemed to have it under control, so he left him to it.

He proceeded to check out the rest of the house.

Wandering through the traditionally furnished living room, Matt absorbed every detail. Very tidy, very feminine, peach and blue chintz armchairs, a blue-and-white striped couch. White lace curtains adorned the windows. A crystal bowl of decaying roses on the mahogany table gave a sweet respite from the fetid air, allowing him to temporarily remove the handkerchief he'd used as a mask. Although it reminded him of a funeral home, the aroma was a welcome relief from the effluvium of death.

What kind of woman would have lace curtains and fresh roses in one room and a dungeon from hell in another? *A very mixed-up young lady,* Matt thought, feeling a sudden rush of sympathy for the victim.

The tiny kitchen contained a stove, refrigerator, small table, and one lonely chair. Traces of white powder were scattered on the table and sprinkled on the floor. Wetting his finger, Matt tasted it: definitely not Splenda. It was cocaine.

Several periodicals had slipped under the table. He knelt to pick them up. *Shit!* The contents were similar to the leather-and-lace magazine they'd found at Sherrie's house, the one with Michael Harrington's number on it.

Matt read the names of the magazines: *Kinky People, Places, and Things; Bondage Times; Whipping Post;* and *Screw.* Leafing through the pages, they all looked the same. Sex and more sex. Toys for sex, 900 numbers for sex, bondage parlors for sex, an abundance of lewd photos with a graphic S&M theme, and there were hundreds of personal ads from all kinds of people seeking partners. He was sure when they checked her computer they would find plenty of the same shit downloaded from the Internet. In all, there were a whole lot of sick, lonely people out there craving all manner of pleasure and displeasure.

All the sex papers contained pictures of naked women and men twisted into every contortion imaginable, some being tortured by various implements.

Then he noticed several ads encircled with black marker. All were dominant males in search of submissive females.

Angelle entered the room. "What is it, Matt?"

"Look at this, Angel. She was definitely looking for love in all the wrong places." He handed her the *Screw* magazine.

Turning the paper sideways, Angelle stared at the picture of a fat man mounted upside down on a wooden post, his legs extended by a rope tied to the ceiling. "How do they do that? Why do they do that?"

"Do you really want to know?" Matt moved on.

Angelle explored the refrigerator door, pointing out several pieces of paper attached by obscene magnets. "The girl was obsessed with sex."

"Check out the powder on the table, Angel," he said. "It's coke."

She tasted it. "You're right."

Matt rifled through more advertisements, noting the ones marked with black ink. He whistled softly. "I wonder if our killer's in here, Angel."

"I dunno, but I think our victim is." Angelle handed him a newspaper clipping from the refrigerator door.

> Darkness Seeks Master
> Submissive SWF, 21, looking for experienced, imaginative master. I fantasize about worshipping your body and fulfilling your every wish. Your slave, Darkness, will accept your punishment gratefully. I patiently await your lash. Make me suffer, please. Fully equipped dungeon on premises. Anything and everything acceptable except exchange of body fluids. AK42/361

"Wow, she's really out there. Okay, Angel, we've gotta figure out which magazine this came from and who answered the ad."

"I don't think it's that easy," a new voice said.

Matt turned. It was Dan Coleman, the Hollywood detective.

"The 'drag rags' have a complicated system of receiving and distributing answers to their ads. They don't open the letters before delivering them to the advertiser."

"Dan Coleman, this is my partner, Angelle Bentley."

"I'm pleased to meet you, Dan." Angelle shook his hand.

Dan continued. "But that isn't our biggest problem." He jerked his head toward the hallway. "Did you see those two guys who just barged in? They work for the victim's father. They want the house cleaned of all indications she was into S&M. Apparently, her family doesn't want the scandal."

"That's out of the question." Matt was outraged.

Dan raised his hands, palms up. "The mayor just called. I gotta do it."

Matt shook his head in disgust and gestured to the table. "There's cocaine on the kitchen table, Dan."

"I'll get somebody right on it."

Carrying the newspapers, Matt followed Angelle into the living room.

After reading the clipping from the fridge, Dan joined them, shaking his head.

"Contrary to her ad, Darkness, aka Bonnie-Sue Rattner, was only nineteen years old. Does the name Harley Rattner mean anything to you?"

Of course it did. "Senator Harley Rattner."

Dan nodded.

"The Bayside Yacht Club." Angelle made the statement.

"Yup," Matt agreed. "All roads lead back to Bayside."

"Anyway," Dan Coleman continued, "my orders came from downtown to put a gag on any and all information. The crime scene is to be sealed, immediately. No statements to the press."

"That's not going to be easy." Matt parted the lace curtains and looked outside. "Marcia Waters is already out there with the Channel Three News van. And every reporter in town will be here before long."

"Shit." Dan headed for the front door. "If you want to go through the house again, you'd better do it now."

"Ready, Angel?" Matt asked.

"Sure." She winced, noticeably.

Tom Wilson passed them in the hallway.

"Tom?" Matt asked. "You figure she's been dead how long? A couple of days?"

"At least that long. It looks like time of death occurred sometime on Tuesday. I'll know better after the autopsy."

So, that means George Fisher died on Monday afternoon, Sherrie Weston was murdered late Monday night or Tuesday morning, and now Bonnie-Sue Rattner was killed one week later. But it all started six months ago with Allison Graham, followed three months later by the death of Cindy in San Francisco. All of them had the same MO. That was four murders, and he was not counting the hit-and-run on Ray Jennings. Only God knew how many others were in between. He addressed the medical examiner. "Tom, let me know as soon as you can if the murder weapon matches."

"I can tell you right now, Matt," Tom said, "if it isn't the same, it's close. All three mutilations were carried out with a long narrow-bladed knife—like I said before, probably a filleting knife."

"As far as I'm concerned, that makes it official. This killer's a serial, but now he's graduated from hookers to the big time."

"Sorry I couldn't be of more help, Matt." Tom turned to leave.

"You did great. I owe you one." Another commotion at the door claimed Matt's attention.

Before he could be stopped, a tall obese man rushed headlong down the hallway. Matt recognized him at once. The agony carved into Senator Harley Rattner's face looked as if it would remain forever.

Protesting loudly, Dan Coleman followed him. "Sir, Senator, sir, you don't want to go in there."

The man came to a halt and turned around, stopping Dan in his tracks. "Just what do you mean, son? Will it be worse than seeing my daughter lying butchered in a plastic bag, her poor body cut to ribbons? What could be worse?"

Dan shook his head. "I don't know, sir."

"Well then, son." He gestured toward Matt and Angelle. "It's going to take a whole lot more than you and your friends to keep me out." The senator lunged into the death room with the ferocity of a pit bull.

"Senator Rattner." Dan hurried after him.

The sounds of fury reached them in the hall. Matt rushed in to see what was going on. Angelle followed.

No longer lit by police spotlights, the room and its hideous contents smoldered in the glow of a red lamp. Harley Rattner was ripping the devices off the wall, and with them smashing the mirrored ceiling into a thousand pieces. Sweat, mingled with tears, dripped down his crimson face as he vented his rage on the instruments of sexual torture adorning his daughter's chamber.

Senator Rattner was literally tearing apart the crime scene, and Matt was afraid he would have a heart attack. But he totally understood the depth of the man's pain. What father wouldn't feel the same way? Matt tried to imagine what it would be like to find his daughter, Julie, like this. It was too much for him. He couldn't even conceive it.

He turned to Dan, who'd grabbed the tail of the Senator's white shirt and hung on, trying to pull him back. But it was all to no avail.

Matt joined him in his attempts to subdue the thundering giant, but even their combined efforts couldn't slow him down. Bonnie-Sue's father simply dragged them both from one contraption to another on a savage mission of destruction.

Within minutes, Matt and Dan were joined by the officer at the door along with two other uniforms he'd enlisted. Finally, the five policemen restrained him and cuffed him. The crazed father crumbled to the floor, his mammoth body trembling.

Angelle sank to her knees on the bloody carpet and cradled his head.

Matt lingered at the door while Dan and the others silently left the room. The only sounds left in the dark obscene chamber were the sobs of a heartbroken father.

# Chapter 25

Even though Kathleen looked like she was about to faint from terror, Megan still wondered why she'd agreed to accompany her on this dumb boat cruise with Michael Harrington, instead of taking her to view the two condos she had selected for her.

Megan knew Kathleen was nervous about her meeting with Michael, but this was ridiculous. Even before leaving the club, Megan had watched her friend gulp two glasses of courage in the form of white wine, and it hadn't diminished a single one of her apprehensions.

Later, as a demure, poised Kathleen sat on the white cushions curved behind the steering wheel of Michael's sailboat, Megan realized how good her friend was at faking her feelings.

"You guys ready for a sunset cruise?" Michael asked, his brilliant azure eyes lighting up his face.

"We won't be long, will we? I have a showing at six." Megan didn't mention her all-important date with Matt and was suddenly aware she no longer viewed Michael's body with lust in her heart.

Her thoughts were solely on Matt Donovan.

But Michael paid her no mind as he addressed Kathleen. "We'll get her home in time, won't we?"

Kathleen didn't answer.

"Are you okay?" he asked with concern.

"I'm fine, thank you, a little nervous, maybe." Kathleen dropped her eyes.

"We can fix that. I'll get you a drink. What would you like? Wine? Martini? Margarita? That's my specialty."

Kathleen fairly glowed. "A margarita sounds wonderful, thank you."

"Megan?"

"I'll have a Diet Pepsi."

Michael disappeared below.

And Megan asked herself one more time what in the world she was doing here.

"I'm scared," Kathleen whined, acting out her hysteria by tearing apart a ratty tissue. "I don't want to go."

"Look, I'm here with you, and I'm all yours for …" Megan looked at her watch. "One hour and forty-five minutes, so don't lose your nerve. Michael is not going to murder you, and you're too old for white slavery."

Kathleen appeared to calm down a little.

In an effort to relax herself, Megan took in the scene.

The late afternoon sun glistened on the water, creating tiny crystals of light on every ripple. Dozens of boaters and their families floated on the water in all manner of craft, taking advantage of the gorgeous weather. Megan leaned back and stared upward at the two tall masts decorated with flags.

Maybe this wasn't such a bad idea after all.

The engine sputtered. Started again. Purred.

Their host emerged from below, carrying a tray of drinks. "Here we are, Michael's marvelous margaritas."

Kathleen sipped on the salt-rimmed glass. "Perfect." She smiled.

Michael handed Megan her Pepsi and then sampled his own drink, licking the salt off his lips.

"What's the name of your boat?" Kathleen asked.

"The *Moon River*."

"Oh, what a beautiful name," she exclaimed. "How did you decide on it?"

Michael's voice took on a dreamy quality. "Have you ever seen a full moon suspended just above the ocean at night? It leaves a silvery river on the sea. That's my *Moon River*, a shimmering pathway to adventure. Someday I'll follow it wherever it takes me." He smiled.

"Oh, that's so romantic," Kathleen gushed.

Michael responded with a sheepish grin.

*Give me a break.* Megan didn't know if she could stand all this true-romance stuff.

"And how big is the *Moon River*?" Megan asked.

"Thirty feet, but she's beamy. I've got lots of room below. Want to see?"

"No thanks, maybe later."

"Are you ready to go, honey?" Michael directed his question to Kathleen.

She nodded, her whole body quivering.

Michael set down his drink and, just like the swashbuckler he was, leaped over the side onto the dock. "Okay, matey, cast off. We're headin' out to sea!"

Rolling her eyes, Megan settled down for the ride.

Matt made a quick stop at the station after he left the crime scene in Hollywood.

Joe was waiting for him with a stack of information about the Bayside members that seemed to pop up every time they had a question—namely David Feinman, Brian Mason, Charlie Grant, and Gino Rosario. No one had a criminal record, and there were no charges of abuse or violent acts. David Feinman had written many brutal screenplays and was familiar with police procedure but had not a single blemish on his name. In fact, they all checked out, except for a speeding ticket here and there. Charlie's man Sy Neang's immigration papers were all intact. He had been sponsored for citizenship by Charles Grant many years ago and had an exemplary record ever since. Other than Brian's activities with Ray Jennings, there was nothing to indicate he had broken the law. Ray Jennings had no criminal record, either.

"I'd like you to start checking out the help at Bayside. That includes everybody: kitchen helpers, dining room crew, dockhands, parking attendants, even management, and the people who work in the office. Don't leave anyone out."

"Right, Matt." Joe headed for his computer.

He spoke to his partner. "Angel, I want you to check again with the rental office and see if Allison or Cindy or anybody else was ever on the lease during the last year, or was included as a tenant. I really need to go home and get some rest. Last night was a little rough, and I didn't even get a chance to change before the trip to Hollywood." Matt headed for the door. "I'll talk to you later."

After an hour-long cruise, Megan was relieved to be off the *Moon River* and away from Kathleen, who had taken to fawning over Michael Harrington.

As she drove down Ocean Avenue on the way to her six o'clock showing, Megan thought about the young couple she had called when she'd first listed Helen Jennings's house. They'd fallen completely in love with it and arranged tonight's appointment to show his parents, who were donating the entire down payment.

Arriving at the house early, Megan checked her watch: five forty-five. Helen's car was not in the driveway. She must be at the club for dinner. Good. She didn't want the owner coming back in the middle of the showing, and Megan had to be home by eight for her date with Matt. She knew she was pushing it. The clients were due at six.

It would all work out. It always did.

Before opening the door with her key, Megan checked the alarm. It was off. Strange. Would Helen be that careless? It was still light outside, so the house wasn't totally dark, but it sure felt spooky.

Suddenly, she heard a noise. She knew the butler was not there. Helen had given him the day off because of the showing.

"Helen? Is that you?" she called. "Helen?"

Loud rattling sounds came from the rear of the house.

Someone was there. She knew it.

The first thing Megan did was hit the silent emergency button on the security system. Next, she charged into the living room and armed herself with a poker. Clattering about, she made a lot of noise in hopes of scaring away the intruder.

A loud bang, and then everything was quiet.

Terror swept over her as she considered the possibilities. It was obviously a thief, a home invader. Anyone who was supposed to be there would have answered her call.

Then a terrible thought occurred to her. *Maybe it's the Bondage Murderer.*

But why would the killer be here at Helen's house?

She stood quite still, listening.

Surely he'd heard her.

Tiptoeing into the dining room, the first thing she saw was Helen's bar. And suddenly she craved a drink as she never had before. Fear had a way of doing that.

Megan couldn't stop staring at the row of shiny liquor bottles for what seemed an eternity. *Stop that, woman.*

Slam. Noise again. Objects were falling.

Megan reached for the Smirnoff bottle and grasped it as a weapon. "Helen? Are you there? I've called the police," she yelled, trying to scare whoever it was away.

Slowly, Megan inched her way down the hallway, poker in one hand, vodka bottle in the other. The office door flew open.

Someone rushed toward her in a flash of black leather.

It all happened so fast.

Was that a hood? A mask? She was down. The bottle shattered.

She heard feet, running. The front door slammed.

Silence. Empty silence. *Thank you, God.* Terrified, she sat on the floor for at least three minutes, eyes wide open, teeth clenched, her arms hugging her body. She was stunned.

Finally, reeking of vodka, Megan slowly clambered to her feet.

She staggered into the den. It was a shambles. Books, videotapes, DVDs, and audiocassettes were scattered everywhere. Helen's magnificent desk was ransacked, its contents strewn on the floor.

Her head swirled with questions. Who was the weirdo in black? And why the damn mask? But what was the leather-faced man looking for?

The doorbell rang. She jumped.

Pulling herself together, Megan headed for the door.

First, she peered out the window. Two police officers had their guns drawn. One was tall and thin, the other short and fat.

As she opened the door, Megan was acutely aware of the stench of alcohol exuding from her clothes.

The short, fat one spoke first. "We came in response to the alarm."

"You can put your guns away. I'm the real estate broker. We had an intruder, but he's gone now." On her way to the living room, Megan tried to explain about the masked man and what had happened.

Exchanging bewildered glances, the officers followed.

She could see they were trying to figure out how much she'd had to drink and if her story had any merit.

"A masked man, you say?" The thin one eyed her with suspicion.

She was trying to convince them of her sobriety when Helen Jennings arrived home. "What's going on here?" she demanded, in typical Helen fashion.

"We received an alarm and came to investigate, ma'am."

Without a word, Helen dropped her bag on the floor and rushed down the hallway to the office.

Megan followed, a little more slowly.

Standing in the doorway, she observed Helen, rummaging madly through the drawers of her desk. Apparently finding what she was searching for, a smile of satisfaction spread across her face.

"Helen?" Megan asked. "Do you know what he wanted?"

Helen slammed the drawer shut. "I have no idea. But I had some cash and jewelry in my desk. I wanted to see if they were still here."

"Are they?"

"Yes, thank you." Then, obviously remembering Megan's distress, she put on a big show of concern. "But how are you, dear? Can I get you anything?"

The doorbell rang.

"Oh my God, it's the clients. I have to clean up. Get this place tidied up, Helen. I'll see if I can hold them off." Megan flew down the hallway, yelling at the two security cops. "Go out the back way. Hurry, please. My clients are here."

Megan ran to the powder room and splashed some water on her

face. She reached for one of several perfume bottles arranged on a mirrored tray and sprayed herself from head to toe. She couldn't decide which was worse, the smell of booze or Helen's heady no-name fragrance. The reaction of the buyers would soon let her know.

As she walked toward the front door to meet the buyers, she couldn't help asking herself one question. She knew that Helen had a great big safe in her bedroom where she kept her cash and jewelry. So what was she really hiding in her desk?

# CHAPTER 26

Megan was still in shock from her experience at Helen's house, and it wasn't until after she had taken a hot bath and dressed for her date with Matt that she even heard about the death of Bonnie-Sue Rattner on the television.

The information on the evening news was sparse, so she didn't know many of the facts. *Dear God, Bonnie-Sue's poor mother and father must be devastated.*

The doorbell chimed. It was Matt.

He stood at the door like a little boy, a small dog in his arms. "It's just a mutt," he offered instead of a greeting.

"Oh, really." Megan smiled. "Well, bring it on in."

"Do you know who it belongs to?" he asked.

"Nope, I've never seen it before. Where did you find it?"

"In the alley near the parking lot." Matt raised his intense blue eyes and held her gaze. "I heard him crying and whining. At first I thought it was a kid."

Melting from the mournful look in Matt's eyes, Megan took the little puppy in her arms and held it to her breast. "It's beautiful." The dog seemed clean and well cared for, but it had no collar or tags. It was probably just lost. "What are we going to do with it?"

"I don't know. If we can't find its owners, maybe you could keep it for a little while."

Megan stared at him askance. "Ma-a-att. I work too many crazy hours to look after a puppy like this."

"I could help you." He gave her that look again.

Did that mean he planned to be around a while?

"I tell you what, just keep him until we check in the newspapers and see if there are any notices posted looking for him." Matt checked the puppy's rear end. "Her. It's a her. If we can't find her owners and you still don't want her, I'll give her to my daughter, Julie. She's going to be home in a couple of weeks."

A daughter? Matt had a daughter?

Suddenly, Megan realized she couldn't take care of the dog this weekend. She was leaving for Catalina on Saturday morning with Alex and Charlie Grant. "Okay, I'll keep her but only if Alex lets me take her on the boat. Otherwise you'll have to baby-sit till I get back." She set the puppy on the floor in the kitchen and fetched some water. The dog lapped it up. "You're thirsty, aren't you, baby? And hungry. And I sure hope you're house-trained."

"Yes, I am."

She glanced up and smiled. "I meant the dog."

Matt smiled too. He knew what she meant.

"Look, I don't really feel like going out, anyway." At that moment, Megan decided she didn't want to spoil the evening by discussing her frightening encounter at Helen's house. Maybe she'd tell him later. "Why don't you go get us a pizza and some dog food? Then we can stay home and take care of the puppy together."

Matt grinned from ear to ear. "Great. Do you like anchovies? I hope."

"Yes, I love 'em. So hurry. I'm starving and so is our friend."

He was jubilant. "Fabulous. I found the only girl in California who loves anchovies, puppies, and old cops."

"Go. Get pizza," Megan said, cavewoman style. "Move it, Officer, I'm starving here."

"I am, I am." Matt left the house, laughing.

The darling little puppy looked up at Megan with bright golden eyes, its tail wagging appreciatively, and she lost her heart completely. The dog was a reddish tan in color, and the thought struck her that it might be a golden retriever. She knew how much it would grow and wondered how she would be able to keep it in this small apartment. *Look at me, I'm already taking ownership.*

By the time Matt came back with the food, Megan knew if they didn't find her owner very soon she had acquired a puppy, no matter how much it grew.

Matt placed a bottle on the table. "I brought some wine."

"I don't drink." Megan reached into the kitchen cupboard for a wineglass.

"Not even wine?"

Should she tell him? Why not? "I'm allergic to alcohol."

"Do you go to meetings?" he asked.

Obviously, Matt knew what she meant. "Yes, as a matter of fact, I do. I still go a couple of nights a week." She poured the wine.

"AA is a great program. One of my ex-partners, Jack Madison, was a member of AA for twenty-five years."

Megan was grateful for Jack Madison. It saved her a whole lot of explaining. "Oh, really? Where is he now?"

"He retired and moved to Oregon." He picked up his glass and carried it to the living room.

She followed with the pizza.

Matt helped her clear off the coffee table to make room for the pizza box, and that's when she saw it—a gold wedding band on his left hand. *What the—?* "Are you still married?" she asked impulsively.

"My wife passed away three years ago. I guess I should take it off." Matt slipped the ring off and put it on his right hand.

"Oh, I'm so sorry." Megan was embarrassed. Why did she always have to open her big fat mouth?

After they'd finished the entire pizza and settled in the living room with coffee, Megan pulled the puppy onto her lap.

It was Matt who brought up the subject of Bonnie-Sue's murder. "How well did you know her, Megan?"

"I saw her around Bayside. I don't know why her mother and father made her go to so many club events. She always looked like she was ready to break and run."

"Yeah, but she had a fine house her grandmother left her in the Hollywood Hills."

"Bonnie-Sue was deep into the Goth scene, and she had dozens of piercings. Her parents were continually trying to change the way she dressed."

"Did you notice any male club members hanging around her?"

"No, in fact it was the exact opposite. Everybody steered clear of her, especially the guys. Most of them knew she was a lit fuse just waiting to go off. Her father is a very powerful man, and nobody wanted to be compromised by Bonnie-Sue's promiscuous behavior." Megan leaned back, and the puppy snuggled deeper in her arms. "I feel so sorry for her mother. When are these killings going to stop, Matt?"

He shook his head, a pained expression on his face.

After a moment's silence, he spoke. "I hate to say this, but I believe all the murders have a direct connection to the yacht club. I find it real hard to believe Bonnie-Sue's death was a coincidence, or that she accidentally picked up the same nut through her ads or off the Internet."

Megan looked at him, aghast. She had to ask, "Is Brian a suspect?"

"No, not yet, but we would like to know where he was the night of Sherrie's murder. He said he was on his boat. Is that true?"

"I can't answer that. He told me he spent the night there. But I don't know for sure."

"What about the night of Allison's murder? Can you remember that far back?"

"I'll never forget it." That's one thing Megan was definite about. "I was terrified when Gino Rosario announced it on the late news. Brian was gone that night."

Matt sat up. "All night?"

"But he often stayed on his boat. So that doesn't prove anything. Does it?"

"Unfortunately, no it doesn't." He sounded bone weary. "We'd need some physical proof or a witness to place him on the scene at the time of the murder."

"Matt?"

"Yes?"

"I don't want to get him in any more trouble, but I think Brian was stalking me last night."

Matt sat at attention. "What happened?"

Megan told him how Brian had rammed her car in the parking lot and then followed her to the club.

"I'll speak to him." His face was grim.

"There's something else."

"What?"

"It happened tonight, at Helen's house. I had a showing, but the house was dark when I got there, and the alarm was off. But Helen's a bit of a dingbat so I didn't think much of it at first." Nervously, she squeezed her elbows. "Anyway, I heard this noise, and I realized someone must be in the house. I grabbed the poker from the living room and some vodka from the bar."

"Vodka?" he asked, disbelievingly.

"A bottle of vodka? You know, to protect myself?"

Matt nodded. He got the picture.

"I went back into the hallway, and suddenly this figure came at me, all dressed in black leather—and a black mask."

"Did he say anything?"

"No. He knocked me down and ran out the front door. It all happened so fast."

"Did you report it to the police?"

"I'd already rung the alarm. The police came." Megan began to shiver. Was she having a delayed reaction?

As the puppy slipped from her grip, Matt pulled her to his chest and held her there for the longest time. "You've had a rough coupla days, haven't you, Megan?"

She felt so safe nestled in his arms. She wanted to stay there forever. For a moment Megan began to cry but immediately swiped the tears away with her sleeve. She wasn't the "damsel in distress" type, and she had a lot more to tell. "There's one more thing, Matt. It's about Kathleen Rosario." Hating to leave the comfort of his arms, Megan pulled away so she could see his face. "She found a photograph of Gino with two women. It was taken on George Fisher's boat, the *Happy Hooker*."

"Were they the murder victims?"

"I think one of them was that Sherrie person."

"Where are the pictures now?"

"Alex burned them. She thought it would be best for Kathleen."

Matt looked disgusted. "Too bad." That would have been physical proof.

She might as well tell all. "And I heard the guys talking about a divorce party."

"Brian Mason already told us about it. Sherrie and Cindy, the woman who was murdered in San Francisco, were the live entertainment. Several other members of BYC were there. We're acquiring more new suspects every day. We haven't spoken to all of 'em, but we will. I expect to see Gino Rosario tomorrow." Leaning back into the couch, he smiled. "But thanks for telling me."

Live entertainment? So that's what those bastards were up to. Gino's divorce was just another excuse for a sex party. How could they? Now she didn't feel so badly about the boytoy.

And then she told him the rest. "And there's Rachel."

"Rachel Feinman?"

"Yes."

"Go on."

"Wednesday night I went to her house to see if she was all right. It was late, but she'd been acting strangely at George's funeral, and I was worried. Anyway, when I arrived, she was taking off in her car." Megan went on to explain how she had followed Rachel to the address on Pacific Coast Highway.

Matt snapped to attention. "You mean the House of Destiny?"

She nodded. "I had the idea she might be looking for her husband, David. You see, last week she caught him in bed with another woman."

"I met his girlfriend, Sonja."

Seconds passed. *Go on, Megan, tell him the truth.* "I went there myself the next night."

"I thought I saw you. But I didn't want to believe it was you." He couldn't wait for her explanation.

"I just had to know what was going on up there. I was worried about Rachel. Maybe she was trying to find David. I don't know what she would have done if she'd caught him a second time." She paused. "Pretty stupid, huh?"

"Stupid is right." Matt took her hand. "Is there anything else you should be telling me?"

"I found Destiny La Conte's phone number in Brian's address book."

"We know that. According to Brian, he went up there once with a couple of the guys."

Megan heaved a sigh of relief. It felt good to get everything out in the open, everything except the boytoy stuff. She wasn't about to go into that. "Matt, I'm really glad you're on this case. I just know you're going to solve it."

"I'm trying, Megan, I'm trying." He looked terribly distressed. "They were all so young, about the same age as my daughter, Julie."

"How old is she?"

"Nineteen. Julie's a model, lives in New York. Scares me, you know?" Matt's smile was weak.

"Do you have a picture?" she asked.

"Yes, I do." He pulled out his wallet and handed it to her.

"She's beautiful, Matt." Megan studied the picture of father and daughter, saw the love in their eyes for each other.

She gave him back the wallet. "You must be very proud."

Grinning from ear to ear, he put it back in his pocket.

*Oh, my, he is so cute, and look at those eyes.*

*Come on, girl, it's only a date.* But Megan couldn't remember when she'd felt happier with someone, and it was only the first date.

But she had to be on guard. Cops got an awful lot of bad press when it came to relationships. The rotten little voice was at it again.

But this time Megan knew things would be different.

When he left, Matt did not try to kiss her; instead he took her hand in his and gently squeezed. "I'd love to do this again, Megan. But in any case, I'll have to come back for the dog when we find the owners."

Clinging to the dog, she kissed him lightly on the cheek. "I had a really nice time, Matt. I'm glad we didn't go out for dinner, and now I've got an extra bonus."

He took the dog in his arms and ruffled his head before handing him back.

"May I call you again?" he asked.

"Of course, Matt, I would love it."

When she closed the door, she was smiling.

## CHAPTER 27

Early Friday morning on the ride to the Hollywood precinct with Angelle, Matt could think of nothing but Megan Riley. He tried to process his feelings. There was something extraordinary about her, but he couldn't define it. He only knew that last night was the most pleasant evening he'd spent with anyone since Constance had died.

Megan had made him feel so comfortable.

And he loved her honesty. He loved how she came right out about her drinking problem like she did. That couldn't have been easy.

And the way she'd taken to the puppy.

"What are you smiling at?" Angelle asked, breaking into his thoughts.

"Huh?" He'd almost forgotten she was there. "Oh, just thinking."

She continued to tease him. "Well, it must be something nice. You've been grinning for the last ten minutes."

They lapsed into a comfortable silence until Angelle spoke again. "Matt, have you read Joe's report on Michael Harrington? He put it on your desk this morning."

He shook his head. "No, I haven't, not yet."

She coughed, clearing her throat. "Apparently, Megan Riley showed up yesterday afternoon."

Amidst the loud blaring of horns, he slowed down the car and pulled over. "Are you serious? Megan Riley was on Michael's sailboat?"

"He tried calling you last night but you weren't home, so he figured it could wait until this morning. Anyway, she wasn't by herself; she was with Kathleen Rosario. They had a drink and then went for a short cruise. They were back in a little over an hour."

*Damn.* Just when he was beginning to trust Megan. Why hadn't she told him? She'd spilled everything else.

And what the hell was going on with this Harrington dude? First, he met up with Rachel Feinman, now Kathleen Rosario and Megan. How did these women get involved with this asshole?

Maybe Michael was a drug dealer—or a friggin' gigolo. Now he was again having second thoughts about getting involved with Megan. He knew there would be serious career consequences if he were to get caught.

But it was too late; he'd already made his choice.

Matt focused again on Angelle. She looked troubled. He wondered if she suspected he was interested in Megan. *Better wait and see.*

They had a second date planned tonight, and he would ask her about Michael Harrington. Until then, he would give her the benefit of the doubt.

"There is one more thing, Matt."

"What?"

"After the two women left, Michael took off on his motorcycle." Angelle looked really uncomfortable.

Matt waited.

"He rode down Abbot Kinney Boulevard toward Santa Monica, and you know how heavy traffic is around dinner time? Well, I lost him."

Matt slammed the car into gear and started back down Santa Monica Boulevard. Michael could have been the intruder at Helen's house. But he had no idea how he could prove it.

"I'm really sorry, Matt."

"It's not your fault. These things happen." *I only wish Megan hadn't been there.*

Matt was relieved when they arrived at the Hollywood station.

Checking his watch, Matt followed Angelle into the briefing room at Hollywood Division.

It was eight in the morning.

A long blackboard ran the full length of one wall. Dan Coleman sat directly in front of it, on one of the small combination desk-chairs, sifting through a file.

"Hey, let me get you guys some coffee." Dan stood up and called out the order to one of the blues outside the door.

Minutes later, Matt sipped his coffee in silence. Angelle made small talk with Dan Coleman.

An intercom buzzed. The FBI agent was announced.

Dressed in a charcoal pin-striped suit and carrying a sleek briefcase, the agent entered the room. "Agent Kotowski here." He shook hands, first with Dan and then with Matt. He turned to Angelle and nodded politely.

"Detective Bentley."

To Matt, the guy looked like a damn stockbroker.

The intercom buzzed again. This time it was Senator Harley Rattner, trailed by a diminutive man in a navy blue-and-white checkered suit, made more ludicrous by red lizard cowboy boots.

"Shit," Matt groaned. "Who invited him?" Even though the senator appeared to have much more control over his emotions, he felt awkward discussing the specifics of such a horrific crime in front of a victim's father.

Dan shrugged. "He insisted. And the governor called."

Senator Rattner wore a dark brown suit illuminated by a tie the color of lime jelly. His immensity filled the entire corner of the room. "I'm Harley Rattner, and this is Dr. Edward Napoleon," he bellowed to everyone in general, extending a giant paw. The FBI agent's fingers disappeared entirely into the fleshy confines of the senator's hand. "He came to me highly recommended by the chief of police."

Continuing his introduction, the senator gave the doctor's credentials. "Dr. Napoleon here is a sexologist specializing in sadomasochism, and a doctor of psychiatry. He has also published a book, *Sex and the Criminal Mind*. I thought he might be of help in your investigation."

Matt saw the FBI agent glance quickly at Dan Coleman, but the Hollywood detective wouldn't meet his gaze.

He observed Senator Rattner more closely. Small eyes the color of weak tea were pressed into his lumpy face, like raisins in a doughy bun, and a pug nose sat a little off center above soft, weak lips. He oozed self-confidence, unlike yesterday, when he'd cried like a child in Angelle's arms. Matt knew that grief had many faces, and the stricken father had tried then, and continued to try, to take command of a situation over which he had absolutely no control.

Matt shook Dr. Napoleon's outstretched hand. "Detective Matt Donovan, Venice-Pacific. This is my partner, Detective Angelle Bentley. We have two of the murders in our precinct."

The doctor nodded and took a seat.

Senator Rattner attempted to squeeze himself into the small wooden desk, like trying to put toothpaste back in the tube.

When he was tightly contained, his voice rumbled, "Doctor?"

The doctor stood up and cleared his throat. He appeared to be searching for the right words before speaking. "I'll try to make this as brief as possible. The phenomenon of sadomasochism was first addressed in the 1880s by a neuropsychiatrist named Richard von Krafft-Ebing in his book *Psychopathia Sexualis*. You undoubtedly know the word 'sadist' was taken from the name of the infamous Marquis de Sade. De Sade was a novelist whose writings equate pain, dominance, and cruelty with sexual pleasure. I'm quite sure you've all heard of his books? *Justine* and *Juliette* are the most famous."

Justine? Of course, Justine was the password for the House of Destiny. And Justine was the name of the woman dragged out in chains. Very creative.

Dr. Napoleon continued. "Not commonly known, the word 'masochism' was derived from another nineteenth-century novelist, Leopold von Sacher-Masoch. His book *Venus in Furs* reveals a sexual preoccupation with pain, submission, and humiliation. There is another term for these conditions, algolagnia. *Webster's Dictionary* defines algolagnia as pleasure in inflicting or suffering pain. This would indicate, as some psychiatrists believe, that the phenomena are two sides of the same coin."

"Why the hell would someone, like my daughter, turn to this crap?" Senator Rattner asked. He seemed perplexed.

The good doctor shook his head. "I don't know the answer to that, sir. Not yet. I do know that since the advent of the AIDS crisis, more and more people are engaging in this type of sexual activity. They see bondage and dominance as a way to achieve high levels of sexual satisfaction without the exchange of body fluids. As you know, more and more leather bars are being opened in big cities, like New York, Los Angeles, and Chicago, and the S&M parlors are flourishing as never before."

"And not just in the homosexual arena," Matt said, recalling the House of Destiny.

"That's right. There's a large subculture, very much underground, of S&M, B&D, whatever you choose to call it, in the heterosexual community, mostly practiced at private clubs and secret sex parties. But private assignations are often arranged through the use of personal ads in the papers your daughter subscribed to, not to mention the thousands of chat lines and websites now available on the Internet."

The senator remained silent, but Matt could see it was an effort.

"Look"—Dan Coleman shifted in his chair—"this is all very interesting, but we really need to get on to something that can lead us to the killer."

"It's important to note," the doctor continued, ignoring Dan's outburst, "the average devotee of S&M deals only in fantasy. Your killer obviously went over the edge from fantasy to reality and now obtains his sexual release from the actual death of his victims. Whether he has an agenda, other than the sexual sadism, we do not know."

"Why do you think he removes the right breast?" The question came from Angelle.

Agent Kotowski took the floor. "Serial killers of this type often display inexplicable behavior when it comes to mutilation of the bodies."

"Could they be ritual killings?" Angelle asked.

"You mean a cult?"

She nodded.

"Unlikely, but anything is possible. I can only go by what we've learned from past serial killers." The agent removed the files from his briefcase. "I agree with everything Dr. Napoleon said. And Detective Bentley may be right. It could be a ritual killing. But as an investigator of sexual crimes, I look at the matter from a different perspective. Officers in our Behavioral Science Unit have interviewed many sexual murderers who kill for pleasure. As a result, we've come to certain conclusions that assist us in producing criminal profiles of this type of killer. I will attempt to inform you, as coherently as possible, how we reach our conclusions. Victim risk in all your cases is extremely high. Three victims were prostitutes." Agent Kotowski paused. "The fourth openly advertised in pornographic newspapers for sadomasochistic sexual partners."

"Now just a minute," Senator Rattner objected.

"Sir, please. I know it's difficult to hear these things about your daughter, and you have tried very hard to erase all of what you regard as the stigma of S&M surrounding her death. But if you intend to remain in this conference, please, no further interruptions." Agent Kotowski was firm. "Offender risk is remarkably low, which would indicate the killer is highly intelligent and probably well educated. He is extremely selective of his victims and will more than likely continue in his killing mode unless in danger of being caught. If that becomes a viable possibility, your killer could turn into a mass murderer. He might place himself in the position of being shot by police, in which case he would take with him any bystanders. Or, at some time in the future, he could simply discontinue his present behavior and we may never find him." He added as an afterthought, "The last scenario is highly unlikely. I'd say he's escalating, rapidly, judging from the condition of Miss Rattner's body."

Senator Rattner grimaced.

Matt asked, "Is it possible he knew all the victims before he killed them?"

"Yes, I think he fantasized for a long time before the perpetration of the first crime. Take the time factors in each case. According to pathology reports, he spent approximately four to six hours with each of the women and removed the right breast postmortem. This would indicate he researched his victims and crime locations well. Evidently, the killer knew he had all the time in the world to carry out his fantasies, finish up with the mutilation of the bodies, and still have time to shower and clean the place up before he left." Kotowski added as an afterthought, "Of course, we don't know the exact location of the crime scene in San Francisco."

"This animal operates with premeditation and skill," Dan growled.

Angelle leaned toward the FBI agent. "Why do you think he removed Allison's body from the house?"

"It's my guess the killer believed he could be traced in some way. Or he could have had an accomplice who helped him dump the body on the beach."

"Ray Jennings could have been his accomplice," Matt said. "Maybe that's why he was hit-and-run in San Francisco. He knew too much."

"Entirely possible," said Kotowski. "This guy is extremely organized. And, according to our theory, the organized killer plans his murders, targets his victims, and strives to gain complete control over them. When they're at his mercy, he proceeds to act out his fantasies of sexual torture, dismemberment, and mutilation. Often he has his own ritualistic oddity—in this case, the removal of the right breast."

"But what has any of this got to do with my daughter?" The senator appeared impatient.

Matt glanced at him sideways. "Are you a member of the Bayside Yacht Club?"

"Why yes, I am."

"That may be the connection," Matt said, emphatically.

"The common denominators are the MO, the pornographic literature—and the Bayside Yacht Club," Angelle added.

The agent nodded his agreement.

Angelle fiddled with the inkwell on the desk. "Agent Kotowski?"

"Yes?"

"Could such a man be living a normal life? You know, have a family, a job, and a prominent place in the community?"

"Yes, it's quite possible he has a wife and/or a girlfriend, and he's probably in the middle-to-upper income bracket. Very often this type of killer lives a double life. His personal life would be completely at odds with his criminal behavior."

"But what makes a person so perverted?" Angelle asked.

Dr. Napoleon answered her question. "Sadomasochistic behavior usually begins at an early age. I once treated a young man—I'll call him Rory. He was punished by his father in various diabolical ways. For instance, if he was caught masturbating, his father locked him in the closet for days on end. Over time, Rory associated the pleasures of sex with being locked in the closet. As an adult, the only way he could attain sexual release was to spend time in the closet, masturbating."

The doctor continued. "One young woman was sexually abused and verbally debased by her alcoholic father. She learned to attach pleasure to humiliation. As a result, she was sexually addicted to masochism by the age of fifteen."

You could hear a pin drop in the room.

Kotowski broke the silence and brought them back to the Bondage Murderer. "Most serial killers have at least two of three problems as a child: bed-wetting, fire-setting, or acts of torture and mutilation of small animals."

"Sir," Angelle hesitated, "could the killer be a woman?"

Kotowski shrugged his shoulders. "It's highly unlikely, but possible."

"What kind of weapon do you think he used to mutilate the bodies?" Dan Coleman asked.

Agent Kotowski answered. "The ME said it could be a filleting knife?"

"Filleting knife? Like a fisherman's knife." Matt pondered for a moment. "The rope binding Sherrie Weston to the bed was nautical line, and we've got a whole yacht club of suspects. I'm up for questioning every member of Bayside."

"But, as of now, you don't have proof to charge anyone, let alone convict them," Agent Kotowski said. "You have nothing, except the pubic hairs in the bathtub at the house on Beachview, and you can't be sure if they belong to our killer. I'm thinking you'll need a witness to put this killer at the scene."

"Or we'll have to wait until he or she does it again." Angelle emphasized the "she."

The FBI agent nodded his agreement.

"Stan, what makes you think the killer is in a middle-to-high income bracket?" Dan asked the agent.

"Several reasons: Miss Rattner's wallet, checkbook, plus a lot of jewelry and cash were left in a drawer of the dresser. Nothing was missing from Sherrie Weston's house, except maybe her address book." The agent paused. "And the killer probably drives a decent car, or it would have drawn attention in Miss Rattner's upscale neighborhood."

Dan Coleman agreed. "True. I spoke to neighborhood security in Bonnie-Sue's area. There were no suspicious-looking automobiles on or around Balmoral Avenue on the night of the murder. We checked out any surveillance tapes that were available. Nothing suspicious."

Matt rubbed his forehead. "What about his age?"

"I'd guess somewhere late thirties to late forties, give or take a couple of years." Agent Kotowski was silent for a moment. "Let's put it together. The perpetrator is probably a male. He may or may not be working alone. More than likely he was physically and sexually abused as a child. He is well educated, organized, married, and/or has a girlfriend. He reads S&M magazines and works the porno ads. He likes bondage sex, wears a condom and gloves, so he leaves no semen or prints. On the other hand, he could have a medical problem, which would explain the lack of semen. He may be associated with boating because of the filleting knife and the nautical line he used to bind Sherrie. He could be a yachtsman, a sailor, a commercial fisherman, a butcher."

"I'd say that narrows it down to about 20 percent of the California population," Matt said gloomily.

Then he thought about Megan's confrontation with the intruder at Helen's house, the intruder who wore black leather. There had to be a connection to the Bondage Murders. Did Mrs. Jennings have something the killer wanted? He decided to pay Helen another visit.

Dr. Napoleon offered a suggestion. "Why don't we ask the press to make a plea for the murderer to come in? Tell him he'll get the psychiatric help he so desperately needs?"

Senator Rattner glowered at the doctor. "Is that all you can come up with for the five grand I paid you to come here?"

"The procedure has worked on many occasions," Kotowski said crisply. "But I'm not sure it will in this case, at least not at this stage."

"I agree," Dan interjected. "We're in the process of putting out warnings to all the advertisers in the various bondage rags. We're checking the S&M bars and the bondage parlors. Sooner or later we'll come up with something. I don't think it's the right time to plead with him to come in. For one thing, I don't wanna see this asshole cop an insanity plea and end up in a sanitarium waiting for some jerk-off psychiatrist to let him out. No offense, Dr. Napoleon, but I've seen it happen too many fuckin'—I mean damn—times."

"He's absolutely right," the senator wheezed. "We'll go along with Detective Coleman's recommendations for the time being." Then he dropped the bombshell. "I'm putting up a $200,000 reward for any information leading to the arrest of my daughter's killer."

*Dammit*, Matt thought. That'll bring the crackpots out in full force. He began to speak but felt a gentle pressure on his arm and knew it was Angelle telling him to cool it. He stood up to leave. "Dan, I'll call you later. Tom's putting a rush on the autopsy report."

"Right you are, Matt."

Matt turned to the FBI agent. "Agent Kotowski, I'd like to fax you some names, members of Bayside. Would you check on their military records?"

"Sure thing." The agent took a gold case out of his pocket and handed Matt a card. "Here, this has all my numbers."

Matt and Angelle said their good-byes and left the room. Outside the station the members of the press were clamoring and running alongside them with cameras and microphones.

Marcia Waters led the pack. "Detective Donovan, Detective Donovan," she hollered. "Do you think this is another Bondage Murder? Is the deceased really Senator Rattner's daughter?"

How the hell did Marcia Waters know they were meeting here? These reporters were uncanny when it came to a good story. "Sorry, Marcia, please let us pass." Matt took hold of Angelle's arm and pushed their way through the gaggle of reporters, bypassing microphones, cameras, and hungry faces.

Marcia did not give up easily. "Detective Bentley, could these be ritual murders? Maybe a cult?"

*Damn, she knows about Angelle's background in Florida.* "Sorry, no comment. Please, let us through. Thank you. Sorry."

By the time Matt climbed into his car, he felt as if he'd passed through a feeding frenzy of killer sharks. "Can you believe it?"

"Wait till they hear about the $200,000 reward," Angelle remarked. "It's going to be a circus."

# Chapter 28

Joe's investigation of the help at Bayside had come up clean, except for a parking lot attendant, a dockhand, and one of the dining room waiters. He was presently at the club interviewing each one. But their best suspect was still Michael Harrington.

So once again, Matt Donovan was on surveillance at Michael's marina. He relaxed in the green 1982 Ford he'd commandeered from the police motor pool. Eyes half-shut, he was listening to soft rock on the radio when an old blue Volkswagen pulled into the parking lot.

A thin blonde Matt immediately recognized as Mrs. Alex Grant exited the old car, which probably belonged to her maid.

He wasn't a bit surprised when she strolled down the deck to Michael's boat. He did think she looked pretty ridiculous climbing out of the beat-up Volkswagen, wearing fancy designer clothes, alligator loafers, and carrying a matching bag. But he had to admit she was classy-looking. A little skinny for his taste, but cute all the same.

By now, nothing shocked Matt; he was just glad it wasn't Megan. He'd already figured Michael had a different woman for every day of the week. Who knew, it might be every day of the month. He just hadn't been tailing him long enough to find out.

Michael had been up to his ass in varnish all morning, so he knew they weren't going anywhere on the boat. And since neither of them looked like they were up for hitting the sack, Matt didn't even get out of the car.

When he finally did and stood at the fence near the entry gate of the dock, Matt couldn't believe his eyes. He would never have pegged Alex Grant as a worker, but there she was, rubbing away at the teak rails with a hunk of sandpaper, wearing what were obviously somebody else's cutoff jeans and T-shirt.

Fascinated, Matt watched her sweat for nearly an hour, every now and then wiping her brow with the edge of a dirty, ragged towel. He'd sure as hell like to know Harrington's secret. He must be a friggin' Houdini, with the magic he performed on women.

Matt checked his watch: eleven twenty. They were doing an awful lot of laughing and giggling down there. *Uh-oh, looks like they're breaking for lunch. Or* maybe Michael was taking her below for a little fun and games. Maybe all that varnishing shit was some kind of weird, yuppie foreplay.

But young Harrington's behavior was without reproach as he walked Mrs. Grant to her car and gave her a chaste kiss on the lips.

Matt jotted down the license plate. He wanted to know who owned the car.

A half an hour later, Joe arrived to take over.

He spent time with Joe, going over the results of his interviews with the three employees at Bayside who had records. Joe felt satisfied they had alibis for the crimes, and he no longer considered them as suspects. So that brought him back to Michael and the four members of Bayside: Brian, David, Gino, and Charles. And all they had from these guys was contemptible behavior, cheating on their wives, and hiring hookers. It remained to be seen what else would come up.

Later that day, Matt met up with Angelle and was back in the parking lot at the marina, carrying a cardboard container holding three cups of Starbucks coffee.

Joe was hunched over in the front seat of a battered white Caddy, devouring a messy burrito. "You're not gonna believe this," he said, his mouth bleeding red sauce. "Dude's got the second shift down there."

"Waddya mean the second shift?" Matt asked.

Joe wiped his face with a napkin. "Yeah, he had that blonde you told me about this mornin'. Then right after you left, this redhead shows. I think this one's really got the hots for him." He stuffed the rest of the burrito into his mouth.

Angelle laughed and shook her head. "Our Michael is undoubtedly a gigolo."

Matt was not amused. Opening the back door of the Cadillac, he gestured to Angelle to enter. He handed her the coffee and then joined her in the backseat.

Withdrawing a sheaf of papers from his inside pocket, he offered them to Joe. "It's Bonnie-Sue Rattner's autopsy. No surprises. Death occurred late Tuesday night, about the same time frame as the others. It's the same MO." The fact that all three murders had taken place on Tuesday nights had not escaped him, and he was very interested in what Joe had to say.

"I hope one of those is for me," Joe said, pointing at the coffee.

Smiling, Angelle handed him the tallest paper cup. "One latte coming up for Joe. I had it made to order." She took one for herself and proceeded to pour five small bags of sugar into it.

"Shit, will you stop it with the sugar, Angelle? It's not good for you." Joe opened the little flap on his own cup. "Why do you eat so much damn sugar?"

"That's what makes me so sweet, Joey." Angelle gave him her phony grin.

Ignoring their bickering, Matt continued to discuss the autopsy. "Bonnie-Sue Rattner died between approximately eleven o'clock on Tuesday night and ten o'clock Wednesday morning."

Joe snickered. "Maybe it's the killer's weekly night out with the boys, and instead of goin' to the bowling alley he goes lookin' for a hooker and does a little bondage." He took a sip of his coffee.

Rubbing the frown lines between his brows with his right index finger, Matt tried to maintain his cool. After working eleven days in a row, his head was throbbing, and he felt like blasting Joe right out of the goddamn car.

Angelle spoke up. "Does this clear Michael Harrington?"

"Not necessarily." Joe took a big slurp.

"Why not?"

"Number one, we didn't start tailin' him till Wednesday, and the senator's kid was murdered on Tuesday night." Joe gave her a nasty grin. "Number two, I'll give ya odds the asshole was schtuppin' her. He's screwin' everythin' else in sight. An' number three, I bet he don't have no friggin' alibi. He still don't have one for Frisco."

"Look, Joe. Once and for all, Harrington had nothing to do with the San Francisco murders." Wearily, Angelle replaced her coffee cup in the box and began counting on her fingers. "The airlines have no record of him flying to San Francisco. His school's records say he was present at all his classes during the entire month of April. And, since he doesn't have a car, he would have to drive four hundred miles, after school, on his motorcycle, rent a car, kill Cindy, and drop off her body in the empty lot." She took a deep breath. "Hit-and-run Ray Jennings, take the car back to the rental company, with no bloodstains on it, drive all the way back to Los Angeles, and still show up for his ten o'clock class the next morning. Give me a break."

"But suppose Ray Jennings really was an accident." Joe was like a dog with a bone. "The killer wouldn't have to be in San Francisco that long to kill Cindy."

"You're really pushing it, Joe." Angelle sounded very ticked off. "What happened to the idea of a kinky couple?"

"That was before all this other shit came down."

"Maybe it's a woman," she teased, retrieving her coffee.

"Yeah, in your dreams."

"Enough, enough," Matt snapped. "It's time to get serious about Michael Harrington, check his whereabouts at the time of Bonnie-Sue's death." And, speaking almost to himself, "We've got to find out why he's shacking up with all these women." He flung the car door open and got out.

As Angelle exited the car, Matt leaned in the window toward Joe. "You stay here and keep tailing Michael until Angelle gets back to relieve you. We're going down there right now to find out what the hell is going on. And after we're done with Michael, we're going to look up Gino Rosario. Then we're going to find that flake Brian Mason again."

Walking down the dock, Matt had a clear view of the sailboat rocking gently in the afternoon breeze. Michael was reclined on the white leather seat behind the steering wheel, his arm around a beautiful redhead.

Deeply involved in a catalog spread across their laps, neither Michael nor the redhead saw them approach.

Matt knocked on the side of the hull.

Looking up, Michael smiled. "Hello, Detective Donovan. Back again?"

He was a little too cheery for Matt's taste. "I'm afraid so, Mr. Harrington."

After handing the catalog to Kathleen, Michael stood up. "This is Mrs. Rosario."

Kathleen nodded.

"Yes," said Matt. "We've met."

"Nice to see you again," she said, tugging at the hem of her yellow sundress.

Matt went straight to the point. "Does the name Bonnie-Sue Rattner mean anything to you, Mr. Harrington?"

The catalog slipped from Kathleen's fingers, and she leaned over to pick it up.

"Nope, never heard of her," Michael answered.

"What about a girl named Darkness?"

Michael laughed and sat down. "Darkness? Are you kidding?"

"She's dead."

Obviously, Michael Harrington hadn't seen the news on TV yet.

Matt was surprised, because their attempts at keeping the murder under wraps had totally failed. Marcia Waters had even announced the S&M connection to Bonnie-Sue's death.

"How about you, Mrs. Rosario?" Matt asked softly. "Did you know Bonnie-Sue Rattner?"

"Yes, I do from the club." Kathleen's hands were shaking in her lap, and her eyes welled with tears. "Are you saying Bonnie-Sue is dead?"

Michael put his arm around her shoulder to comfort her.

Angelle posed the next question. "Where were you on Tuesday evening, Mr. Harrington?"

"You're not going to believe this." He shook his head.

"Don't tell me." Matt quipped. "You were alone?"

Michael gave him a defensive look. "Well, I'm alone a lot."

Kathleen jumped in. "He was with me."

Even Michael looked surprised, but he didn't deny Kathleen's statement. He just held her more tightly.

"All night?" Matt asked sharply.

Kathleen nodded.

"Would you swear to that, Mrs. Rosario?"

The redhead's little button nose jutted up. "Why wouldn't I? It's the truth."

Matt gave him another chance. "Mr. Harrington?"

He didn't bat an eye, just fiddled with the collar of his Hawaiian shirt. "Yes, Kathleen was with me, helping me study."

"Well, I guess that's it then." Matt was about to leave, but instead he turned to Kathleen and looked directly into her eyes. "You wouldn't perjure yourself, would you, Mrs. Rosario?"

Kathleen stared back at him defiantly. "No."

It was obvious the woman was infatuated with Harrington, from the way she nestled in his arm. Matt was equally certain she hadn't been with Michael the night of Bonnie-Sue's murder. The lovely redhead was trying to protect her boyfriend by providing him with an alibi. "Are you still married to Gino Rosario?" Matt asked.

"I'm divorced." She lowered her lashes.

Angelle posed the question. "What exactly is your relationship to Mr. Harrington?"

"I ... er ... we're dating."

Kathleen's hesitant answer was too much for Matt. "What the hell is going on here? Don't you think the two of you had better tell us the truth?"

"I don't know what you mean, Detective Donovan. I've told you everything I know." Michael removed his arm from Kathleen's shoulder.

Matt glared at him.

"Now," Michael said, standing up again, "unless there's anything else, I'd like to continue selecting my fall classes."

"There is one more thing," Angelle said. "Where did you go after Mrs. Rosario and Ms. Riley left your boat yesterday afternoon?"

Even Kathleen stared at Michael questioningly.

Harrington looked surprised, but his answer was prompt. "I went to pick up a pizza."

"All the way to Santa Monica?" Angelle asked.

"Yes, I go to this place on Main Street." He looked from Angelle to Matt and back to Kathleen. "I like their pizza. Is that a crime?"

"No." Matt shook his head. "But breaking into Helen Jennings's house is a crime. And I have the feeling that's where you were."

"What the hell are you talking about?" Michael went on the offense. "Why would I break into Helen Jennings's house when all I have to do is ask her and she'd invite me in?"

"Is Mrs. Jennings another one of your girlfriends?" Matt asked sarcastically.

"No, but she is a client of Party Favorites." Michael turned to Kathleen. "In fact, that's where I first saw Kathleen, at Mrs. Jennings's house."

"You've got a regular stable, don't you, my friend?" With that, Matt stormed off the boat, stopping only to help Angelle over the side. "You'll be hearing from me again. Soon."

Deep into his own thoughts, Matt hurried down the dock.

*Dammit.* Something very strange was going on with Michael Harrington, and he couldn't figure it out. Hell, he couldn't even ask Kathleen about those compromising pictures of her ex-husband and the two prostitutes. Not without breaking Megan's confidence.

† † †

When Matt and Angelle finally got to Bayside Yacht Club, Brian Mason's sailboat, *Dreamer*, was no longer tied to the dock.

According to his next-door neighbor, Mason had left for Catalina and would not return until Sunday or Monday. Since this was the club weekend in Catalina, many of the members had already headed to the island, located about thirty miles off the coast.

This information got Matt to thinking. Hadn't Megan told him she was going to Catalina this weekend with the Grants?

Did it bother him that Brian Mason was going to be there, too? Damn right it did. But he'd have to deal with it later.

Angelle asked for directions to Gino Rosario's boat. But it took ten minutes of wandering through a maze of expensive yachts before they finally found it.

Gino's long, sleek racing craft had the name *Sexcess* emblazoned in crimson letters on the side. A streak of mottled gold surrounded the whole boat. Shiny chrome fixtures were polished to the max. *It takes a massive engine to move this mother,* thought Matt. He figured a hundred grand would be lowballing it.

A dark-haired man could be seen working in the inner cabin.

Matt called to him from dockside. "Mr. Rosario? Can we speak to you for a moment?"

"Of course." Gino flashed his million-dollar smile, just like on the eleven o'clock news. A pregnant woman, about twenty-three years old, followed him from the cabin to the afterdeck.

*Some looker,* thought Matt, *but barely out of her teens. Old Gino must really like 'em young.* He pulled out his badge. "Detective Donovan, could we speak to you in private?"

"You can say anything you like in front of Jennifer," Gino bragged. "We're going to have a baby, Jennifer and I." He patted the steering wheel of the boat. "And this is my other baby. Forty-one-foot scarab, *Thunder*. High-performance engines. I bet I'll get this little hot rod up to seventy miles an hour when we cross the open sea to the Island."

"Yeah, nice boat," Matt said unenthusiastically. After only two minutes in his presence, he loathed Gino Rosario and couldn't help wondering how Jennifer and her unborn child would fare, rattling all the way to Catalina at seventy miles an hour. "We'd like to speak to you about Sherrie Weston and Cindy Smith."

Gino couldn't get away from his girlfriend fast enough. He walked them down the dock. "It might be better if we didn't upset Jennifer."

"How well did you know the two girls, sir?" Matt asked.

"Hardly at all. The guys gave me this surprise party, and you know how it is." Gino kept winking at him.

"Is there something in your eye, Mr. Rosario?" Angelle asked innocently.

"Look, I don't want any trouble. George hired those two women, and I got so drunk I didn't know what the hell I was doing. Somebody snapped those pictures, and I hid them in my golf bag and forgot all about them until I heard about Sherrie Weston's murder." He scowled. "Kathleen gave you the pictures, didn't she? The bitch."

"Kathleen?"

"Yeah, my goddamn ex-wife."

"Does Mrs. Rosario have pictures? We didn't know there were any pictures—until you just told us." Matt rubbed it in. "Mr. Mason told us about your 'divorce party,' and we're interviewing everyone who was there."

"Did you have any contact with either of those women before or after the party?" Angelle asked.

"No."

"You realize they're both dead," Angelle said.

No response from Gino, but he turned kind of gray-looking. Matt pushed him even further. "Have you ever used the house at 42 Beachview Avenue for assignations?"

"A couple of times." His voice was sullen. "But only with Jennifer."

"Are you aware there was a movie camera hidden in the closet?"

"You're kidding." Gino's eyes widened and, looking even more scared, he nervously slicked back his hair with an open palm.

"Mr. Rosario?" Matt asked. "Have you ever participated in any sadomasochistic activities?"

"Absolutely not." Gino shook his head vigorously. "S&M is definitely not my bag."

"Do you know if any of your friends are so inclined?"

"I don't go around asking people about their sex lives." He looked back at his pregnant girlfriend. "Look, will there be anything else? I don't want Jennifer to get worried."

"Ever been to the House of Destiny?"

Gino's face shut down. When he answered, his voice was flat. "Once, with David Feinman and Ray Jennings."

"Are you sure you didn't go there with Allison Graham?"

"I'm sure. Can I go now?"

"One more thing." Matt wouldn't let up. "How well did you know Bonnie-Sue Rattner?"

A look of panic crossed his face. "Hey, I had nothing to do with that crazy bitch. Not that she didn't try. She was always hitting on somebody. Why don't you speak to Brian Mason? Last time I heard, he was Bonnie-Sue's flavor of the week."

*Brian Mason, huh?* Matt let it pass.

"How did her parents react to this behavior?" Angelle asked.

"It was like Harley had blinders on. And her mother was worse. She was always trying to get her to dress differently, as if that was the only problem. If you ask me, the girl was a stoned nymphomaniac." Gino glanced back at Jennifer, who was standing on the deck, a concerned look on her pretty face. "Look, I've told you everything I know. Can I go?"

"Yes, go." The guy was a fucking creep, Matt decided, as he watched Gino scurry back to his boat.

"Waddya think, Angel?" he asked, walking up the dock.

"He's covering his ... you know what." Then, climbing into the car beside him, Angelle added, "I've got a plan."

That's when his cell phone rang. It was Dan Coleman from Hollywood Division. Matt talked for several minutes.

"So?" she asked when he hung up.

"There's nothing new on that end. No prints. The bathroom was scoured, nothing in the drains. Dan checked with the smut papers, and he was right. The personal ad departments forward the responses to the paying client, who then decides which ones to answer. Also, somebody leaked Bonnie-Sue's sexual preferences, and the press knows. So get ready for more flack."

Looking pained, Angelle nodded. "I already heard it on the news. Poor Bonnie-Sue sure picked herself a nutcase."

"Yeah, this one's a mail-order Mr. Friggin' Goodbar. I'm meeting with Dan on Saturday night. We're going to hit the leather bars and bondage parlors in Hollywood." Matt checked his watch. "Why don't you go on home, Angel? Spend some time with your kid. But first, I want to hear your plan."

"First thing in the morning, I'm going to cross-reference the personal ads we found in the sex papers at Bonnie-Sue's house with the ones in the magazine at Sherrie's. I'm also going to troll the chat rooms and S&M sites on the Internet. See if anything turns up."

"Good idea, Angel. But I don't want you going anywhere by yourself, you hear?"

"Is that an order, boss?"

"That's an order."

He let Angelle out at her car, which was parked in the lot at Pacific Division next to a row of black-and-whites. She leaned into the window. "We're going to find him, aren't we, Matt?"

"Yeah, we sure the hell are, Angel."

When she left, he picked up the telephone and dialed. "Hi, Megan, Matt here."

She sounded pleased to hear from him. "I really enjoyed last night, Matt."

"How's our puppy?" he asked.

"Great. But he chewed up one of my slippers."

"He did? So I'll buy you some new ones." Matt's face broke into a grin. "Still want to have dinner tonight?"

"I'm looking forward to it."

"Fantastic. I'll be there at eight fifteen." He'd worry about what Megan had been doing with Harrington later, but not now. He was too happy to hear her say yes.

# CHAPTER 29

A FEW MINUTES AFTER Matt rang the bell, Megan opened the door, looking very sexy in a black T-shirt minidress.
*Great legs and that incredibly curvy body.*

Just then, the puppy clawed its way up the legs of Matt's best gray pants, yapping continually. He picked it up and carried it to the living room.

Megan smiled at the dog like a doting mother. So, the puppy hadn't been a bad idea after all, despite the chewed-up slippers.

"Can I get you a glass of wine, Matt?"

"Love it," he said, stroking the dog's silky fur.

"You look done in. Why don't you sit down and put your feet up?" She headed for the kitchen.

"Yes, I guess I am." Still holding the dog, he dropped onto the white settee and stared out the window. Because of the boardwalk lights glaring back at him, Matt couldn't see the waves breaking on the sand, but he could hear them. Funny how he felt so good being with Megan. Maybe he'd finally begun to recover from Constance's death.

After handing him a glass of wine, Megan sat next to him on the couch, nursing her cola. "Do you mind if we stay home? I've been gone all day, and I hate to leave the puppy again. I thought I'd fix a little dinner."

"Dinner? You're really cooking dinner?"

She laughed. "Actually, I'm defrosting dinner, if that's okay?"

"Perfect, makes me feel right at home." Matt grinned and scruffed the little dog's head. "You hear that? We're gonna stay home with you."

"You look awfully tired, Matt. Why don't you lie down? I'll call you when dinner's ready." Megan took the puppy from his arms and turned off the reading lamp beside the couch.

As he watched her disappear into the kitchen, a soft breeze wafted in through the sliding doors, cooling the darkened living room. The soothing sounds of the surf eased his tattered nerves, and he felt a million miles away from the grimy aspects of police work. He kicked off his shoes and lay down on the sofa. Closing his eyes, Matt melted into the soft, downy cushions.

He awoke to the sensation of gentle hands stroking his hair.

"Matt. Wake up. It's time for dinner."

The touch of her cool fingers lingering on his forehead was like balm to his soul. Wanting it to last forever, Matt kept his eyes closed. Softly, gently, she soothed his brow. Her caress was healing, repairing his heart, a heart so brutally crushed the day Constance had died. He wanted to stay there, but something licked his face with a wet, gravelly tongue and kept on licking.

And it definitely wasn't Megan. He could hear her laughing.

*Damn.* It was the dumb dog.

Matt jumped up from the couch, wiping the puppy's saliva off his face. Then he too began to laugh.

A little while later, he stood in the doorway and watched Megan work around the tiny kitchen. While he was napping, she'd changed into an emerald silk robe that brought out the green in her eyes. Her movements were sparse and calculated as she tossed the salad. Two plates of steaming fettuccine topped with broccoli and chicken were already on the table.

Megan smiled and set down the salad bowls. "Julia Child I'm not."

"I'm so hungry anything would taste great."

"Thanks for the vote of confidence."

He grinned. "Sorry."

Dinner was congenial. And as Matt sipped his wine and watched her eat, he relived the precious moments earlier when she'd stroked his forehead.

Megan stood up. "If you are a very good boy and finish everything on your plate, you just might get dessert."

Matt leered at her. "But I like being a bad boy."

"My best dish is yet to come," she promised.

"Oh? And what might that be? Everything I've sampled so far has been pretty damn great."

"Eat."

He did.

While Matt cleared the dishes and fed the leftover chicken to the dog, Megan prepared her famous Chocolate Quick Fix.

She carried the dessert to the living room.

When the last smidgen of ice cream was gone, Matt complimented her on every aspect of the meal. That done, he posed the question he'd wanted to ask all evening. "Megan, what's going on with Michael Harrington?"

"Michael Harrington? Are you sure you want to know?" She looked pretty embarrassed.

But he persisted. "Yes, I do."

Megan squirmed in the chair. "Well, the girls hired this guy—what I mean is, I didn't think we'd find one. But, you know, Rachel got the idea to hire a time-share lover." She mumbled the word "lover." "I didn't actually get in on it."

He couldn't believe what he was hearing. Surely she didn't say what he thought she'd said? "You hired a what?"

"A time-share lover. You know? A boytoy." She tried to laugh it off.

But Matt was not laughing. He was truly pissed and showed it. "Are you out of your friggin' minds? Do you have any idea what kind of dangerous game you're playing?" Maybe he should tell her he suspected that Harrington was the one who broke into Helen's house. "The son of a bitch could be a goddamn serial killer."

Megan made a face. "That's ridiculous."

"What's ridiculous? Michael Harrington is my number-one suspect for the murder of four women and one man." Jumping up from the couch, Matt began to pace. "How come every woman involved with this case is hypnotized by this asshole? Even my goddamn partner is always defending him. The guy's a friggin' gigolo."

"Don't get chauvinistic on me, Matt Donovan. I'm trying very hard to explain something that must be difficult for you to understand. And I know it sounds crazy." She paused, lowering her voice. "To tell you the truth, I never thought they'd go through with it. Timing, it was timing more than anything else. Everybody was so upset with the men in their lives, and it seemed like such a fun idea. It all started out as a joke."

"Some friggin' joke."

"I'm not going to say another word until you change your superior attitude." Megan scooped up the dog and placed it on her lap.

Maybe he was overreacting. Maybe.

*But why am I so pissed off? Jealous? Possibly.*

"Look," she explained patiently, "Rachel's the only one who's gone to bed with him. Kathleen and I simply went for a cruise on his sailboat, and Michael behaved like a perfect gentleman."

"You never went out with him alone?"

"No, I didn't." She looked into his eyes. "Honest. I haven't told the girls yet, but I didn't even send him the check. I have no intention of seeing him."

At least that made him feel a little better. "Do you think Mrs. Grant went to bed with him?"

"Absolutely not. But she did visit with him this morning. She told me she helped varnish his boat. Can you imagine? Alexandria Grant, varnishing anyone's boat?"

"Yes, I know. I was watching them …"

Megan looked startled but didn't say anything.

"Do you think Kathleen Rosario hit the sack with him?"

"I doubt it."

Matt wasn't so sure. "Judging from the way she was hanging on to him when I saw them on his boat, I'd say she did."

But Megan shook her head. "You don't know Kathleen. She's very moral."

"Did Michael know Bonnie-Sue Rattner?"

"I don't think so. He's not a member of the club." A quick intake of breath from Megan.

"What?"

"The shower. Bonnie-Sue attended the wedding shower at Helen's house."

"Yes, Harrington told me Mrs. Jennings was a client of Party Favorites, which used to be her ex-husband, Ray's, company."

"I don't know where he came from, but Michael did perform his strip routine at the shower." Looking thoughtful, she added, "And Bonnie-Sue was definitely there. In fact, she got very excited. At the end of the show she even followed Michael into the house. Do you think she made a date with him?"

"She probably did. From what I hear, Bonnie-Sue was no shrinking violet; she went after what she wanted."

"Oh, God, you think he killed her." Megan held the puppy to her cheek.

But Matt was already into the next question. "Is it possible Kathleen was with Michael the night of Bonnie-Sue's death?"

"When did she—"

"The medical examiner thought it was late Tuesday or early Wednesday morning."

"I don't see how she could have been with Michael."

"What do you mean?"

"As far as I know, none of us even met Michael until the day of Ginny's shower—that was on Tuesday, the same day Bonnie-Sue was murdered. We all had dinner together, and then we split up, so unless Kathleen slept with him that first night, she's lying."

"Then Michael has no alibi."

"Only if Kathleen admits she lied, but I don't think she will." Megan sounded morbid. "I think she's fallen for him, and if that's true, she'll defend him to the death. She's very codependent. Kathleen doesn't fall in love—she takes hostages."

"This damn case gets crazier by the minute," said Matt, stroking the dog.

*Boytoy? Shit.*

"Oh, dear God." Megan suddenly looked terrified.

"What's the matter?" he asked sharply.

"Kathleen left for Catalina with him."

"When?"

"Tonight. They're sailing across on Michael's boat."

"Jesus." Matt flashed on the bloody scene at Bonnie-Sue Rattner's house. He turned cold thinking about the same thing happening to Kathleen.

"Matt, we've got to do something. I'll try her cell phone."

"Do you think she will have service way out in the middle of the channel?"

Megan picked up the telephone. "We can try."

No answer, but Kathleen's answering service responded. She left a message asking her to call back.

He reached for the telephone. "The coast guard will find them."

Megan suddenly brightened. "I know, I'll call the Grants. They're sleeping on their boat tonight. Maybe Charlie can reach them by radio." She called Charlie on the *Ecstasea* and gave him the phony excuse of trying to reach Kathleen regarding the sale of her house.

Charlie agreed to put out an open call on the ship-to-shore radio.

Five minutes later the telephone rang. Megan grabbed it up. "Hello?" She pushed the speaker button so Matt could hear the conversation.

"Charlie Grant here."

"Did you reach them?"

"I did. They're more than halfway to the island."

"Did you speak to Kathleen?" Megan sounded anxious.

"Yes, dear, I did. She said they didn't have cell phone reception so she couldn't call you back. Maybe when she gets to the island. But she said she's fine. In fact, she insisted on continuing to Catalina. She didn't seem to care about the sale of her house. Her friend Michael said they'd head back if there was a problem."

"He did?" Megan's surprise showed in her voice.

"That's about all I could do, Megan."

"I'm sure it was, Charlie. Thanks." She changed the subject. "I'll see you in the morning then, six o'clock at the dock?"

"That's right. I want to be leaving the marina by seven o'clock. Better get a good night's sleep." Charlie hung up.

As she replaced the receiver, the puppy squiggled out of her arms and buried herself in the cushions. "I guess Kathleen's okay. It sounds like she's determined to stay with Michael. I'll be seeing her tomorrow."

Matt sighed. "My hands are tied right now. We have no real evidence to arrest Michael Harrington."

There was silence between them for the next few minutes, a silence broken only by the thundering crash of the waves.

He found himself staring at Megan. Unable to stop himself, he reached for her.

She came to him. Their lips touched.

He pulled her hard against his body and kissed her hungrily.

Megan gently moved away, scooped up the puppy, and took his hand.

All the way upstairs the little dog struggled in her arms.

Megan was grateful for the small Tiffany lamp that graced her dresser and cast strange colored shadows on the bedroom wall. It was just enough light.

She came to a halt at the foot of the bed as the puppy wriggled out of her arms, scampered under the bed, and stayed there. Before she could decide what to do next, Matt's arms encircled her waist and untied the sash holding her dressing gown together. Gently, it slid off her shoulders, forming a pool of green silk on the floor.

She turned. Standing before him, she felt cherished and beautiful.

His hands shaped her shoulders, and then, like the kiss of a butterfly, his fingertips brushed her nipples.

He twisted out of his shirt. She felt him, skin on skin.

She groaned as he lowered her to the bed.

Megan's whole being opened up to him … and she was lost.

# CHAPTER 30

The *Ecstasea* left Bayside Yacht Club a little after seven o'clock on Saturday morning under overcast skies.

Megan had chosen to sit outside on the flying bridge where Charlie Grant had stationed himself to steer his yacht out of the slip and into the main channel of Marina del Rey. Charlie's wife, Alex, was still asleep in the master cabin, below decks.

A cool dampness pervaded the air, and the tart, briny smell of the sea encouraged Megan to breathe deeply. As they reached the outer breakwater where hundreds of seagulls and pelicans made their home, the odor turned to one less pleasant.

Rounding the breakwater, Charlie headed south.

A hazy fog dimmed the horizon and prohibited Megan's view of Catalina Island, but winds were light and the water tranquil, promising an easy crossing. Although her real passion was the silence of sailing, she found the throb of the engines on Charlie's yacht comforting. So did her new friend, Silk.

Silk. Yes, Megan liked that, and she loved the fact that she and Matt had chosen the name together. As she stroked the puppy's honey-colored fur and trailed her fingers along its smooth, shiny tail, Silk snuggled deeper into the blue cashmere blanket draped across her knees.

Her thoughts switched to Kathleen. Before leaving the marina, Charlie had checked with Harbor Patrol. The *Moon River* had arrived in Catalina Harbor late last night with Michael and Kathleen safely aboard. Megan had even spoken to Kathleen, who informed her she was well and "deliriously happy" with Michael.

"Are you warm enough, Megan?" Charlie asked, sticking his hand in the pockets of his red all-weather jacket. He stood in front of the large instrument panel positioned at the forefront of the flying bridge.

Seated directly behind Charlie on a bank of navy-blue leather seats, Megan hugged her dog. "Thanks, I'm plenty warm. The weather's perfect." She and Silk snuggled even deeper into the white cable-knit sweater she wore over her black sweats.

"Yes, it is." Silence, and then he said, "Too bad Brian isn't here."

She gave him a hostile look, even though he couldn't see it.

He turned, adjusting his captain's hat over his eyes. "I take it you're all finished with Brian." It was more a statement than a question.

"Absolutely, and if you must know, I don't feel bad about it." She looked him directly in the eye. "I guess that makes me a heartless bitch."

"No, I think it just means you did the right thing by breaking it off." After setting the automatic pilot, Charlie sat down beside her. Absentmindedly, he stroked the dog and stared at the wide foamy wake unfurling behind the yacht. "Alex tells me you're seeing Detective What's-His-Name."

"Donovan. Matt Donovan. But it's nothing serious," she lied. "We're only at the getting-to-know-you stage."

"He seems like a nice fellow. I spent a while talking with him the other day."

"I was there the day you met him. Remember?"

Charlie nodded. "Yes, of course."

"And then I ran into him at George's funeral." She chuckled. "Literally."

"You know that he questioned Brian?"

"No, I didn't," she lied again, suddenly realizing she had to be careful not to reveal anything Matt had told her in confidence.

"I heard he was asking about Ray Jennings's sex life."

"That must have been a dull conversation." Megan changed the subject. "I listed Helen's house yesterday."

"Good for you. How is she?"

"She's most anxious to sell."

"What does she plan to do?" He seemed surprised to hear Helen was selling.

"I think she's already bought a house somewhere in Florida. She's being awfully closemouthed about it."

"Florida, huh?"

"That's what she said."

"I don't suppose she needs to worry about money."

"Oh, dear, I'm glad you reminded me. I have to call Home Funding on Monday. I think there's an error on the loan amount owing."

"Really? What?"

"Helen said she took a mortgage on the house for $500,000 to pay off Ray. But the loan company told me the balance was at least half that amount. She apparently made a couple of big payments in the last few months." *Dumb, Megan, dumb. You shouldn't be discussing Helen's private business. Not even with a mutual friend.*

"Maybe Ray had an insurance policy," Charlie suggested.

"It's possible." She had to get Charlie off the subject. Heaven forbid he should think she was in the habit of divulging her clients' financial secrets, especially now that his own company might be in trouble. She lifted Silk in the air. "Don't you love this little cutie? Matt found her in the alley."

He nodded and fondled the puppy. "They say the life of a cop's wife is pretty damn tough, Megan."

"No worse than being married to a drunken dope addict. You saw Brian the other night. He's in worse shape than he was before he got sober. Alcoholism is a progressive disease, you know. No one ever gets better, and that includes Brian."

"Yes, I know. My mother was a chronic alcoholic." Charlie's expression darkened. "She wasn't easy to live with."

Before Megan could comment, he continued. "Brian looked pretty bad the last time I saw him. But how are you? Are you still attending your meetings?"

"Yes, I am, almost every day."

"Is it necessary to go so often?"

"My sponsor told me to attend ninety meetings in ninety days, so that's what I did. Now I try to get there at least every other day." Megan sighed. "I wish Brian would go back to the program. Not that it would make any difference between us, but at least he'd get some help. Don't you think he's been acting kind of crazy?"

"Yes, and I can't imagine what's gotten into him. But that's enough about Brian." Charlie patted her hand. "Just promise me you won't turn into one of those reformed drinkers and try to convert us all."

She laughed. "Don't worry, Charlie, I promise."

"Do you find it difficult when everyone's drinking?"

"Occasionally, I do." Megan thought about it for a moment. "But most of the time it doesn't bother me."

"Well, I think what you are doing is commendable."

"Thanks."

Charlie returned to his position at the wheel and, after turning the autopilot off, manually steered the boat.

For the next hour or so, Megan lay full length on the navy cushions, alternating between staring at cloudy skies and dozing.

The rolling motion of the boat finally lulled her to sleep, and she did not wake up until Sy Neang leaned over her, coffeepot in hand.

"Miss Megan. You like coffee?"

"Oh, yes, please." As she swung her legs off the seat, a loud squeal came from the dog that had been sleeping in her lap. "Sorry, Silk, time to get up."

Suddenly, a golden sun burst through the clouds, clothing the sea in robes of sapphires and diamonds. And Megan caught her first glimpse of the dark hulk that was Catalina Island, looming through the morning mist.

"The Indians on the mainland used to describe Catalina as 'mountains that rise from the sea,'" Charlie said as he steered the *Ecstasea* to the westernmost end of the landmass.

Megan nestled the puppy in the blanket and stood up. "It's magnificent." She was always awed by the wonder of the magical island each time she saw it.

She gazed up at the tall, rugged mountains reaching for the heavens, their jagged peaks lost in a fleece of cumulus clouds. Leaning over the ship's rail, Megan watched as thick, foamy whitecaps crashed against the base of the craggy cliffs.

The ocean held such power; it left her breathless.

Off to her right, a proud armada of billowy clouds sailed across the horizon, like a fleet of Spanish galleons. Somehow, on this bright, sunny morning, her perception appeared sharper, and colors seemed brighter, more dazzling.

Was she seeing through the eyes of love?

*Oh, come on, girl, you've only been with him twice.*

But her body heated up as she recalled last night's lovemaking with Matt.

Returning to her seat, Megan picked up the puppy and whispered, "Matt is so special, isn't he, baby?"

Silk gave an agreeable whine and burrowed deeper.

"Eagle Rock ahead," Charlie called.

The *Ecstasea* rounded the tip of the island, where conflicting currents swirled around the massive rocks. Brian had told her it was called "a confused sea."

"Good morning, Megan. Good morning, darling." It was Alex, dressed in her white terry robe. She swayed from side to side, trying to find her sea legs.

"Well, sleepyhead," Charlie kidded, "you finally woke up, did you?"

"It's only nine o'clock." Alex dropped on a deck chair.

"My wife gets up at the crack of nine and not a minute sooner, don't you, darling?"

She smiled at Megan. "I hate to get up in the morning."

"Yes, I know." Megan laughed. Everybody knew.

Alex took the puppy from Megan's arms and cuddled her. "You are such a pretty doggie. Yes, you are. Silk. What a sweet name."

Sy Neang appeared again, carrying the coffeepot along with a large tray of raspberry Danish. He balanced everything expertly, even in the rocky sea.

"Passing Iron Bound Cove," Charlie yelled. "The water will settle down soon."

Megan leaned back on the cushions and studied the towering cliffs. In comparison, the Grants' huge yacht looked miniscule.

"Ribbon Rock," Charlie said, ever the tour guide.

No matter how many times she saw it, Megan was overwhelmed

by the complexity of Ribbon Rock, where each stripe of color told its own story of evolution. Here, the island's 120 million–year geological history was literally cast in stone. Millennia of wind and rain had molded these bluffs into myriad shapes and colors, as wave after wave of blue and white water slapped the base of the cliffs, slithering into every cave and crevice.

The sea calmed as the *Ecstasea* continued east to Catalina Harbor.

When the yacht rounded the bluffs, a sheltered bay came into view. Megan caught her breath at its pastoral beauty. Surrounded by precipitous cliffs on the left and softer sloping hills on the right, the cove was spattered with dozens of boats bobbling like corks in the gentle breeze.

Entering the small harbor, Charlie eased back on power and slowly motored to a private mooring can placed strategically in front of Bayside Yacht Club Beach House. Directly opposite was a similar facility owned by California Yacht Club.

Above them, on the sloping hillside, several buffalo grazed and leisurely crossed the hiking paths to find more luscious patches of green. In the winter months it was not unusual to find these hulking beasts feeding near the road, but it was quite rare during summer. Megan knew that a recent brush fire had depleted the vegetation on the upper slopes, which caused the buffalo to seek food at lower levels.

Sy Neang pulled up the spreader lines and, before long, the yacht was secured.

Megan caught sight of the *Moon River* anchored near the cliffs. Kathleen and Michael, who were sunbathing on deck, stood up and waved. It was a reassuring sight, and she happily returned their greeting.

Relaxing now, having seen for herself that Kathleen truly was safe, Megan admired the pristine beauty of the small bay.

She'd been here many times before and knew it well. She'd crossed the narrow band of land that separated Catalina Harbor from the Isthmus Cove dozens of times and passed within inches of the buffalo that roamed freely in the colder months.

Commonly called Two Harbors, the location was a moviemaker's dream, and in the 1930s such timeless movies as *Mutiny on the Bounty*, *Treasure Island*, and *The Sea Witch* were filmed here. In later years, *McHale's Navy* and numerous movies and TV shows had also been shot here for the same reasons: Catalina Harbor's towering cliffs, sandy beaches, clear blue sea, and endless horizons. One such movie company had brought the original buffalo to the island, decades ago, and throughout the ensuing years they had proliferated.

Suddenly, Charlie cut the engines.

Silence. The whole reason Megan loved being there. She loved the magnificent stillness of the island. Softly stroking Silk, she listened. The only sound to be heard was the distant bleating of goats foraging for food.

How she wished Matt was here beside her.

She closed her eyes. Even Silk was quiet.

On the Grants' yacht, cocktail hour was in full swing before Megan could find a private moment with her girlfriends. Eventually, she spoke to Rachel, clad in a bright yellow clown outfit and crowned by a curly golden wig. She sent her in search of Alex. In the meantime, Megan rounded up Kathleen, who had been very easy to find in her Raggedy Ann costume. But she had to practically drag her away from Michael, who was dressed as her Raggedy Andy.

Finally, the four friends came together in Megan's cabin.

Kathleen blustered, "Why do we have to have a secret meeting? I was having a good time."

"We need to have a discussion about Michael." Megan made no bones about it. "Did you know that he's the number-one suspect in the Bondage Murder case?"

There was complete silence for at least fifteen seconds.

Then they all spoke at once.

"That's the stupidest thing I've ever heard," Kathleen said.

"Who told you that?" Rachel asked, ever the inquisitor.

Alex assumed her aloof socialite voice that perfectly matched her sequined Harlequin suit and platinum wig. "I don't believe a word of it."

"Well, it doesn't matter much what you believe." Megan had

never seen a designer-clad jester before, and she felt pretty stupid in her own slapped-together-herself getup that only faintly resembled a clown. But she didn't let her discomfort change her opinion of Alex's dumb statement. "Matt Donovan told me last night that Michael is the prime suspect. That's why I was so worried about Kathleen's moonlight crossing in the middle of the night."

"So-o-o," Alex drawled, finally seeing the light, "that's why you had Charlie call them on the radio last night."

Megan nodded.

"I think Megan's just trying to spoil it for me because she hasn't had a chance to go out with him." Kathleen's tone was accusatory.

"I don't have any desire to be with Michael. I've been seeing Matt Donovan." There, she'd told them. "In fact, I didn't even send Michael a check." She waited for everyone to jump on her, but no one seemed to care. They were too wrapped up in themselves.

"You see," Kathleen declared, "she's been influenced by that detective."

"At least I didn't provide an alibi for the guy that could very well have murdered Bonnie-Sue Rattner." Megan's temper was getting the better of her. "Because of you, Kathleen, any one of us could be next."

Rachel objected strenuously. "Kathleen wouldn't do anything like that. You're mistaken, Megan."

"I am not. She told Matt she was with Michael last Tuesday night. Now we all know it was Tuesday evening when we met him at Hal's Restaurant and made our proposal. Unless Kathleen met up with him later and spent the night with him—"

"Did you spend the night with him, Kathleen?" Rachel asked.

"Well, no. But—"

"There are no buts about it," Rachel ranted. "You lied to a police officer. You put yourself and every one of us in danger. What the hell is wrong with you?"

"I knew we'd all end up arguing over this guy." Exasperated, Megan took Rachel's arm in an effort to restrain her. "Please, let's not fight amongst ourselves. We've got to figure out what to do."

"I should have known he was a damn phony." Rachel's emotions ran rampant. "He gave each one of us exactly what we needed. He knew which buttons to push, emotionally and sexually."

"So you did go to bed with him," Kathleen cried, clearly shattered by this newest revelation.

"Well, I didn't," Alex complained. "It cost me a thousand dollars to varnish his damn boat."

Kathleen opened the stateroom door. "Megan, it doesn't matter what you or your detective say about him. I don't believe it. Michael is the kindest, most gentle man I have ever met, and someday, I intend to marry him." With that little bombshell, Kathleen stepped into the corridor and slammed the door.

Megan sighed. "I don't know why I'd expect her to behave any differently. You know how she was with Gino, in total denial all those years. 'If you don't learn from your mistakes you're destined to repeat them.'" The others glared back at her, provoking a need to explain. "That's just a little gem from my AA sponsor."

"Really?" Alex said, obviously unimpressed.

"Well, I think we'd better get back to the party." Patting down her yellow hair, Rachel pulled a jeweled lipstick case from her voluminous pocket and coated her lips with ruby lipstick. "Michael Harrington doesn't strike me as a killer." She rubbed her lips together.

"I wish I could get my money back," Alex grumbled on the way back to the party. "It's the principle of the thing."

But Megan felt compelled to keep an eye on Kathleen.

# Chapter 31

Saturday night, Matt met up with Dan Coleman, the detective from Hollywood Division, and together they made the rounds of more than half a dozen sewers with names like Devil's Den, House of Horror, and Torch. They were trying to find someone who matched the psychological profile of their killer. Maybe he had visited other bondage parlors in the past.

The last stop was a house run by a local madam who'd been in business in Hollywood for years. Matt had been informed by vice that she kept a clean, drug-free house and for the most part was left alone by the LAPD.

Mistress Lara's Flesh Emporium appeared sedate and quiet.

Hidden behind a ten-foot fence and tall thick shrubs, the colonial-type residence was definitely discreet. Matt guessed that even inquiring minds wouldn't know what lechery lurked behind the doors of this elegant, pillared mansion.

Mistress Lara greeted them at the door, looking more like a Viking queen than a madam. She wore a black leather bustier with two strategically placed steel cones. Alas, the silver cones were much too small and totally incapable of containing those mammoth breasts, and fleshy mounds of pale skin toppled over the tops and sides.

The overflow was a sight to see, and Matt found it impossible not to gawk.

Lara rolled her eyes when she saw the badge. "Look, you guys, I already gave. Check with Tom Bristol."

"We're not interested in busting you, Lara. We just want to talk to you about these S&M murders." Dan paused. "It's in your best interest. You wouldn't want one of your girls getting hurt."

Moving out of the doorway, she let them in and introduced herself by her real name. "Betsy, the name's Betsy Bradford. This isn't the best time to come calling, you know. It's Saturday night."

The living room was set up a lot like Darkness's dungeon, with soft lights, mirrored walls, and blood-red carpet, producing the Stygian atmosphere favored by S&M patrons.

Matt's eyes widened at a naked bald-headed man who hung on the wall. His wrists were secured with steel manacles, and metal clamps were attached to his genitals.

"Yes, Mistress. More, Mistress," the guy screamed to the witch who was ministering to him.

Dan put a protective hand over his crotch. "Ouch," he said to Matt.

In another corner a senior citizen, at least seventy-five years old, was locked in a pillory. The man's head and hands hung from holes drilled into the wood. He wore only a smile of pure pleasure.

*I'd bet money the old boy's on plenty of Viagra.* "Do you have any private rooms, Betsy?"

"Yeah, you interested?"

"For me? No, thanks."

"We got six rooms upstairs. Some people dig being out in the open, though."

Dan interrupted. "We need to talk in private."

The mahogany-paneled den Betsy led them to was so unlike the rest of the house it could have been on another planet. Oriental rugs graced a dark planked floor, and the walls were lined with books. Matt scanned the titles: *S&M for the Male*, *S&M for the Female*, *Venus in Furs*, *The Writings of the Marquis de Sade*, *Bag of Toys*, and many more hardcover books on similar subjects.

Betsy asked them straight-out, "Okay, what's up?"

"Have you had an unusually vicious client show up here during the last few weeks?" Dan asked.

"Only one." She gave a loud cackle. "That was a joke. We did have one sick bastard a couple of weeks ago."

"Can you describe him?"

"Average height, he wore a trench coat and a fedora. Underneath he had his own leather getup already on, including the mask."

Sounded to Matt like the same man the bartender at Club Damnation had described. And whoever the hell he was, Matt knew they were moving closer.

"You mean you didn't actually see what he looked like?" Matt asked.

"I didn't see his face. Sometimes people want to be anonymous, so we respect that. Anyway, this guy wanted a private room and a small blonde."

He exchanged glances with Dan before asking, "Are you sure it was a man?"

"I just assumed it was. We don't get a lot of women here. Occasionally we do, but not very often."

"Who did he see?" Dan asked.

"He ended up with Roxanne, and he was pretty damn rough, too."

"Where's Roxanne now?"

"She went to stay with a friend in Chicago for a couple of weeks, to heal an' all. Her back was all torn up from his whip."

Matt was becoming more and more convinced this was their man. "How badly was she injured?"

"It was pretty bad, enough to scare the shit out of her. If she hadn't been here in the house, it could have been worse."

"Didn't she cry out?" Matt asked.

"He used a gag on her."

"Jesus H. Christ," Dan said, under his breath.

The middle-aged dominatrix shrugged. "It's an occupational hazard."

Dan shook his head. "Do you have a number in Chicago where we can reach Roxanne?"

"No, I don't, but she'll be back here tomorrow night. You can talk to her then."

"Thanks, Betsy. We appreciate the help." Dan headed for the door, and Matt followed.

"We'll be back tomorrow evening to talk to Roxanne." Matt turned back to the madam. "Oh, and if she calls in, get her number."

"I'll do anything I can if it'll help catch the bastard."

On the way out to the car, Dan pinched his thumb and forefinger together. "We're this close. I can feel it. Roxanne just might have that one piece of information we need to catch this bastard."

"Yeah." Matt felt it too. "Let's just hope he lays low until we can talk to her."

☥ ☥ ☥

Megan's feet ached, and no wonder. She'd played hostess for the club's Bring on the Clowns party for the last three hours—since eight o'clock, to be exact. Helen Jennings, chairperson of the event, had taken her own sweet time letting Megan off the hook.

The clubhouse was gaily decorated with balloons and ribbons, giving the room a festive air. Even though the party was still going strong, Megan was bored. Yacht club functions had lost a lot of their charm since she'd quit drinking. And she knew why as the noise careened through her brain, carousel music blaring from speakers and Bayside employees hawking hot dogs, peanuts, and saltwater taffy. The bartender hollered, "Last call," and the rowdy merrymakers lined up for yet another round of punch laced with Myer's Rum.

Megan sipped on her Shirley Temple, observing the variety of clown outfits worn by the eighty or more guests. Surprisingly, few were repeated. Many of the clowns who attempted tricks, such as riding a unicycle or juggling balls and skittles, had gotten a little tipsy and, as the evening progressed, became less and less proficient.

Uh-oh, somebody else went down.

Dr. Henderson? On stilts?

In her attempts to help the good doctor, she spilled her drink all over her own costume. *Damn.*

Brushing off her own baggy red pants, Megan asked, "Are you all right, Doctor?"

"Yes, thank you," but he stared at her rather stupidly. "Now, don't you look cute, Megan."

Before she could respond, the doctor dropped his stilts and limped toward his wife, who was seated beside Helen Jennings.

Making her way through the crowd, Megan paused to admire the dancers. Raggedy Ann and Raggedy Andy, locked in each other's arms, twirled to the strains of a calliope waltz. Kathleen looked positively radiant, but the minute she saw Megan watching her interact with Michael, she flashed a defiant smile.

Megan smiled back. She understood. Kathleen was in love, and she didn't want anyone raining on her parade. No one would ever make her believe Michael was anything other than her knight in shining armor. He was one of the heroes from Kathleen's favorite romance novels. Not a gigolo.

And she would never believe he was a killer, even if they brought her the proof.

Megan caught sight of Gino Rosario sitting on the sidelines, beside his pregnant girlfriend, eyeing the happy couple with malice. Unexpectedly, he jerked from his seat and staggered across the half-empty floor toward his ex-wife.

From the look on her face, Gino must have said something nasty, and Kathleen began to cry. Gino stormed out of the clubhouse.

Only a week ago, Kathleen would have run after him, pleading with him to come back. Instead, she allowed Michael to lead her to a corner and hold her gently in his arms. It was a tender scene.

Megan prayed Michael was everything he seemed to be at this moment.

On her way to the French doors, she heard Rachel and David arguing at a nearby table. Sadly, Megan recalled how she'd once believed theirs was the perfect marriage. Certainly, the last few weeks had proved otherwise. Abruptly, the fight ended with David kicking back his chair and wheeling off to the bar, while Rachel marched to the ladies' room.

Megan started after her and then changed her mind and headed for the outside porch, overlooking the harbor.

At that moment, Charlie Grant entered the clubhouse. "Got a minute?" He grabbed Megan by the arm.

She pulled away, surprised at his roughness. "You're all out of breath, Charlie."

"Listen, I just came back from Doug's Harbor Reef at the Isthmus. Brian was there."

"Was he alone?"

"Alone ... and ripped."

"I hope he doesn't come over here."

"He was talking about it."

"I'm leaving." Megan could not deal with Brian tonight. "Tell Alex I'm going back to the boat."

Too late, Brian staggered up to them. "Watch out for that bitch, Charlie."

Megan flinched.

"So what the hell is that supposed to mean?" Charlie, usually the master of restraint, appeared to lose his cool.

"She knows exactly what I mean." Brian stumbled into the clubhouse with Charlie two feet behind him. "Ask her about telling stories to her cop boyfriend."

Megan escaped to the veranda, just as she heard chairs and tables crashing, glass breaking, Helen Jennings's voice, and then Brian's and Charlie's. They were arguing.

The music stopped.

As she stepped back into the shadows, Brian lurched past her into the night, trailed by Charlie Grant, who was trying to calm him down.

Megan remained there in a dark corner of the porch for the longest time. Lately, Brian was drunk most of the time. His behavior was appalling. Not her problem.

She gazed out over the harbor. Silver-lined clouds hovered above the island, hiding the moon. From where she stood, Megan could see the anchor lights of the boats repeat themselves in the blackness of the water and glimmer like reflected stars. Mast lights, high atop the sailboats, rocked back and forth with cradle like precision, and a couple of serious powerboats, almost as big as Charlie's, were garishly lit with colored bulbs. Several other yachts, safely anchored in the shelter of the cliffs, were discernible only by the glow of a table lamp in the salon or an overhead fixture on the aft deck.

And then she remembered.

It had felt the same. She was standing on the porch at the house on Beachview. It was dark. They had gone there for drugs. That was it. Brian needed cocaine. He was wasted; she was, too. But he'd made her drive there anyway. It was all so clear now. She remembered the picket fence, the pathway, the three steps to the porch, a glass-paneled door. Someone answered his knock. A woman—she knew it was a woman. But who? She couldn't remember. Megan racked her brain, but nothing came.

Maybe she'd been in a blackout. *God knows ...*

Suddenly something caught her attention.

Who was that? Someone was leaving the clubhouse.

A window of light beamed across the person's head, and Megan recognized Helen Jennings's tacky red wig. Now why would she sneak alongside the building like that? Reaching the end, Helen moved away from the shadow of the clubhouse and headed for a dark craggy trail, curving upward around the edge of the bluffs.

Then, another figure emerged from behind the restrooms and followed Helen. From the outline of his build, Megan assumed it was a male.

Megan had hiked that same trail a few times, so she knew it climbed the rugged hillside and ended abruptly on the top of hazardous cliffs, facing out to sea.

The path was narrow and dangerous, even in daylight.

Curious, Megan followed, keeping her distance. Up, up the steep grade almost to the top.

Helen finally stopped at a dark projection of land cantilevered over the murderous rocks below. As if it was preplanned, a second figure approached her and spoke, animatedly.

Megan scrambled for cover under a scraggly bush—and lost her footing. She slid several feet down into a small gully running along the hilly side of the pathway.

Had they heard her?

She waited. She listened. She heard nothing but the resounding crash of the waves breaking against the walls of the cliffs. She saw the two silhouettes against the starry night sky. Suddenly, Helen laughed. It was not a pleasant laugh.

The other person mumbled and gesticulated wildly. Helen screamed back, her words lost in the wind. They argued.

Megan heard words like "blackmail," "money," "bitch," and "truth." Suddenly, the dark figure grabbed Helen by the neck.

Stunned, Megan panicked. She had to do something. She tried to climb back up to the path, but she lost her footing. She fell all the way down to the bottom of the gully this time, smack into a pile of buffalo dung. *What a God-awful smell.*

Again, Megan scrambled up the side, her fingers clawing desperately at the gravel. She slid again but kept trying to get back on the path.

Soon her fingernails were torn and bloody.

Finally Megan crawled up the crevice until she was just a few feet below Helen and her antagonist. She peeped over the ridge.

Helen was down, on the very edge of the cliff, but moving. She was still alive. The attacker wheeled away from his victim and stalked directly toward Megan.

*Oh my God.* She ducked. Had he seen her?

She heard him rail again. "You bitch."

Megan peeked again. The assailant had turned back to face Helen, who had crawled back from the edge.

"You haven't heard the last of me," Helen croaked.

*Keep your damn mouth shut,* Megan silently pleaded.

But the attacker said nothing more. Instead, he passed within inches of Megan's hiding place, kicking gravel in her face. But she remained absolutely still.

Assured now that Helen was alive, Megan continued to cower in the gully, reeking of animal dung. She didn't want Helen to know she'd been spying on her.

She heard a rustle at her feet. *Oh my God, snakes.* Poisonous snakes.

She curled up in a ball, terrified of what might lurk in the darkness.

When was she going to leave? But it seemed like an eternity before Helen pulled herself upright, from her knees, and tottered down the path again.

With Herculean effort, Megan dragged herself up the unstable grade. She tried desperately to brush away the waste caked on her clothes but only managed to spread the stench. Giving up, she started back.

On her descent to the clubhouse, her mind was filled with questions. Was Helen blackmailing someone? Or was it the other way around? Then she remembered the low balance on Helen's loan and decided Helen must be the culprit. She was paying off her loan. But who could she possibly be blackmailing?

Then Megan remembered the intruder. Of course, that's why the man was searching Helen's office. He was looking for pictures or whatever else she had that would incriminate him. She felt a sudden chill. Helen Jennings was in grave danger.

She must speak to Matt. Maybe she should warn Helen.

Returning to the dock, Megan found Sy Neang waiting with the Grants' Boston Whaler.

"Want to go out to *Ecstasea*, Miss Megan?" Sy asked.

"Yes, please. Have Mr. and Mrs. Grant returned yet?"

"No, miss." He helped her into the craft. Making no comment about her disheveled appearance, or the foul odor she emanated, Sy revved up the engine, and they headed for the yacht.

Within minutes Megan climbed aboard and went to her stateroom while Sy returned to shore to await Alex and Charlie.

At least the puppy was glad to see her.

Then she attempted to reach Matt on the cellular phone. No luck. She left a message. While she waited for him to call back, Megan jumped into the shower to clean off the dust and stench. Finally, comfortable in her pajamas and robe, she tried calling him again.

But it was quite late when he finally answered his home phone. "Hi," she said. "It's me."

"How are you, Megan?" Matt sounded happy to hear from her.

"I'm fine. But I think Helen Jennings is in a whole lot of trouble. I think she's blackmailing someone."

"Are you sure?"

"I followed her up this pathway to the top of—"

"You did what?" Matt showed such anger in his voice. "Megan, do you realize what a chance you were taking?"

"Yes, and I did it anyway." Silk snuffled her arm.

He seemed to sense her impatience. "Tell me what happened."

Rubbing the puppy's silky fur, Megan felt much calmer after she'd told him exactly what had occurred.

"Did Mrs. Jennings ride to Catalina with you and the Grants?"

"No, she came with the Hendersons."

"Do you think she returned to their boat?" Matt asked.

"I don't know. I came right back to the *Ecstasea*. I had to. I stunk like the inside of an animal cage."

She could tell he was making an effort not to laugh. "It's all right. You can laugh if you want to. But this information is important, isn't it?"

"Yes, Megan, it's great. But I'd feel a whole lot better if you were here, safe and sound. When are you coming home?"

"Tomorrow evening. I'm going snorkeling with Charlie in the morning." She changed the subject back to Helen. "Matt, do you think I should go and talk to her?"

"No, absolutely not. You've done enough."

"She'd probably deny blackmailing anyone. But are you sure I shouldn't confront her? Tell her she needs protection?"

Matt sounded panicky. "Listen to me, Megan. Do nothing. Do you hear me?"

She gave in, mainly because she was too tired to argue. "Oh, and there's one more thing about Michael Harrington." She paused. "I don't know if I did the right thing, but I told the girls that Michael was a suspect."

"I think that was probably the right thing to do. How did they react?"

"Well, Kathleen ended up in hysterics, but she did admit she wasn't with Michael the night of Bonnie-Sue's death."

"I was pretty sure she wasn't, but I couldn't prove it."

Megan continued in her thoughtful manner. "It appears to me that Michael Harrington seems to know exactly what each woman wants. Rachel needed someone powerful to sweep her off her feet. He did that, to the point where she lost total control of herself." Silk happily licked Megan's fingers.

"Go on."

"But with Kathleen, he appears to be the exact opposite. Romantic. Tender. I mean, Kathleen has really flipped for this guy. She says she's going to marry him."

"Jesus."

"I feel partly responsible, Matt. Kathleen would never have done the boytoy thing if I hadn't agreed to go along with it." The lump in her throat hurt as she tried to keep from crying.

"Of course it's not your fault, honey." Matt was emphatic. "Everyone makes their own decisions. What about Mrs. Grant?"

"Alex? I have no idea why she was working on his boat; that's something she'd never do with Charlie. I mean, they have servants all over the place. Maybe it brought back memories of happier times when she didn't have all that money. Who knows?"

"My partner's right. The son of a bitch is a gigolo."

Of course, it was true. But what the hell had they expected? The guy was a stripper, a lady's man. And he had no trouble taking their money, with his own added stipulations—living expenses, indeed.

"Look, honey," Matt said. "Try to get some sleep, and call me when you get in. Promise?"

"I promise."

"I'll pick you up at Bayside and take you to dinner, okay?"

"I'd love it, Matt. See you tomorrow."

"Yes. Good night ... darling."

He'd whispered the "darling" part, but Megan was thrilled to her toenails. Darling. Matt had called her darling.

She held the puppy to her cheek. *Did you hear that, Silk?*

Later, she tried to fall off to sleep, but her mind wouldn't quit. Thinking back on the entire evening, Megan realized not one person at the club cocktail party, nor at the clown party, had mentioned Bonnie-Sue Rattner's murder—even though it had been splashed all over the papers and talked about endlessly on the cable channels. The promise of a $200,000 reward had made it the news of the day.

Megan put if down to group denial. Talking about death might spoil the evening.

Then, Megan remembered she hadn't told Matt about her feelings of déjà vu and the revelation she'd had with regard to Sherrie Weston's house on Beachview Avenue.

She didn't relish telling him she'd gone there with Brian Mason to buy drugs. Thank God she'd told him she was in AA. At least he knew she didn't practice that kind of insanity anymore.

Holding the dog close to her chest, Megan climbed into her bunk.

# Chapter 32

On Sunday morning when Matt arrived at the station, Angelle was already seated at her desk surrounded by smut publications, writing letters to the box numbers.

Every guy in the office held a paper or magazine in front of his face, and Matt was damn sure none of them were the Sunday *Times*. Comments like "Hey, man, look at this" were repeated several times as the bondage papers changed hands and loud guffaws rang out.

Matt beckoned, and Angelle followed him into the conference room to find Joe seated at the table, rifling through the trillion leads they'd already received on the Internet. Senator Rattner's $200,000 reward had caused every nut in Los Angeles to crawl out of the woodwork. But who the hell knew? Maybe they'd get a live one.

Taking a seat beside Joe, Matt told them about Mistress Lara's Flesh Emporium and Betsy, the Viking madam.

"Hey, I think I know that broad," Joe said, scratching his balding head. "Betsy Bradford? Big, hefty blonde, right?"

"Know her in the biblical sense?" Angelle teased. "Were you the whipper or the whippee, Joey?"

"No, I ain't kidding." Joe shook his head. "Betsy's a good old broad. Into S&M now, huh?"

Unable to resist, Matt got into the act. "So, she was one of your old girlfriends?"

Joe just sat there, looking really uncomfortable.

Matt grinned. This was the first time he'd ever seen Joe Schumann without an answering wisecrack in all the years he'd known him.

"Look, pal, why don't you go see if there's any more leads comin' in on the Internet?" As soon as Matt let him off the hook, Joe took off quicker than a humming bird.

"You need to lighten up," Matt said to Angelle, pressing his lips together.

She burst into gales of laughter. "It's different when the shoe's on the other foot."

Matt finally broke down and smiled. "Okay, let's get serious. Did we hear anything from the FBI about military records?"

"Not yet."

"Any interesting leads from the hotline?"

"No."

"Okay. Right now, I want you to check even deeper into family backgrounds on all of 'em: Michael Harrington, Brian Mason, Gino Rosario, Charles Grant, and David Feinman." Matt ticked the names off on his fingers. "Especially Sy Neang and Helen Jennings."

"Helen Jennings?"

"Let me tell you what Megan overheard last night …" Matt told her the story of what he suspected was Helen's blackmailing career.

"Okay, you got it. I'll get everything together as soon as I can." Picking up a sheaf of papers, Angelle left the room.

Matt contemplated the wall—that's what the guys in the unit were calling his array of information charts and suspect lists.

He had nothing new on Michael Harrington. Nothing new, period.

Any and all methods of shit work had already been done.

Before long, Angelle would have complete files on the Bayside members who interested him. And she was hard at work on the personals in the bondage rags and all the Internet websites and chat rooms she could handle.

It was fucking amazing how many weirdos were into this crap.

Megan awakened in her stateroom on the *Ecstasea* with Silk nuzzling her neck. She took the little dog in her arms and wrapped her up in the sheets. The puppy wrestled her way out of the covers, and they played happily on the bed for at least an hour.

Then, dressed in an old pair of shorts and an oversized T-shirt, Megan headed topside. She was looking forward to going snorkeling with Charlie and planned on a light breakfast. Neither Charlie nor his wife, Alex, was in the salon. Obviously, it was way too early for Alex; she never got up before nine o'clock.

Sy Neang brought in a tray of croissants, coffee, and a small plate of dog biscuits. The man never missed a beat.

Megan laughed. "Look, Silk, Sy brought you some cookies." She noticed a smile flicker across the smooth, sand-colored face of Sy Neang.

"Is Mr. Charles up yet?"

"Yes, madame, he helping Miss Kathleen's friend."

Surprised, she asked, "You mean Michael Harrington?"

"Yes, Miss. Miss Kathleen, she in one stateroom. Mr. Charles is gone, trying to fix Mr. Harrington's sailboat."

"What's wrong with it?"

Sy Neang shrugged his shoulders.

Grabbing a croissant, Megan went in search of Kathleen.

As she entered the causeway, leading to the staterooms, Kathleen appeared.

"Good morning, Megan." Kathleen looked ready for the runway in a blue cotton shorts outfit. Her red hair was pulled up and twisted in the latest casual fashion and held by a tortoise-shell clip.

"What happened to Michael's boat?" she asked.

"The steering broke." Kathleen shoved past her into the salon. "Is there any coffee?"

Following her, Megan asked, "What do you mean the steering broke? You mean the steering wheel or the rudder itself?"

Kathleen poured a cup of coffee and then curled up on the couch. "I think it's the rudder. Anyway, we're riding home with you guys 'cause Michael needs a special part to fix it."

Filling her own cup with coffee, Megan decided the afternoon's ride home would prove very, very interesting.

Lobster Bay was Megan's favorite place in the whole world to dive. The small cove south of Cat Harbor teemed with flame-colored

Garibaldi, darting through the giant strands of seaweed—seaweed that reached for the sunlight with arms thirty feet long.

When she first hit the water, her body was freezing cold, even in her wet suit. But after a few minutes of shivering, Megan's body adjusted to the water temperature.

With powerful strokes, Megan swam some distance from the boat where Charlie was painstakingly hooking bait to his fishing lines.

As she neared the cliffs, she rolled over on her back. With not a living soul in sight, she gazed up at the precipitous rocks towering above. Nursed by the soft swells rocking her body, Megan dreamed she was all alone in the world before time began. Her thoughts swung to Matt, as they always did when she enjoyed a special moment. How she wished he was there. She wanted to share everything with him.

Suddenly, Charlie called out, "Megan, you okay? Where are you?"

She raised her arm and waved. Then, spitting on the glass of her black rubber face mask, she rinsed it in the sea to clear the condensation caused by her body heat. She shoved the end of the snorkel into her mouth and was ready. Rolling over, she scrunched her body and propelled herself into the depths. Driving herself down, she hit the rocky bottom in seconds and then quickly catapulted back to the surface, snaking her way through the wafting seaweed.

Knowing that Charlie patrolled the surface in his Boston Whaler gave her the freedom of a dolphin to explore the sea's depths. With a quick intake of breath, she dived again. But this time when she broke the surface, she heard Charlie yelling for her to stop.

He'd put away his fishing tackle and driven the Whaler to her location. Pulling her diving flag, he pointed to an area about half a mile beyond.

Megan climbed back into the small Boston Whaler and scrambled over Charlie's fishing equipment.

That's when she could finally see what had caught his attention.

A rubber dinghy carrying a man and a woman hugged the cliffs. They were crying out for help and waving. "Let's check it out," Megan said.

Charlie gunned the engine. "It looks like an accident."

Megan removed her mask and snorkel as he swung the boat around and headed for the cove, where the other boat drifted.

As he pulled the Whaler alongside the dinghy, Charlie called out, "Ahoy there, need some help?"

The couple were wearing royal-blue wet suits, with masks and snorkels to match, and were hunkered together on the one and only seat in the dinghy. "We think there's a body down there." The young man cuddled closer to the girl who was whimpering softly. "My wife's real upset. Do you have a radio? We need to call harbor patrol."

Charlie reached for the ship-to-shore radio, but Megan had other ideas. "I'll go down and check it out." Quick as a flash, she donned her mask and snorkel.

"No, Megan." Charlie's voice was harsh, and he even put out a hand to prevent her from leaving the boat. "You stay here."

But Megan would have none of it. She dived over the side.

On her second descent she saw the body, suspended in twenty feet of water.

It swayed, tall and limp, arms dangling like a grotesque puppet, a large rock tied to its feet. The painted white face was hideously ravaged, its empty sockets staring sightlessly at myriad multicolored fish. Soggy red hair floated around its bloodless head and drifted with the seaweed in the undulating rhythm of the tide. Back and forth. Back and forth. Shock rendered Megan immobile, and for a heartbeat, she hung in the water, face-to-face with the lifeless, doll-like creature, its smeared, red mouth grimacing menacingly through a haze of green water.

As the bizarre clown pulsed with the movement of the tide, the red baggy pants moved toward her in a gruesome parody of animation. Megan panicked. It was all she could do to stop herself from opening her mouth to scream. Under the diving mask, her cheeks puffed with air. She compressed her lips, wanting desperately to breathe.

Suddenly, the current pushed her forward into the bloated corpse and shocked her into action. She began to backpedal. Kicking her way to the waterline, her foot became entangled in the waterlogged hair. Enmeshed in her toes, the wig broke away from the corpse. Soft and gummy, it clung to her foot like a living thing.

She couldn't shake it off. She tried and tried.
A silent scream ripped through her mind. *Oh my God.*
Kicking ... kicking ... kicking.
Megan broke the surface with a terrifying howl. "It's Helen Jennings."

## CHAPTER 33

Early that evening, as the *Ecstasea* motored out of Catalina Harbor and rounded the point to Lobster Bay, Megan sat in stunned silence in the enclosed afterdeck, unable to rid herself of the vivid pictures of Helen's body. It was almost more than she could bear.

She shivered and reached for Silk, who was napping on the floor.

Why hadn't she approached Helen after the scene on the hilltop? Begged her to speak to the police? Megan tried to talk herself out of the guilt, realizing Helen couldn't have asked for help, especially if she was blackmailing someone.

Megan cursed her own impetuous acts. She must be a crazed adrenaline junkie diving for a dead body, slinking into the House of Destiny, hiring a damn boytoy.

Silently, Kathleen tried to cover her with a cashmere throw, but nothing could relieve the jumbled emotions Megan was experiencing at that moment.

She stared out the window.

Pale shadows, like dusky heralds, stood sentinel on the rugged cliffs of the Island. Another time, another place, it would have been breathtaking. She caught sight of the cove where Helen's body was found, and it all came back.

No matter how many times she'd told the coast guard and harbor patrol about the mysterious person who had followed Helen up the hill, there was no proof it ever happened. She'd begged them to call Detective Matt Donovan. He would give them the facts on the murder investigation. As far as she knew, harbor patrol had not talked to him yet. They suspected that Helen had committed suicide. But Megan didn't believe that for one minute.

There was a rock tied to Helen's foot.

How could they possibly think that was suicide?

The body had been found far beyond the pathway that curved around the edge of the cliffs, where she'd seen Helen the night before. No, Megan was sure someone had killed her elsewhere, carried the body to Lobster Bay, tied a rock to Helen's foot, and dropped her into the ocean. There was no other explanation. Why would Helen walk all the way to the very top of the cliffs and then jump into the sea to commit suicide? Especially when she'd hiked up the same path only hours before, almost got pushed over the edge, and then struggled back to safety. The suicide idea was ludicrous.

And what about Michael Harrington? Where was he when Helen was killed?

Megan had already called Matt and left a message on his voice mail, telling him that Helen was dead. Maybe she should call him again.

Passing by the cove, Kathleen stood up and craned her neck, obviously trying to get a better look at the coast guard cutter cruising along the water's edge by the cliffs.

Megan grabbed her arm. "Sit down, girl, there's nothing to see. They took the body away hours ago."

"Well, what do you think they're doing?" Kathleen asked.

"How do I know? They're probably looking for clues." Megan paused. "Was Michael with you last night?"

"Of course he was. Didn't you see us dancing at the club?"

"No, I mean after that. Did you sleep with him all night on the boat?"

"Yes. But we got up early. He wanted to fix the rudder. He brought me over here and—"

"What time?"

"About five in the morning."

That would do it. Michael had had plenty of time to meet Helen and kill her.

Kathleen dropped her gaze and mumbled, "I think I'll take a nap. I feel sort of ill. Can I use your cabin?"

Megan softened her voice. "Of course, honey. But where's Michael now?"

Kathleen stood up and stretched. "I think he's with Charlie, steering the boat."

When Kathleen left, Megan rested her head on a downy pillow, cuddling with the puppy. She had an urgent need for silence.

Her thoughts were befuddled, and she tried to sort them out.

She recalled the break-in at Helen's house, the weirdo in black. Was he the blackmailee? But why did he wear a mask? And what the hell was he looking for? Maybe he'd hoped to find whatever evidence Helen was using against him.

Obviously, Helen's office had been the only room searched. Megan had never checked the upstairs, and Helen hadn't volunteered the information. In fact, she had told the police officers there didn't appear to be anything stolen and not to make a report. She'd told Megan that making a fuss about it would be a bad idea, especially when they were trying to sell the house.

Regrettably, by her silence, Megan had tacitly agreed. What had she been thinking? That's when the fear, guilt, and god-awful pain rose to the surface, and Megan wept uncontrollably.

She should have done something to help Helen.

† † †

After listening to Megan's rambling message, Matt rushed to Helen Jennings's house. He sure as hell didn't want anyone else getting there before him.

It was dark when Matt reached the fancy Santa Monica neighborhood north of Montana Avenue. The street was unlit, except for areas where individual spotlights shone on ancient trees, exotic bushes, and flower beds in full bloom.

It didn't take him long to get in. Megan had given him the alarm code.

The house was in darkness, except for a couple of table lamps in the living room, obviously to deter burglars. Better late than never.

He began his search in the office. Megan had told him the burglar had entered the hallway from the office and that Helen headed directly to her desk when she had arrived home after the incident.

Matt knew it was no ordinary robbery. He had the distinct feeling that the thief knew exactly what he wanted and had a pretty good idea where he could find it.

Entering the office, he flicked on the light switch near the door. Paperwork covered Helen's grandiose desk. He shuffled through it. Nothing interesting. The top drawer was filled with more papers. He checked the other drawers—nothing much. He found a couple of yellow legal pads, both blank, and a few pens and pencils.

More junk in the second one.

But the bottom drawer was shorter than the other three. How come?

Matt knelt down and fooled around with the back of the drawer. Suddenly, a panel popped open. He reached inside and pulled out the contents.

It was a DVD in a clear plastic case. There was a familiar label stuck on the corner that read "Fantasy Films." *Bingo.*

Hold it. What about a search warrant? Matt knew that whatever he discovered would be inadmissible evidence if he had to use it in court. *Screw it.* Megan might be in danger, and he was past caring. Matt removed the disk from its cover and headed for the TV.

A piece of paper fell to the floor. He picked it up.

It was a note, dated two weeks before Ray's death. It read:

> Helen,
> I am sending you a film. If anything bad happens to me, forward it to the police and tell them everything I told you.
> Ray

"But Helen didn't listen to you, Ray, old buddy. And now she's dead." Matt slipped the disk into the video drive.

No credits. The bedroom of Sherrie's house popped on-screen. A naked woman, dragged into the picture by an unseen assailant. A thick chain attached to a black studded collar clasped tightly around the fragile neck of ... Allison Graham.

Matt jumped from his chair. He knew what was coming.

Allison was obviously stoned out of her mind. Then, a dark apparition moved into view, and Matt turned cold.

Clothed in a black outfit, not unlike a loose-fitting wet suit, the assailant's head and face were concealed by a leather hood, its zippered mouthpiece closed. Long cuffed gloves covered both hands and arms. Matt couldn't even tell the color of the person's skin, let alone the gender.

Leatherface handcuffed Allison to the bed. Then the son of a bitch really went to work. Matt's mouth tightened as the action accelerated, but he forced himself to watch the DVD to the very end.

When it was over, he was sickened to the core, and Allison was dead. He sat in the chair for several minutes, unable to move, unable to think.

His mind jumped to Megan. The thought of that animal being here in this house with her almost blew him away.

When Matt finally pulled himself together, using his handkerchief to avoid destroying any prints, he picked up Helen's crystal telephone and called Hollywood station.

"Dan Coleman, please." Minutes later, Matt had related all that had happened. "I'll be there in a half hour, and we'll head for Lara's Flesh Emporium. With any luck, Roxanne will be back from Chicago and she'll recognize the guy on the tape."

☨ ☨ ☨

Megan awoke with a start. It was dark, and she was still lying on the enclosed rear deck of the *Ecstasea*.

Casting aside the blue cashmere throw, she peered out of the surrounding windows. Total blackness. The only sound was the humming of the engines.

How long had she slept? Surely, they were almost home?

With the dog wiggling in her arms, Megan headed for her cabin. "Silk, we're getting off this boat as soon as it docks. But first we'll wake up Kathleen."

But Kathleen was not in her bed, so Megan figured she had to be with Michael in another cabin. Megan glanced in the mirror. "What a wreck!" she cried, running her fingers through her disheveled hair.

In the reflection, she saw the puppy's tail disappear through the open door. "Silk, come back here. Where do you think you're going?" She tried to grab her.

But the dog ran as fast as her little legs could carry her, tumbling down the ladder to the deck below. Righting herself, Silk headed toward the crew's quarters.

Megan followed close behind, down the gloomy causeway of the lower deck to where the puppy had disappeared. She called Silk's name at every doorway. Finally, she found herself in the dimly lit engine room.

The massive diesels were deafening.

"Silk. Here, Silk. Come on, sweetie." Megan heard frantic yelping from somewhere behind a large duct. It ran from the air-conditioning unit along the starboard bulkhead, disappearing into the next cabin. Crouching down, she followed the puppy's yips. Silk had somehow managed to squeeze through the opening made for the pipes and was in the next-door cabin, unable to find her way back.

Megan left the engine room and reentered the hallway.

She could still hear the dog barking. Opening the door to the cabin next door, she fumbled for the switch and turned it on.

The fragile glow of a single yellow bulb cast flickering shadows on the cold, steel walls. A rancid odor, one Megan could not identify, permeated the room.

The cabin was empty, except for a built-in bunk … and a puppy. Silk was in the corner, baying and snuffling at the door of a closed locker. Balancing on her spindly back legs, she scratched at the wooden door with her claws, snarling and yapping at whatever was inside.

When the little dog realized Megan was there, she stopped what she was doing, scrabbled across the cabin, and lapped happily at her ankles.

"Miss Megan." Sy Neang stood in the doorway.

Megan whirled around. She hadn't heard him come up behind her. "I—I was looking for the dog." She picked up Silk and began to push past him.

Sy put his hand on her arm. "It not be wise to come down here alone. You maybe get hurt. Find things … not good." His voice was one even sound—monotone, like a chant.

"I beg your pardon." She looked down at his hand on her arm and up into his cold obsidian eyes. *Don't panic,* she told herself. *We're talking Sy Neang here.*

But Megan felt threatened and really frightened.

The dog growled.

Megan held her breath.

Sy moved aside and let her pass.

Relieved, Megan hurried toward the steps, taking them two at time. At the top, her heart was pounding so hard she had to stop, but only for a second. She was determined not to spend one more minute in the presence of Sy Neang. He was hiding something, and she sure as hell didn't want to know what it was. It could be another damn body, for all Megan knew. There were enough of 'em floating around. Floating. Thoughts of Helen's dead body sent her stomach churning.

Tucking Silk under her arm, she went in search of her friends, checking first the salon and the bridge. When Megan opened the door of the cabin next to her own, expecting to find Kathleen, she got quite a surprise.

Snoring on the bed, fully clothed, was Brian Mason.

*How did he get on board? That damn Charlie probably invited him.*

Come to think of it, where was Charlie? And Kathleen, Michael, and Alex? Megan hadn't seen a soul except for Sy Neang.

Fear swept over her one more time.

Quickly, she made her way back to her own stateroom, clutching the dog even tighter. Her hands trembled as she slammed the door and locked it.

She heard footsteps down the hall. They got louder. They stopped outside her door.

Megan froze. Was it Sy Neang?

She'd always thought Charlie's man was a little strange, but a killer?

# Chapter 34

After Dan Coleman had viewed the murder tape at the Hollywood precinct, Matt drove them both up Coldwater Canyon to Lara's Flesh Emporium.

Dan didn't utter a word all the way up the hill.

The Hollywood detective also had a teenage daughter, and Matt knew exactly what he was feeling.

Lara, aka Betsy Bradford, answered the door. Her outfit had changed from black leather to red leather; otherwise, she looked the same as she did on their last visit.

Matt and Dan trailed the Viking queen to the den.

Passing through the living room, Matt was surprised to see it empty of customers. Just a couple of pale-skinned girls, dressed in leather S&M gear, smoking and playing cards.

Betsy left them in the paneled den and went to summon Roxanne.

Matt walked to a tall wooden credenza that held the TV equipment and slid Helen's disk into the drive. Then he took a seat and waited in silence.

Dan Coleman lit a cigarette but hurried to stub it out the minute the door opened to reveal Betsy and Roxanne.

Sweetly plain, Roxanne didn't look anything like a hooker.

Small and skinny, she had a pleasant face marred by several yellowing bruises under her eyes and on her chin. Her bleached blonde hair was long, reminding Matt of an old Veronica Lake movie.

Roxanne was not young. She was probably about thirty, thirty-five—older than their killer normally picked.

Introductions were made, and Betsy left the room.

"We want you to look at this video and see if it's the same person who attacked you," Matt said gently. "It's pretty gruesome, Roxanne. Can you handle it?"

"Yeah, I wanna see you get the motherfucker." Her voice was brittle as ice.

Her coldness of tone assured him Roxanne was indeed a hooker and hard as a rock. Matt pushed the start button.

Minutes into the tape, she said, "I think he's the one."

"Are you sure?"

"I recognize the outfit. It's the same, silver studs on the gloves, zippered mouth on the hood. It sure does look like him. The bastard seemed hyped, like he was wired on speed." She clasped her arms across her chest, hugging herself. "Shut it off, will you?"

"Are you positive it was a man?" Matt asked.

"It never occurred to me it wasn't." She looked perplexed. "When he spoke, it sounded like a guy. But I really don't know. I guess a woman coulda faked it."

Dan Coleman cut in. "We'll assume it was a man. Try to remember everything he said, even if it sounds unimportant to you. It may mean something to us. Think, did he mention a name?" He hit the off switch on the disk player.

"Ecstasy. He said his name was Ecstasy. You know, like the drug. That's what he said, and then he gave me a coupla Ecstasy pills, some uppers, and a fair amount of blow. I was pretty much wired as he was. Then he tied me to the bed." Roxanne took a deep breath. "He used a lotta sex toys, all kinds of shit, stuff he brought with him, stuff I ain't seen before. Then he damn near killed me with his fucking whip." She slipped off her blouse and showed them multiple lash marks that were still healing. "I couldn't cry out for help. The gag …"

Ecstasy was a drug commonly used by young people at dance clubs and raves. Its main ingredient was MDMA, an amphetamine with some side effects, but throw in a few uppers and a couple of lines of cocaine, and she had to be really out of it. Matt guessed the perpetrator was not as high as Roxanne thought; otherwise, he would be unable to function as effectively as he did. Plus, he had to drive his car when he left the brothel.

Suddenly, something else clicked in Matt's mind. "You're sure he said his name was Ecstasy?"

"I'm sure. But a lot of people use made-up names when they're doing their bondage thing."

Matt was already aware of that: Ecstasy, Darkness, Destiny.

And then he knew. Matt jumped from his seat. "Son of a bitch, we've got to get to the marina." He grabbed the tape and rushed out the door. "I think I know who the fucker is, Dan. Let's get outta here."

"Why the marina?" Dan asked, running behind him.

Matt told him.

"I'll get us a chopper." Dan pulled a cell phone out of his inside pocket. "They can pick us up at the Hollywood station house.

† † †

It seemed like ages before Megan got enough nerve to leave the cabin again.

*Dammit.* Somebody had to be out there.

With the squirming puppy in her arms, she ventured down the causeway one more time and headed for the Grants' stateroom.

No sign of life anywhere, not even Sy Neang.

"Alex, Alex. Where are you?" she called, wandering down the passageway.

As she approached the master stateroom, the door flew open and Alex stuck her head out. "Hi, Megan, we were just wondering if you were still asleep."

Megan pushed past her friend into the cabin.

Kathleen lay on the bed reading a romance magazine.

"I think Sy Neang is the killer," Megan blurted.

Alex gaped at her in stunned silence.

"He followed me down to the engine room and acted really intimidating." Megan tried to explain what had happened.

But Alex was not convinced. "Honey, he just didn' want you gettin' hurt. A lot of accidents can happen down there when we're under way."

"You're the one who said Sy Neang is harmless," Kathleen reminded her. "Now all of a sudden he's the killer. I think you're overreacting, Megan."

"I'm not. I'm not," Megan said, at the same time hoping they were right. "There was a really foul odor in there, Alex. I'm telling you there's something very wrong."

Alex put her arm around Megan to comfort her. "You're just distraught, honey. Who wouldn't be after seeing Helen's dead body floating in the water? I'm sure it was real upsetting."

Twisting out of Alex's grasp, Megan added, "How the hell did Brian get aboard?"

"Oh, my dear," Alex said, with a quick glance at Kathleen. "Charlie and me found him sleepin' in the clubhouse. The poor man was so drunk we just couldn't leave him on the island by himself. If Brian tried to sail *Dreamer* home, God alone knows what would have happened to him."

"And what about Michael? Where is he?" Megan directed her question to Kathleen.

"He's helping Charlie steer the boat."

Megan rolled her eyes. That makes three of them steering—Charlie, Michael, and the automatic pilot. But maybe Michael was the one who approached her door.

Megan was really worried. Something didn't feel right.

And she hadn't heard from Matt, either. She decided to try calling him again.

Checking her pockets, she couldn't find her cell phone. *Damn.* She'd left it on the rear deck. Handing the dog to Alex, Megan assured her, "I'll be right back."

When she left the cabin, Megan heard the lock click behind her. Despite her loud protestations, Alex wasn't taking any chances, either.

† † †

Matt put his hand over one ear to drown out the noise of the helicopter. "Angelle, it's me," he yelled into the mouthpiece. He had to reach her; he needed her help badly.

"Matt?" she called out loudly.

*Damn.* She sounded far away, like she was in a wind tunnel. "Look, I'm headed for Bayside in a chopper." He continued, even though he wasn't sure she could hear him. "Roxanne ID'd the guy. Said his name was Ecstasy. I'm waiting to hear from the FBI before I know for sure. I want you …" There was more static on the line.

"I can't hear you, Matt," she yelled above the crackling noise.

*Please don't quit now.* He shook the handset. "One, two. One, two. Any better?"

"Yes, much better. Go on. I hear you."

"I want you to head for the marina right now. I've contacted the coast guard, and they're going to have a cutter ready. Call Joe. He'll go with you." He was speaking fast in clipped tones, trying to get his message across before the line went out again.

"What's going on?"

"All hell broke loose. Helen Jennings is dead. They found her body floating in some bay in Catalina. She was strangled and dumped in the ocean. Megan saw the body, and I guess she's pretty shook up. The Grants' yacht is on the way home as we speak, and I need you to meet them. I think I know who the killer is." More static interference drowned out the sound. "Angel, are you there?" he yelled.

No response. The line was dead.

*Damn. Damn. Damn.* Matt slammed the handset into place.

† † †

As Megan tiptoed down the shadowy hallway in search of her cell phone, the engines were deafening, and the yacht creaked and rolled with each swell.

Suddenly, a door slammed. Someone was there.

She turned around and headed back toward the sound.

Passing Charlie's office, she rattled the door. Locked.

She tried the cabin on the left, the one Brian had been sleeping in. Empty. The bed was still unmade. Now, where the hell had he gone?

Quietly, Megan closed the door and continued down the passageway.

The salon was dark and empty, and a single outside light caused quivering shadows to dance like dark flames on the bulkhead. She switched on a table lamp.

Nothing. She tried the overhead light. Nothing. Obviously, the power was off.

Squinting, Megan peered around. "Hello? Hello, anyone there?"

No response. No sign of life. But she doubted anyone could hear her over the roar of the engines. She returned to the hallway and, keeping her back to the wall, retraced her steps.

There was a sudden movement to the left, behind her. Pain in her head. She flung her arms over her head defensively. Too late—she was down.

Curling herself into a tight little ball, she tried to protect herself from the beating.

Whack. Her fingers were hurt. One more whack and her head screamed with pain. She attempted to get up and was hit again. Extreme pain blurred her vision.

Rolling on her side, Megan spit out the vomit. Then nothing. Silence.

The attack had stopped. But she couldn't see anything.

Then she heard sounds of a struggle. Was someone else here, defending her?

More fighting. Grunting. And then, something heavy hit the ground.

Groans—not hers. More silence.

Megan tried to get up again. Whack, on the back of her head. Blackness.

# Chapter 35

Megan came to on the floor. The room was in total darkness. She was curled on her side, her right arm mashed against her breast.

The floor was cold, hard, vibrating. A screaming sound rattled through her head, her ears, her teeth, like a train rushing through her brain. She struggled to get up, but dizziness overcame her, forcing her back to the floor.

She rested for a moment, trying to gather strength.

Her hands and legs were free. But the taste in her mouth was dreadful. And that smell? Something was rotting. She raised her fingers and wiped her mouth. Wet.

Sweat or blood? She tasted it. The wetness was blood.

Then it all came back. She was on the Grants' yacht. She was in the hallway. She'd been attacked from behind. She was hit on the head, over and over. Fingering her scalp, Megan felt several lumps and a long open gash behind her left ear. Whoever it was had done a real number.

She began the long climb to her feet, resting every few seconds to alleviate the vertigo. Which way to the door?

Reaching out her arms, Megan rotated her body to measure the space. The enclosure was not large. Maybe a closet?

Something fell and landed on her feet. She ran her hand along the wall, feeling for a light switch. Found it.

A red glow suffused the tiny area. Was she in a closet?

She glanced at the clammy object lying on her foot.

She retched. Wiping her mouth with her sleeve, Megan looked again. It was a hunk of rotting flesh. She heaved. A long dry heave.

Revolted, she kicked it away. Clawing frantically at her foot, she tried to erase all trace of it. She rubbed her hands on her jeans, compulsively, and clenched her fists.

She had to force herself to stop.

Fighting panic and nausea, Megan placed her head between her legs. After a few seconds, she straightened.

The nausea was gone for the moment. But the panic remained. She inhaled, exhaled, inhaled, tried to regain some kind of control. Oh, God, the stench.

Slowly, Megan pulled herself together and attempted to interpret her surroundings. On the back wall, a single red bulb cast a crimson triangle of light over an oil painting. Beneath it was a small table laden with dozens of unlit votive candles.

It looked like a shrine or an altar.

Megan strained to read the title at the bottom of the canvas: "Amazon Woman."

What the hell was that supposed to mean? She studied the picture.

A beautiful fair-haired woman stalked barefoot alongside a river. Hooked over her left shoulder was a rawhide quiver of arrows and, trailing behind her, a tired-looking male, his hands secured by brown leather thongs.

The warrior-woman wore only a tattered scrap of leopard pelt wrapped around her hips. Her upper body was bare. Megan caught her breath.

The woman's right breast was gone, replaced by a vicious red scar.

Megan turned away quickly and examined the shelves on the wall. One of them held a wig form displaying a repulsive leather mask. Its eye slits were elliptical, almost oval in shape. The silver zippered mouth grinned at her with icy mirth.

She stared, almost transfixed. It looked exactly like the death's-head hood and mask the intruder had worn at Helen's house. Folded neatly beside it was a black leather suit. And next to the suit was an array of bondage apparatuses: whips, chains, clips, straps, all kinds of sexual paraphernalia.

With effort, Megan roused herself and continued her search for a way out. Bile rose in her throat as the combination of decomposing flesh, diesel fumes, and her own vomit made her dizzy. *Get a hold of yourself, girl.* But she knew she was going under.

Megan fought the fainting spell with every ounce of willpower she possessed.

She finally righted herself.

She found the door and rattled the latch. It was locked from the outside.

*Dear God, please let me out of here.* With a strength born of desperation, Megan slammed her shoulder against the door and thanked God it wasn't metal. Her shoulder surely would have been broken. It looked like it might be wood.

She kicked it with her foot. Kicked again. And again. It finally gave way.

The boat suddenly pitched, and the door flew open, spitting Megan out of the closet into the darkened room. Unsteadily she made her way to the door.

Using the wall for support, she staggered down the passageway to the stairwell.

Climbing the stairs was painful. Her legs had no strength at all. Lying in a cramped position for God knows how long had numbed the muscles. She stopped for breath. Pain shot through her head, her arms, her knees, her shoulders.

Then she was moving again, slowly.

At last, she reached the main deck.

Weaving her way through the furniture in the salon, Megan approached the short ladder that led to the pilothouse.

Cautiously, she ascended.

"Charlie?" she whispered.

The instrument panel was lit, and an eerie green glow radiated from the bank of computers. The person hunched over the wheel was unrecognizable.

Suddenly, the figure whirled toward her.

The face was hidden in shadows, but Megan clearly saw an upraised hand holding a shiny fisherman's knife. The long, thin blade mirrored a single ray of moonlight.

She turned and fled down the steps. She heard the pursuing footfalls.

The yacht lurched, pitching her to the left. Her legs quivering, Megan dodged through the salon. The *Ecstasea* tipped again, hurling her into the coffee table.

She crashed to the floor and stayed there for the longest moment, listening.

Someone was cursing. Close. Too close. *Slam. Won't you come home, Bill Bailey? Won't you come home?* Someone had hit the player piano. The music. The deafening engines. The grunts of her would-be assassin.

Then a glass, or a maybe a wine bottle, crashed to the floor in front of her.

Pain, she could feel the pain. Blood trickled down her arm. Sobbing, Megan crawled along the teak floor on her hands and knees, crunching her way through the jagged glass till her hands were gouged and bleeding.

She lost a shoe. No time to look. Quick as she could, Megan clambered to her feet and limped toward the open door. As she crossed the threshold, a blast of cold air hit her in the face. Then she was outside, gulping fresh sea air.

Shaking her head to clear it, Megan examined her arm. A large shard of dark glass protruded. She yanked it out and tossed it into the sea. Hearing no footsteps, only the pounding in her ears, she sagged against the bulkhead.

Her arm throbbed painfully. She checked it. More blood. Pressing her fingers to staunch the wound, Megan tried to get her bearings. She could see lights along the shore. And in the distance a beacon flashed. Could that be the breakwater? Putting every ounce of faith at work, she prayed it was the entrance to the marina.

Her breathing eased as sea spray cooled her cheeks.

Suddenly, an arm clamped her neck. Squeezing. Choking.

She couldn't breathe. She was going under.

*Help me, God. Help me.*

A surge of adrenaline coursed through Megan's body, and she smashed down on her attacker's instep with her one shoed foot.

Her assailant grunted, loosened his grip. Megan tore free.

With not even a glance back, she stumbled along the causeway, clutching her bloody arm.

By the time Megan reached the stateroom, her arms and hands were covered with blood. Crying out, she slammed her body against the door and banged as hard as she could with her fists.

It opened. And she fell into Alex's arms.

"Lock the door. Lock the door," she yelled.

Alex kicked it shut.

The dog ran around in circles, barking and yapping.

"Oh, my God." Alex screamed. "What happened?"

Megan heard herself mumble, trying to explain.

"Kathleen," Alex took command and led her to the bed, "there's a first aid kit under the sink. Get it."

Kathleen rushed off while Silk tried to claw her way up the bedspread.

Megan reached out with a shaky hand to comfort her puppy.

Carrying a white box and two white towels, Kathleen reappeared. "You must have had a terrible fall, Megan."

"I didn't fall. Somebody attacked me." Megan couldn't stop shivering.

"Why would anyone do that?" Alex demanded, holding a towel to the injured arm.

"I'll tell you why, because your damn houseman is the Bondage Murderer. That's why he chased me away from that cabin earlier. And when I didn't stay out of the way like a good little girl, he bopped me on the head and stuck me in that infernal closet of his with … with all those body parts."

"Body parts? What are you talking about, Megan?" Alex cried.

"Body parts, as in pieces of skin. I don't know what the hell they were, and I didn't stop to find out. All I know is they must have been there for a while, because the smell was god-awful."

"Pieces of skin?" Kathleen rocked back and forth on the bed like a child. "Oh, Megan, what are we going to do?"

"Stop that, Kathleen," Alex snapped. Turning to Megan, she almost pleaded with her. "You must be mistaken."

Suddenly, there was a loud pounding on the door of the stateroom. Megan glanced quickly at Alex, who appeared glued to the floor.

Trying to stand up, Megan's knees shook so much she almost fell, dropping the dog.

"It's me, Charlie. Let me in."

"Thank heavens." Alex rushed to open the door.

Charlie stood there, a dull gray gun resting in the palm of his right hand. His fleshy face was grim, his small black eyes unnaturally bright.

"Megan says that Sy Neang is the murderer. But he isn't, is he, Charlie?" Kathleen cried.

"Oh, come on," Charlie scorned.

But Kathleen ranted on. "He attacked Megan and left her in an awful cabin. Then she fell down. And look at her arm. It's cut really badly. And besides that, somebody hit her on the head."

Charlie turned to Megan. "Is that right?"

"Somebody chased me." She dropped her eyes and watched the dog lapping at her fingers. "I couldn't see his face."

Charlie paced the cabin, flicking the safety of the gun on and off. "But I've known Sy Neang for almost thirty years."

"Charlie, where's Michael?" Kathleen whined. "I really must see him."

Alex turned on her. "Will you shut up about Michael?"

"How about Brian?" Megan asked. "Where is he? When I first saw him in the cabin, he was asleep. But later, when I checked again, he was gone." A cold chill crept through her bones. Could it have been Brian? Did he attack her?

Megan shook off the thought. But something was going on around here. People were dying and disappearing right and left.

Her fingers grazed her bruised neck. Whoever did this to her had to be strong.

But who was it? Sy Neang? Brian? Michael?

Charlie shook his head. "I didn't see anyone. I've been on the bridge, steering the boat since we left Cat Harbor."

How could he have been steering the boat? Hadn't she just …?

The door banged open, and Sy Neang walked in.

Charlie lifted his gun and aimed. "Stay where you are."

"Mister Charles?" Sy Neang's startled black eyes darted from

Charlie's face to the little gray gun and back to Charlie. The boat rocked. Sy Neang swayed forward.

The gun exploded with a deafening roar.

Sy's face mirrored Megan's own surprise and horror as he clutched his chest and sank to the floor.

"Charlie," Alex screamed. "Why did you do that?"

"He's the killer."

In her present state of numbness, Megan could barely comprehend what was being said. She heard the words, but nothing really registered. In the back of her mind she knew she'd gone into shock but felt powerless to do anything about it.

After a moment's silence, Alex mumbled, "But Sy was unarmed."

"I didn't know that, did I?" Charlie nudged his houseman's body with his foot.

"You said he wasn't the murderer." Alex's voice was flat.

"But you girls convinced me," Charlie snapped. "I couldn't take a chance. He might have had a gun, and we wouldn't be alive right now."

Megan gazed at the corpse, at the blood, at the staring eyes.

Charlie reached for Sy's pulse. "He's dead. You have nothing more to fear."

"We can't stay here with him," Alex moaned.

"Alex, the man is dead. He can't hurt you." Charlie's voice was cold. "Stay in the cabin. The autopilot is on, and I need to set a new heading."

"You can't just leave him there," Alex cried, staring at the growing pool of blood surrounding Sy Neang.

"Walk around him," Charlie spat.

"I can't." Sobbing, Alex covered her mouth with her hand.

Charlie dragged the body into the passageway. "We'll turn him over to the police when we get back to the marina. Now you girls relax." He disappeared.

Alex was still trembling. And Kathleen started rocking again. Slowly, Megan began to piece things together. What she concluded seemed impossible.

# Chapter 36

Matt passed over Beverly Hills in the chopper and then past a cluster of tall buildings that was Century City. His nerves on edge, he tried to contact Angelle again. No luck.

More minutes dragged by before the towers of Marina City Club loomed ahead and then a multitude of boat slips. The dock and restaurant lights and those from thousands of boats twinkled, like stars in a midnight sky, leaving shimmering waves in the inky water. Matt directed the pilot to Bayside Yacht Club.

The Grant slip was empty. *Goddamn.*

The *Ecstasea* hadn't returned yet. He looked out to sea.

Following Matt's thumb, the helicopter veered off toward the breakwater.

† † †

By the time Charlie returned to the master stateroom, Megan had managed to struggle to her feet. Catching a glimpse of herself in the mirror, she was shocked. Despite Alex's attempts to clean her up, her hair was stained a deep crusty red. "Oh, God," Megan gasped, "I look terrible."

Charlie stood with his back to the door.

"Is everyone else all right?" Megan asked. "Michael? Brian?"

"They're fine," he said. "They'll be down here soon."

"But where exactly are they now, Charlie?" Megan insisted. "On the bridge, in the salon, in their stateroom—where are they now?"

Voices babbled as Alex and Kathleen both spoke at once.

Megan walked toward him. "I think I'll go and find my cell phone. I'd like to call Matt." She watched Charlie's expression change, contort into something feral.

He blocked her path. "You know, don't you?" Charlie raised the gun and aimed it at Megan's chest.

"Know what?" A chill descended upon her. "Know what, Charlie?"

"You saw the picture, didn't you?"

"What picture? Oh, you mean the picture in Sy's cabin?" She was stalling for time, because deep inside, Megan knew the truth. And it horrified her.

"Maybe it wasn't his cabin." Hatred filled Charlie's squinty eyes and exploded from his every pore.

Megan put out her hand and inched toward him. "Why don't you give me the gun, Charlie?"

He clicked off the safety. "Don't move another fucking inch."

Megan had no doubt she was in the middle of a terrible nightmare. "I was only just—"

But Charlie didn't allow her to finish. "I almost had it made. But you had to spoil it—didn't you, Megan?—with your female snooping. Now, you'll all have to die." His last words rose to a hysterical pitch.

Alex looked baffled. "Charlie?"

Her worst fears were confirmed, and Megan panicked. Not knowing what else to do, she went for him. "You bastard," she yelled.

Charlie's fingers squeezed the trigger. "Stay where you are, Megan," he demanded. "I will shoot, you know?"

She stopped and stood perfectly still. "Okay, Charlie. Okay." Megan held out her hand in a halting gesture. "See, I'm right here."

"What are you doing, Charlie?" his wife whispered. "You can't shoot Megan."

"It was you, wasn't it?" Megan took a step forward and tried to keep him talking. "But why, Charlie? Why did you do it?"

"Does there have to be a reason?" he sneered. "Maybe I just like it."

Alex began to catch on. "Charlie, what are you saying?"

It was only then that Megan realized what she had found in the closet, and the ramifications of that find. *Oh my God, the pieces of flesh must have been women's breasts. And all the porn stuff and that leather outfit belonged to Charlie.*

His eyes were cold chips of flint. "Just stay where you are, bitch."

"The portrait? This all has something to do with that woman in the portrait, doesn't it, Charlie?" She tried moving closer.

His eyes glazed over. "The Amazon woman was the ultimate bitch. Like my mother, like the rest of those whores," Charlie snarled. "I kill bitches."

"What are you talking about?" Alex cried. "Charlie, please stop this."

"He's joking, Alex," Kathleen tried to reassure her friend. "You didn't kill any bitches, did you, Charlie?" Her voice wound down. "Just Sy."

He turned to his wife. "She was a hooker. The first one in Cambodia was just a hooker. It was an accident, unavoidable. But when she died it was too late. Sy Neang was my man in Cambodia. He helped me get rid of the body. That's why I brought him here to America. Don't you see, Alex? He helped me with the bodies." Charlie's eyes pleaded with her to understand. "I had to do it. The breast was the most important part."

But Alex simply stared at him with her hand over her mouth, unable or unwilling to comprehend what her husband was saying.

"Charlie, you need help." Megan moved toward the bedside table. "You've been under a lot of stress, trying to sell the condos and all."

"Too many bitches." Charlie shook his head. He appeared to be having some kind of psychotic break. "Too many bitches."

"But why did you kill Bonnie-Sue Rattner?" Megan asked, still unsure about what she was going to do next. She only knew she had to keep him talking.

"The sleazy bitch threw herself at me." Charlie smiled, a manic glint in those cold eyes of his. "She led me on for months. They all did."

"And Helen Jennings." Megan inched forward. "Why did you kill Helen?"

He spoke as if he were describing a day in the park instead of the murder of all those human beings. "It took me a while to figure out who was blackmailing me. At first I thought it was Ray. Then I was sure it was Sherrie. But when I finally figured it out…. Stay back, Megan!" Charlie grabbed Kathleen and thrust the gun to her head. "Don't make me do it, bitch."

"Charlie! Charlie! Let me go." But no matter how much she fought, Charlie held her in a death grip. In desperation, Kathleen screamed, "Michael! Michael!"

"You're not going to get any help from your asshole boyfriend, so you might as well shut your mouth." He hit her head with the gun.

The yacht tilted, and he lost his balance.

Screeching, Kathleen broke free.

Megan made her move. Pulling the bedside lamp from its socket, she flung it at Charlie. It crashed into him. The gun hit the floor.

Megan and Charlie both scrambled for it and knocked it across the room. It landed at Alex's feet. She seemed paralyzed and just stood there, staring at the gun.

Megan dived for the weapon.

With a demonic shriek, Kathleen flung herself at Charlie.

Kicking and scratching, she stayed on the attack, but he finally shook her off and came up from the floor, brandishing the fisherman's knife. Roaring like a wounded beast, he snatched Kathleen up again and pressed the knife to her throat. Blood trickled down her neck as Charlie dragged the wide-eyed woman into the corridor.

Megan lunged after them, but Charlie pulled the door shut.

It slammed on her fingers. She ripped them out of the door, and pain shot up her arm. Her good arm. She doubled over. *Damn the pain.*

Her hand was swelling fast. But, gripping the gun with a shaky right hand, Megan opened the door.

*Easy, take it easy,* she told herself. The bastard had Kathleen.

There was no one in the darkened passageway, just the dead body of Sy Neang.

She moved slowly along the wall, trying to avoid touching the corpse. And then she caught the strong odor of gasoline. Was the engine leaking? That couldn't be good.

Thud. Thud. She jumped. Someone was kicking the door inside Charlie's office.

Opening it slowly, Megan pointed the gun.

Brian was laid out on the floor, bound and gagged. Behind him, handcuffed to a pipe on the wall, was Michael Harrington. His head was battered and bleeding, his shirt soaked with blood. Michael's glazed eyes told her he had a serious concussion. Charlie must have tied them up when he left the cabin after shooting Sy Neang. He'd known then it was all over, and he planned to get rid of them all.

Megan's whole body began to shake. She struggled to gain control of herself, and with trembling fingers, she removed the filthy rag from Brian's mouth. She undid the bindings on his arms and legs. He grabbed his twisted right arm and tried to get up.

Neither he nor Michael appeared to be in any condition to help.

"Jesus, Megan, it's Charlie. He poured gasoline all over the place, and I saw him start a fire in the engine room. The whole goddamn boat is ready to go up in flames," Brian croaked. "After that, I tried to stop him from beating you up, but he knocked me out and I woke up here." He tried to move his shattered limb. "I think my arm is broken."

"It looks really bad." She gestured toward the semiconscious Michael. "Untie him, and go get Alex and Kathleen. Bring them to the deck. Hurry, hurry, and don't forget my puppy." Then she moved back in the hallway.

Screams were coming from the upper deck.

Megan climbed the spiral staircase, her knees folding like spaghetti. Suddenly, she stopped. *I can't do this. He's planning to destroy the yacht. We're all going to die.*

It took several frenzied seconds before Megan could continue her climb.

Crouched on the top deck, her heart tried to batter its way out of her chest. The night air was cold and damp. She shivered and gasped for breath.

There was lots of noise. Engines. Big engines. Blades beating the air. She looked up. A helicopter hovered close by.

Someone leaned out. She could almost make out his face.

The chopper moved in even lower, keeping pace with the *Ecstasea*.

It was Matt Donovan. What little strength Megan had left melted from her body. She grabbed the railing to keep from sinking to the deck. *Thank you, God.*

Spotlights from the chopper flooded the deck.

That's when she saw Kathleen, tied to a cleat and straddled by Charlie, his long knife pressed at her throat.

Lifting a shaky hand, Megan took aim with the gun.

She wanted to blow the son of a bitch away.

But the yacht lurched, and the shot went wild.

Charlie turned to face her and grinned. He slid the silver blade across Kathleen's throat. She screamed and thrashed, trying to get away from the blade. More blood.

"Drop the gun," Charlie growled.

For a split second, Megan hesitated and then obeyed. The gun slid away from her reach.

An explosion! From above.

A bullet crashed into Charlie's back. His body folded face forward onto Kathleen.

Screaming and yelling, Kathleen bucked her hips, trying to push him off. She was splattered from head to toe with Charlie's blood. Megan rushed to her aid.

She tried to untie Kathleen's hands. *Dammit.*

A male voice, hollow and loud, blasted through an amplifier. "Megan, this is Matt. The boat's on fire and it's on a crash course. Get off the boat right now. Do you hear me? Get off the boat now."

She knew about the fire. But what did he mean? Crash course?

Megan stood up. All she could see ahead was blackness and what appeared to be a tent of lights. She squinted.

Oh, dear God, it was a huge tanker, obviously laying at anchor. And the *Ecstasea* was headed straight for it. Panic energized her. Desperately, she looked around for something to free Kathleen.

She saw the knife.

Grabbing it from Charlie's hand, she hacked at the ropes on Kathleen's wrists.

Freed, Kathleen sprang to her feet, screaming hysterically. "Where's Michael? I want Michael."

"Brian is bringing him. He was knocked out."

Megan turned to see Alex rushing toward her with the dog in her arms, until she saw Charlie's body. Then she stopped. Transfixed, Alex stared at her husband.

"We're about to crash," Megan yelled above the sound of the chopper. "We have to jump, Alex." But as Megan stepped over the body to reach for the dog, Charlie grabbed her leg.

*Holy shit.*

Purely out of instinct, her foot lashed out. Kicking. Kicking. But Charlie's grip was firm. She fumbled for the knife. Clasping it in frozen fingers, she brought it down, over and over and over, but Charlie wouldn't let go.

A shot rang out.

Michael stood two feet away, Charlie's gun extended.

Charlie slumped over. But then he tried to climb to his knees, holding on to the gunshot wound in his belly. He stretched out a bloodied hand toward his wife.

Michael fired again.

This time Charlie went down—and stayed down.

Megan struggled to her feet, trying to maintain her balance as the deck pitched and rolled. The *Ecstasea* careened toward the tanker at breakneck speed. Megan tried to grab Alex and yank her toward the railing, but she fought back like a madwoman.

"Come on, Alex, Charlie's dead. Please, please, we have to go. The boat's on fire." In desperation, Megan even tried to pick her up.

But Alex pushed her away.

Dropping the dog, Alex broke free and ran back to Charlie. She flung herself on top of her dying husband. Megan looked around. Now the flames were belching out of the stairwell from below decks.

Clutching his injured arm, Brian was poised on the rail. Then he was gone.

Michael, holding Kathleen, leaped over the side.

Alex lay prostrate on Charlie's body. The tanker loomed.

From above, Megan heard Matt yell, "Jump, Megan, jump!"

The noise of the helicopter's engines tore at Matt's eardrums.

Imprisoned in the damn bird, he was totally helpless as the grim scene played out before him in terrifying sequence. Beneath the harsh glare of the spotlight, he saw the ferocious flames roar through the entire yacht and begin to devour the top deck.

He watched Brian hurl himself overboard.

He saw Michael grab Kathleen and jump into the sea.

But not Megan—she was searching for something.

"For God's sake, Megan, jump!" The flames were getting closer.

Then, she moved. He saw her scoop up the puppy and, seconds later, vault over the side. She was quickly lost in a swirl of water.

Resurfacing, Megan fought the waves. Then she was gone.

"Quick, take 'er down." Matt grabbed a couple of life jackets and jumped from the helicopter into the sea.

The shock of the icy water stunned him. He felt the pull of the tide and total powerlessness as the sweeping waves carried him aloft time after time.

There was a lull as he rode the wave. He couldn't see Megan.

And he felt fear, a fear he'd never known, even when his own life was in danger. It overpowered him with such ferocity he could not seem to act.

Another huge swell carried him high in the air, and Matt caught a glimpse of her, just yards away. Frantically, he swam toward her. But Megan disappeared again.

He swam for his life … and hers, praying, praying. He promised God the world.

*Please, please, God. Don't let her die. Please, I've only just found her.*

She bobbed up again. Only a few feet more. Swim. Swim.

And then he had her. Weak with relief, he pulled her close.

Silk wriggled and squirmed, but Megan clung to the bedraggled puppy with the same determination Matt clung to her. "Where is everybody?" she sputtered. "Kathleen and Michael? And Brian? Oh, Matt, Alex wouldn't leave Charlie. She's still on board."

"Shhh, Megan. It's too late, honey."

The dog whimpered. Megan began to cry, and Matt held her close.

He held them both in the circle of his arms and caught his first glimpse of the coast guard cutter.

Meanwhile, the blazing yacht barreled toward the tanker.

The helicopter veered toward land.

Suddenly, there was a shriek of sirens from the oil tanker. The hideous tidal wave of noise drowned out the sounds of the departing chopper and dulled the roar of the rescue boat.

That's when the horizon erupted in flames, and a million sparks mingled with a million stars. Flames leaped up the sides of the tanker into a gaping hole caused by the explosion. Tongues of fire reflected in the black water for miles as the pits of hell opened to receive the monster on the *Ecstasea*. And Matt was glad.

Though the heat scorched his nostrils and the stench of burning fuel almost overpowered him, he trod water, holding his precious burden, and prayed no oil would escape from the tanker. God help them if an oil slick caught fire.

The flaming yacht exploded again. And again.

In slow, slow motion, the inferno, all that remained of the mega-yacht *Ecstasea* slid down the side of the towering ship and slipped quietly into the sea.

The coast guard cutter pulled alongside. Joe Schumann stood on the bow, still and sturdy, a senior citizen figurehead.

Angelle was aboard, holding blankets.

Someone leaped into the water and took Megan and the dog from Matt's arms, half-carrying her up the ladder to the deck.

Joe cried out, "There's somebody else out there."

Still standing on the ladder, Matt turned. He heard Megan shrieking as the spotlight picked up two people clinging together. It was Michael, holding Kathleen's head above water.

Another cry rang out. "There's another one."

Within minutes the crew had them all aboard—Matt and Megan, Kathleen, Michael, and finally, Brian.

"Look, look, there's someone else out there," yelled Michael. "It's Alex. It must be Alex."

The coast guard crew quickly went into action and pulled a weeping Alex from the sea.

He saw Megan's compassion as she threw her arms around Alex, trying to console her. He could not imagine how it would feel to find out that someone you loved was an evil monster, a monster who had tortured and murdered God knows how many women. He was sure that Alex's pain was unbearable and, sadly, far from over.

Hot blankets were passed around, and steaming mugs of coffee.

Soon, Matt found himself rolled inside his own heated blanket along with Megan and Silk. He held her tightly against his chest and vowed to himself he would never, ever let her go. "I love you, Megan," he whispered.

Megan raised her eyes to him and said, "I love you too, Matt Donovan."

Matt smiled. This was the only place on Earth he wanted to be.

# Epilogue

*Four Months Later*

MEGAN WAS TOUCHED. The *Moon River* was decorated with twinkling Christmas lights, and garlands of white poinsettias were strung on the lines and halyards. Magnificent cream orchids from Hawaii intertwined a sparkling white trellis set up on the afterdeck.

The bride wore an antique lace dress and an abundance of pearls. She held a small bouquet of white roses and orchids mingled with baby's breath. And you could see she was a little bit pregnant.

*This truly is a miracle,* thought Megan.

The groom was striking in a navy blazer and cream slacks.

"I now pronounce you husband and wife." The minister blessed them, and Mr. and Mrs. Michael Harrington kissed.

Two young women tossed rose petals at the smiling couple as they faced the small audience of less than a dozen people.

"I've never seen Kathleen look happier," Megan whispered.

Rachel made a crack. "I think he's too much like Gino."

"Maybe you're just jealous," Megan commented dryly.

"Absolutely not; one evening of adultery was enough for me. But it did force me into realizing that my marriage was over."

"Working at Venice Legal Clinic has been good for you." And it was. Rachel looked like her old self again.

"Yes, I feel like I'm really doing something worthwhile." Rachel grinned.

"And I really want to thank you for all the legal work you are doing to help Mothers in Recovery."

"Megan, you're the one who raised more than a hundred thousand dollars at the luncheon. I think you should be very proud of yourself."

Megan smiled. She was pleased. Now Mothers in Recovery had a very healthy down payment on the house next door. The new babysitting center would be up and running sometime next year.

"I miss Alex, don't you?" Rachel asked, her eyes filling with tears.

"Yes, I do. But I can understand why she had to go back to Florida. It would be difficult to face her friends, knowing the crimes her husband committed." Add that to the fact that Charlie was more than three hundred million dollars in debt when he died, and it would take an army of well-paid lawyers to unravel the mess. "Maybe she'll come back sometime." But she knew that was wishful thinking.

"Having a lot of money is very important to Alex. She'd find it hard to go on without it, especially here."

"Okay, ladies," Matt said, handing them drinks. "Here's a Coke for you, Megan, and champagne for Rachel."

As he stood beside her, Megan watched him sip on his Coke.

Since they'd made a commitment to each other, Matt had chosen not to drink in her presence. And she loved him for it.

In fact, she loved him totally, completely.

"Matt, have you figured out why Charlie turned into such a monster?" Rachel wanted to know.

Before he could answer, Megan interrupted. "Rachel, this is not the time to—"

"It's okay, honey." Matt sat on the sailboat's rail. "We're still unsure what precipitated his first kill in Cambodia. He had not yet developed the ritual of taking the breast. But we now know that Charlie was physically abused by his mother. Apparently, she was an alcoholic and some kind of religious nut. Since his father was a womanizer, the mother took out all her rage on Charlie. She beat him relentlessly and, when she caught him masturbating, she locked him in the closet."

Rachel was insistent. "But why did he mutilate the bodies the way he did?"

"Charlie regarded his mother as all-powerful." Matt was beginning to look uncomfortable. "She kept that picture of the Amazon woman in her bedroom, and it became a masturbatory tool for Charlie. Somehow, in his screwed-up mind, he linked the Amazon with his mother, and together they were the object of his hatred and desire."

"Why did he have to cut off their breasts?" Megan shuddered at the thought.

Matt explained, "Legend tells us the Amazon women cut off their own right breasts so they wouldn't get in the way of their bows and arrows during warfare."

"That's why he kept the picture of that Amazon in his cabin. The one I saw—" Megan stopped. The memory of that night in the darkness of the cabin, the stench of rotting flesh, the pieces of … Megan caught her breath.

"It was all part of his ritual. He took the body parts as trophies. We're still trying to untangle what happened," Matt said. "And some of it we may never know."

"What about Sy Neang?" Rachel asked. "What was his connection?"

"As far as we can figure, Sy just helped with the cleanup. He had a slavish devotion to his boss and did everything Charlie asked—for a price. It turned out that Sy Neang had a very healthy bank account, almost two million dollars. Undoubtedly, he was well paid for his efforts. But Charlie's money was about to run out. He was being blackmailed and was faced with the threat of losing all his money and assets. These things combined were the final stressors on Charlie." Matt moved to Megan's side and put his arm around her. "You okay, sweetheart?"

"I guess Charlie had a whole other life that none of us could even imagine." She leaned into Matt's arm. "Not even Alex knew what he was really like."

Matt nodded his agreement. "Charlie kept a secret apartment in San Diego. No one in his family even knew about it. He often crossed the border from there, and we believe he was responsible for the deaths of numerous prostitutes in Tijuana. Most of the time, Charlie killed for the sheer thrill of it. Keeping the breasts as a trophy was all part of the ritual. We're still checking it out with the Mexican authorities. There may be as many as a dozen murders linked to Charlie through his MO."

Rachel finished her drink and set the glass on a small table. "I still don't understand why he killed Helen Jennings."

Matt filled in the details they had hypothesized. "She was blackmailing him. Helen's ex-husband, Ray, accidentally videotaped Charlie when he murdered Allison Graham. Ray was terrified when he realized what he had. That's why he moved to San Francisco. Besides getting away from his wife, he was also trying to get as far away from Charlie Grant as possible. But Charlie thought Ray was blackmailing him, so he ran him down with his car. We now have the rental car as evidence. After he killed Ray, he had a little fun with Cindy. She's the other girl who performed with Sherrie at Gino's divorce party. He believed that Ray had shared the DVD of Allison's murder with Cindy."

Matt twirled his glass and looked directly at Rachel.

"But, when he received another blackmail letter after Ray had died, he became convinced Sherrie Weston was the blackmailer. He killed Sherrie and still didn't find the DVD, so he decided it must be Helen Jennings, that Ray had given the DVD to her and she had decided to collect. When he tried to search Helen's house, he was interrupted by Megan and had to find another way. On the way to Catalina, Megan let it slip that Helen had paid off most of her mortgage with a lump sum of cash, cash she had recently extorted from Charlie Grant. That was all he needed to know. Charlie didn't waste any time. First he confronted Helen, and then he got rid of her."

"And, on the way back from Catalina, when I finally figured out he was the killer, he decided to get rid of us all by burning and sinking the *Ecstasea*." Megan would never, ever forget that moment when she realized that Charlie Grant was the Bondage Murderer. She had been sure he hadn't been steering the yacht like he said; he'd been attacking her with a knife, because whoever was steering had chased her down. And then when he shot Sy Neang in cold blood, in front of them all, she knew he had done it to deflect suspicion from himself. In fact, the more Megan had thought about it, the more everything fit.

"The way he planned it, Charlie would have been the sole survivor of a fire at sea." Matt pulled her close. "If it wasn't for Megan's courageous actions, things might have turned out very differently."

That's when Michael Harrington yelled, "Hey, you guys, Kathleen's going to throw the bouquet."

"I sure as hell don't want to catch it," Rachel said and pushed Megan forward.

Kathleen tossed the bouquet of white roses and baby orchids.

It flew into Megan's hands.

Matt smiled and pulled her into his arms. "There's an important question I've wanted to ask you, Megan, and this looks like a very good time."

# The End